THE TRAIL OF FLAME

THE SEVEN ISLES
BOOK TWO

A.R. KNIGHT

CHAPTER 1

THE FLYING SEAS

The lithe man held the rapier point-forward, the silver blade destined to strike right at Wax's heart. With his hair tied back, his face as narrow as his sword, the Kance fighter looked every bit the Windmaster his isle proclaimed him to be.

Wax bobbed his feet, rolling them with the ship's own shimmering silver-and-wood deck. The Kance ship cut through the waves, all its edges blinding in the sunlight as the rough-and-tumble regularity of a sea voyage found itself thwarted by cunning construction.

Wax himself lacked that beauty, his weave not doing much to keep him warm in the slicing sea breeze, his loose pants snapping, his climbing shoes biting at the surface in the one effective accessory he had.

Oh, and his Foti blade. The blue sword picked up the ocean's reflection, carrying the sea in its waved steel. Thicker than the Kance man's rapier, the Foti blade would have to use its strength to make up for its stubbier length.

Bets to that effect danced the deck around them, the sailors not actively steering the ship taking their midday break to see how badly their friend could beat Wax up and down the vessel.

One call in Wax's corner came from his right, where his older brother Quik, holding onto one of the many rope loops against the Kance ship's railing, hollered sage advice: don't stand still.

Beside him, her bamboo staff sticking up over her back like some tree sprouting from her shoulders, stood his sister. Bliss held a nervous look, like she had almost the entire journey, and Wax tried to offer up a confident grin.

The man wouldn't kill him, after all.

"Ready?" The Windmaster asked, reedy voice mashing with the crackling splash the ship made as it danced through another wave.

"Always." Wax shifted his stance, brought his right foot forward and put the blade into a double grip.

Last time he'd lost his weapon, sent it skittering across the deck to leave a divot in the polished wood side. They'd had him scrubbing the dishes every night since, and Wax wouldn't want to see what further punishment the Kance might devise should his Vis clumsiness do any more damage.

Then again, what did they expect? Wax wasn't born on the seas. He was a jungle man, made for vines, for swinging through treetops and dashing into leafy groves.

The Windmaster cared not, and came on with a fast three-step, cutting the distance between them to a hair. As the man's angle predicted, the rapier came in for a heart-stopping strike, one Wax batted away with his own sword.

A too-heavy parry. While he'd moved his thick blade all the way across his chest to knock the rapier aside, his opponent merely needed a wrist flick to get the stab back on target.

For once, the Kance ship gave Wax an out: on the backside of its latest wave slice, the ship dipped forward into the valley between the rolling monsters. Wax used the momentum, cutting left and forward with his shoulder. The rapier snipped a loose thread with its thrust, but missed Wax's body, giving Wax a solid charge right at his opponent's chest.

That Kance swiftness didn't help here, the impact barely slowing Wax down and throwing the Windmaster into a flailing backpedal, one that should've ended the fight save for his opponent planting his right leg hard, then leaning forward and placing both hands, rapier slapped down in the left one, on the deck.

"Don't let him recover!" Quik's voice rose over the jeers and cheers, collectors and betters sensing an imminent opportunity.

Wax went on through the shoulder charge, taking his brother's advice and bearing down on the Windmaster. He brought the Foti blade up for a two-handed smash, a fatal end. Surely the man would yield, throw up his arms and give up.

Instead the Windmaster slipped his left hand low, on the rapier hilt's very end, and with his wrist, popped the blade's point up, right where Wax ought to run himself through.

Or would have, if the fighter didn't pull the point away, swiping the blade left and letting Wax catch himself, come to a stop as the ship began to climb into the next wave.

"Your brother gives you bad advice," the Windmaster said, standing. He tapped Wax's blade with the rapier. "Position is everything, whether your sword is nimble or slow."

"I'm sure I'll learn that sometime." Wax looked at the

blue blade. He'd yet to win a fight with the damn thing. "At least I caught you with the shoulder?"

The Windmaster chuckled, "At least that."

THE TRIO TOOK their last dinner on the ship's deck, calming seas as the vessel approached Foti allowing them a sedate meal beneath the ethereal sails. Kance had a way with blues, and the cerulean colors faded to white and purple depending on how the sunlight hit their thin canvases. More long than wide, the sails found the wind like Wax might've a vine in the jungle's heart: with swooping precision.

Even now the sailors, stationed at three separate tills along the ship's length, barked out calls to one another to keep the vessel flying across the water.

As the ship's captain had told them upon leaving Vis: Rana might flow on the seas, but Kance would float above them.

Wax's home? Kitaye preferred the ships to come to it. Seafarers could be found on the far coast—the thought of them bent Wax into a frown—but their craft, svelte boats built from cultivated, fallen leaves wouldn't last long in the ocean's rough-and-tumble grasp.

Then again, three days out and Wax already missed the feel of loam between his toes, of trees above and cooking spices lingering in the air.

"Better than this, anyway," Wax muttered, sipping another leek soup spoonful. The thin liquid barely qualified, though the Kance captain made clear Wax could barter for something tastier.

As if Wax had anything to barter with.

"You muttering to yourself again?" Quik asked.

"Maybe." Wax refused to admit what he'd really been doing: talking to Pan, picturing his friend with them, ready to join Wax in critiquing the culinary malfeasance forced upon their bodies. "Do you like this?"

"I accept it." Quik shrugged. "When we're out on long hunts, we live on what we can scavenge. This isn't much different."

"Thought Renewals would get something better."

'Take it up with Noctia,' Bliss signed. His sister finished her soup, kept tilting her eyes towards the ship's bow, as if she could spot Foti first. She looked less green now that the ship had passed into flat seas. 'Maybe they'll give you a salmon if you ask real nice.'

"Probably only if I give them this first." Wax reached up to his chest, where the ever-present warmth lingered. There, slotted into a copper-colored necklace, sat a fragment of Vis. A bright emerald no larger than Wax's thumb, the skar tickled Wax's nerves whenever he touched it, like brushing a numbing leaf. Its faint voice now whispered nonsense in his head in the quiet moments, an insect he couldn't silence but had learned to ignore. "How many do you think I'll get?"

'Every single one,' Bliss signed. 'I didn't join you to see you fail.'

"Makes two of us," Quik added. "Finish the soup, Wax. The next step starts tomorrow."

CHAPTER 2
BELOW

The cave ate their footfalls. Svarde and Kivi, the rock-lizard ferrite, walked at the small column's head. Svarde's torch sputtered in his right hand, its glinting flame finding and destroying shadows in the jagged tunnel. Maena's information said this cave would keep going deeper and deeper, far along to a point where every explorer failed to return.

Down there, somewhere, was the fiend's source.

The cave wasn't dead rock. Mosses and mushrooms poked out from crannies. Water dripped and joined them here and there, sluicing along through the earth. For the first hour, too, the Rana sailors broke up the journey with songs.

That ended when they reached the Aegis.

Like a spiderweb built from silver light, the Aegis ran along beneath the seven isles, protecting them. A gift from the gods in their last moments, or so the Circle and the Najahn declared. Svarde hadn't ever seen it before, and the lines splitting the air before his face, catching the torchlight but not bending in its flame, forced a halt to the march.

Maena, the Rana captain, decked out now in her full deep blue leather and emerald cuirass, matching blue-and-green pants, joined Svarde at the lead while sailors grumbled behind.

"So this is it," Maena said, reaching out and touching the filaments. A hand-length apart, the lines ran through the rock, and Svarde guessed if he chased them all the way, they'd lead right back to Catya, there in that prison.

"Beyond here we'll have no protection," Svarde said, his right hand going up to the axe on his back. "The fiends will be undeterred."

"Are you scared, Guardian?"

"I'm not a Guardian anymore." Svarde didn't look at Maena, kept his eyes ahead into the gloom. "My name's Svarde. Call me that, or nothing."

"The march making you sensitive?"

"I'm keeping it simple. You should, too."

Maena jerked her head back towards the column, the eyes peaking past torches to look at their leaders.

"All of them understand we're likely to die down here, Svarde. They all have their reasons for coming, reasons that came from the lives they've led. Don't ask them to throw that away."

"All I'm asking is for their swords and crossbows when the fiends come."

Maena nodded, "That, I think, they can deliver." She stepped back from Svarde, faced her sailors. "After this, the songs stop. We move in quiet. Watch for danger, keep your feet steady. Trust your friends, your wits, your abilities, and we will not fail."

Kivi snorted. Svarde agreed. Grand speeches always paled against harsh realities. Maena's would fare no better down here.

Walking past the Aegis didn't clear the air, didn't make Svarde feel any lighter, heavier, sicker or happier. It did, though, raise the hairs on his neck, set his eyes to sweeping the cave on a constant patrol.

For a long time the cave had offered them nothing. Only a single path with winding turns, some steep and shallow sections. After the Aegis, though, the makeup changed.

The earth went wild.

Not five minutes after the filaments the tunnel burst open into a sprawling cavern, one broken up by towering pillars, irregular rock stomping on one another in a purple-pale mash-up. Lines carved by unnatural means scraped along the walls as Svarde and the crew poured into the broad space, fanning out with torches held high. Rocky teeth hung down from the ceiling, some dripping water onto equally large spires rising from the floor, some as tall as Svarde and twice as wide.

"A man could get lost in here," Svarde muttered, waving his torch around, scouring the wet ground for a sign.

A sign of what, Svarde didn't know. But he'd take a fiend's trail. The monsters had to come from somewhere down here, and a claw track might lead them right to where they needed to go.

Might lead Svarde to where he'd wanted to be ever since Catya picked up that last skar, ever since becoming the Aegis went from fanciful dream to iron certainty.

Ever since he'd given up the one he'd loved for seven isles that didn't give a single damn about her.

Maena broke Svarde's reverie, calling for a break, a chance to drink some water, eat some of the salted meats they'd brought along. Svarde and Kivi rejoined the crew, found their several dozen setting up in their clicques, torches planted where they could.

The Rana sailors had a different cast about them now. Their tanned, sea-sprayed bodies hunched, their eyes roaming like scared beasts. A hand free was a hand on a saber hilt. Others checked once, twice that their crossbows were loaded.

"They're scared," Svarde said to Maena, the two of them, as they often were, sitting apart from the others. "We're not even one day along and some look like they might crack."

"Few have been in a cave before, Svarde. Much less one that runs this long." Maena frowned at her own dull white fish strip. "Reality gives us a different taste than our dreams."

"We're far away from dreams now."

"They'll come around. Give them time."

Kivi snorted, Svarde nodded. Time was all well and good, but they didn't have time to give. Already, new sounds trickled up through the rocks, not the dripping water, the whistling wind, but the scrabble of claws on stone. The far off cries as beasts found battle, or purpose. The clicks, clacks, coughs as things unimagined took notice of their next meal.

Svarde stood, drew his right axe and held it aloft. It caught the torchlight, drew the eyes from every Rana sailor. Heaped over with Whent furs, his Guardian Foti-forged gear beneath, Svarde hulked. The weight gave him fortitude, bolstered his purpose, and he let the sailors find some solace in his form.

"Brothers, sisters," Svarde began as the Foti often did. "Where we go now, monsters await. Demons, even. Creatures for which we have no words. I look at you and see what might pass as fear in lesser people, but that must now be turned to courage. For remember, you travel with soldiers, with fighters." Svarde nodded at his axe. "We will see the worst before this is done, but when it is over, it will be the fiends that know fear. Not us."

A few heartened grins caught Svarde's ending, some others held up their swords, their waterskins. For a brief moment, the grand speech had its hold.

Until a howl, rising from the deep and coming closer, stole it all away.

CHAPTER 3
WHAT RISES MUST FALL

The Wound descended at Ami's feet, its darkness dropping far below anyone's sight. Sticks, stones, and even some lit torches tossed down vanished without sound into the Wound's all-consuming black. Nothing thrown that way ever returned.

But plenty rose up.

"Be ready," Catya whispered, the Aegis moving back on her stone chair, settling on the cushions and looking as frail as ever. Her robes looked to bury her body, too large by half, but no doubt measured right not long ago. "They are coming."

The Aegis's warning was unnecessary, as the flashes around the dimming necklace at her chest worked well enough as clues to what approached. The seven skars resembled dull rocks now, their faint colors the slightest reminder of what they once were.

"Wards," Ami said, drawing her sword and bringing both hands to grip the great blade.

Foti-crafted, etched with glimmering orange topaz along the center, Flamebreak earned its namesake. The silverblack blade seemed to draw in the torchlight, glowing in its reflection.

The two Wards, Najahn guards in spotless purple-black plate armor, chakrams hooked into their backs and voulges at the front, stepped from their watchposts inside the dome.

They stood on rock, albeit clean rock, and the smooth gray surface let the trio spread out to cover the Wound. Ami put herself before Catya, while the two Wards took opposite sides, forming a triangle around the pit.

The scrabbling drew closer, raking as large paws and claws dug into stone and loosed it from the walls. Heaving lungs growled and huffed with every pull.

They were close.

Ami drew in a breath, felt Flamebreak's wrapped hilt beneath her hands. Her armor sat heavy, perfect on her shoulders, her legs. A recent addition, that: with the fiends coming more frequently, Ami had to assume any day might bring a breakthrough.

At least this time she was here, ready to fulfill her role.

"Glad I get to be your Guardian one more time," Ami said without looking back to Catya.

"Hopefully not the last." Catya's words almost broke Ami's heart, not because of what she said, but the sheer brittleness in how they sounded.

With luck, the Renewal would happen soon enough to give Catya a few days, a week, a month without her burden.

With luck.

The fiend gave no warning. The claws scratched below, and then its shape flared free from the Wound, jumping at the Ward ahead and to Ami's right.

Every fiend was a unique horror, and this one bore its claws along eight spindly arms, each one emerging from a wooly, long torso. Gnashing teeth and sharp sapphire eyes dominated one end, while its rear found room for a snapping, stinger-equipped tail.

The damn things were getting worse.

The Ward fell back at the fiend's leap, using her voulge and its curved point to block the swiping claws. Where the spear's heavy haft couldn't go, the Ward's armor took the hits, gouges appearing in the metal.

The Ward to Ami's left slapped his voulge into the ground, swiping both hands behind him to draw the chakrams. Taking a side-step, the man spun, building up momentum and launching the discs one after another. The sharp circles gashed into the fiend, each one shearing off a leg and leaving the monster howling.

Standing up on its two rear claws, the beast lunged forward, putting its full weight on the defending Ward and bearing her to the ground. The Ward called for help, and the third guard made his appearance, running in from outside with his voulge ready.

The one who'd thrown his chakrams glared at Ami, his face asking why, with that huge sword, she'd yet to move.

The answer came from the Wound, where claws still made their nasty sounds.

The second fiend leapt out, its legs spreading wide as its teeth snapped towards Ami, as if planning to enclose the Guardian in an awful embrace.

Bad idea.

Ami brought Flamebreak up to her shoulder, then swiped the blade in a diagonal slash across her body as the fiend closed. The sword, true to its namesake, left sparks in the air as it went, those hot embers lining the fiend's body as the sword bit in hard.

The creature squealed, the damage done to its midsection, and those gnashing teeth pulled back in a wild howl. The legs landed around Ami, the fiend's bulk pressing her back a step even as its vitals leaked free from the wound.

Ami sidestepped left, setting her right foot hard as she did so, whirling Flamebreak from her ankles up around her chest in a spinning cut. The swipe snared a couple reaching legs, barely slowing her swords momentum as it sliced clean through. Again the fiend howled.

And again, Ami set herself. Finishing her spin, Ami brought Flamebreak up to her shoulder, point forward. The fiend thrashed, its sapphire eyes lighting on her, showing nothing close to sanity.

Time to put the monster down.

"For the forge," Ami growled, kicking off with both feet in a short sprint at the fiend's body.

Clawed legs tried to buffet her, but the talons bounced off her hard shoulder pads. The fiend opened its mouth wide, intending to swallow Ami's head whole.

The bite never made it. Flamebreak struck first, pushing in, lifting the fiend's torso skyward. Ami kept pushing the scrambling, dying beast towards the Wound. When she saw the blackness beneath the monster, Ami pulled back on the blade, letting Flamebreak burn its way free.

The fiend couldn't do more than burble as it fell deep into the dark.

Ami tracked her look to the other monster, similarly dispatched, although with many more cuts. Voulges whirled, chakrams littered the ground, and the fiend's slow demise played out as the monster settled into its forever sleep.

The Ward who'd drawn the fiend's initial rush knelt on the ground, her wounds already getting patched by her fellow guards. The post-battle quiet, a sacred silence, descended.

"You haven't lost a step," Catya whispered, coming up behind Ami, leaning on her shoulder. The thin Aegis felt like a feather, making Ami flinch. Every touch confirmed Catya was so far from what she'd been, so far from . . .

No. Those dreams only led to nightmares.

"As long as I'm protecting you," Ami said, sheathing Flamebreak, "I'll never stop getting stronger."

Ami faced Catya, forced herself to look at her friend. Memories clashed with the current moment, Catya's eyes showing old curiosity as they trailed to Ami's sheathed sword.

"Foti's skar still burns?" Catya asked.

"Still." Ami nodded.

"Mine die so quickly, yet yours sparkle with so much life."

"I'm not protecting all the isles with mine."

"Trade?"

Ami laughed, shook her head. Stopped herself from saying what she felt.

Never, Catya. Never would Ami pay that price.

"Then, can I ask you something?" Catya said, stopping to take breaths between the words. She'd need a nap soon. Ami flicked a glance to the Wards, nodded at a straw-covered patch near the stone chair. They'd find cushions, a blanket.

"Anything," Ami replied.

"I need to know, here at the end, was I too weak?" Catya reached up, clutched the necklace. "Was I the wrong choice?"

How do you answer a question like that?

The Catya Ami knew, the one she'd grown up with,

would've never asked it. Would've assumed she was the perfect person for anything she chose to do. That's how you earned the Aegis in the first place: unshakeable belief in your abilities.

But here Catya was. Barely a decade since she'd put on the necklace and withered up. All but spent. Not just physically, but, clearly, her soul too.

Ami needed to answer her. Give Catya something to hold onto. Ami cast a net, glanced left and saw nothing save the canvas dome and slate gray stone. Looked right, found an opportunity.

"They fight for you," Ami said, nodding to the Wards. "I fight for you."

"Because the Circle demands it."

"Those Najahn blowhards hold no sway over me." Ami put her gauntlets, careful, on Catya's shoulders, drew her in tight. Again the lightness, the barely-there weight sent shivers. "I'm here because I love you. Always have. Always will."

Catya's sniff muffled against the thick mail. "You don't hate me for being so weak? For dying so fast?"

Ami pulled back, "You're not dead."

The sniff, the red-rims around Catya's eyes turned into a dire, thin laugh.

"Ami, I died the moment I put this necklace on."

CHAPTER 4

THE GAMBLER

Foti's obsidian towers emerged through the fog like a giant's chipped teeth. Looming and dark, they nonetheless filled wax with calm after days on the open sea. A clear horizon was beautiful, sure, but having a reference point was a nice change. Helped ground him to know how fast they were skipping across the water.

That water had been home to waves and little else, save the occasional passing bird or cloud. Now the sea grew crowded as Wax, Bliss, and Quik watched near the Kance vessel's bow.

If Kitaye had Vis's trade all to itself, Foti, and the city they headed towards, a smoke-and-steel town called Smythe, made the jungle isle's commerce seem like children's toys.

Giant Foti galleons brushed up alongside the Kance vessel, towering overhead with their dark wood and metal bodies, massive sails blotting out the sun as they swept along. Wax and Bliss shrank back every time one came near, even though the Kance sailors assured them no collision could happen, not with their ship so lithe.

Quik, for his part, put on a false smile and stood, arms crossed, daring this new world to shove him around.

Smaller cutting ships abounded too, casting their fishing nets or setting about with harpoons in favor of larger game. Ships from other isles, like Noctia's swooping gray sloops and Rana's flowing cutters, dashed in and out of Smythe's sprawling port. As they closed, the air picked up an iron tang, Wax's lungs itching.

Coughs spread around the ship as the sailors settled into the new way of things.

Berthing lacked grandeur: ropes appeared in hands, slipped over posts on one pier among many, the docks forking out into the ocean. Someone dropped an anchor and the captain, a man who'd never bothered to give Wax his name, wished them a dismissive farewell.

The trio took their satchels and stepped off, feeling the hard wood shiver.

"I, for one, could use some land beneath my feet," Quik said.

"Race you to it?" Wax nodded towards the dock's end, a run crowded with crew and cargo.

'You're on,' Bliss signed, the first bright grin Wax had seen in days springing up.

The seasickness had turned Bliss into little more than stewing sludge. Good to see her fun coming back.

"Not this time," Quik killed the idea. "This isn't home. We're visitors, and more than that, Renewals. We can't act like idiots."

"Why?" Wax asked, starting the walk towards shore anyway.

Not as fun as a race, but land was land, and he'd gone long enough without it.

"Because unless you know how to get Foti's skar, we'll have to get help from someone here."

"There's not, just, a guide? A sign?"

"Did we have one in Kitaye?"

Quik twisted his voice a certain way when he wanted to make a point, a distant mocking inflection on the words. Wax didn't answer right away as they walked, dodging around crates and carriers filled up with sacks and satchels. The answer to Quik's riddles would always be apparent, if he just thought about it enough.

"Okay, so we knew Vis," Wax said, homing in on the answer. "Because we lived there, we'd all heard the stories, seen the Renewals before. But we've not done that here, so we'll need someone who has."

"Look at that, Bliss. Our brother's not hopeless after all."

'Don't know if I'd go that far.'

Wax reached up, pulled out the necklace so the emerald skar sat on top his green-tan weave. "Hey, who's the important one here? Be nice."

Quik snorted, Bliss rolled her eyes, and Wax felt new stares fall on him.

Looks that'd been cursory before, confirming perhaps that these three really were Vis, now looked harder and no longer at Wax's face, his weave. The skar drew the stares, held inspections.

Wax tucked the necklace back beneath the weave. The looks went away, and Wax breathed again. He hadn't realized he'd stopped, hadn't realized how odd his nerves felt under the press from all those wandering eyes.

"Good call," Quik said, low. Wax noticed his brother's hands had drifted towards the gauntlets at his waist, the hand-covering mauls ready to be slipped on in a second. "Not sure we should be advertising who you are."

"I'm getting that, but why not?"

"Because the skars can be used for more than Renewals, my new friends," a voice announced, the source a man lounging on a crate just off the dock's end. Several days stubble lingered on a sun-drenched face, shiny black and purple leather breeches and boots gave way to an ashen tunic. At his hips, duel rapiers—Wax could recognize the weapons now after all those Kance duels, lay ready. A pipe sat steaming in one hand.

And the most intense eyes Wax had ever seen, almost purple in their look, locked on him. The man waved with a pipe to an open spot on the rock next to him, where dirty water lapped against the bare stone shore. No beaches here.

The trio stopped, Quik going one step further to put himself just a hair between Wax and this new man. If a threat, though, presented itself, none of the commerce near them detected it: crew and cargo continued their inexorable progress.

"Who are you?" Quik asked, the hunter taking over. "And why were you waiting for us?"

"Name's Cassignol, and I come here every day watching for clueless travelers." The man grinned. "There's good trade to be had helping the lost find their way."

"How do you—" Quik started, stopped when Wax went past him, stepped right up to Cassignol.

"We're not lost," Wax said, squaring up to the man. Cassingol, despite his fancy clothes, didn't have much stature to him. No brawls in the backstreets for this one. "But we could use a pointer or two, if you're inclined to provide one."

"Can do, can do," Cassignol said, nodding several times

over. "I'll give you this one for free: You're in Smythe, jewel of Foti's southern coast, and the biggest mining town in the Seven isles. Anything you want that requires heat and ore, you can find it here." Cassignol stood up off his crate, waved at the city behind him. "Fortunes are made by your skill with the hammer and tong in this city."

"Or by your slick tongue?" Wax curled up a smile.

Cassignol gave him a slight nod. "As it is everywhere." The man squared back up to the three. "Now, I can get you whatever it is you're looking for, but, in trade, you must do something for me."

"Which is?"

"A game, my friends. A simple game."

Cassignol spun on his heel, began walking up the sprawling avenue. Wax glanced back at his two Guardians, who shrugged. A game might not be what they were looking for, but they had few other options. No other leads.

"Guess we play," Wax said to his siblings, and they started off after the man.

The Seven Isles had their differences. Wax learned this young, as did everyone, simply through the ships pulling into Kitaye's harbor. While everyone spoke the same language, the slang differed, the phrasing morphed, the accents changed. Babble on Smythe's streets came in coarse and straight, hammer blows hitting every syllable, a dialect that made sense as the noise from smithies, docks, and hard work filled every gap.

For the first time in his life, Wax felt molded brick beneath his feet, laid cobblestones—Cassignol threw out the details as they walked—proving hot on Wax's toes despite the cloudy day. Avenues broke off on either side, all flanked by homes, businesses, people living out unrecognizable lives.

No communal cook fires, no fragrant spices, no whoops and dances. Not that he didn't see happiness on the faces, not that the Foti people didn't have springs in their steps, but here it came with grime and grit, heavy muscles and laden backs.

Blades, axes, knives, and worse clung on every waist. Leather and steel cloaked chests and legs, while many back on Vis worse next to nothing at all save their earned inks.

"Quit your gawking," Cassignol said as they cleared a large square, this one dominated by a hammer statue, its massive gold-gilded head slamming down into a marble slab. "Everyone can see you're outsiders, but they don't need to hate you for it."

"Hate us?" Wax asked. Quik and Bliss seemed content to follow, to let Wax lead the conversation. "Why? We've never seen all this before."

"You like being watched, boy?"

Wax glared. "I'm not a boy."

"Here your skin's too clean to be anything but. Earn a few ember scars, work some more ash into that hair, maybe we'll see you as something more." Cassignol's smile took on an edge. "Till then, you're nothing but a mark."

"That's what I am to you?"

Cassignol shrugged, took a hard right towards a squat, long building. A shingled roof looked like it'd collected its own ash coating over the years, the flakes falling here and there over the scorched stone exterior. Wax didn't see any fires, any forges nearby, so how the building earned its color seemed a mystery.

Cassignol guided them through the main doors, and inside sprawled something new: the Najahn barracks back on Vis had looked something like this, long tables placed side by side, chairs around every one. Here, though, those tables were occupied, and not by food. Instead, strange instruments lay along them all, with men and women surrounding each, bellowing out numbers, colors. Some threw small cubes into square boxes, while others spun wheels while the table's other occupants looked on, taking sips from ale flagons before cursing or shouting in glee.

Shiny clay chips passed from hand to table and back again as the cubes hit their numbers, the wheels stopped their spinning.

"Welcome," Cassignol said, turning to face the trio and spread out his arms, "to Smythe's pride and joy, The Anvil's Arms." Continuing his slow twirl, Cassignol pointed at the machines, the crowds clustered. "Here you can win a new life for yourself, can have the most fun you've ever enjoyed. The possibilities are limitless, and with those full satchels, I invite you to take advantage."

"More like, they take advantage of us," Quik muttered, coming up beside Wax. "The man's playing you, brother. We should leave."

Cassignol tilted his head, put on a pout even Wax could tell was false. "Ah, but my friends, you promised me a game, did you not?"

"And you promised us an answer," Quik reminded the man.

A glittering grin rekindled, Cassignol nodded, "Play a few rounds and we'll see about getting you on your way, perhaps with a heavier load than before."

The first two days at sea, Wax burned hours staring off at nothing. Pan, his best friend, the one who should've been in his place, kept whispering that his death was Wax's fault. Sawi, Wax's love now separated by duty and distance, drained away the zest, the happiness that'd brought springs to Wax's every step.

For those first two days Quik and Bliss tried, failed to make a dent in that sorrow. Towards the end of the second, a Kance sailor, that duelist with a rapier, suggested Wax could break his mood by embracing the adventure. Turning his life into something new.

So when Cassignol suggested diving into a game, Wax found he didn't much care what it was. They were on Foti, a whole new isle, embarking on a ridiculous quest to save the world.

Quik's caution stank of old thinking, of the boring and the slow.

CHAPTER 5

BOLTS AND BLADES

T he tunnels gave Svarde and Maena time to engage a defense. The two shouted orders, at first contradictory and then aligning, setting the sailors into a close circle, using the pillars to make tight gaps. Torches stacked in the center, the bright glow shining out towards any oncoming creatures, hopefully blinding their approach while making shots easy to take.

On the ring's outside, the sailors most confident in their sabers and their armor. On the inside, crossbows at the ready. Maena, ignoring Svarde's suggestion, stood next to him at the absolute front line. Kivi snorted at Svarde's feet, chewing on a pillar's base between glances towards the approaching noises.

Roars, hisses, claws on rock. The usual fiend symphony.

Svarde had both axes ready, their fresh edges gleaming in the orange-yellow flickers. On his right, Maena held her saber in one hand, the other with its wrist slung through a thin duelist's shield. She had her hair tucked beneath a Rana cap, a smooth helm so slick it'd deflect just about any smack delivered unto its shiny gray self.

Svarde knew that quite well, from memories he'd rather forget. Fights from a life long since past.

"Ready?" Svarde growled Maena's way.

"If I wasn't, I should've stayed topside," Maena replied. "This is what we've been working for, Svarde."

"What's that?"

"A fight on the fiend's home turf. They've been the invaders all this time." Maena's voice rose. "Let's kick their asses all the way back home."

The sailors took up a cheer. The shouts echoed around the cavern, a brief confidence. One buried mere moments later.

The fiends didn't deal in subtlety. The slobbering things crawled from the dark, two massive arms pulling a rounded torso, a spider's mandibles along the ground. As Svarde took in the newest horror, he noticed a green trail leaking behind them, smoke rising where it touched the ground.

Not only were these monsters ugly, but they had surprises.

"Don't let their blood touch you," Svarde hollered as the first crossbow quarrels shot over his shoulders.

The bolts, shorter than the arrows he saw on Vis, went straight ahead with malicious force. They bit hard into the clambering fiends, spinning the monsters around, driving them to the ground, or finishing their fight with a well-placed strike to the fiend's savage face. Clicks abounded behind Svarde as the ones who shot reloaded, those precious seconds opening a window where the next fiends, their hands and bodies steaming, burning from the acidic ooze of their fellows, swam forward.

Svarde went to meet them.

His first target found Svarde's eyes on approach, the monster declaring Svarde's demise with a harrowing roar, its spit flecking onto Svarde's face, followed by a mighty swipe. Svarde met the arm with his left axe, an upward deflection that should've sheared the limb off at the wrist. Instead, the axe bit in only a fraction, the crushing blow continuing right on through and throwing Svarde to the ground.

His right knee banged hard on the stone, his shoulder's impact cushioned by Svarde's armor. His right hand, gripping the axe, wasn't so lucky: the fiend planted its own left hand on the sprawled limb, pinning it to the ground. Its teeth spread wide, sought victory.

And found a mouthful of ferrite instead.

Kivi jumped on and leapt off Svarde's back, curling into a ball as the ferrite slammed into the fiend's open mouth, cracking those incisors and forcing the jaw wider still, a morsel too large, too dangerous for the fiend to eat.

Kivi went to work, her claws and snorts, her lava-hot vents forcing the fiend into a haphazard retreat. Svarde pulled himself upright, confirmed Kivi seemed to have the better of that matchup, and felt the next quarrel wave shoot past him into the dark.

More fiends howled, more collapsed, and the air suffused with an acrid tang. The smoking blood swamped the floor, and Maena called for a backpedal, a closing in around the torches.

The fiends, too, seemed to hesitate, their battle cries dying to whimpers, coughs, sniffs from the dark beyond.

Svarde counted eight monsters dead, another half that injured and being put down by precision shots.

Unnecessary.

"Save your ammo," Svarde said, back-stepping to the line. "We won't be recovering quarrels from these beasts."

Kivi joined him a moment later, soaked in the sizzling

offal, the goop thankfully unable to penetrate her hard shell. The ferrite snorted at Svarde, disdain evident in her sharp attitude.

"I'll be more careful," Svarde apologized. "You're right. You shouldn't have to save me every time."

The ferrite snorted again, taking up its place at Svarde's shins. He took the ceasefire to check the crew, found only a couple minor injuries, though three sabers had been lost to the boiling blood. An unforeseen problem: how many spare arms had Maena brought?

If the captain seemed bothered by the events, Maena didn't show it. She continued delivering commands, straightening out the circle, tightening its gaps to make up for the pillars they'd left behind. No natural walls buttressed their circle now, just dense human will.

It would have to be enough.

The smaller circle invited a new strategy, and the fiends proved they had some brains inside those meaty skulls, the monsters making noise aplenty as they spread throughout the cavern, those clawed arms scratching upwards towards the ceiling and behind them on the walls. Shadows moved at torchlight's edge, their jerking, angry strokes an unnatural sight.

More than a few sailors muttered prayers to Rana, more than a few whispered doubts about their decision to come on such a foolish quest.

Svarde would have to show them they were not doomed.

"We break them," Svarde announced. "Strike before they're ready. Aim for their heads, watch the arms. Don't doubt yourself or your fellow fighters. We are together." He clapped his axes, then shouted out a Foti battle cry.

Solid as steel. Hot as a forge.

If Maena doubted his strategy, she didn't counter it, and the Rana sailors parted like an exploding fire. Sabers and daggers drawn, the sailors closed at speed with the fiends. The bigger creatures proved less nimble, their dual arms large and deadly, but not so quick to adapt to slashing strikes, surprised stabs from corners unseen and unexpected.

Svarde, with Kivi at his heels, drove straight into the darkness, letting the torchlight's edge highlight his target, a fiend mid-climb up a stone pillar, in shadow.

Taking one step, planting his right foot, Svarde jumped high, slashed with his axe, and caught the creature's smoking end. Like with the wrist, as Svarde had hoped, his axe bit in and held, letting Svarde's leap carry him on and pull the fiend down with him. The great creature landed on its side, just in time for Kivi to barrel into its gnashing maw.

This time, Svarde landed with a roll, rising, turning and dashing back to strike the vulnerable beast from behind. A double whack with his axes, coupled with Kivi's mauling, put the fiend down. Splatters smoked on Svarde's furs and leather, but that didn't stop the Guardian from picking his next victim and moving on, voice rising into a Foti battle chant.

This first victory would belong to the humans.

Most fights felt longer than they were, mere seconds ending lives that'd lasted for many years. Svarde's axes, Kivi's teeth and claws found fiends aplenty to sink into, but most monsters already bore wounds, were fleeing more than fighting from the Rana's nasty stabbing daggers and slicing swords. The growls and howls dwindled as the last creatures were cornered and put to final rest.

And yet, two Rana lay dead, one to snapping teeth, another to an unlucky spray of the foul blood.

In the heaving aftermath, the two bodies and several more wounded were put near the torches. The remaining Rana without more than scratches gazed at their friends while Maena led a seafarer's blessing.

Svarde tuned it out, looked at the bodies and didn't see them.

How many times now would corpses litter his path?

Kivi must've sensed the dour direction Svarde's post-victory thoughts were taking, because the ferrite tugged at Svarde's leather greaves. A look down found Kivi's eyes sending Svarde in another direction. One away from the Rana funeral, from the plans to carry the bodies back to the surface for proper casting into the sea.

"What'd you find, my friend?" Svarde asked, following Kivi deeper into the cavern, in the direction the fiends had come from.

A monster's body lay there, one of several. A quarrel, or what remained of its withered, melted shaft, protruded from the skull, speaking to the fiend's early end. What had drawn Kivi's attention, though, came soon enough: the blood Svarde had seen before the fight, the answer made clear. A deep wound along the fiend's backside, a gash too straight and clean to come from a claw or a narrow rock.

Svarde knelt, careful to keep his knee from the smoking blood, and studied the line. The fiend's skin, a sickly yellow, looked torn clear, but blackened, too, at the edges and within. Some poison, then. Further evidence against accidental injury.

"GOING OFF ON YOUR OWN ALREADY?" Maena asked, the Rana captain coming up behind him.

Svarde pointed at the wound, described it, found nothing but cold in Maena's eyes.

"Don't you find it curious?" Svarde asked.

"What I find curious is how a member of our band could wander away while we pay our respects to our dead." Quick as a flash, Maena had her glittering, curved dagger out and held to Svarde's throat. "We are in this together, Svarde. You and all of us. When one dies, we see them off as one. Or you can leave now, and take your chances in this grim dungeon alone."

Svarde found no joke, no room to wriggle in her expression. Found only an answer to give.

"I've spent a long time avoiding people, because I've seen enough of them die." Svarde rose, reached and took a gentle hold of Maena's hand and the dagger's hilt. "I thought I could avoid awakening those memories. Perhaps I was wrong."

"You were."

Svarde bowed his head, apologized, and the dagger found its way home just as fast as it had appeared. Behind them, the sailors split into two parties, a small few accompanying the wounded and the dead back to the surface.

Fifteen left to continue the journey, replenished with what supplies they could scavenge from their departing friends.

As for the long wound, when Svarde showed it to Maena, the Rana captain had no answers. Only more questions.

"The Dark Below won't give us much else, I expect," Maena said, the troop gathered, torches again lighting the way on. "At least, not till we reach its rotting core."

"And carve it to pieces," Svarde added.

At that, at least, a rumbling agreement made its way through their force.

With torch in one hand, an ax in the other, Svarde again took up his spot at the front, marching out the cavern's far side and down, always down, into the dark.

CHAPTER 6
IN WORDS, IDEAS

Every Isle told its history in a different way. On Foti, big events had their details carved into stone, the tablets stacked and displayed in the immense hall in the Great Forge at the isle's northern end, Foti's hot beating heart.

Ami wasn't after Foti's stories, though. Noctia, thankfully, had an easier way of recording moments. The isle seemed to take its minimal resources as a sign to invest in more developed things, and the same spires serving as home to the Najahn and the Circle housed, too, the Seven Isle's foremost, and only, university.

Leaving Flamebreak and her armor behind, the latter getting some touch-ups courtesy of Noctia's inferior blacksmiths, Ami felt the chill through her purple-black Najahn robes as she wandered into the crowded intersection. Past the first gates, where the guards gave her solemn nods, Noctia swapped from bustling seaport and thriving civilization miasma to something more sedate, yet more exciting.

The goods here came by way of conversation, and they flowed back and forth through the air as men and women launched treatises, ideas, and data at one another. Benches and tables strewn about the cobblestoned square found themselves occupied despite the chill, steaming coffee mugs—imported beans from Vis and Kance arrived daily—masking the nastier seaport smells from further down the crater's mountainside.

Shops took on a different air here too, displaying trades for paper, pen ink and quills, books, and gear meant for a battlefield Ami had little experience with. Yet she wandered into the first one anyway, glancing at the shelves.

Letters came back at her, long titles on leather-bound volumes declaiming this and that. Ami found her bottom lip a good target for chewing, nervousness touching her. Reading as a skill wasn't exactly prized in Foti, wasn't required to bring a Renewal around the isles and earn the Aegis.

"Anything I can help you find?"

Ami almost jumped at the mousey voice, the shop's sole clerk appearing behind her with more stealth than a Kance assassin. Instead of whipping a backhand and stepping aside to buy herself time, Ami forced up a smile. The clerk looked every bit the scholar, his robes bearing the golden tassles reserved for Noctia graduates. A single lens hung from his neck, ready to assist with any close up scrutiny.

"History," Ami said.

"Ah, well." The scholar nodded at the shelf Ami was inspecting. "You've found the right place. Any particular events you're looking to study?"

"The Renewals."

"Joining in on the fun, eh?"

"The fun?"

The scholar chuckled, made an absent wave towards the square. "Every time a another one is announced, we have our scribes get to copying new editions of them all." The scholar moved next to her, reached and pulled out a thin volume, a gold-lettered name, Demion, on the spine. "But I'm sensing you're not the average student looking for answers to their next quiz."

He held the book towards her. Ami looked at it, kept her hands at her sides.

"Who's that?" Ami asked.

"The one that matters more than all the others," the scholar said, his voice picking up a certain reverence. He ran his fingers over the cover, unadorned save for the name, again done in gold on the black leather. "You want to understand what this is, then you must start at the beginning."

Ami frowned, took the volume, then looked back towards the shelf. "I was hoping you might have something more recent."

"The last few Renewals have their editions near the entrance. You would've walked—"

"I want the real stories, not what the Circle decided to publish." Ami flipped open Demion's volume, expecting and indeed finding the Circle's mark, their approval stamped and signed inside. "Everyone knows they control the message."

"If that's what you believe, then why are you seeking answers in a Najahn bookstore, my friend?"

"Because I don't know where else to look."

The scholar nodded. "Books aren't a simple endeavor. They take time to write, resources to be made whole. Noctia and the Circle control what we do because we are the only ones with the means to do it." The scholar turned around, but as he walked towards the front counter, he threw a look back Ami's way that said follow, so she did, tucking the Demion volume, and its Circle marking, under her arm.

The scholar pulled out a tiny paper scrap, one stained by a rogue coffee drop. Dipping his pen in the small ink well at his elbow, both now resting on the slim stone counter, the scholar wrote out numbers, a name. An address.

"It wasn't always this way," the scholar said, "and there are still those who do what they can to preserve an unvarnished history. Ask for Mattimo."

Ami took the paper, double-checked that she could read the scholar's scribble. Barely. She moved to set the volume on the counter, but the scholar pushed her hand back.

"Edited it might be, but this one is far from false. Give it a try, Guardian."

Ami blinked, stared at the bookkeeper with sharper eyes.

"You know who I am?"

"I wouldn't be much of a scholar if I didn't recognize the Foti swordmaster whose been stalking our island for the last decade, now would I?"

"Then you'll tell the Circle what I've been asking about."

The scholar shrugged, "Will I risk my life and well-being for you, Guardian? No, I will not. But neither do I see a need to go running to the Circle and tell them all about my day. Don't give them a reason to come knocking on my door, and I won't knock on theirs."

Ami didn't open the book till she had her lunch, till she sat alone on her slim balcony looking over the downward slope to Noctia's main city. The morning gave her a day free from strong winds, rain, or the awful smells accompanying the massive Whent ships and their manure.

The weather gave her an opening, the fiends climbing up the Wound gave her the motivation.

Demion, the first Aegis, didn't leap off the pages. Whomever scribed the volume took things from legend and said so, creating a woman who'd embarked not out of some grand vision but instead a desire for power, for protection. The Isles were a dangerous place then, with humans moving in packs, creating what weapons they could from scavenged sticks, rocks, slain fiends and their claws.

Demion sought something greater, not unlike every Aegis that came after.

Ami flipped ahead, skimming as she went. Details weren't important. At least, she hoped not. The scholar seemed to force the book on her, so something ought to be gleamed from its pages, but poring over words while Catya died felt worse than useless.

Demion found her first skar on Kance. Fascinated with its power, she—

Ami blinked. Reread the words. Power? Her look traveled to Flamebreak, sheathed and leaning against the wall near her room's door. That the skars held some elemental strength was known—though who knew what those beer brewers and gamblers on Tamas found in their tokens—but aside from the Aegis, the little stones were party tricks. Flamebreak trailed some fancy sparks when it swung. Hardly the stuff to change the world.

Demion, though, didn't seem to see it that way. She tore up her tribe, forced them over seas and lands to find more skars, fiends be damned.

According to this book—Ami flipped to the end, the day was wearing on and she needed to get to the address the scholar noted—Demion fashioned the Aegis necklace herself to hold the stones, witnessed the effect going up by accident, and promptly camped her remaining people right here on Noctia.

What a nice ending. A new home, a shiny necklace, and a curse that'd chain the isles to the skars forevermore.

The book, though, held no discourse on what Demion's search for power did after she became the first Aegis.

"Did you stop?" Ami closed the volume, looked out over the ocean. "Or did you keep looking for more?"

If one set of seven covered the isles in a fiend-destroying shield, what might two or three accomplish?

A polite knock, three soft cracks on her door, canceled the musing. Behind the dark wood waited a woman almost as sturdy as Ami herself, though this one had the dry skin and dead humor local to Noctia. You never could get enough water on the island, and it showed.

"Guardian, I presume?" the woman asked.

Ami hesitated before answering, taking in the woman's full form, namely the massive armor set engulfing her body. Full Foti-forged plate, though the orange emblems and silver badges had been replaced by Noctia purple and gold. The voulge and chakram seemed to be missing, but the ridged gauntlets on the woman's clasped hands told Ami such weapons weren't necesssary.

"You've found me," Ami answered.

The woman nodded, no surprise there. "I'm Terrevin, Catya's new Shieldwarden."

Terrevin made the statement as though Ami should've grasped its meaning without further explanation. Like a drawn blade.

"You mean the Aegis." Ami frowned. "Only her friends call her Catya."

Terrevin's mouth slipped to a straight line. "Catya's her name. That's what I'll call her." The formal Noctia diction dropped away, Ami detecting more than a few years spent on the docks in Terrevin's past. "The Circle's decided to step up Catya's protection, and I drew the lucky deed."

"Good. Fiends made it through this morning."

"I heard. It'll happen again, too, but next time we'll have more than a couple green Wards to greet the ugly things." Terrevin let her hands drop, tilted her head. "Reason I'm here is to warn you that you'll have to clear your visits from now on."

"Clear my visits? I'm her Guardian."

"Right, and we're all thankful for that, but Catya's in a fragile place. Your visits, according to the Wards on duty, rile her up. Can't have that, what with civilization at stake. Best thing for her is rest, peace."

"There's no peace at the Wound."

"There will be now." Terrevin popped up the same placid smile she'd greeted Ami with. "You have any questions, concerns, Guardian, feel free to take them up with the Circle. Till then, you enjoy your afternoon."

Ami stewed for precisely two Terrevin footsteps, jangling heavy things thudding down the hallway.

"Are all Shieldwardens so rude?" Ami called after Terrevin, who flashed a grin back.

"There's only one Shieldwarden, and you're talking to her." Terrvin shrugged again. "So yes, I guess we are."

THE NAJAHN SECTION ran down the mountainside all the way to the water, cut off from the main city by a sloping wall. Periodic gates allowed flow watched by guards either focused or flippant, depending on their mood. At the seaside, the Najahn and the Circle kept a small several docks for themselves, docks full as the day neared dinnertime.

Ami looked over the ships resting there. One Tamas skiff and two Whent sloops, the latter the smallest vessels the Whent, with their love of hulking monsters, made. Anyone keeping an eye on what boats came in and out of this port could deduce which isles held the Circle's favor, or which were begging for it.

Off the docks, the Najahn's waterside warehouses were few and small, buttressed on their sloping sides by the oldest houses on the island. These held sharper angles on their roofs, looking more like arrows than the curated swoops farther up the hillside.

Cats, all collared in purple and gold, roamed the streets here, hunting rats and other vermin stowaways. The yowls, meows, and occasional hissing played backwater to the lapping surf. Nothing quite as unique as Kivi, but the ferrite held a place all her own.

Ami pulled the hood up around her face, hiding her smile. She missed the rock lizard and her skeptical snorts. Missed, too, Kivi's devotion to keeping them all alive. Of course, when Svarde announced his departure, Kivi chose him and adventure over the staid day to day on Noctia, but all the same . . .

This wasn't quite the adventure Kivi preferred either, but Ami's pulse quickened as she slipped down the small side street noted on the scholar's slipped paper. She'd left Flamebreak back in her room, the blade a bit too obvious to go carting around on a walk like this. Only a Foti dagger on her hip now, its blue edge catching a sapphire fire whenever the slimming sunlight found it.

A narrow door marked the address, a candle lamp flickering outside its sodden oak body. Black moss, a damp weed, clawed for purchase around the entry, cut ends showing a mild respect for appearances. The numbers matching the paper sat carved into the grey stone, jagged lines showing a hasty, haphazard job.

Ami knocked, bare hands hitting hard twice. Waited. Knocked once more.

"Coming, coming," came a muffled reply, the words clipped the way the Kance tended to, as if always in a hurry to the next one. Ami stepped back, her right hand moving to the dagger's hilt.

A latch unclicked, then a second, before the door swung open wide. No fear—wait. Ami fought to keep her mouth from dropping at the sight: a stocky man, shirtless to the waist, with wine dribbling off a scraggly gray beard. He held a book in one hand, the goblet hanging from his mouth, placed there to give him a hand free for the door.

"What're you knocking for?" the man asked, curiosity beating back the tone.

"I need some answers," Ami said. "I was told you could help me out."

"What kind of answers?"

"I need to know why the Aegis is dying so fast."

The man nodded, sniffed, then turned his head back into the house. "Friends, the lady has come to us with questions. Do we have answers?"

At least five voices, covering all kinds, rose back in a rousing affirmative.

"Well then," the man said, "I think you've come to the right place. Welcome to the Najahn Historical Society, Guardian."

CHAPTER 7
A MARK

Bliss watched Wax take to the games in the Anvil's Arms with gusto. Her brother soaked up the rules, broke open his satchel and slapped bets down with dried fruit, salted meats, and nuts courtesy of Kitaye's parting gifts. The Foti players, their motley beards and tied off pony-tails sucking in the light with their ash flakes, countered with metals, ores, and raw root vegetables.

Dice, strange white cubes with narrow curves cut into the sides, bounced around. Hard chits with symbols carved front and back flipped up and down. Ales in beige earthen mugs slopped everywhere. A steady drumbeat cascaded along in the background, undercutting constant cheers and jeers.

All beneath a glowering, smoke-stained roof. Despite the vaulting, its dark presence closed on Bliss, crushing in with the bodies buffeting her side and back. Quik didn't seem much better, though her brother's bigger frame and gruff frown seemed to push away accidental contact. Maybe if she drew her staff, delivered a few hits . . .

Wax threw up his hands, let out a vine-swinging

whoop, one accompanied by groans and grins from the seven others at his long table. Another win, and that meant Wax wouldn't want to leave. Egos loved egos, and few loved theirs more than her brother.

"You want to leave?" Quik asked, leaning down and delivering what should've been a whisper as a shout. "You don't look happy."

'You do?' Bliss signed back, her left hand working while her right fended off a drunk stumbler.

"We're his Guardians, Bliss. Guess we do what he wants, now."

'If that's what you believe, then you're a moron.'

Quik grinned, "Look, we've all had it tough. Pan, the fiends, Kitaye getting attacked. Wax looks like he's having fun, so I'm going to let him." He nodded towards the exit. "How about you do some recon, see if you can't find a good way from here to Foti's skar?"

That, at least, seemed like an appealing prospect. Not only the skar but a chance at some food. Bliss had a full satchel, but days of soup, dried fruit, and jerky begged for something different.

'You sure?'

"Just check back in after a while, see if we're still here." Quik tapped his chin. "We'll be outside by dusk if not before. Plan on meeting here by then."

The late morning—Bliss blinked at that, given the party inside—infused her spirit with vigor with its bay-blue sky. The views around her didn't do so much, the soot-covered bricks and stone leaving little for the Vis native to hold onto. As if Foti regarded green things as optional, unnecessary, a waste.

Her own weave seemed to be drying out, too, in the Foti air. They'd have to find some local clothes soon or their outfits would match the ash drifting along the streets. The air wanted them to cover up, the chill sharper as they traveled north, although the constant forges churning away mellowed the breeze with fiery flashes.

Commerce churned about Bliss, big cargo barges trundling by on metal-laid tracks, with people on either end working levers to keep the things moving. One rail zipped towards the port, carts laden with refined ores, with crates stacked and labeled. Others went the reverse on a parallel track, these holding stickered boxes, random lumps to be delivered somewhere, to someone.

The trade on offer seemed absurd, beyond anything Bliss could've wanted. Who needed all this stuff, who wanted to trade it, and why? Was Foti so unable to satisfy itself that they needed so much sent to other isles?

Or was there something Kitaye was doing wrong, with its market stands flush with a few found delicacies and little more?

Well, Quik wanted knowledge, and Bliss wasn't going to find it standing outside the gambling hall.

She took off down the misshapen stone street, its branches increasing with every stride further from the docks. The splits led to small alleys and larger boulevards, with squares popping up here and there dominated by statues of grand leaders Bliss neither recognized nor cared to know.

The city's character changed, too, as she distanced herself from the docks. Fewer sailors, more citizens, people eking out a real living on the isle. Small gardens appeared as forges gave way to homes, to shops catering life's necessities. Those metal tracks stayed with her the whole way, often splitting off or catching small stations where posted people would weed through the contents, adding and removing crates as needed.

That, at least, seemed more efficient than Kitaye's method, where everyone had to go get what they wanted themselves. Bliss watched an older woman waiting for a cart receive her package, a slim box handed right from the cart to her hands. No need for her to walk to some ship.

Where, how, the bartering occurred for all this, Bliss didn't know. Didn't care overmuch to find out, either.

The skar remained paramount.

Bliss had hunted all manner of critter and creature, but she'd never gone after information before. Where would someone find a detail like the Foti skar's location?

Her first instinct ran with the Najahn, those purple and black soldiers and their mysterious ceremonies, icy stares, and distant attitudes. They tended to flock to skars like flies to a carcass, yet Bliss hadn't seen a single one since the trio had landed on the isle.

So maybe they'd landed on the wrong part? A long walk ahead?

Bliss went to the next square's center, looked around at her options. The main avenue continued, finishing not far ahead at some large granite block, a building made from sharp edges and sturdy slates. The split-offs went in murkier directions, sidling along smaller houses or shops. Taverns, things Bliss only identified because the Kance sailors talked them up so much, dangled offerings with swinging charred wood signs.

"Looking for something?"

The question came from her left, and Bliss turned, saw an arms-folded, ash-stained woman offering her a kind smile.

"Not often we see a Vis this deep in the city," the

woman continued, her voice as smokey as her breath. "You stay bottled up in your jungle, as I understand it. What's pulling you out here?"

Bliss pointed to her mouth, shook her head. The woman's eyebrows quirked up before she settled into an understanding smile.

"Who among us doesn't have a special gift," the woman said.

While Bliss wasn't sure she'd call her muteness a gift, she did have a way to counteract it. Reaching into her thigh pouch, Bliss pulled out the stone plate she used to scratch out words, along with the sharp rock to make the etchings.

"Now we're onto something," the woman said.

Bliss hesitated, took a longer look at the woman. Beyond the outfit, she had a strong satchel filled with who knew what. A hammer lay looped into her belt. Rugged boots and thick pants beneath the tunic suggested a working day in unpleasant conditions, an idea backed up by the inky smudges on the woman's cheeks, her forehead. Her hair, save for a few escapist curls, lay tucked beneath a flat deep green cap.

Definitely not Najahn then, and not the flowing flowery foppery of Cassignol either.

"Don't worry, I won't bite you," the woman said. "Name's Carrilee. I work in a smithy back that way, like everyone else around here."

Bliss took the sentence to etch out a quick word, 'Why?'

"Helping you?" At Bliss's nod, Carrilee shrugged. "Curious, I suppose. As I said, we don't get Vis back here, and you looked a little lost."

Bliss smiled, gave a slight shrug. Carrilee wasn't wrong. She started to scratch 'skar' into the stone, Carrilee guessing at the word before Bliss finished.

"Well, I'll be torched," Carrilee said, "I was thinking you didn't look like a trader, even though that satchel looks plenty full. No greed in your eyes, you see. Learn to read that real quick around here, what with everyone on Foti looking for their next mark."

'Mark?'

"Someone to fool, take in, rob blind. All those lovely things." Carrilee shook her head, cast her eyes about as if to say such thieves could be anywhere. "The fiends are making it worse, putting everyone against everyone else when we ought to stand together."

Carrilee doused her grim assessment with another smile. Stretched her arms, then pointed off towards the big stone building.

"You want to find the skar, you've gotta go that way. Not the ore house, I mean, but a long trek beyond it. Through the lava tubes and across the Wastes, then you'll get there, so I understand it."

'How far?'

"Depends on how you want to travel. Walking, you're looking at a few weeks. You're on one tip of the isle, my friend, and you're needing the other." Carrilee nodded back towards the port. "If I were you I'd march right back to the water, see if you can't get a ride on some ship. Save you time."

A fair plan. Bliss gave Carrilee another nod, put her hand on her heart and then pointed towards Carrilee. A sign most people figured out, even if they'd never encountered someone like her.

"Now," Carrilee said, "it's about lunch time, and you're not liable to catch a boat leaving this late anyway, so how about I treat you to a meal and you tell me more about your little isle?"

Bliss hadn't had anything other than an apple from her satchel since the early morning on the boat, so the thought of a real lunch sounded pretty damn good. Trading stories for a meal also seemed like a good deal, though Bliss wasn't quite sure how patient Carrilee would be with the etching: one or two word questions were one thing, a long tale quite another.

Nevertheless, that wasn't Bliss's problem. If Carrilee wanted stories, Bliss would tell them, one word at a time.

Carrilee led Bliss off the square down a side street, past several taverns and their lunch time wafts. Carrilee wrote off the smells as false advertising, saying any real local would know crap posturing as perfect.

"The real goods are just a little further on," Carrilee said. "Assuming you want an authentic Foti meal, that is."

'Sure'.

"That's the enthusiasm I'm looking for." Carrilee laughed, then her eyes lighted on Bliss's staff. "That what I think it is? Bopping people on the nose?"

Bliss grinned, 'Yep'.

"Looks like it'd be mighty good at it."

As they walked along, the houses dwindled in size. Multi-floor stone edifices, carved symbols Bliss couldn't parse decorating the outside in oranges and reds, slowly shrank to single-story shanties, with thin roofs and piled block walls looking like a swift breeze might wipe them out.

The people, though, stayed resolutely the same. Most carrying hammers, many smeared with ash and grit, bright eyes and strong frames all around. Some reminded Bliss of Svarde, albeit a dirtier version. Taller and larger than the people on Vis, if often fatter and prone to coughing fits.

Overhead, the sky stayed blue. The smoke tendrils dissipated as they moved away from Smythe's center, leaving the air cleaner. Every breath no longer felt like Bliss had sucked in burning sand.

"Here we are." Carrilee turned towards a squat restaurant. Its dangling sign had an axe and hammer crossing hafts over a plate, though what food that signified Bliss couldn't tell. "The Workman's Table. Not the most creative name, but you don't need a fancy title when you've got the goods like this place."

A man smoking some long pipe leaned against the wall near the shaky wood door. He gave Carrilee a familiar nod as the two went by, his stare lingering on Bliss for a long second, the man's thin lips stretching into a strange smile.

Through the door, the Workman's Table offered cozy confines. A half-dozen small stand-ups and a long bar along the restaurant's back. Brick ovens boiled, sizzling meats and tubers filling the air with a stomach-rumbling smell.

For being lunch time, the restaurant held only three others beyond the cook at the back. Those three held their own table, ale mugs sitting before picked-over plates. All turned as Carrilee led Bliss inside.

"Guess what, friends, we have a new visitor today," Carrilee stepped aside, gave Bliss a hand-waved entry. "Say hello to my friend Bliss, who's traveled all the way from Vis to our fair city."

Bliss offered a half-hearted wave. Received nods in return as the trio went back to their plates, their ales. A relief, that, as Bliss had no desire to try explaining herself to all these people.

"Can't expect much more than that from this crew," Carrilee said, guiding Bliss to the restaurant's bar. "They've been chopping rock all night, and as soon as they're done here, it'll be a few short hours asleep before it's back to the mines."

'Hard life.'

"They're all hard here, honey."

Carrilee dashed through an order to the chef, promising Bliss she'd like what she had, and when the food plopped down, rosy sausages, glistening potatoes, roasted carrots, and a half pint, Bliss found she couldn't disagree. Everything carried with it new flavors, the heady char, the smoked aftertaste with every bite. Grill plates on Vis were rare, and always carried the campfire scent on everything cooked. This, this held a metallic tang, an industrial edge.

Better than home? Bliss wouldn't go that far, but as something different, Foti cuisine took the trick.

The ale, too, had its own life. Vis alcohol came sweet, made with fruits into wines and rattlers, saisons and sugary sips. Foti's tasted like autumn, malty and smooth, a loose finish settling on her tongue after every drink.

She would've asked for a second, her plate cleaned, had Carrilee not held up her finger.

"Now, you can't deny we've shown you a good time," Carrilee said. "Foti hospitality, right here."

Bliss narrowed one eye, tried to parse the sudden change in Carrilee's tone.

"You're here looking for our skar with that thick satchel of yours," Carrilee continued, and as she spoke, Bliss realized the table behind her had fallen quiet. A glance that way confirmed the pipe-smoking man had moved inside, right in front of the door. "So, Bliss, tell me now. Are you Vis's Renewal?"

Bliss shook her head.

"A Guardian, then?"

Bliss hesitated. Carrilee's smudged face didn't look so

much like the kind worker now, an intense shape taking over her features. Would lying to someone like this be dangerous?

"That's an answer if I've ever seen one," the cook said, his elbows planting on the bar across from Bliss. "Think you've found a good one, Carrilee."

Bliss flicked her eyes back and forth between the two. A good one for what?

"Don't get yourself worked up, Bliss," Carrilee said, her mother's tone no longer fitting. "You're far away from home, and the rules change. We don't need nothing much from you, understand. Think of it as payment for your food."

'What?'

"Bliss, sweetie, I need you to lead us to your Renewal. There, we'll make a simple trade: your life, for the skar they're carrying. Then you can follow the directions I gave you and be on your way." Carrilee dished out a sympathetic frown. "It's a favor. Who wants to be the next Aegis, anyway? Stuck on that miserable island?"

Bliss turned back to her cleaned plate, the fork next to it. She felt, heard her heart pumping. Her staff leaned on her back. She nodded slow, her hands slipping the tablet and the scratching stone back into her pouch.

"Good choice, Bliss," Carrilee started.

Bliss grabbed the plate and flicked her wrist, sending the hard ceramic flying right into Carrilee and knocking her off the stool, the shattering dish clattering around her.

The cook reacted quick, reaching for Bliss with sudden fire in his angry eyes, a fire quenched with a pained yelp as Bliss caught the outstretched arm with her fork. The cook yanked it back, cursing.

Chairs slid behind her, feet pounding on the stone floor.

Three coming from behind. Bliss planted her palms on the counter, lifted herself off her stool and kicked it, sending the railed seat scattering back into the charging group. She heard it strike shins as Bliss scrambled onto the counter, her right hand flying up to her staff, drawing it from the back holster in a wide swing, one catching the cursing cook across the face and sending him tumbling back into the still-hot grill.

Even Bliss winced at that.

Carrilee remained on the ground, holding her face and wanting no part of the fight. Two of the table toughs watched her, hands now gripping a couple hammers. The third sat on the floor, extricating himself from her thrown stool.

The pipe smoker stayed where he was, covering the door and watching Bliss with what looked like amusement.

He, then, was the most dangerous one.

Bliss brought her staff into a double grip before her chest, parallel to the ground as she stood on the bar counter. The two thugs looked between their battered knives and the distance to the bar before matching stares, deciding to come at Bliss together.

Perfect.

Setting her feet, Bliss launched off into a straight dive, pushing the staff ahead. The bamboo stick, as tall as she was, clubbed the goons across their faces. Bliss swung her legs up at the impact, catching her stopped momentum on the restaurant's sloppy floor.

With her right hand, Bliss let the staff loop over her palm to smack into the thug on that side, laying him out from his grunting, groaning grounding. The other, cursing, flailed with the knife, its blade catching the staff's left and knocking a chunk off the rear cap.

He'd pay for that.

Sliding the staff into a double-grip on its left end, Bliss swung it across her body. The thug tried a feeble block, saw his knife get swatted away, then saw little else as Bliss knocked him into a temporary oblivion.

"Okay, okay," said the pipe man into the moaning silence. He took another draw as Bliss settled back into her stance, confirming with a quick sweep that her enemies stayed down. Even the thug who'd been caught up in her stool seemed reluctant to re-enter the fray, scooting his back up to the bar, his hands empty. "We get the point. You're not an easy mark."

Bliss pointed to the door behind him, glaring fire all the way.

"Leave?" The man shrugged. "Why not. Though you might regret it."

Bliss narrowed her eyes. Regret what? Not bashing this guy's skull in too?

"You're guessing by now that Foti isn't some paradise," the pipe man said, not moving from the door. "If you can't forge, you'd better fight. We choose to pick our battles with clueless visitors than the beasts out in the isle. Can't fault us for that." The man reached into his pocket, pulled out a silver-looking chit. "This here, it's a marker. Says I'm owed a small piece at a smithy just down the way." He pointed the silver rectangle at Bliss and her staff. "You take that thing outside here and it'll get snapped in two by the first ferrite you find."

The rock monster Svarde had kept on Vis? They ran around Foti? Bliss shouldn't have been surprised: the hanokos on Vis weren't any less deadly.

"So I'll offer you a deal, Guardian. What you've done in here, I've no doubt you can do again out there, with an audience. I'll get the promoting going, you put on a show, and this chit's yours, and plenty more besides."

Bliss tilted her head. Did another sweep, confirmed no strike to the back was on its way.

"Then all you need is to bring us back a skar," the pipe man said, grinning. "You take one for your Renewal, sure, but snag an extra one for us. It'll cost you nothing, and it'll mean everything for our little band."

Wax had detailed the exploits to get the skar on Vis, the climb up the sana stalk, the competition with the other candidates. Dangerous, but none of that danger revolved around getting an extra skar.

Then again, if the skars were so far away, how would Bliss get one back here? She spread her hands, staff in her left, and put a puzzled expression on her face.

"Don't worry," the pipe man grinned. "We have people all over the isle. Once you've got it, we'll find you. Hand the skar over, we'll give you something extra for your trouble. Deal?"

The chit shimmered in the firelight. Bliss could just walk forward, smack the guy with her staff and steal the thing. Maybe the comment about friends everywhere was a bluff, maybe she wouldn't have to worry about getting stabbed in the back some night.

Or maybe she should take the man up on his offer, get some more practice whacking these Foti thugs around.

Wax kept saying this was all about adventure, and with all these bodies on the floor, wasn't she having one?

CHAPTER 8
THE LONG DARK

The fungi pulled away easy from the stones, smooth and wet in Svarde's hand. He held the torch close, looked over the purple-gray mossy mushrooms and tried to decide if eating one would kill him or not. Behind him, Maena's troop spread out into another small cavern, taking a midday break—a time chosen more by feel than any actual knowledge—from their downwards climb.

They'd avoided any further fiends since the fight up above, whether by reputation or luck. Strange sounds still cascaded through their tunnel, but none bothered approaching. The tension faded with every step, letting the mind turn to more mundane problems.

Like food, and where to find it.

Their satchels held supplies aplenty, but who knew whether it'd be enough. The Dark Below hadn't been mapped, could go on for days, weeks. The turn-back point would be a few days from now, a point they could push back further by effective foraging. Water was plentiful, easy to heat up over a small fire to purify then toss in a skin for later drinking. Food was another matter.

Nobody wanted to eat the fiends, so they'd left those carcasses behind.

"Are you ever not glowering?" Maena asked, coming over to join Svarde at the troop's vanguard, near the cave's continued path.

"Suits me," Svarde replied.

"How would you know, if you never smile?"

"Trying to be friendly again after threatening my life?"

Maena, her once-clean face dirt splattered and sweat marred like them all, her hair splitting and bedraggled, flashed a sharp grin. "Being an effective leader, nothin' else. You'd do it too."

Svarde shook his head, glanced again at the mushrooms, then stuffed them down his gullet. Thick, chewy, tasted like nothing much at all. A good sign, that.

"Never led any damn thing in my life," Svarde said after he chewed the mushrooms to oblivion. "Thing about leading is you're not in the fighting."

"Did you see that last battle? Fairly certain I was, as you put it, in the fighting."

"All the while you were thinking about who needed to be where, what needed to be done. I got to watch my axe take out a monster."

"Is that what really makes you happy, Svarde? Slaughtering mindless beasts?"

So what if it was?

"Not mindless. Just angry." Svarde stood. They ought to get going soon. Lingering anywhere invited hungry visitors. "The fiends all seem to hate us."

"If you ran into the Aegis, wouldn't you?"

"Thing is, these ones, we fought'em below the shield. They weren't scarred yet."

"Not by the Aegis, perhaps, but by something else surely." Maena caught Svarde's stance, put her fingers to her lips and blew a bright long note. The crew sprang into a different action, swiping up their gear into satchels, stomping out fires. "These fiends were as hurt as any we'd seen. I'd like to know why."

"Maybe they fought among each other."

"And then flipped into a concentrated, organized assault on our band? Not likely."

"Then add it to the pile of mysteries we're trying to solve and let's be about it."

KIVI AND SVARDE CONTINUED LEADING, marching down from the cavern to intermittent wonders. The path they trode bore hallmarks from fiends past, scratches and deep indents as feet and hands, claws and hooves laid themselves to stone. The fiends, though, held little interest for the natural marvels scattered throughout: the expedition went through crystal caverns, rooms that seemed coated with broken diamonds—some, Maena's crew stuffed into their satchels for later trading. They journeyed through bleached chambers broken into irregular sections, as if something large had once burrowed out a nest only to abandon it. Long steep slopes running alongside waterfalls, shallow walks overlaid with sticky mosses and mushrooms aplenty.

Their torches burned bright and gave sight to things never before seen by explorers from the Seven Isles.

At least, none who'd made it back to the surface. And

Svarde believed they would, at least some of them, with the fiend's source crushed beneath his heavy axes.

With that deed done, maybe Catya would find her life returned. Maybe questions long cut off could be answered. Or maybe Svarde was foolish to hope.

"What do you think, Kivi?" Svarde asked the ferrite prowling beside him. "Am I stupid to wish for another chance?"

The ferrite, as she often did, snorted back at him. A sour note, putting a damper on his fancy.

"Right," Svarde muttered. "Keep the focus on where we are, not where, or when, we might wish to be."

Kivi, at least, was having a great time. The different rocks, each presenting a new meal, gave the ferrite a munching abundance. Kivi's crunching accompanied the troop's marching scuffle like a natural drumbeat, a gravel guide.

Without daylight, tracking time became a measure of exhaustion. When feet could go no further, or the mind became so blurred that steps began to slip, Maena would blow a whistle at the next cavern and the group would settle in, sleep with a posted watch, and start again. All the while, Svarde measured the looks around him, the expressions fading from determined, excited, to drained and drawn. More and more looks went back the way they came, calculating just how far back they'd have to go to reach the surface.

On the fourth night, that calculation hit a hard number.

After a meal of moss and mushrooms, a small salted fish slice gifted to each, the fifteen sat beneath their torches as Maena spun another seaside tale. One Svarde, going by the bemused expressions, guessed everyone had heard a time or two already. At its conclusion, with some poor sailors having lost their cargo to a swindler pirate and her mischievous tricks, polite laughter rattled through the cavern, dying off to a dripping quiet.

"Know how much farther it is, then?" Asked an older sailor, a sapped spotter called Fairstrike.

"Nobody knows, including you," Maena replied. Eyes shifted between the two. Everyone knew a power struggle when they saw it. "It might be a day before we're truly in the Dark Below. Might be a week."

"Not gonna last that long." Fairstrike grabbed a mossy handful from near the fire, held it up. "Lest you think we'll be living on this for a month, listening to our stomaches growl."

"Better than listening to you talk," Svarde added.

Fairstrike threw the man a sneer, "I came on this same as you, to set things right. What I've seen so far is a lot of rock and a few fiends that tossed my friend into the next life. I'll allow this as an experiment, but it's clear we're off. I say we turnabout, get more gear, more people like us, and come back proper."

"You want to fit an army in this cave?" Maena asked.

"Better an army than our starving selves."

A few agreeing grumbles there. Svarde's own stomach murmured its opinion. The moss and mushrooms weren't filling, and they'd found too few cave fish to supplement the meals. Soon enough, they'd start to grow weak, tired, easy snacks for the fiends.

"Is that what you want, then?" Maena asked, throwing the question around the room. "To give up already, head back to the surface and admit you're not up to it?"

"Not giving up," Fairstrike snapped in a hurry. "Playing it smart. We come back better, now that we know what we're doing. It's the way to go, captain."

"I'm not going back," Svarde said, his eyes on the fire. "Do what you want, but I came here with a purpose, and I'll see it fulfilled."

Fairstrike laughed, "Then keep on going. Your life's yours to waste as you want, Foti."

"Hands," Maena called. "Those who want to head back, and those who want to keep going. I'll not have dissent, not have complaints, so make your choice now."

The calculation had been done. There was no hesitating. All but two declared their surface-bound desire, and Maena gave them their marching orders. Return to the surface, get more soldiers, and come back after them.

The four, Svarde, Maena, and two weathered fighters named Rasslebeck and Pennifer, filled up their satchels from the departing troop. Watched the larger party leave by torchlight, heading up on the long journey home.

"Now it's a real adventure," Svarde said in the real, deep void.

Kivi, her pulse always on point, snorted.

CHAPTER 9
DEVIANT DELIGHTS

The cards slapped, the chips fell, and Wax won and lost and won and lost and reveled in all of it. The cheers, the jeers, the curses and the whack on the back as the Foti dice rolled along the table. Every time Wax moved the clay chips, each decorated with a carved number and a spiral swirl, Sawi and Pan vanished further into his memory.

At least until Quik pulled Wax away from the table, much to the groans and complaints from the Foti gamblers sharing the space with him.

Wax shrugged Quik off, made to go back to that place, that lovely void where he wasn't the Renewal, wasn't anything at all.

"Hey," Quik growled, pulling Wax back. "It's past dark. You and I haven't eaten in hours."

"So?" Wax ignored his stomach, which was indeed protesting. "We're not supposed to be anywhere."

"We're supposed to be crossing this isle to get a skar, Wax."

Amid the casino's bustle, the jostling ale trays, the

bouncing music played by a three-piece drums-and-flute band, the growing crowd seeking to wipe away another ordinary evening, the idea of hunting skars seemed so remote, so terribly uninteresting.

"Yeah, we'll get to it." Wax pushed Quik's hand off his wrist. "Not like we're leaving tonight."

"Is there a problem?" Cassignol, the man who'd led them here from the docks, came up. He carried two mugs frothing with ale, pushed one each at Wax and Quik. "Nothing that can't be solved with a little ale, I hope? On the house."

"Why?" Quik asked, eyeing the ale. Wax took the mug, drank a mouthful. His fourth of the day, spaced out enough with the betting so the shallow warmth hadn't spread to his fingers. "What'd we do to earn this?"

Cassignol waved his hand across the casino's width. Crowded tables caught the gesture, but Wax realized stares aplenty were already directed at him and his brother.

"Word's spread," Cassignol said. "Two Vis here, and playing? A marvel." He leaned in. "We'll make more with you two here drawing a crowd than any ale you could ever drink, so enjoy."

Quik frowned. Wax clinked his mug against the second Cassignol still held out.

"See, brother? We're famous already." Wax looked down at his stomach, then back at Cassignol. "Any chance the hospitality extends to some real food?"

"You need only ask," Cassignol said, bowing his head just a smidge. "I'll have the kitchen whip up some Foti specialties." Shoving the mug into Quik's hesitant hands, Cassignol bowed again and scurried off towards the kitchens.

"See?" Wax said. "We're eating free, drinking free, and

—" He stopped, noticing his brother stood alone. "Where's Bliss?"

"She left hours ago," Quik growled. "Like me, she doesn't like this place. Wanted to go find out where Foti's skar was. Because she cares."

"Right, right. She cares. I'm just blowing this whole thing because I'm taking a few hours to have fun." Wax rolled his eyes, sloughed more foam from the mug into his mouth. "You don't have to be so serious all the time."

"Wax, being a Renewal is as serious as it gets. People are dying from fiends while we're sitting in here. People that you could save."

Wax squinted at Quik, tried to parse the accusation. Was his brother really saying that Wax trying, just for a few hours, to live a life not filled with grief and danger was somehow a sin against the planet?

He reached inside his weave, pulled out the Vis skar. As ever, it bled warmth into his hand, the sapphire stone catching torchlight and dazzling. He'd been about to throw the stone at Quik, tell him to take over, if his brother felt so strongly, but holding the skar twisted that logic.

The stone had looked much the same when Pan handed it to him, there at the sana's base as his friend lay dying. Wax had made a promise. No chips, no bets, no free food would change that.

"Okay," Wax said. He tried to throw off the ale's lingering blurs, failed. Leaned into them instead. "You want me to take this more seriously, fine. I will. But I'm not you. I'm not the most serious man alive. You want to be my Guardian, you're going to have to live a little. Laugh a little."

Quik reached out, closed Wax's fist over the skar.

"That's yours, brother. As am I. We're all with you, and we're all depending on you."

"No pressure, then."

Quik tried a half smile. It didn't really work.

"There's six others, Wax. But none of them are as good as you."

"You know that, huh?"

"Absolutely," Quik clacked his mug against Wax's. "Because I taught you everything." Wax shoook his head, grinned. "Now, how about we eat whatever garbage they're going to shovel at us, then go find our sister?"

"Does that give me enough time to win a few more games?"

Quik sighed, Wax winked, and returned to the table's siren song.

THE FOOD, though, proved an effective interruption. That and, while Wax ate, Quik snagged his brother's chips and cashed them out, turning in the clay sliders for salted meats, dried fruits, and some other supplies. Neither knew where Foti's skar happened to be, but they'd need food enough to get there.

The Foti specialties turned out to be roasted pies, stuffed with meats and root vegetables, overdone with fluffy browned crusts. They smoked as Wax, using a metal fork for the first time, poked them open. An amber sauce coated them, slightly sweet with a tongue snapping tang. A far cry from the fruit and fish that'd been his life's mainstay.

After, pushing away Cassignol's begging to stay, Wax and Quik left the Anvil's Arms and stumbled out into Smythe's lantern-lit streets. The stone gleamed, embers and ash still drifted down here and there, the always-working forges pumping fiery gouts towards the dark sky. Carts rumbled by, even more than in the morning, taking advantage of the quieter streets to increase traffic.

"Where do you think she went?" Wax asked as he and Quik looked up and down the main avenue. "Back to the docks?"

"She wanted to find the skar." Quik pointed towards Smythe's far off city center. "I'd say further in. Might be a Najahn office or someone else that'd know."

If the jaunt to the casino showed them Foti society lived on hard labor, the late day walk proved they celebrated equally. Taverns and restaurants bustled, rough-and-tumble drumming music, singing, and shouting pouring into the streets. Ale barrels rolled off the carts and into the buildings, most greeted with wild cheers from those inside.

Behind it all, the ringing of hammer on metal provided Smythe's heartbeat.

"Don't think I could live here," Wax said as they walked, his eyes following smoke into the too-open sky. "Too much noise, too few trees."

"Can't breathe without coughing, either."

"Maybe you get used to it."

Quik scrunched up his face, "Don't think I want to."

They made it to a larger central square, one dominated by side streets. Quik, noting that Bliss was supposed to meet them back at the Anvil's Arms, looked more and more frustrated with himself. His hands clenched, his lips turned into a permanent grimace.

Wax flipped his the opposite way.

"She's not a little child anymore," Wax said as they stood in the square's center. "She'll be fine, Quik. Maybe she got lost, or she's having buckets of that Foti ale."

"Not something Bliss would do."

Wax had to give Quik that. Bliss hadn't been one to dive into the parties back on Vis, no reason she'd change that here.

The challenge of finding another way to cheer Quik up died, though, when Wax surveyed the square, looking for options. There were people and carts milling about, yes, but a steady stream seemed to be headed one way, down a side street to their left. Murmurs rising from the passing people buzzed with verve.

"Something's going on that way," Wax said, pointing. "Want to check it out?"

Quik sniffed. "Last place. If she's not there, then we go back to the Anvil's Arms. See if she turns up."

"Deal."

Hooking up with the growing crowd meant catching conversations. The charred, sweaty, tired folks kept going on about a new brawler on the streets, one doing something different than the old street slugger style.

That new brawler turned out to be Wax's younger sister, holding court in the side street's center—no cart tracks down this way—surrounded by a crowd and facing off against a man at least twice her size.

"Is that?" Quik asked as they drew close, found books between people to catch glimpses into the makeshift cobblestone arena.

"Getting herself into trouble, yep," Wax answered.

Neither Bliss nor her opponent had weapons. Bliss's staff and satchel were gone, and she bore the hallmarks of a busy afternoon making hands: bruises walked up and down her arms, sweat beaded on a dirty brow, and a thin red line trickled from a puffy lip, but Bliss's eyes seemed bright, her body in a hunter's careful stance.

The man opposite her had his size sprawled out, his arms wide, as if he meant to go in and give Bliss a devastating hug. The match must've been on for a while, because he bore his own marks along his legs, bare chest, and a cut over one eye. Both breathed like they'd been running hard.

"This has to stop," Quik said, starting to muscle through.

"Hold up." Wax grabbed his shoulder. "She's got this."

The bigger man went forward, spitting on the ground between him and Bliss. Wax's sister stayed still, let the man close the distance.

"This isn't right," Quik said, glaring back at Wax. "Even if she wins, even if this gets her some dumb prize, the risk isn't worth it."

"What, because if she gets her leg broken, she can't be my Guardian?"

The crowd called for the man to charge, and with a wild roar, he did just that. Two long strides and a sweeping grasp, one Bliss undercut by darting in, delivering a quick jab to the man's throat. The hulk's arms closed around Bliss, the man sputtering out into a hacking, gasping cough. At first, Wax thought the man might crush Bliss anyway, and the crowd did too, going by their cheer, till it became obvious the man was leaning on Bliss, his face turning purple as he tried to breathe.

Ducking out from her opponent's flimsy arms, Bliss put her hands out, let the man fall to the ground, where he found his breath at last. The crowd made its booing opinions known, and satchels all 'round slipped open as bets changed hands.

"And all was well," Wax said to Quik, who'd once more put on a glower. "Bliss knows what she's doing."

The crowd began clamoring for the next fight, but the

noise died out as another voice, from a speaker Wax couldn't see, called out that the duels were done. The night's champion had been crowned.

Bliss, newly anointed, crashed into her brothers as the people parted. Her hugs were tight, fierce, happy. Wax threw out congratulations, while Quik grumbled his own. Their attention shifted, then, from Bliss to the one coming up behind, a man holding a pipe in one hand, and Bliss's staff, and satchel, in the other.

At first Wax didn't recognize Bliss's weapon. The bamboo seemed barely there, covered and interwoven now with metal ends and a strong middle grip. Orange lines cut through the tanned wood, providing patchwork strength.

Bliss took the rewards, leaned in to catch a whisper from the pipe man, then turned back to her brothers.

'Not what you expected, right?' Bliss signed.

"Understatement," Quik said.

"Pretty awesome," Wax added.

Bliss beamed, 'And guesss what? I know where we've got to go.'

CHAPTER 10

EXODUS

Knowing the way and walking it turned out to be two very different things. Using Bliss's winnings, the trio scored a room and board for the evening at an utterly alien inn called the Bluster's Beard. Circular tables and sloshing soups occupied their dinnertime, replete with Bliss's signed retellings of her various victories over Smythe's street-fighting Fotis.

In her words, the effort boiled down to fighting like a Vis, not like a brawned-out wrestler. Quik tried to take offense at the characterization, his own biceps seeming to bulge in defense of his fellow muscle-bound maulers, a reaction diffused when Wax tuned up an imitation of the same with his lanky form.

Quik laughed, reached over and squeezed Wax's arm, "Guess that's why you've got us for Guardians, brother. Strength and a staff on your side."

'I'm more than just a staff,' Bliss signed, then pointed at her stuffed satchel. 'Who bought you dinner?'

"She's right, Quik." Wax put his arms behind his head,

leaned back in the hard wood chair and took a deep breath. "Bliss is tops so far."

"Is this a competition?"

"Why not. Winner gets a mention in my victory speech."

'I'll pass.' Bliss stood up, finished her ale. 'And I'm exhausted. They said they have a bath here, and I've never tried one before. Catch you two back in the room.'

Taking her satchel, and therefore robbing the night of any wild spending sprees, Bliss headed off.

"She's too good for the sea now?" Quik asked once Bliss had moved from ear shot.

"You see any oceans around here we could swim in?" Wax countered. "After this round, think I'll take after her, start the journey clean."

"Won't last long."

Wax grinned, lifted his flagon to his lips. "I'd be disappointed if it did."

SMYTHE'S MORNING ground into being, carts and forges hammering and squealing to life. A different orchestra than the jungle birds, but Wax, who'd spent the night trying to figure out how people slept on straw mattresses, could see the similarities: the music of home.

"The faster we leave, the sooner my ears will stop screaming at me," The Renewal said to his two bleary-eyed Guardians. "The Foti are fun, but I can't take much more."

If last night's amusement kept the grimy air and discordant sounds in check, leaving the inn stone sober let Wax, Quik, and Bliss embrace the cold iron Foti life. Around them, shops opened up to take in visitors looking for breakfast, for tools, for trades. Criers claimed stoops in the squares to shout the morning's news, which, as Wax heard it, seemed mainly focused with the going rates for various ores and metals. The giant carts trundled without mercy, pushing pedestrians to dash away as they rambled along.

Yet the trio had a direction, north, and Bliss took up her guiding mantel, that metal staff a nice totem to mark her path. The three walked alongside one another, their Vis weaves already worn after days at sea without a good oiling. Their feet, too, bore new scratches from the some-times-rough cobblestones. Somehow Foti's stone canyons brought windy gusts and, with them, a chill cooler than what Vis found even in Winter's thin heart.

Bliss seemed to catch the group's mind when she turned, held a shop to their left in her eyes. Dusty windows—parts looked like they'd been cleaned that morning, but good luck keeping up against the grit onslaught—showed through to clothes heavy and light, real fabrics spun from cottons and better.

"Feels wrong to abandon our home so early," Quik said, but he followed Bliss and Wax into the store nonetheless.

It would feel worse to freeze to death, Wax assured him as they tried out new outfits. With Bliss once again serving as their patron, the trio left the shop not long after in thicker get-ups. Bliss and Quik opted for orange and silver tunics, thick pants billowing out around the ankles. A classic Foti outfit for traveling days, according to the shopkeeper.

Wax kept it flashier, throwing on a collared gray jacket with golden seams, matching heavier pants with deep pockets. A Foti foreman's getup, made for carrying both tools and respect.

"Feels right," Wax said at his sibling's stares. "I'm your boss, remember?"

Quik glanced at Bliss, "Should I knock some sense into him?"

'Not yet. Wait till he has the skars first. Then we can take-em.'

"You can try." Wax pointed at the billowing pants. "You're going to trip over those things."

Yet, much to Wax's annoyance, neither one did. Bliss and Quik strode without issue, the three moving with more confidence and drawing fewer stares with their tattoos covered, their clothes matching Foti fashion.

Smythe offered little else on their way out, the buildings rising towards the center's huge smithy and government building—the trio blinked at that, Kitaye's elders tended to prefer campfire chats along the beach to drive their city along—and then falling again as the group wound northward, towards land that only seemed to grow more turbulent.

If Vis hid its rolls and roils beneath verdant greens, Foti laid itself bare. Once Smythe's buildings dwindled, a narrowing ending with a stout gate and a stone wall cutting between two opposing ridges—both, Wax noted with some satisfaction, shorter than the sanas back home —the expanse before them seemed to stretch on forever.

A dull watchwoman drank from a steaming coffee mug as the trio approached the gate, a lonely place with not a trader in sight. No travelers either. A mystery solved by the watchwoman when she read their questioning looks.

"Everyone knows the sea's a better way," she said, not bothering to get up from the rickety chair and stone table. "You want to cross the isle on foot, you're either looking for something or running from someone."

"The first one, then," Wax said. "We're heading north. Will this road take us there?"

The watchwoman shrugged, "Suppose it might. Never walked it myself." She squinted, eyes peeking from beneath a thin ash-marred cowl. "You're not locals, then."

"What about it?" Quik asked, folding his considerable arms.

"Just saying you might want to watch yourselves out there," the watchwoman sniffed. "Lot of ways people can go missing out on the floes, and don't think anyone'll come find you. Least not to do more than loot your bones."

"Aren't you a bit sour? It's not even noon yet," Wax asked.

"Watch this lonely gate all day, every day, and tell me you wouldn't get a bit . . . sour." The woman waved them on. "Better get moving. There's places to stay if you make it far enough. There's fiends to find you if you don't."

The scrub brush plains beyond Smythe turned dark before they'd walked more than a couple hours, the trodding no longer done on stone but flattened earth. Small critters, lizards and the like, darted away as the three marched along. Biting flies darted in, found themselves thwarted by the covering outfits, and buzzed off to seek easier meals. Unbound by obstacles, the wind took up a chaotic turn, gusting and snapping Bliss and Quik's pants like tiny flags.

At least the weather kept cool, the sun a weak tan up in the frosted blue sky. Wax could take long swingings through the jungle shade in heavy heat, but a slow walk on a boiling day was a form of torture he wasn't sure he could stand.

As it was, Wax asked Bliss time and again why they couldn't have jumped on a boat. The answer was always the same: the skar wasn't seaside. It lay north of the isle's center.

"But could we not have found a more fun route to go?" Wax asked, sighing as the scrub brush died away, replaced by hard black rock. "It's getting more boring by the minute."

The Floes, as the Foti called them, turned the road's straight-on gait into a winding game of ups and downs. Several strides would bring them to a warm gully, where hot steam and smoke leaked from cracks, and sweat threatened to make an appearance, then seconds later they'd again be blasted by Winter's breath. The lizards and bugs vanished, and only a few tentative weeds broke through the lava rock.

"We're lucky," Quik said as they crested their third roiled ridge. "Vis is much better than this."

"Agreed. What I wouldn't give for a good vine and some fresh fruit." Wax fished out his water skin, took a drink. "What're the odds this runs dry out here and we shrivel up, lost like that watchwoman said?"

'Not very good,' Bliss signed. She'd gone a few paces ahead and bent over, studying a rock. 'They've carved a sign here. The path splits.'

Reading wasn't a skill especially prized on Vis, but the letters scrawled on the stone seemed to be city names. Arrows marked the direction, one north, the other west.

"You're sure they said north?" Wax asked his sister. "If you're wrong, that's definitely putting Quik on top."

Bliss rolled her eyes, fingers flashing, 'I'm not wrong.'

The northward path, though, didn't keep to the rolling fashion. It dove down, winding deep into a gap between two immense, yet smooth, lava rock hills. The destination became clear enough before they'd reached the bottom: a cave's mouth, wide and rippled, as if the lava had burst out from its hole and cooled many times over. From above, the cave seemed smaller than the one Wax and Bliss had entered back on Vis, the one with the fiend, where Pan—

"Lucky us," Wax announced as they closed with the hole, banishing the memory. "This must be the lava tubes we heard about. Means we're on the right track. Way to go, Bliss."

'Told you.' Bliss replied, unlimbering her staff and planting it on the ground before her.

"What's that for?" Quik asked, and Wax seconded the question.

'Last time we went in a cave, a fiend came after us. I'm just being prepared.'

Wax glanced down at himself, the blue Foti blade on his belt. The knife that should've gone to Pan hanging opposite. The Vis skar hung near his chest, its warmth near his own heart. He'd come a long way from the weave-wearing, tree-hopping whooper who would've looked at a fiend and ran.

"What do you think, Quik, are we prepared?" Wax asked, reaching and drawing the blade. Its sapphire metal shone in the sunlight.

Quik grunted, tying on his gauntlets. "Any fiend finds us, it's going to realize it's made a big mistake."

"Then, Guardians, into the tube we go."

CHAPTER II
HIGH SOCIETY

From the first step inside Ami figured this was not the place for her. Cushions—cushions!—lingered about the building's first floor, piled in red and purple clumps instead of chairs, tables, or anything else. Seedy carpeting, coated in splotchy wine stains, ran into corners where threads frayed into half-built spiderwebs. Stone walls glimmered behind lit candles, the bricks etched with scrawling poetry. Bodies moved in the shadows, some raising glasses to toast Ami's entry, others keeping heads in books or snuggled up with one another, positions Ami very much did not want to investigate.

"It's a bit much, I understand," said her greeter as he joined her in surveying the rooms. "You'll get used to it though. Our motto, after all, is freedom of the body, freedom of the mind."

Ami took a breath to steady herself. A mistake, as the incense wave coming with the inhale had her coughing hard enough the man slapped her back twice to bring the fit to a close.

"Another unfortunate first time effect," the man said,

leaning into her view with a concerned smile. "It'll pass in a few minutes, as it has for everyone else here. As for me, you can call me Mattimo. The others, you'll learn their names as they decide to tell you."

"Ami," she gasped, swallowed, and forced herself to stand up straight. She'd fought fiends, faced disasters and horrors the likes these people couldn't comprehend. A few candles wouldn't bring her down. "I need to find a book. I was told you'd have it here."

As she spoke, another man in slipshod deep blue robes sashayed over carrying a goblet brimming with deep crimson. He held it towards Ami with a slight bow, "A welcome gift for the Guardian."

Wine in unusual situations sat in Ami's box of bad ideas, but she felt eyes tracking the moment. Refusing seemed in bad faith. She'd take the goblet, then, but let the cup keep its drink.

"Thank you." Ami accepted the glass, raised it to the room, received another chorus of chopped welcomes.

"Please," Mattimo called into the house, "bring up the music again. I love you all, but I am sure the Guardian would rather hear something more pleasant than our hobbies."

Maybe Ami would be drinking that wine after all. She took a taste, nutmeg cherry lingering on her tongue. Not bad, all things considered.

Mattimo waved her in from the door, one he shut and bolted behind her. Normally, Ami might see that as a trapping sign, something to be wary of, but the people she saw around her were as far away from thieves and warriors as she could imagine.

"Now then," Mattimo said, leading the Guardian across the room and into a thin hallway. Paintings lined the stones here, and Ami expected to see self-gratifying portraits, but instead she found artful renditions of ancient songs, clips of poems done up against watercolor woods or misty mountains. "You were asking about a book?"

How much to trust a man? Ami kept people on a private sliding scale. Most, at first blush, started in the middle. To be accepted as who they were and given little of value. Soon, though, actions dictated a slip or a climb, a move towards confidant or cock-up. Yet, enduring whatever this was only to walk away with nothing wasn't an option.

Ami would be having more drinks tonight, alone and on her balcony, and she'd be doing it with the prize in hand, damn it.

"What do you know about Demion?" Ami asked Mattimo as the man led her to the house's opposite side, a kitchen overflowing with food and drink, though all seemed to have been delivered from elsewhere. At her words, Mattimo frowned, then waved the other three people in the kitchen out of it.

The power structure fell into place as the trio obeyed without question, slipping past Mattimo and Ami with glazed eyes and glassy grins.

"A strange name to start with, Guardian," Mattimo said, heading to a narrow wood shelf overflowing with wine bottles, most opened and half drank, as if people couldn't be bothered to finish what they started. Mattimo, at least, poured from an open red much the color of Ami's. "Most only know Demion from their childhood stories. The first Circle, the first Aegis."

"I want to know what else she found." Ami reached into the pouch at her waist, pulled the book she'd skimmed and held it up. "This feels forced."

Mattimo, crystal goblet in one hand, took the book with

his other and sighed as he read the front cover. "Some things are written to please the reader. Others are written to please the ones in power."

"What's missing?"

Mattimo handed her back the book. His face held a different complexion than the jaunty party-host he'd been a minute earlier. Calculations ran through the wrinkles, the sloppy cheeks and graying hairs.

"What are you digging for, Guardian?"

"Hope. For my friend."

"The Aegis?"

"My friend, Mattimo. That's what she is to me."

The man nodded. His eyes flicked towards the door, towards his wine glass. Ami had the impession of a nervous mouse wishing he could leave. Then Mattimo straightened, spine found.

"We hold these parties down here because it avoids eyes," Mattimo said. "Despite what you might be thinking, it isn't all this. We burn days in discussion, writing and deliberating things no sailor, no miner, no Najahn soldier has time to think about. We advance our civilization here."

"Great. What does that have to do with my question?"

"I'm saying that we are free here to discuss things that aren't said elsewhere, not because the Circle gives us license, but because prying eyes and ears aren't around." Mattimo tipped the goblet, drained the glass in one go and refilled it. "The Najahn are like any society. We keep secrets, some more potent than others."

"What I'm asking for is a secret, then?"

"Enough of one that to reveal it would be to risk myself, to risk everyone here and what we do."

"Risk how? That I might tell someone?"

Mattimo slipped up a small smile, "That you might tear apart what we hold so dear."

Ami reached past Mattimo, set her goblet on the shelf. She straightened, standing over the smaller man, and put on the soldier's face she'd worn guarding Foti mines from bandits and worse. The look tended to get people to choose her way, but Mattimo didn't blanche, didn't budge.

"I see what you're doing, Ami," Mattimo said. "Don't think I wouldn't tell you, but it would mean my death were it found out. Yours too, and possibly everyone here."

"Hiding it means the Aegis is dead."

"She was always going to die, as will the next one and the one after that."

"Ten years, Mattimo. Only ten years." Ami put a pointed finger against Mattimo's chest. The man looked at it, gulped down his second glass of wine. When he turned to fill it again, Ami pushed him, locked him against the shelf. "The Aegis before that lasted twelve. How long till we're dealing in weeks, days? A constant string of kids lining up to die to keep the fiends at bay?"

Mattimo's weak smile persisted, "You and I will be long dead by the time that comes to pass."

"You'll be long dead by midnight if you don't take me seriously."

"I do, Ami, I do." Mattimo's expression changed, his eyes flicking up and lighting with a new hope. "You're trying to do what, then? Save the Aegis somehow? I can tell you now no secret will give Catya her years back."

Ami pulled her hand away, trying to deny to herself that's what she expected. The skars held power, and yes, some part of her believed they might be able to turn back Catya's clock, give her a second chance at what she'd lost. Without that . . . without that this was about the future.

"Then I want to make sure she's the last one like this," Ami said.

"Again, an impossible promise. What I know are only suggestions, whispers, and they may have nothing to offer you."

"May is better than what I've got."

"And what do I have, Ami?" Mattimo's look changed again, a man of many moods. His voice, though, morphed with it, no longer a beggar, a defier, but now a dealer. "Risks can't be taken for nothing."

"Helping the world isn't enough for you?"

"If it was, would I be here?" Mattimo chuckled, and this time Ami didn't stop him as he refilled his goblet. "I've tried to convince you otherwise, but if you want this information, then you'll have to find something I want."

"Something that I can give, you mean."

"Just so," Mattimo said. Ami had a sudden flash of where they were, the kinds of awful filling this place. Her glare made Mattimo flinch. "Nothing gauche, please. In fact, what I'd really prefer is something much more plain."

"And that is?"

Now Mattimo's eyes really twinkled, and his words flowed less like honey and more like sharp tacks, stinging their target with every syllable.

Back in her room, Ami did indeed pour herself a glass. White, and cool in the evening weather. Winter approached, a slow thing on Noctia, but the ocean breeze could take the temperature and do with it what it would. Ami let it blow her ember locks across her face, her eyes looking out over the cliff but not seeing it.

What Mattimo asked for wasn't going to be easy.

Wasn't going to be right. But it was something, perhaps, Ami could get her hands on. Was it worth risking her station, her ability to help Catya? Mattimo's information might be nothing, might be as vague and frustrating as the book.

But to do nothing was no option either.

Ami spun her look to Flamebreak, leaning against the wall. She'd been given the sword as a gift, to use it for glorious purpose. Time, perhaps, had come to take it up again, only in service of saving the world, not dooming another poor soul to a slow death.

Okay, Mattimo. She'd get his little letter, no matter who she had to toss aside to do so.

The world required that much.

CHAPTER 12
INTO THE HEAT

Caves didn't seem quite the same after the adventure back on Vis, what with a fiend charging from the water and chasing, nearly killing Wax and Sawi. The lava tube didn't match that cave's darkness, thanks to orange and yellow lines running along the great arched rock's floor, roof, and sides. The veins entranced the trio within their first few steps, drawing in their eyes with its flowing, mesmerizing color.

"Not exactly normal, is it?" Quik said.

'Bet it is here,' Bliss signed back. 'Foti wouldn't have a path going through this if it wasn't safe. Let's go.'

"Why are you in such a hurry?" Wax asked.

'Because I'm not keen on spending the night out here,' Bliss said. ' The people I spoke to—'

"You mean the ones you beat up?" Wax interjected.

'Yeah, those. They said travelers weren't the only ones out on the Foti pathways, especially at night.'

"Like who?" Quik kept his eyes on those flowing veins. Like orange stars smeared in a line.

'Bandits. Monsters. I didn't get specifics.'

"I think we're prepared," Wax shrugged off the complaint, but picked up his pace anyway. Bliss had one thing right - staying out in Foti's barren wilds wasn't the goal. Wax wouldn't mind sleeping somewhere else besides the rock tonight.

On Vis, you could always find a canopy to snuggle up in, an inviting leaf or sana flower to provide a comfy bed. Wax winced as he looked at the brittle ground: here wouldn't be so comfortable.

The lava tube, at least, killed the biting wind that'd plagued them on Foti's rolling outer hills. Unfortunately, that wind was replaced with a dead heat, one that grew as they moved in from the tube's entrance. Soon they stuffed their outer layers back into their satchels, returning to their Vis weaves.

"How the Foti don't melt in here, I don't understand," Wax muttered as sweat advanced down his brow.

"Don't see many of them down here, do you?" Quik asked.

"Guess we know why."

Bliss took over leading, with Quik adopting the rear. Wax wondered if this was going to be the new normal, his brave sister and her metal staff acting as his vanguard. He and Pan had gone in a pair, Guardian and Renewal together.

That hadn't worked out. Might as well try something new.

As the day drew into the afternoon, the lava tube continued its sliding descent, scaling deeper into the Foti earth. As it did, those veins grew brighter, spidered through the gray-brown rock until it seemed they were walking more on a rocky river over lava than in a tunnel.

The rock itself changed character too, sprouting new

shimmering black patches, some of which bore a pickaxe's marks, as if some tentative mining had been done then quickly abandoned.

"What's the cost there?" Quik mused as they passed the first one, "A bit of whatever that is at the risk of punching one of those veins and ending up a melted man?"

"Depends on how desperate you are," Wax said.

"Who'd be that desperate?"

"Don't know if you were paying attention back at the Anvil's Arms, but there were more than a few who looked like they might consider taking an axe to that thing."

"Nobody on Vis would be that lost."

"Not on Vis, brother, in case you haven't noticed."

Bliss kept to herself. Maybe she'd seen more than a few similar folks during her streetside brawls. Who might jump at fights like that except the bloodthirsty or the broken?

Wax shook off the thought. Grand adventure seemed much more palatable without getting lost in the darker sides of where they went. His job wasn't to solve Foti's problems, but to save the Seven Isles.

Or, if he didn't make the Aegis, to have a good time traveling.

'Stop.' Bliss help up her right hand, her staff in her left. 'Something's moving up there.'

"Where's 'up there'?" Wax asked, bringing himself beside his sister.

She pointed the staff towards a circular stone patch on the tube's ceiling a few strides distant. Ruby red lava veins ran around the circle, a curious bent considering everywhere else the lava simply cut straight through. Adding to the oddity, the light reflected from the veins tended to bounce off the rock, shimmering and otherwise leaving a dark center. A grim moon in the tube's charcoal sky.

"What do you think it is?" Quik asked.

'No idea,' Bliss signed, then waved the staff along the right wall. 'But I don't think it's been there long.'

Her sister's eventual placement as a hunter gained more credence as Wax followed her staff's point. Narrow chinks in the lava tube's rock wall climbed up from a wide vein at its rightward side, the chinks themselves shining with faint yellow, lava bits running down like dripping ale from an overfilled flagon. Those divots climbed all the way up the wall to the ceiling, where they continued across in a steady line to the circle patch, a spot Wax now noticed was centered right over the tube.

"I'm getting the sense this might be a trap," Wax said.

"Then you're not an idiot," Quik added.

'Wouldn't go that far,' Bliss signed, continuing on before Wax could add a rebuttal. 'I'll trigger it. Quik, be ready.'

"Of course." Quik slipped on his gauntlets, tying the red thread around his wrists. "Wax, stay back."

"Why would I stop my Guardians from doing their jobs?"

"Because you've already done it twice already."

Again Wax would've offered something to counter the insult—a devastating comeback should, no doubt, have found his lips—but Bliss killed the conversation with a hard dart forward, lowering her head, holding the staff in both hands, and barreling on.

As she neared the patch, the shimmering sides unfurled, spreading out in dark bunches against the ceiling. The thing, whatever it was, seemed as wide across as Bliss's staff, and as it unfurled, lava dripped from its center, a center opening into a circle flush with yellow, steaming teeth.

The creature dropped. No, pushed, its many legs shoving off from the ceiling and looking to make a swift, deadly intercept with Bliss. Wax shouted, Quik ran after his sister, and Bliss dove.

No, more than that. Wax gawked as Bliss used her staff, driving its front end into the rock to propel herself faster, cutting beneath the plummeting bug-like thing and winding up on its far side. The creature landed with a lava-scattering crash, embers flying as it scuttled—Wax estimated its legs as 'many', and on all sides around a sloping central shell. The mouth seemed set its middle, those teeth grinding into the rock without apparent harm.

Bliss swiveled as she landed, bringing up the staff into a guard and studying the monster as it rotated to face her, if such a thing really had a face.

Quik used the opening.

Lowering his left shoulder, ignoring the burning flecks splashed onto his skin from the fall, Quik scooped into the creature with his left hand, bending his legs, flexing his intense arms in a shoveling flick that sent the creature tumbling over. Quik's right hand sent his gauntlet across his face, catching newly-flung embers on the oiled wood.

Bliss didn't need a tip to know what to do, swinging her staff in a hard cut across her body to smash the lofted lava bug. The bamboo, metal-reinforced, cracked against the things scuttling legs, sending it flying into the lava tube's rightside wall. The smack crackled, rock and carapace flying everywhere.

But those legs kept scuttling, those teeth, now exposed, clacked as the bug sought to free itself.

A clacking that seemed awfully loud, now that Wax thought about it.

He blinked, freed himself from the action—Bliss

heading towards the captive bug with her staff ready to deliver a smushing end—and checked his right, where that wide lava vein sat.

And groaned.

Another bug, many legs glowing amber from the lava's heat, crawled free, one limb at a time. Every pointed end hit the rock with a chipping, awful sound, lava pooling from the step and melting the stone.

When a second clicking, clacking sound came from behind, Wax closed his eyes for a brief second, offered up a prayer to Vis, and drew his blades. The Foti sword and knife took up a brilliant blue hue in the lava's light, sparking up some hope as Wax turned to face the thing coming in from behind.

"We've got more friends!" Wax shouted, choosing to gain some distance from the side bug by charging the ambusher at the rear.

Unlike the black and shiny monster from the ceiling, these one bore charred green speckled lines along the beetle's shell. Wax took those markings at first for randomness, much like a hanoko's fur, but as he neared to a sword stab's length, the truth revealed itself: these were the same scars Bliss had described on the fiends back on Vis.

Not native things to Foti, then, but more horrors from the Dark Below.

"Good," Wax said, swinging his sword in a crossing cut towards the bug's front dozen legs. "Won't feel guilty about killing you, then."

The bug took the sword with a screeching chirp, its legs sheering off as though Wax was cutting through flower stalks. Resistant to lava these things might be, but a sharp slash? They had nothing.

Except raw surprise.

The bug jumped as it lost its legs. Wax's swing left his arm across his body, the Foti knife in his arm down by his left waist, in no position to guard against the bug's sudden leap. With embers flying, a toothy maw soared towards Wax's face, a surefire kill. At least, it would've been on anyone not trained to dodge sudden branches, vines, and all manner of ugly the jungle could throw at you with high speeds.

Wax threw out his left leg, using what remained of his swing's momentum to fall on his side, hitting the lava tube's floor with his left shoulder. The bug landed beyond him, trying to slow down with legs that no longer existed. The creature rolled, its gnashing teeth exposed to the ceiling.

Planting the Foti knife and his left hand against the ground, Wax lunged back towards the bug, jabbing down with the larger sword, sticking its pointed end right into the bug's nasty mouth. The sword bit in, a shivering stab, and for a moment the monster jerked, forcing Wax to drop his knife and hold on with both hands till the critter stopped its struggling.

Letting go of the sword's hilt, Wax sat back, looked to see Quik finish off his insect by throwing the torn, battered bug against the ground over and over again till the creature stopped moving.

'You okay?' Bliss signed as she sprinted up next to Wax, sliding in on the rock next to him with concern plastered over her features.

He grinned, "You're lucky I know how to fight."

Bliss frowned, looked him up and down, 'Guess so. Sorry, I should have expected more.'

Wax lay back on the rock, a move that proved spending

a night on the hard ground would be a terrible play for their tired bones.

"We don't know what to expect Bliss. Not from any of this. I think that's why so many Renewals die on the journey." He looked at the ceiling, those rich colorful veins no longer seeming quite so beautiful. "We grew up thinking the isles weren't so dangerous, but I think we were wrong."

Wax felt his sister grab his hand, was surprised when she pulled him up, breaking his momentary reverie.

'Then we'll get better,' Bliss signed once Wax stood up. Flipping her staff to her right hand, she reached and drew the Foti blade from the dead bug, ignored the lava gout following the pull, and handed the steaming, but still whole, weapon back to her brother. 'This is only the beginning.'

Wax laughed, "Where'd you learn to talk like that, Bliss?"

'Isn't that how Guardians are supposed to sound?'

"Like Svarde?"

'He got Catya to the Aegis, didn't he?'

That thought wasn't as comforting as Wax wanted it to be.

JARL'S TOOTH. The name carved into a rock that looked, well, like a large chipped tooth. It jutted up between the glowing veins a few hours after the beetle battle, a welcome sight for a trio too tired now to contemplate struggling along much farther. Wax had spent the last twenty minutes trying to imagine a way to sprawl out his satchel on the rough ground.

At least it wouldn't be cold down here.

Sweat covered them all, mingling with a day's march

smell that begged for a bath. No ocean would be offering its reprieve here, though, which meant Jarl's Tooth better have something, even if that something was just plugs for their noses.

The lava tube bringing them to the town opened up, its graceful cylinder faltering into a bubble rock dome, one pierced by several other large caves.

"A meeting of the tubes," Wax muttered as they took in the immense underground cavern.

Normally, caves would be pitch dark this deep, but they didn't need to light a torch: those brilliant veins spidered all over floor and ceiling, swooping along hanging rock and crawling back on up. Some split wide enough to spit molten flame out, tiny geysers not getting above Wax's shins but still beautiful, in a fiery, horrible fashion.

"This is the opposite of home," Quik said, Bliss nodding right along with him. "I hate it."

Wax took a deep breath, stretching his arms up to offer a counterpoint, but the acrid odor coming with the inhale prompted a coughing fit instead. With both his siblings looking at him, faces tilted and eyebrows narrowed in concern, Wax waved towards the clustered buildings.

"Let's just get inside."

Jarl's Tooth offered five houses, each one sporting an addition like a workshop, a pen for small animals, or a sheltered garden flush with mushroom-like plants. Beyond those, the only thing on offer was the inn.

A massive structure looking like someone had pounded flat several large obsidian discs and stacked them on one another, the Jarl's Tooth inn—conveniently also named the Jarl's Tooth—sat square in the cavern's center. All paths led to the thing, and for the first time all day, the trio saw other people. Real, live humans.

And yet, to see the people lounging outside the Jarl's Tooth was to do a triple take. The miners and working folk in Smythe had ash everywhere, worse grease and sweat like honor badges. The collective milling about outside the Jarl's Tooth, all with pipes in their mouths, puffs of blue and white smoke rising with every breath, looked like they'd emerged from, well, the lava tubes.

Whatever their skin color might've been before, it was all charred black now, a thick coating slathered and burned onto anything exposed, and given the heat, the men and women out there didn't wear much. Tight bands wrapped hands, while thick boots clad feet up to their knees. Shirts and shorts, loose and filthy, completed the ensemble, the only standout feature Wax saw being small emblems stitched across their chests.

If the Vis trio inspected the people of Jarl's Tooth, then the people of Jarl's Tooth certainly inspected them. Slow looks became fastened stares as the three walked into town, satchels full and heavy, their faded weaves decidedly not the local fashion.

"The inn, then?" Quik mused as they past the first houses.

"Is there anywhere else?" Wax replied. "I'll answer that: no."

Not a soul bothered to come up for conversation as they approached, their mouths sticking to their pipes, eyes only flipping away when Wax sought to counter the look with one of his own. The views didn't seem hostile: no frowns, no narrowed eyes or shifting of hands to the hammers everyone seemed to have hanging from their waists. Curiosity, then. Even a faint bemusement as lips made slight hints towards smiles.

"Getting the distinct impression we're not supposed to be here," Wax muttered.

"The only place we're supposed to be is Vis," Quik said. "That's part of this whole thing. See the isles, learn about them, become the worldly citizen before you take up the Aegis's mantel."

"You keep talking like I'm going to be the one doing this."

"You will be."

"Damning your brother to a life lived on that terrible island, huh?"

Quik's retort, if he had one, was canceled when Bliss pushed open the Inn's main door. The wrought-metal slab should've been heavy, its char-crusted coating suggested, but as Bliss pushed, gears wound, sliding the door inward with a pleasant industrial grind.

Wax wasn't sure what he expected from a Foti inn stuck in a lava tube's innards, but what he saw seemed to break those slim ideas.

First and foremost, the expected heat didn't materialize. In fact, a cool wave washed past Bliss, over Wax and his brother. The sweat everywhere chilled, prompting a confused shiver. That air's source became apparent real quick: a massive ice chunk, stretching from floor to far up ceiling and encased in a glass-silver cage. Water dripped down from the chunk, running into thin, grate-covered pipes along the inn's floor. No guesses, then about where the small hamlet found its water supply.

Beyond the ice, an observation Wax took his time making, as he'd never seen snow and ice save from afar on the absolute tops of Vis's mountains in Winter, the Jarl's Tooth offered the standard long stone slab tables they'd seen in Smythe. Ale flagons dominated, as did smoked meats and heaping root vegetable piles. Dried fruits stood on offer too, completing a tasty ensemble, at least going by the looks.

The people engaging in the Jarl's Tooth dinner took the Smythe worker vibe and maximized it, crusting over like the ones outside and barreling through their food with the gusto of those who'd spent all day using every muscle they had. Conversation rattled between hawked spit into precisely placed spittoons, the several servers hustling between tables with manic fervor. One dared give the Vis trio a double-take before nodding towards a smaller, empty circular spot.

The stone stools on offer lacked comfort, but after a day on his sore feet, Wax didn't much care. They set their gear beside them, leaning up against the Inn's front wall. A few eyes wandered their way, sticking for long seconds before getting drawn back into their day-to-day.

'I don't think they'll attack us,' Bliss signed as the three turned from the room and back to their table. 'I don't see weapons.'

"Funny that's the first thing that comes to your mind, Bliss." Wax leaned forward, put his elbows on the table. Solid gray-black granite. "Don't think everywhere on the isles is a death trap."

'So far, hasn't it?"

A server, a gaunt man who looked about a day away from turning to dust, approached and gave them an exhausted introduction. Yes, the man said, his voice wispy gravel, this is the Jarl's Tooth, and yes, I know you're not from around here. No, it's not uncommon for visitors to wander through as we're in an intersection, and yes, the ice is remarkable. It comes from Rana's northern floes, lasts about a month, and we get a new piece delivered.

"The standard ale and supper for all three?" The waiter concluded, having refused to let any of them get a word in.

"What're the rates?" Quik asked, and the waiter flicked a look towards their satchels.

"Cheap enough for you, I expect," the man replied.

"Then let's go with it," Wax said. The waiter nodded, turned to leave, and Wax leapt on his intuition. "You're not from here either, are you?"

The waiter looked back at Wax, appraised him with, this time, a smile a tad more genuine,.

"A Kance refugee, I'm afraid. Gave up the wind for this deep down hole."

"Why?"

"Why does anyone leave their home?" The waiter asked. "Because they have to."

The man strode off, leaving Wax to turn to his siblings.

"Was that a real answer?" Wax asked.

"Seemed glib to me," Quik shrugged. "His call, though. At least we're getting food and some real drink."

'Not too much. Ale, I mean,' Bliss shot a pointed look at Wax. 'We've got a long way to go.'

Wax grinned, "Bliss, you know me. I can control myself."

THE LAVA NEVER DIMMED, no matter the time. Wax stood outside the Jarl's tooth inn, waiting while Bliss and Quik took their turn at the rock-sculpted latrine—using it required a fortified soul, as the hole led straight to a flowing lava river. The pipe smokers dwindled as the evening wore on, a more sure time teller than Wax's old intuition, which seemed useless underground.

The ale played a minor racket in his skull, hitting harder

than the sweet stuff on Vis. The hearty meal made up for it though, and, more than the potatoes, the skar. Wax held it in his right hand now, careful to keep his palm cupped over the gnarled sapphire.

Warmth came off the gem in soft waves, caressing his skin and offering, like a spider web's sticky touch, the chance to pull. Quik and Bliss didn't know it, but Wax had found a little tug here and there felt like taking a quick nap. Rejuvenated, recharged, any alcohol effects gone. With them, too, went the slight burns from the beetle battle earlier.

If the skar cared, Wax didn't see it. The warmth felt as strong as ever, the deep blue shade as full as the moment he'd picked it off the giant sana on Vis.

What else could he do with it?

Wax flicked his eyes up, followed a dark speck in an overhead flow as it ran along the ceiling. Pulled along by forces it couldn't control, that thing.

Not him, though. Quik and Bliss were his guardians, not his guides. The Aegis, all that puffery, ceremony . . . Pan's request played over, drawing Wax back down the sapphire. The skar.

For now. For now he'd go along with the adventure, enjoy every minute he could. Wax owed Pan that much.

But if they asked him to put on the chains, to sit in that desolate prison on Noctia?

Wax slipped the skar back inside his loose Foti tunic. He didn't have to answer that question now, and hopefully never would.

CHAPTER 13

CHANCE MEETING

Quik blamed his restlessness on being the older brother. The one responsible if things went wrong. Which was why he sat, leaning against the warm stone wall in their cramped room, watching Bliss and Wax sleep on their stiff beds. No straw or leaves here—too likely to burst into flame, according to the innkeeper below—so they slept on hard cots, smoothed stone with a ratty pillow. No need for blankets given the heat, but both Bliss and Wax threw their weaves on themselves anyway. For comfort, for home.

Quik eyed his own bed again, shoved up against a corner. A narrow window over it, barely large enough for a squeeze-through escape, offered the omnipresent orange light, the glow coming through and planting a yellowed square on the dusty gray stone floor. Voices carried through too, murmurs from below, even though Quik figured the hour had passed into early morning.

Then again, hard to follow the day and night when you didn't have a sky, a sun.

Quik had done the same dance all the Kitaye kids went

through: early years bouncing from tree to tree, doing as his elders asked and finding what he loved, letting that guide his first inks, all putting him on a path to join the hunters. Not because he loved the violence, but the thrill. The moments stalking a game bird, or spying out a fish to spear brought life into focus, a clarity he couldn't find at the cooking fires or helping his mother man the trading post.

Quik wasn't finding it much here either. Save for those beetles—a lapse, there, letting Bliss be the one to catch out the threat first—the journey so far had felt like a greasy babysitting job. Foti ale was fine, but its malty caramel tasted better as a celebration, not a way of life, and at this rate, Wax was going to have them drowning in the stuff before the week was out.

And in between the drunken bouts, they'd do what, meander through these ever-lit tubes?

Quik scratched at his leg. His eyes burned, something in the air eating at them. The room stifled his every breath, and without thinking about it, Quik stood, opened their door, and stepped into the circular hallway.

Their room sat on the third disc, the rounded floors encircling the hulking ice in the center. Immediately, the cold ran over him, washing away the sweat, bringing life back. Quik could handle the heat as well as anyone on Vis, but something about the dry, baking pressure here beat him down, sucked his will, demanded water.

Despite the hour, when Quik descended the central stair running alongside the ice, he found people aplenty still in the inn's dining room. A few drinking, their ales frothing over, but more sitting in clumps engaging in quiet conversation, as if Quik had come upon some social hour.

Glances flitted Quik's way as he hit the ground floor, and in that moment Quik realized he'd left his satchel back in the room. Without goods to trade, he couldn't ask for much. Not even a cool water cup, filled from that great crystal's run-off.

His indecision met its end when a table, and a woman somehow decked out in working leathers, waved him over. Two others, both equally clad for duty, their gear marred in a workman's way, sat at the table, leaving one more seat for Quik.

"What'll you have?" The woman asked as Quik approached.

"I have nothing to trade?"

"Isn't what I asked, islander." The woman nodded towards the empty chair. "Interesting visitors are scarce enough round here, worth paying for a story."

Quik eyed the three, found the woman's partners equally interested, though their eyes bore exhaustion's glaze. How long any story would hold their attention seemed a debatable question. Drinks, on the other hand, were drinks.

"What would you like to know?" Quik asked, after a similarly sleepy bartender—no more waiters this late— took his ask for a water.

He expected the usual, questions like the ones he and Wax had fielded in Smythe's casino. How do you survive in the jungle, what's it like swinging through trees, and all that ilk.

"Which one of you's the Renewal?" The woman started, cracking a smile. "I've bet on you, she's going for the girl, and he's wagered his last obsidian shard on the boy."

Quik's hand tightened on the water mug. He flailed about for a response.

"What Renewal?"

The woman laughed, and after a moment, the other two

joined in, their soft chuckles a distant background to their leader's guffaws.

"Don't ever try to lie again, my friend," the woman said as the laughter died. "It doesn't suit you, not the way those mighty fists do."

Quik didn't know what to say, so he drank the cool water instead. Let his look creep back to the stairs. A quick goodbye, a return to—

"Let's try a different way," the woman said. "The name's Sledge." When Quik blinked at her, she nodded at him. "Now you tell me yours."

"Quik."

"There you go. Not so hard, was it?" Sledge leaned on the table, never taking her cinnamon eyes off him. Up close, he noticed dark freckles, burn scars scattered here and there on her face. A patch of what would've been deep red hair looked torched off above her right ear. "I'll ask you again, to settle our wager. Which one's the Renewal?"

The minutes between the first ask and the second proved enough for Quik to settle himself. Like finding his footing on a dipping frond. He wasn't in some fight, but in a populated inn at a trading crossroads. Quik could hold his own.

"My brother, Wax," Quik said. "He's carrying the skar."

The man pounded his fist into the table, "I knew it. The kid's got the look."

"What look?" Quik asked as the other two nodded.

"Purpose." The man shook his head as he spoke. "It's a damn curse, feeling like you've got destiny draped all over you." The man stared into the table then, lost in some past memory.

"Don't let him get you down," Sledge said as the other woman put her hand on the man's shoulder, gave the leather pad a squeeze. "Old Loggren here's never got over his own shot at the skars, even though it's been near twenty-five years."

"Hard to forget when you had a chance to be the Aegis," Loggren muttered, before slipping into a sigh.

"We tried," Sledge reminded him. "There's a reason nobody from this half of the island's ever been the Foti Renewal. Too far away. If we wanted a crack at it, we should've moved north." Sledge turned back to Quik. "Which is what you three should be doing."

"We're walking that way, as best we can find."

"Walking, he says," Sledge laughed again, the other two joined her. "Hope you like pounding stone, Quik, because it's a hike."

"We'll get there."

"Is that what you think?"

Quik hesitated. What kind of response was that?

"All Sledge is saying," jumped in the other woman, "is that there's dangerous roads between here and the Great Forge, where the skar's at. There's a reason most sail the journey. Less risk, especially with fiends about."

"And other things besides," Loggren added.

"Things that might see your boy Wax and decide there's something easy for the taking," Sledge continued. "Don't know if you Vis understand, but a skar's a valuble thing. Plenty wouldn't mind taking it off your hands."

Quik sat back. Put room between his chair and the table. He could flip the furniture, put Loggren and the other woman on their backs and leave him one on one with Sledge, a fight Quik figured he could win.

"Relax," Sledge said. "We're not going to rob you."

"Not yet," muttered Loggren.

"Try, and you'll regret it," Quik said.

"Funny, you acting like we have much to lose," Sledge waved at the inn around them. "Spending our days mining away ore to send to Smythe, our nights drinking in the Jarl's Tooth. What a life to risk throwing away for a chance at something better."

Her tone changed, the light in her eyes going from an ale's dimming sight to one sparkling. Loggren and the other woman too sat up straighter, their looks at Quik less a buzzy genial and more the edged evaluation, a hunter's stare.

"Is this how Foti treats its visitors?" Quik asked. "If you came to Vis, we wouldn't threaten you, we wouldn't make you feel like you might be stabbed at any moment."

"Because you've got an isle of plenty," the other woman replied. "We're an isle of work. Of sweat and crud and dust. Spend some years here and see if you feel different, if you don't give a wanderer a kind look and a free drink."

"All we're saying, Quik," Sledge said, "is that you've got a hard road ahead. One better taken with good sleep and a sharp eye."

"Then I'll thank you for this, and say good night." Quik drained the water, stood from the table. Sledge raised her glass in goodbye, the other two didn't bother looking his way.

Quik checked back as he reached the stairs, saw the trio immersed in conversation, not a glance looking after him. Sledge laughed at something again. Maybe the veiled threats had just been warnings, maybe his heartbeat could slow down, his nerves could relax.

The staff nearly took Quik's head off when he came through the door. Bliss adjusted the swing, sent it low and killed its strength so that it only left a nasty sting as it smacked Quik's chest.

"What're you doing?" Quik asked, rubbing the spot and seeing Wax, off to the left, with his Foti blade drawn.

"You left and didn't come back," Wax said, sheathing the blue-glowing blade. "For a few minutes, we let it go. Then, we wondered if you'd found trouble."

"I'm not you," Quik snapped back. "I needed some water, and I found it."

'Long time for some water,' Bliss signed, setting the staff back against the wall.

Left without much choice, Quik relayed the story. Wax and Bliss listened, before both dismissed the downstairs trio as nothing more than worked up workers.

'People in Smythe told me the same thing,' Bliss signed. 'It's like Foti make a habit of warning visitors that they're in trouble.'

"Maybe so when they rob us, they can claim we were warned." Wax grinned, slumped back on his bed. "Clears their conscience, you know?"

"Whatever their words, I didn't like them," Quik said. "I felt like prey. Not a pleasant sensation."

Bliss, who'd taken up a spot near the doorway, signed back, 'We're like no prey they've ever hunted, brother. If they try us, we'll show them how wrong they are.'

His sister was right about that, at least. Quik reached for his satchel, found the carved gauntlets on the floor next to it. The wood glazed, cleaned, and sharp enough to bite through anything less than stone and metal.

CHAPTER 14

CAVE WALKING

By the third closed tunnel, the walls clearly cut apart and caved down to seal off the rightwards path, the foursome knew they were being guided. By what, to where, were questions Svarde didn't have the answers to, neither did Maena, Pennifer, or Rasslebeck, and all four chose to keep silent about the matter, stewing their growing fear with curiosity as the pattering steps brought them deeper and deeper.

Only Kivi, with her snorts and tentative bites at the barriers, bothered to question events. At this latest one, an impressive brown and pink collage battering shut a passage, Kivi stuck back when Svarde and the others made to move on through the only tunnel open to them. Instead, she scratched at the wall, bit at the stone, notching grooves in the collected rubble.

"Going to need a lot more than you to get through it," Svarde said, kneeling by the ferrite as the others watched. "Bit too much rock even for your gullet, I'd say."

Kivi snorted, kept at it. Svarde watched the lizard, tried to sort out the idea, the point. Until Kivi's scrabbling registered a different note, one that took longer to find its home in Svarde's memory only because he'd never seen the ferrite show it before.

"You scared, Kivi?" Svarde asked, low and quiet. Had to preserve the ferrite's standing among the group. "Scared of whatever we're walking towards?"

Kivi stopped her scrabbling, snorted twice, then backed up the path, her eyes and tongue peeking the way they'd gone.

"Can't do it," Svarde said. "Even if we wanted to, would be hard to scrounge enough supplies to make it back to the surface now. We're committed, as are you." Svarde reached behind his back, patted the axe haft. "Don't worry, you're not alone down here. We'll protect you."

Kivi's beady look said the offer didn't provide much comfort.

"Your ferrite coming along, Svarde?" Maena asked, down the tunnel, holding the torch aloft. They'd been able to find plenty of burnables in the gloom, at least. The forever dark held at bay for now. "We've got some hours yet before a break and I'd like to use them."

"She's coming," Svarde said, standing. "C'mon, Kivi. Let's go find what's been closing off these ways. Maybe it's a friend."

Though not a soul in the party believed that to be true.

The stone took on a life this far down, a changing world just like any forest or tundra up above. The smells and sounds changed, with heat rising as they went down, enough to make the foursome abandon their Whent furs. Rana cloth made its return, the light outfits tearing as they snagged on stones and ill-placed footfalls. Odd rock formations grew more common, as though the earth down here had yet to settle on a plan, with caverns popping up and dying away quick, making up shapes at odds with what Svarde would've considered natural.

"Fiend work," Pennifer, the crossbow-wielder, dead-eyed and prone to dark observations, said.

Whether the monsters did indeed carve out their own dens in the deep was a question they hadn't yet answered, but without another option, the label stuck with the group as they continued. Crystalline alcoves, swift streams, bubbling noxious pools and lichen-crusted ledges interrupted their steady steps. Boring, the journey was not, though Svarde did find himself wishing for an open sky.

He'd never felt much love for the stars before, but not seeing them now for so many days seemed to put a cloak on his hope, his happiness, and left only resolve.

Which was more than enough.

"Hold," Maena whispered, leading the crew through the tunnel to a new opening.

At the torchlight's edge, the rock walls spilled away again, offering up another cavern, and then yanking away those expectations with a brutal surprise.

All throughout the journey down gashes lit up the walls, with broken fiend parts found here and there. Another set shouldn't have been shocking, save this time the destruction didn't seem random, didn't seem the product of ritual cleaning, culling.

To Maena's left and right, the cavern's scalloped walls had their bases decorated with bones. Not randomly placed collections, either, but end-to-end laid out, as if lining a tunic's skirt. And stretching up those walls were markings, long and short lines, some at angles. They split and came together, the bones themselves serving to divide the markings into columns.

"Into verse, if I have my guess right," Maena said, the

party now into the room and looking at the scribblings. "This isn't any language I've seen before, but it's definitely that."

Staring at the scratched verse prompted no further understanding, so after some minutes tracing the markings along the walls, Maena whistled the foursome together. The Rana captain held a different guise about her now, the determined explorer muted by introspection, a look Svarde feared was starting to creep in on his own person.

This was a mission of vengeance, destruction. Getting its clear goals colored with side stories wouldn't do. Wouldn't serve Catya.

"Ideas?" Maena asked into the dripping, soft torch glow. "The caves go on, but if I make my mark right, it looks like we're entering a home."

"A home we've been led right to," Rasslebeck said. "Not like we were intending on interrupting the business of whatever's in here, but it didn't leave us much choice."

"We could go back," Maena offered. "Two breaks, I think, was our last split."

"Why?" Pennifer asked, her hands, as ever, on the two crossbows at her waist. "Are we scared?"

"It's the goal, is all," Maena replied. "We want the heart. Where the fiends are coming from. There are no fiends here. At least, none like what we're hunting."

Fiends could've made the markings, maybe, but Svarde kept the thought to himself. No doubt the others were already thinking it, were tossing the reasoning aside. Even the smartest monsters from the deep, like the tar thing that'd tried spitting Svarde up on the Whent surface, seemed limited in their cultural abilities. None that he'd ever seen would go about writing a poem or a history on a cave's walls.

But then, perhaps only a certain type of fiend made it up to the surface. Perhaps the unruly ones were chased out by these, the true terrors who made their devil homes in the dark.

"We have to find out," Svarde said. "Whatever this is, if it's a fiend, a monster, or something else besides, we have to know."

"Do we?" Maena countered.

"If it's not a fiend, then maybe it's a friend," Svarde swept his torch towards the bones lining the walls. "Those are fiend parts, unless I'm way off, which means it's got a healthy appetite for our enemies. And if it's a bigger, badder fiend than all the rest carving out a home beneath our feet, then it's best we put it to bed."

"The four of us, you mean," Maena said.

"Five." Svarde nodded at Kivi, which did nothing to improve Maena's straight frown.

"I'm with the Guardian," Flashstrike said. "We knew there'd be mysteries down here. I'm for solving, and killing, them all."

"Agreed," Pennifer added. "Don't like the idea of walking back, wasting time."

Maena nodded once, "Settled, then. Svarde, take the lead. Stay sharp, ready. It's likely our host already knows we're here."

The host didn't offer much of a welcome. Past the opening cave, three tight options gave Svarde a left, middle, or right. The leftward tunnel had an arched bone smashed into the rock above its middle, while the center tunnel had its apex capped with a crimson, dried blood smear. The right offered what seemed like a long, deep groove across the top.

"Kivi?" Svarde asked. "You smell anything interesting?"

The ferrite snorted, burst its steam vents, then scurried forth towards the middle offering.

"Follow the lizard," Svarde muttered, axe in his right hand and the torch in his left burning away.

The middle tunnel didn't stay level long, but curled sharply up. The ground didn't hold to a cave's natural floor, picking up a pebbled composition instead, as if dug out and left to slowly fill in by an unstable ceiling. Svarde glanced up that way, seeing a mangled rock collection hung together over their heads as if by sheer will and nothing else.

He quickened his pace.

The strides beneath that doomed ceiling didn't last long. The tunnel lipped up into a heart-shaped room, split in towards the middle by a glittering pink-and-white quartz. The giant, jagged gem at first had Svarde stopping, stunned as his torch found reflections in every corner, those stars longed for suddenly appearing though no sky existed for them.

"Look past the light," Maena said, moving beyond Svarde into the room.

Her comment's target became clear as Svarde adjusted to the brightness: for all its crystal beauty, the quartz held imperfections, ones not placed there by geology. Instead, clothes, armor, shoes and weapons lay hung off various ends, those diamonds and arrows ending with odd treasures from bodies Svarde couldn't see.

"What are these?" Rasslebeck said as the group moved in and looked over the leavings. "Not Rana, not Whent. Foti, maybe?"

Svarde leaned in to what looked like a chain cuirass, its top hole hanging over a thin skin-pink quartz needle. The ringlets had seen better days, many cut apart, rended and smashed, but even so their craftsmanship didn't match the Great Forge. The metal lacing looked like an awkward fit, the ores not ideal for the purpose.

"It's a poor job if it came from us," Svarde said. "I'd give it to Kance, or maybe some Noctia playing at smithing."

"But, if pressed, you wouldn't call it either of those," Maena suggested, once more glancing about with a musing look. "These shoes aren't much more than scraps, but the stitching doesn't match anything I've seen either."

"Old, then?" Rasslebeck offered. "Some leavings from a party long before us?"

"Not that old," Pennifer, off to the left and holding up a second chain tunic said. "Iron like this would tarnish and fade down here before too long, like it does on our ships after only a few days."

"Which means what?" Rasslebeck asked. "We've found some new people?"

As if in answer to his question, a weeping wind rustled through the room, the air banging the clothes against one another and the quartz, a dire chime.

"No," Maena said. "I think we've found its trophies." She reached to her waist, drew her saber. "And I think we're about to become its newest additions."

THE WIND PICKED UP AGAIN, rustling through the quartz room and sending the garments shifting, those ringlets clinking against one another. Whistles and moans went with it, the air slipping through cracks and crevasses to make its noise. Svarde followed the gust, torch and axe in hand, waiting to see which exit—the room held three, one off each heart's side and the tunnel they'd come in on at the shape's pointed base—the breeze would take.

The wind, it seemed, crossed the heart, coming in on the right and billowing out the left. Pennifer drew both crossbows, Rasslebeck and Maena had their sabers ready, but no monster materialized, and after some long seconds the wind died down, leaving as its parting gift a murmur at its exit.

A murmur just like a dying conversation, muttered words and sharp meanings hidden behind mushy echoes.

"A trick of the wind," Maena said as all eyes went towards that tunnel. "Nothing more."

"A trap, a trick, or a mistake," Svarde replied, heading that way. "Watch my back."

With Kivi at his feet, the warrior held the torch out ahead, following the wind towards its chosen exit. Behind and beside him, the quartz played out its pink ends, the cavern walls opposite a mottled blue-gray. No fungus here, no dirt or rubble left to litter. Something cared for the chamber, that much was obvious.

Svarde slowed up as he neared the tunnel, poked the torch further ahead and hoped its golden hue would find something to reflect. Nothing showed save further shadow, the tunnel curling hard right beyond the room, preventing further sight.

Preventing, too, his companions from seeing what would happen should Svarde venture further. A choice, then. Split up or stay together. The narrow tunnels would cramp a group's fighting, but separating in an unknown place like this, with traps and terrors likely about, seemed the height of folly.

"We go together?" Svarde asked the group. "This way?"

"With no better option, I'm for it," Maena said and the other two agreed. "Form up for a fight. I'll take the rear."

Pennifer and Rasslebeck held the center, the former's

crossbows ready to aim in either direction should the threat reveal itself.

Again, they stalked the dark. Again, the dark seemed to stalk them.

The tunnel performed its curl clean, a snapping wrap that deposited the bunch into a tight, towering hole. At their feet, save for a small pebbled shore, lay a small lake with deep, dark fathoms. Above, darkness flew beyond the torch's light, a rising space leading up who knew how far. The wind still ran around in here, chasing off the walls and brushing the water.

Kivi played tester, dashing forward and dipping a single long red tongue into the lake. Kivi's tongue sizzled as it struck the water, but the ferrite followed up with a lapping lick, then another.

"It's clean," Svarde said, following the ferrite to the shore and kneeling. He leaned over, set his axe down and scooped the clear liquid into his palm. Stared at it in the torchlight. "Perfect."

"No monster's toilet, then," Rasslebeck said, sheathing his saber and pushing a handful into his mouth. "The best this side of Rana, I think."

They refilled their water skins, the quartz room's eerie terror fading next to the unexpected bounty. Even the still-whispering wind took on a jaunty feel, a sort of hello to the group having made it this far.

"An oasis is an oasis, even if we're not in the desert," Maena said as they broke out a quick lunch. "Though I'll still say the beast that owns this place will make its appearance sooner or later."

"Then we'll be fighting it on full stomachs instead of empty ones," Rasslebeck said. "A better deal, all told."

"Don't want to die hungry," Pennifer added.

Svarde held his torch out over the water, trying to see if he could spy a bottom. None revealed itself, neither did a source for the pool. Or what might've carved the opening overhead. More mysteries in the deep.

Too many.

The tunnel continued past the pool, circling to the right and putting the whole bunch back in the quartz room. A simple loop, the pink once more shining before them.

"Two more tunnels back the way we came," Svarde suggested.

They made to head that way when the wind came through again, faster this time, the ringmail making a clashing symphony against the quartz as the gust blew through. And again, following its departure, the muttered tones of harsh conversation through the far tunnel, the one leading back to the lake.

"A play of the air, or a nasty trick," Svarde said.

"If it's a trick, I say we trap the thing," Rasslebeck said. "Two go straight ahead, the others back around. We meet in the middle."

A short enough distance splitting wouldn't be too much of a risk, and yet Svarde hesitated, caught Maena's frown and saw her assessing the same odds.

"We go fast," Svarde said. "Kivi and I head back this way, you three straight ahead. Don't be slow, we meet at the lake."

"It's a chance," Maena said. "One we don't—"

"We put this to bed here," Svarde said. "Either it's the wind, or it's something worse. I'd rather be sure it's not the latter before we turn our backs on this damn thing again."

Maena shrugged, gave Svarde a salute with the saber. "See you in a few minutes, Guardian."

The tunnel back took a sharp left upon leaving the

quartz room, just as it should've. With Kivi walking at his feet, Svarde made each step careful, torch aloft and axe ready. Purple and blue stone. Dripping water in the distance, the wind rising and falling again.

The leftward curl ended, the tunnel straightening out before it should've. Svarde stopped, blinked, sniffed at the air and looked at the smooth tunnel walls. They'd walked this way moments before. No sounds said the earth had moved, and yet as sure as he'd been about anything, Svarde knew this tunnel wasn't the same one he'd just walked down a moment ago.

"Maena?" Svarde called, his voice echoing into the dark. Rolling ahead and behind with no answer. Kivi snorted, nervous. "Something's not right here."

Kivi snorted again, this one an agreement. An obvious one.

When confronted with an unexpected change, best to backtrack. A blind charge forward might be satisfying, and a younger Svarde might've picked up his axe and barreled on with a caustic roar, but this one had seen how badly that could go. Instead, he turned, stomped back the way he'd come.

And found himself again at the quartz chamber, loot hanging from the gem as if nothing had changed. The other three members of his party were gone. No sound of their passage echoed through.

"Maena?" Svarde called again.

No response.

"Then we follow," Svarde said to Kivi, and the two went past the quartz, looked to the tunnel that should lay beyond.

They saw nothing save rock.

Svarde stared at the stone. Putting such a wall up, one

so clean and without seams, would take true tradecraft, would take days and make more noise than a cave like this could hide.

Kivi snorted again. Nervous.

"Think I'm with you on this one," Svarde said.

The wind died. No rustle. The ringmail fell quiet. The drips and drabs, the crackle of dust and rock on the move ceased, the cave falling silent save the snap from Svarde's torch.

The warrior turned 'round slow, looking back at the chamber's middle, at the quartz. Standing there, where there'd been no shape a moment before, stood a man. One with a stiff beard, with scars, with a torch in one hand and an axe in the other. At his feet waited a ferrite, sizzling tongue tasting the air.

"Well damn," Svarde groaned. "This wasn't what I wanted today."

He took a step towards his mirror, and the shadowed version of himself copied the motion. Svarde raised his axe, the mirror man did the same. Kivi snorted and her copy did too.

Svarde closed till he could pick out the flecks in his copy's eyes, count the lines along his cheeks. Time to see if this thing was his imagination or not.

"Sorry, myself," Svarde muttered, his copy's lips moving with his own even if no words emerged.

With a light touch, Svarde brought his torch down towards the copy. The mirror torch came towards Svarde's shoulder, but he felt no heat from its glow. Saw no flames from Svarde's own, real torch light up on the copy.

An illusion, then. A mental trick. Svarde sighed, nodded. These games, he could—

The wind swirled, harsh fast, and gusting around his

torch. The fire snapped once, fighting against the swirl, then died. Utter dark drenched the room, and as Svarde dropped the torch, reached for his second axe, he felt the wind pick up again, felt it rush into his ears, his mouth, his eyes, and steal his breath away.

"Ease up, friend," said the mellow tone, wet and healthy and bored all at once. "Don't rise too fast."

Svarde opened his eyes. Closed them. Opened them again. The view changed not once, showing the pitch dark hadn't gone away since the wind took him. He twitched his arms, his legs. Took a long breath.

He lived, seemed unbroken.

"Kivi?" Svarde asked the air as he sat up.

"Just you and me here, friend. You and me." A soft laugh, like a jester's amusement at his own joke. "Always nice to have some company at the end."

Svarde's fingers felt hard rock. Still in the cave then, though a quick check confirmed his axes were gone, his provisions too. His clothes remained, his boots tied on. Kivi, it seemed, hadn't made the trip either.

Which made it time to investigate the voice.

"Who're you?" Svarde asked, standing and bumping his head on a low ceiling. He cursed.

"Why I said to ease up slow," the man replied, the voice a leathery thing, heavy on the gullet. "This isn't a pleasant space to be in."

"Answer my question."

"Who am I?" The man seemed puzzled. "I think I would've had an answer for you one day, long ago."

Svarde cast about in the dark, tried to find the walls. Succeeded after stumbling around. The chamber was a squat circle, a tight ceiling, a smooth floor, and what seemed like a boulder-sealed door about half Svarde's height. The man, when Svarde found him, flinched away, but the touch confirmed skin, bones, and not an unhealthy feel.

"Where are we?" Svarde asked, the man continuing to mutter about who he was, who he might have been.

"Oh, that one's easy enough to answer," the man replied, laughing a little again. "You're home, friend. Your new home, anyway, and soon to be your only one."

"What're you talking about?"

"At least we can share it, you know. It's been so long, it'll be nice to have company. You should tell some stories."

"Stories?" Svarde went back to the boulder, tried to feel around the edges. "What's the point of stories right now?"

"Because if you don't share them now, you might never get another chance again."

Svarde scoffed, "Something going to kill us then?"

"Oh no. Not kill us. Something far, far worse." The man tittered, broke into a brief sob. "I was once somebody, you know. You will be too."

Svarde shook his head, worked his hands around the boulder, and listened to the drip, drip, drip as water splashed into the room.

CHAPTER 15
SPY GAME

Ami tugged the hood up closer around her face, Noctia's pre-dawn fog coming with the cloth to cloak her in shadow. A chill morning, a wet morning, those rain barrels across the isle filling slow in the drizzle. She leaned against the stone wall, a lit Foti pipe in her mouth, the minty smoke vanishing into its natural counterpart with every puff.

Carts rattled along the cobblestones, taking meals and supplies to where they were needed. Early classes, Circle meetings, Najahn drills and developments. The working class doing its part so the scholars and soldiers could have their day.

A day that, hopefully, would start soon.

A thin door sat at Ami's left, closed and locked. An exit, really, from the tower the door belonged to, and one that would open up as soon as the Tenet who controlled this tower opened the day's business.

Ami repeated the Najahn ranks again, muttering their names, their links. She'd done her best to play light politics in her time here, getting Catya what she needed, ensuring Ami kept her access and was otherwise ignored.

The Tenets served as the Najahn's directors, each one managing part of Noctia's society, part of the Najahn's sprawl. From food to footsoldiers, ships to skars, Tenets monitored them all, and in her experience, Ami found each and every one the same sort of ambitious pencil pusher. Sniveling, conniving, working to get as much for themselves as the people they supposedly worked for.

Which was why, when Mattimo asked her to rob one, Ami wasn't all that sad about it.

AT LAST THE DOOR CREAKED, the sun not yet forcing its way through the morning's misty gray. The dark wood swung open, a Najahn servant in purple robes stepping out with chamber pots to empty into the seaward drains.

The young man threw Ami a surprised glance, caught Ami's glowered glare in return, and kept moving. The drains lay across the street, an easy walk now shrouded by fog. As soon as the scholar started the journey, Ami curled left, through the door and into the tower.

Inside, lamps burned in small sconces, illuminating a stone corridor with grape carpeting running down the middle. To Ami's immediate left a stair began its curl up, while straight ahead offered the rumbled good cheer of a day as yet unspoiled.

Tapping her pipe against the wall, the ashes falling to a pile in the corner, Ami made for the stair and started up. Its spiral gave her a chance to hide from the returning servant, gave Ami a chance to pull back her hood, reveal the Guardian badge on her purple tunic.

She'd tried to enter this tower twice in the last two days, found herself rebuffed both times, told a Guardian had no business here, but if Ami knew one thing, it was that the Najahn had soft underbellies. Get past the first shell, and nobody in this tower would dare confront her.

She hoped, anyway.

The second level offered little more than the first, its offices and anterooms beginning to bustle. The few people in the hallway moving between places didn't give Ami a glance. So secure in their places, their purposes, their power.

Power Catya gave them through her sacrifice.

Ami shook off the snarl, turned back to the stairs and climbed again. Tenets, like all the greedy would-be lords, kept their offices at the tower tops. Ami herself had only ever been to one, the Tenet who ruled the Wards and the Renewals, the one who'd given her and Svarde the rules after Catya slipped on the necklace and trapped herself on this damn island.

That Tenet—himself long gone now, replaced by someone Ami neither knew nor cared to know—had glorified himself in the stone penthouse that was his charge. Walls littered with artifacts not earned but nonetheless boasted of. Gifts and treasures from the isles given to the Najahn, though whether from honest desire or duress, who could, or would, say?

This tower's Tenet ruled over something different. Resources, supplies, trade and science. A grab bag of things that didn't fit in with weapons, monsters, and politics. The tower, as she climbed, seemed to take on the Tenet's duties, its raw gray stone vanishing behind hung maps of the isles, many dotted with trade routes, or framed papers and pictures showing natural treasures.

The theme, at least, was on point.

On the third level, Ami lingered and looked at a hung diagram depicting Foti-forged sapphire. Not really the gemstone, but a product of folded metals and crushed crystals, the Foti specialty was both rare and beautiful. Even Flamebreak didn't carry that forging in its blade. The hung picture attempted to describe how the metal was made, attempted and failed to bring Ami back to the sweltering heat, the singing songs roared out to the hammer's beat. The lava's shifting lights, the water as hot as the air dripping down her throat, sweat collecting in waist-worn skins for later. A community bonded by fire.

One she'd never go back to, much as Ami could credit it with her strength and resilience. Some things were best appreciated through memory, not relived again.

"Guardian?" Asked a tremulous voice, a small man appearing there in the hallway at her side. "Is there something you need?"

Discovery. She'd planned for this. Turning an inquisitive ask was just like turning a blade. Parry and thrust.

"I've never been to this tower," Ami said, putting on her toothiest grin as she looked down at the man. "I've been walking through them all, and finally found a day to see this one. It's fascinating."

The man beamed, vanity assuaged. "Not many would say so." He followed her eyes to the Foti sapphire picture. "Most don't have patience for the gears keeping our world turning."

"I've watched Catya die for the last decade," Ami said. "Patience is all I have left."

The scholar went ashen, gulped through a nod. "The Aegis's sacrifice is the greatest gift someone could give."

Another gulp, a back step. "I hope you enjoy our tower, Guardian."

The scholar turned, quick-stepped away and ducked into the first room he encountered on the right. Ami snorted. Another coward, unwilling to confront the cost of all this luxury.

But then, that'd been the plan. Make any of these fools uncomfortable and away they ran, back to the safety of their books and banter, where consequences could be abstracted away to nothing.

She took to the stairs again.

The fourth level offered a change. Again the hallway, again the hanging pictures, but rather than Najahn scholars puttering about, quiet suffused instead. The doors all seemed shut, each one a thick Whent wood and placed into their arched stone doorways. Bronzed numbers gleamed on each one, assuming the viewer would know what forty-one, forty-three, and forty-five might mean. The even-numbered partners sat on the other site, presenting Ami with a questionable choice surfeit.

The stairs didn't go up any farther, either, so these doors were what she had to work with. Save, of course, the hallway's end and the double-wide passage there to the tower's middle. If this one matched the other towers, there'd be four branches, each with its own room comple-ment. A couple dozen to choose from, and, assuming this was the highest level, one would be the Tenet's office.

How many could Ami open before someone found her, became suspicious?

"Let's find out," Ami muttered, turning to the first door on her left and pressing down on the handle.

With a soft click and a seamless sweep, the door swung

inward, revealing a small room with a single table, several chairs, book shelves and an unlit fireplace. Two thin windows showed the fog still dominating outside. A break room, maybe, or meeting place between more formal spaces.

Ami turned around, angling to go to the next door, only to bump into a large man filling the hallway space behind her.

A glance revealed him, despite the Najahn garb, as Tamas. Loose skin, faraway eyes, too few callouses yet too many wrinkles for his age. A body lost in thought, or in machinations. He doubled Ami's girth, though how much was billowing robe and how much his body remained a mystery.

"Rare for a Guardian to come to our tower," the man said, giving Ami the smallest, neck-only bow. "We are honored with your presence."

"Don't be," Ami replied. She glanced around the man, hunting for more people and found none. "I'm just looking for something."

"And what might that be?"

"A damn spine, for one." Ami put up a scowl. Hopefully this guy was as meek as the other, would go scurrying off as soon as he faced resistance. "You know where I might find any?"

The man smiled, a face-splitting thing that looked either too happy or too scary. Ami couldn't decide which, the man's vibe inscrutable. Enemy, ally, or random wanderer?

"Finding courage in another is often a matter of circum-stance, I've learned." The man backed up a step, gestured down the hall towards the tower's center. "Care to elaborate? Perhaps in my chamber, where listening ears might not be so close."

"Your chambers? Who are you?"

"The master of this particular tower." Again the man did his little bow. On Foti, anyone caught bowing would get mocked behind their back, possibly punched in the face. A reflex Ami had learned to suppress after a few awkward early encounters on Catya's Renewal road. "My name is Gladdring, Tenet of Noctia at your service."

Ami worked fast on the walk to Gladdring's office, at first trying to spin up some lie about why she'd come to the tower, something about seeing the sights, looking at their pictures of Foti materials, but Gladdring's glittering gaze said he bought none of it, so when they settled into his chambers, Ami dispensed with the charade.

Mostly.

"I'm here trying to help Catya," Ami said.

Gladdring waved Ami towards a cushioned chair, one carved from near-black wood. It seemed all curves and curls, inset furls looping around one another. She ignored the offer, instead standing behind the chair with her hands on the back. Gladdring eyed her for a long moment, then went behind his desk. Gladdring's own chair was much the same as Ami's, if almost twice as large, its back looming up over his head. Framed by twin oval windows whose gray light blended with sconced lanterns to brighten up the crowded space.

Crowded, Ami was confused to find, not with books but objects. Shelves stood against the stone walls, their every bit covered in boxes, in glass containers with strange rocks, dried fruits, or insects. A circular globe stood near the far wall, its bright blue surface an estimate of the world and the Seven Isle's tiny place within it. From some distant instrument, a lone trumpeted tune floated up and in.

"Assisting the Aegis is the most noble thing any of us can do," Gladdring said, interlocking his fingers and leaning over the wide polished desk. "How can I help?"

She'd fought fiends by the dozen, she'd stared down the Precept and his Circle allies time and again, had her life put on edge, and yet never once had she been asked quite like this what she wanted. Ami, Guardian, didn't have an answer.

But neither would she say nothing. She paced, taking a slow walk around Gladdring's office and let the steps give her ideas.

"I want a chance to save her," Ami said. "And I think one exists here. On Noctia. In your records. Or your storerooms. Somewhere."

Gladdring tilted his head, "Are you suggesting, Guardian, that Noctia has a way to help the Aegis and is choosing not to?"

"Are they? Are you?"

Again that smile. Gladdring creased it into a shrug, "If we are, I don't know about it. Tenets aren't privy to all Najahn information." Gladdring leaned forward again. "Is there a reason you came to this tower specifically, Ami?"

She hadn't given Gladdring leave to call her by her first name, a protocol breach Ami chose to ignore. Gladdring seemed really interested now, his eyes wide and locked on Ami, as if begging her to speak more. Either the man truly wanted to help the Aegis, or his days were so boring as to make a conversation like this the best part.

Regardless, she couldn't betray Mattimo. Not yet.

"I want to know why the Aegis isn't lasting as long

anymore," Ami said. "Something is changing. Catya's aging faster than any of the others."

"And you think the answer lies with our trinkets? With trade, the price of grain?"

Well, perhaps she'd betray Mattimo, if only a little bit. Dancing with Gladdring wasn't the sword fight she preferred.

Ami narrowed her eyes, approached the desk and put her hands on it, looking down at Gladdring, around him. "I know there's more here than grain, Gladdring. You have the kinds of things that might help me."

"Oh? What kinds of things?"

"Why is it that the Najahn control every place on the isles where skars are found?"

Gladdring chuckled, "Because we seek power, and the skars have it."

"And you have the skars."

Gladdring's eyebrows rose. "Quite the accusation." The mock alarm faded, Gladdring sat back in his chair, the fascination dwindling. Apparently Ami had said the wrong thing. "Those who need to know already understand we take the leftovers. In return, we keep enough skars safe for the next Renewal. This isn't the controversy you think it is."

"But why? What do you want with the skars if they're not for the Renewal?"

"A question, Ami, that I would not ask," Gladdring said. "Some here are not as supportive of free knowledge as I am, and would take your inquiring about such things as dangerous. The skars can't help your friend. Do right by her, lend Catya your friendship, your comfort for the time she has left."

"Then you can't help me, or won't?"

"It doesn't matter," Gladdring said. "The result is the

same. Catya will survive until the Renewal completes, and then she will die, as has every other Aegis. The world will continue as it has before. Best make what you can of it."

Gladdring nodded towards the door, standing as he did so.

"You looked fascinated for a moment there. Interested. What did you want me to ask?"

Gladdring shook his head. "Nothing, no matter. Go on, Guardian."

"Show me out?" Ami asked, leaning back against the far wall. "It's the least you could do."

"The least I could do would be considerably less," Gladdring grumbled, his charm now utterly dead. Nevertheless, he moved from his chair towards the door. Ami followed, sweeping behind the man's desk, her eyes crawling, fingers searching. A thief, however, Ami was not.

"What are you doing?" Gladdring asked, turning back, his eyes glittering with something less than amusement.

"I was hoping I'd find them, the skars," Ami said, making an open show of looking around the desk now. Her hands opened drawers, shut them. "You're saying they aren't valuable, but I want to be sure."

"The skars, if we have them, would not be here," Gladdring said. "Leave off, Guardian, or my politeness will come to an end."

"Oh no."

Amislipped on a cold grin, left the desk behind, and squeezed by Gladdring.

No need to start a fight when she'd found what she needed. Ami didn't pull out the small paper, a badge really, until she'd reached Noctia's streets. Nothing save a single emblem, drawn in runny black ink, with seven circles adorning a frilled shield. A key, if Mattimo was right, to answers.

But why wait for Mattimo to find them?

AMI DEVOURED lunch not far away, socking away seconds in a small cafe. She traded, as ever, on the account the Najahn provided for her, payment for the hours and days she spent by Catya's side keeping her safe. A fruit and fish combination enjoyed on the cobblestones outside, the late morning sun having conquered the fog and brought about a brisk, beautiful day. Scholars and soldiers churned around her, most not bothering a look at the Guardian. Not a soul said hello, offered up thanks for her sacrifice.

Back at the beginning, the crowds would've paid her more respect, would've thrown Ami grateful gifts for all she'd done to bring the Aegis safely home. As the fiends dwindled away, so did anything like debt, Ami fading to irrelevence as Noctia churned on with its life.

For a while, the relative anonymity felt pleasant, a respite Ami could enjoy with Catya and, for a short time before his self-imposed isolation, Svarde. A basking in success, a grooving into life of a new routine. The daily watch, the exercises, the hobbies. The Rat's Fang. But she was too young for her life's tale to dwindle so early, a fact that only became clear as Ami grew older, as Catya grew ancient.

Time, then, to get on with the next era.

She returned to Gladdring's tower, noting the scholars milling around the main door had changed over since Ami's unceremonious departure. The Guardian had looked at the stolen note again over lunch, decided that any secrets opened by such a thing would have to be lower, down into the sloping cliff rock at the tower's base. The building narrowed as it rose, and the foot traffic on those upper levels suggested too lax security. Nobody, after all, had bothered to push Ami on what she was doing till Gladdring himself ran into her.

This time she covered her Guardian badge, letting the Najahn cloak do its work. Ami wasn't sure her warrior's visage could ever convince anyone she'd been spending lifetime among the books, but a moment's doubt was all she needed, was what she earned, walking straight by the scholars into the tower. The eager trio had their mouths barking at one another, caught up in some debate about Whent grain and Rana rice.

The tower's main lobby offered a more impressive entry than Ami's side door from earlier that morning. Gladdring had escorted her down the main stair, a back-and-forth climber that continued down from where Ami now stood. Hallways branched to her right and left, while portraits, including one of Gladdring, lined the walls. A small plaque on her right declared in golden letters that this was the Tower of Trade.

Confidence would ever serve as her companion on missions like this, and it propelled Ami here, sending her feet padding along the carpet to the downward stair. Narrow steps fell away as she descended one, two, three floors. Those all appeared ordinary: more hallways, more hanging art, more hapless scholars. The fourth, by now down far enough so no windows broke the stone walls, offered the stair's conclusion onto a lantern-lit circle. The stair ended in the circle's center, the spaces left and right occupied by chairs and tables more suited to guard shifts than research. Empty now.

Empty, perhaps, because their occupants stood before a

closed, hallway-spanning gate. Not a door, but a wrought iron barrier sporting at least two locks along its rightward side. The two guards giving Ami curious stares stood with arms folded, requisite voulges leaning against the walls on either side. Whether these two had spines at all, Ami found it hard to guess: their faces seemed weathered, their eyes pale and sharp.

Gladdring, apparently, didn't hire the scrubs for his secrets.

Ami stopped as she left the stair, watched the pair as they watched her. An awkward impasse. Burbling conversation drifted down from the upper levels, not a sound from this one. Both guards seemed to hold their breath, as if to twitch would be to break some stonefaced agreement with Gladdring.

"No greetings?" Ami asked.

The left guard frowned, "We don't know you. Are you supposed to be here?"

Ami fished out the paper, held it up. "Got this today. New project."

The left guard reached out, took the paper. The right guard glowered, a nasty stare. No, Ami wouldn't want to get these two in a fight. Not without Flamebreak, at least.

The guard passed the paper to his cohort. Let his folded arms fall to his sides. Kept them loose, as if Ami might jump the man at any moment.

"Clear?" The left guard asked after a long several heartbeats.

"Looks legitimate." The right guard handed the paper back to Ami. "Who gave this to you?"

"How's that any of your business?" Ami asked.

"Everyone going through this gate's our business."

"Gladdring gave it to me." Ami nodded at the gate. "You

going to open that thing? I didn't come all the way down here just to chat with you two, wonderful as you are."

The left guard snorted, fumbled with some keys locked onto a loop at his waist.

"A smart mouth's not the best thing to have down here," the right guard said as the other undid the locks. "This is a serious place."

"I'll keep that in mind." Ami brushed by the guards as the gate slid open.

She felt their eyes on her back as she went down the hallway, as closed doors again offered options to her left and right. Ahead, a dead wall signaled the end. If she tried the wrong one, would the guards know Ami had bluffed her way in? Or maybe . . .

"Care to help me find the right place?" Ami asked the pair.

"Which place is that?"

Ami threw on an exaggerated eye roll, "You know which one."

The guards glanced at each other. The right one sighed, pointed to Ami's left. "First door. It's unlocked."

"Look at that. Being helpful didn't kill you after all."

WITH A PUSH ON THE HANDLE, the chosen door slid inward. Immediately a sparking scent, like something recently burned, flooded Ami's nose. The air rushing past, the echoing sound signaled the room beyond as much larger than any one Ami had yet seen in the tower, an impression amplified by the distant lamps on walls to her right and ahead. The only close side came on her left, a scarred stone slab seeming to push Ami down yet more steps, a half-stair down to what looked like a ringing walkway.

What it ringed became clearer as Ami descended, a latticed barrier cutting between the stone walkway and the room's pit-like center. Down there, another full story below, sat seven large chests. Each one rested on a pedestal engraved with the name of an isle. Three of those chests sat open, their contents glittering inside. A large table dominated the pit's center, one splayed over with strange items Ami couldn't identify. Swirling metal pieces, sparkling in the light. A woman leaned over them now, muttering to herself as Ami approached the lattice and looked down.

Who was that, and what was she doing?

As Ami watched, the woman held up a hand, snapped her fingers, and raced to one of the open chests. One with Foti's isle emblazoned beneath it. Two latches clicked free, the lid popped up and open, and the woman reached in and grabbed a glittering ruby, one with a wrinkled shape Ami knew all too well.

The woman returned to her table with the skar, slotted it into a device the length of a good dagger, where the Foti skar nestled in next to the breezy gray Ami knew belonged to Kance. The woman lifted the device, then slid a small switch between the two skars, linking them with a silver line. That sparking smell filled the air again, and the woman twisted, aiming the device at a standing board against the room's far side.

"Attempt number two hundred and twenty-three," the woman said. "Foti and Kance this time. Let's go."

The woman's arms clenched, as if she were about to draw a blade, and the device hummed, crackled like a leaf beneath a booted foot, and a bright orange line lanced out, striking the board and bursting it into a momentary flame.

Ami gaped. Listened as the woman cheered her own

success. That the skars held some power, that was suspected. That they could—

Hands clapped on Ami's shoulders, spun her around. The two guards stood behind her, one with his voulge ready. Behind them, Gladdring scowled, his flaxen face even more pallid in the dim light.

"Did I not say to forget this, Guardian?" Gladdring asked. "Now, you will wish that you had."

CHAPTER 16

PROTECTORS

Filled with eggs and potatoes, their water skins refreshed from the ice block in the Jarl's Tooth's center, the trio set off northward, once again venturing into another lava tube's glimmering, sweltering tunnel. Bliss took up the lead, her metal staff clacking every time she set its hardened ends on the rocky floor.

For all the walking, for all the oddities on Foti, being on the move inspired a certain vigor in her every step. Purpose, that was it. A drive that'd been sharpening every moment since their arrival on the island. Cassignol and the casino had been confusing, but the bar fight, the brawls in the street, and now the Jarl's Tooth served as a center.

She'd passed her first tests as a Guardian, kept her brother safe and the group on the move. This wasn't something she couldn't do, wasn't a task meant for adults while Bliss ought to have stayed back in Kitaye, waiting for her time to arrive.

Behind her, Wax and Quik muttered about breakfast, about the late night run-in Quik had with the group at the bar. They hadn't been around for breakfast, a quiet affair, one the waiter said was because anyone living there had already embarked on their day hacking stone, tending to animals, or marching off in search of trade.

Hard to tell when you had slept in without a sky, without a sun.

The northward move through the lava tube went without incident for an hour, then two. The steady path offered no twists and turns, just a straight-on shot. The waiter said the journey ought to be long but dull, few interruptions on the way to the Great Forge, where Foti's skars could be found.

"Miss the trees, Bliss?" Wax asked, coming up beside her and leaving Quik to wander in the back.

'I like the rock just fine,' Bliss signed with her left hand.

"Don't tell me the island's getting to you." Wax pasted on a look of mock horror.

'At least I don't have to listen to you whooping every minute.'

"You didn't like that?"

Bliss rolled her eyes, 'The first time it's fun. The twentieth, it gets a little old brother.'

"I'm hurt."

'Then grow a thicker skin. There's going to be worse ahead.'

Wax laughed, "Sounding so wise, little flower."

Bliss stopped, forced Wax into a frown. 'I'm your Guardian now. Not a little flower anymore.'

"Whoa, okay. Sorry."

"She's asking to be treated like an adult, Wax," Quik said, catching up. "That's what she deserves after what she's done."

"Point taken." Wax gave Bliss a quick nod. "Guardian, then. All business, no fun. Got it."

'Don't know about that.' Bliss pointed ahead, down the lava tube. 'Looks like we're about to see the sky again. Seems like fun to me.'

THE PREDICTION HELD TRUE, the lava tube's craggy orange rocks fading to the black rolling land they'd walked after leaving Smythe. Overhead, a clear cool day took over, blue sky showing nothing save a few curious birds circling overhead. Foti sprawled in every direction, cut here and there by low hills, but not enough to interrupt a clear shot to the horizon. Ahead, the path wound through the charcoal straits, though the color line in the distance seemed to change, as if they neared a split between worlds.

"Nothing but the birds," Quik mused as they took a water break there at the tube's end. "On Vis, a view like this would give you more life than you could count. Here's nothing but rock."

"Makes you appreciate home a little more," Wax replied.

'Maybe you need to change your perspective. I think it's beautiful,' Bliss signed.

What Bliss didn't say, what she appreciated about Foti's landscape, was that she could see any fiend approaching from a long way off. No sneaking through the jungle, no darting from hidden corners, no dying lost and alone.

Which meant the trio had time aplenty to consider the ragged wagon train along the path before them. Much like the giant carts in Smythe, these domed tubs trundled on the path in a slow yet unstoppable gait, their wheels—as tall as Bliss—grinding on the dusted rock. The crushing roll announced their presence before Bliss saw the things, coming into view as the group crested a low rise.

Four massive carts and an accompanying party to match. From distance, Bliss counted at least a dozen, most sporting the warmed-over leathers common to Foti people. The travelers ranged about their train, occasionally barking commands at the creatures pulling the carts, creatures Bliss recognized.

"Ferrites," Wax said before Bliss could sign it. "Huge ones."

The rock lizards, two to a cart, grumbled forward, pulling their charges with large chains linked to collars along their necks. Even from afar, Bliss could see the smoke sizzling up as the lizards vented their heat. Every so often, too, the creatures would snap their heads left or right, gulping up a wayward stone.

"Grim," Quik muttered as they closed. "Thank Vis we don't have to treat animals this way."

"We're not moving ore back and forth, brother," Wax replied. "Don't think we wouldn't rope some hanokos into a job like this if we had to."

'As if they'd take it,' Bliss added. 'The cats would kill you before you'd ever get a collar on one.'

The carts didn't stop as Bliss, Wax, and Quik approached. One of the travelers broke off, waited for the three to come near before nodding a soot-coated head their way.

"Don't usually see travelers on the road," the man said. "Much less ones from far away."

"We apparently made a mistake," Wax replied after dishing out their names. "Supposed to take a ship, but we're already walking, so ... "

The man smiled, his teeth a glaring white compared to

the grimed-over skin, "Best you keep going then."

Bliss narrowed her eyes, flashed her fingers at Quik, who translated with the appropriate tone, "What's that mean?"

The man just shook his head, kept up his smile, and waved them on. Quik tried again, received only the same words.

"Guess that's what we'll do then," Wax said, his cheer faltering at the awkward exchange.

The rest of the traders weren't much better, giving the Vis group little more than slight glances or stone-faced stares. The carts never halted, the big ferrites carrying on. Bliss, Wax, and Quik had to move to the path's side, walk in a single file to get around the slower wagons, coughing all the while at the charcoal dust kicked up by the massive wheels.

Only after they'd put a few strides between themselves and the lead wagon, did Wax open his mouth again.

"Well that was awkward," the Renewal said, lobbing one last confused stare behind them.

Bliss kept her eyes forward, the path descending now between two large black lava mounds. The rolls bunched up, the gray-black lathering on itself like poured oil. Those circling birds kept pace overhead, watching in silence. Bliss sniffed, picked up nothing more than dust's sting on the air. Little here to warn them if something wasn't right, save instinct.

She stomped her staff on the ground, didn't stop moving, but Wax and Quik stopped their back-and-forth on how rude the travelers had been.

"What is it?" Quik asked as they entered the narrow valley.

'Something feels off,' Bliss signed, keeping her eyes traveling. 'Too quiet.'

"It's always quiet unless one of those carts is around." Wax followed her look. "Don't see anything. And who'd be out here anyway?"

The arrow struck the ground before Bliss's feet, right where her next step was about to land. It quivered in the rock, crude fletching an insult to any Vis hunter, the broken feathers scraggly and bent. The shaft looked little better, but the arrowhead gleamed.

"Who out here indeed?" A woman announced, looking down on them from above. A bow in her hands, a skimpy quiver on her back.

"Sledge," Quik muttered, his gauntlets staying by their waist. "They have us."

As if waiting for Quik's assessment, Sledge's crew came out from either side, three apiece and all looking like they'd crawled from the rock itself. Their hands held knives, a club, a pitchfork that looked too old for farm work. If these were bandits, they were sadder than any Bliss could've imagined.

So she picked up her staff, took two long steps forward and planted it in the ground.

"I'm with you," Wax said, following her. He picked up his voice, "What does your sorry bunch want with us?"

Sledge drew another arrow, rested it against her bowstring. "Simple. We want the skar. And you."

A mistake. Sledge finished the words with an ominous slime, but they woke a savvy fire in Bliss. If the bandits wanted the trio alive, then they had a chance.

Bliss looked back at her brothers, flashed her fingers, 'She won't fire into a fight. Don't give up.'

Quik's mouth opened like he was about to question

Bliss, but she didn't give him the chance. Sliding her foot, Bliss broke into a hard run towards the valley's exit, scooping the staff as she went and holding it like a lance.

Wax and Quik would either fight and give them a shot, or they would surrender and this journey would end before it ever really began.

Two scruffy men and a hooded woman, the latter off to the left, started at Bliss's sudden run. The middle man, knives held too tight in his hands, stepped forward like he thought he could take Bliss and her staff's far superior reach straight up. Regret struck fast, the man trying to backpedal off his back foot, sliding on the dust. His friend saved him, lunging in with a swipe from . . . Bliss pulled her staff back as the strange device, a pointed metal crescent fastened to a wood haft, slammed down into the space between her and the trio.

Sledge poured words into the air, calling for this and that. Bliss ignored them all, planting her left foot and kicking to the right, letting her left hand guide the staff in a straight thrust at the miner and his odd weapon, one apparently too heavy to pick back up. Bliss smacked the man's chest, leather bending with the hit, the man's face going purple as his breath blew out his lungs.

Something blue flashed to Bliss's left, and as she pulled the staff back she noticed Wax, Foti blade drawn, knock away a darting strike from the woman, who'd pulled a short spear from her cloak. Wax's blade cut off the spear's end, sending the bit bouncing away and the woman into a wide-eyed retreat.

The knife-wielder found his confidence, whirling back into the fray with a three swipe sequence, driving Wax back. Bliss dropped her attack on the right-side miner, swinging her staff in to force the knife man into a dual-bladed parry.

The opening was there, and Wax tried to take it, lunging back in with the Foti blade. A wild strike, and one the knife-wielder dodged by falling back, letting Wax put himself between the enemy and Bliss.

No.

WHAT DO you do when the thing you're trying to protect is between you and the enemy?

Get'em out of the way. Bliss dropped her staff into a hooking swipe, one that hit Wax's right ankle and spun him up and over, landing on the rocky ground with a splat. Her brother cursed, asked what Bliss was doing, remarks she disregarded as the knife-wielder readied his defense. From her right eye, Bliss caught movement as the miner stood back up, shaking his head. The girl, at least, seemed to have no desire to get back in, edging towards the valley's exit, her eyes on the fight's other end.

Hopefully Quik held his own,.

Bliss tried another stab, using the staff's reach to go for a head-smacking strike on the knife-wielder. The man again parried the blow with both blades, catching the staff and forcing it up. This time, he drove forward, stepping on Wax in an effort to shoulder-charge Bliss.

She tried to drop back, pull the staff in, only to feel a heavy weight hit her shoulder, knocking the staff from her grip to the ground as her body followed, collecting scrapes as she hit the cool rock. Before Bliss could roll, could pick herself up, a knife found its way to her throat, the point pressing in on her skin.

"Don't move," the knife-wielder snarled, his voice a husky, smoked mix. "Your damn dance is done."

Bliss considered her options. Tried to weigh whether the knife man would really stab her if she went for her staff. Wax, at her vision's edge, had the miner kicking away his blade. The girl returned now, pulling small ropes from a belt along her waist and tying up Wax's hands.

Already outnumbered, beaten up, there didn't seem to be an out. Back on Vis, the Lira had a principle for moments like these: Wait with both eyes open.

She could do that.

Quik hadn't put up much of a fight on the valley's other end. His gauntlets had power, but the fighters down there had long, tarnished blades and spears. A critical reach deficit causing Quik to hang up his hands almost as soon as the fight began.

Sledge, for all her yelling, didn't seem all that upset with Bliss's spark, coming down to the girl personally and seeing that her knots were tied, shuffling Bliss next to her brothers in a stiff line.

"Spirit's never a bad thing," Sledge said, pulling the knots tighter. Bliss's wrists tingled at the pressure. "Blood still flowing, girl?"

Bliss shook her head. If her hands went numb, there'd be no escape.

Sledge loosened the knots, then leaned in, whispered, "I like you, but try anything, and it'll be your brother's throat I slit first."

Wax didn't seem like he'd fight that too hard. Her brother's bravado looked sapped, the man's constant grin a decided frown, eyes downcast as his Foti blade and knife were torn away and handed to the young girl who'd busted her short spear. Sledge went up to him next, reached inside Wax's tunic and found the skar. Lifted the necklace up and over Wax's head, the knife-wielder keeping his blade drawn and at Wax's back.

"DOn't need to do that," Quik growled, standing nearby, one of the swordsman covering him. "Wax isn't dangerous."

"So I saw," Sledge replied. "Nevertheless, one thing you learn out here is never to take unnecessary chances." She dangled the skar in the air. "First prize of the Renewal." She held the skar up and the half-dozen bandits gave a ragged cheer. Sledge slid her look back to Wax. "Now, don't get all upset. You're not going to die. Our partners frown on that. We're just going to settle you in a nice place to rest for a while, then, when the Renewal's all done, you get to go home. No harm done."

"No harm?" Wax countered, dredging up some soul. "Aren't you costing all the isles a chance at peace with this? You're hurting Renewals, which means—"

"Not hurting Foti's Renewal, are we?" Sledge grinned, stuffed the skar into her tunic. "Worked last time, didn't it? Almost the time before too, if that Guardian hadn't gotten lucky."

Bliss blinked. She barely remembered the last Renewal, hadn't been alive for the one before. Sledge didn't look old enough, though it was hard to tell beneath the dirt, to have slung her bow twenty-five years ago, but what did Bliss know? Maybe Foti sent their kids out to be killers at ten.

"Now," Sledge said, looking over the three again like a mother about to deliver a stern lecture. "We'll be walking a ways, then taking some unusual transportation till we get to the western coast. You act nice, we'll see you there in comfort. Everything will be fine. Not luxury," Sledge laughed, "because, well, we're hardly that, but you won't starve." Her eyes went hard, her smile bent to a frown. "Fight us, make trouble, and things will go wrong for you too. Like I said, nobody needs to die, but my crew comes first. I'm not above feeding one of you to a fiend to keep us safe."

Sledge whistled then, the bandits breaking into prodding action, pushing Bliss, Wax, and Quik on. The three had to carry their own satchels, while the bandits took their weapons. Bliss herself fell to the line's back end, the short spear girl walking with her at the back. As they left the valley through its northward exit, the massive carts caught up to them, entering the valley's southern side.

Sledge threw a wave back towards the wagon train, and those strange travelers, with Wax, Quik, and Bliss tied up in clear view, waved back.

For all Wax and Quik's talk about wanting to see the other isles, Bliss was growing pretty sick about the whole thing.

"Name's Torny," said the girl a few minutes into the walk. "What's yours?"

Bliss had her eyes on the ground, watching her footing. Sledge had them leaving the main road outside the valley, cutting left into some scrub brush foothills. How she found the path, Bliss didn't know, because it all looked like rock and dust to her. The line went in near single-file, Sledge up front with the knife-wielder, while two other bandits covered Wax and Quik, leaving Torny back with Bliss at the line's end.

"Don't talk much?" Torny asked.

Bliss rolled her eyes, put a finger to her lips and shook her head.

"You can't?" Torny's eyes widened. "Wow. That's awful."

Bliss bit her lip to keep herself from giving Torny a well-deserved headbutt. Sure, she'd spent her whole damn life living with people's reaction when they found out Bliss couldn't talk, but on Vis, people accepted it. Most everyone had a quirk, and it was common courtesy to take the discovery as it was and move on.

Foti, apparently, had no such politeness.

"Don't know what I'd do if I couldn't talk,' Torny continued. "I'd probably still be in the mines. Like everyone else."

Bliss wiggled her hands, felt those knots. Sledge might've loosened them, but they weren't coming off, not without some serious scratching, rubbing against a rock or wayward post. Nothing she could do while on the move.

"Knew a boy who couldn't hear right," Torny was saying, Wax's Foti blade now in her hand as the girl waved it in the air, watching the sapphire catch the light. "Everyone kept saying he wasn't going to amount to anything, but know what? He could feel the stone perfect. He's in Smythe now. Has his own forge and everything." Torny stopped waving the blade, slid it back into the sheath now looped onto her belt where the ropes had once been. "Are you like that? You know, real good at something?"

Bliss looked up at the sky, measured the sun's crawl towards twilight. Hours away yet, hours more listening to this.

"Look," Torny said, and Bliss did, as the girl's voice hardened from idle curiosity, "Sledge has us paired for the long walk. Means we'll be together all the time. You can either keep on doing what you're doing, ignoring me and all, but that's going to make this real boring. So how about you decide something different, okay?"

Bliss scrunched up her face, threw a confused look Torny's way. The girl and her friends had just ruined Wax's chance at being an Aegis, torched their opportunity to keep going with the Renewal. How could Torny expect Bliss to be, you know, friendly?

"Hey, there you go," Torny flashed a gritty smile. "A real response. What a thing to see."

Now that Bliss actually looked at Torny, the bandit girl had a bit more than just scrappy leather and indecision to her. Choppy hair led to a dirt smeared face, a small cap adorning Torny's head with a woven orange-and-yellow crosshatch throughout. More personalized than the other hats the bandits wore. Little bits stuck out among Torny's other clothes too, like a silver-seeming bracelet on Torny's left wrist and several dull rings among her fingers. Torny's shoes seemed scuffed, but Bliss realized the girl didn't seem to make a sound as she walked, her feet rising and falling with little dust to show for it. Torny's eyes, too, always seemed active, scanning everywhere while her fingers twitched, as if wanting to grab at something.

Maybe that's why Torny had been waving the Foti blade around. Hard for her not to.

None of that solved how Bliss and Torny could communicate. Wax, Quik and a few others on Vis—Bliss winced as Pan flitted through her memory—took years to develop the signing she employed so fast. The only other option would be the small tablet and scratching stone in the pouch along Bliss's thigh, a device that'd mean freeing up her hands.

Now there was an idea.

"... so it's like this for another day or so, but then you'll see some really cool stuff," Torny was saying when Bliss grunted, drew her attention back.

Wiggling her tied hands, both looped in front of her, Bliss reached towards the pouch on her right thigh. Torny stopped, hand going back to that sheathed Foti blade. Bliss shook her head, reached for the pouch again, managed to snake a couple finger tips around the rope tying it closed and pulled. The pouch opened, the scratching stone and tablet falling to the ground.

"What's that?" Torny asked.

Bliss crouched, fumbled at the stone and the tablet. If she tried, the knots seemed loose enough to give Bliss a chance at writing, but that wasn't the goal. She missed instead, dropping the scratching stone a couple times. Meanwhile, the rest of the party kept moving on, drawing further away while Torny watched.

"Here, let me pick that up." Torny bent down, scooped up the tools. Looked at them, noticing the faded scratches on the writing tablet. "I get it. You write on this thing?"

Bliss nodded.

"I'm not the best reader, but we can try?" Torny handed the tablet to Bliss, who dropped it, wrists and hands not quite fast enough to catch it. Torny started to reach for the fallen object, then stopped, stared at Bliss with a sharper eye. "You know, if I was a bit dumber, I'd loosen those knots more." Bliss raised her eyebrows. Had to keep playing the lie. "But, despite what Sledge thinks, I'm not an idiot. You've got range on those fingers. Enough to make scratches on this thing. So quit playing."

Bliss cocked her head.

Torny pursed her lips, slipped the scratching stone and the tablet into the satchel over her back. She drew out the

Foti knife, Wax's Foti knife, and put its point up to Bliss's chin.

"You know why we're here?" Torny said, the curious girl all gone now. "Because we have nothing to lose. Our lives have been one awful day after the last, and now we've got a chance at getting out of this. I don't want to hurt you, whatever your name is, but I swear, I won't hesitate. This is it for us. Remember that."

CHAPTER 17

CAVE DEMON

Her hand reached down, sparks flying up around them as the lava below surged. Rocks cracked, the cavern walls splintering in the heat. Sweat marred Svarde's hand as he reached out and took the offered help, his boots kicking at the crusted stone cliff for purchase.

She yelled something, words washed out in the roaring crunch, then leaned back and pulled. Svarde's right hand found a notch, his fingernails breaking off as he gripped the hard stone. Between the two, he climbed the last meter, falling onto the stone bridge, the breaking point between the Great Forge and safety. Around them, bodies littered the dirt. Ferrites and fire bats ran, fought, and died. Yet she'd thrown Svarde her hand.

Another woman ran up, angry, cut, and wearing a Foti guardsman's armor. She lifted up Svarde's rescuer, bringing the woman to her feet, and in the motion Svarde caught the orange twinkle, the stone looped around the woman's wrist.

A rival, a—no, Svarde killed the thought as he rose to

his knees. Not a rival anymore. The only one left. The Renewal. The second woman pushed Svarde's rescuer away, sparing one frowning glance at Svarde, one no doubt making sure Svarde didn't intend to pursue, sword drawn in that cursed hellfire cave.

"I did follow, 'course, but with my hands clear," Svarde said in the dark, over the continual drip. "Had to, after that. I'd been a Guardian once, failed, and needed to see if they'd take me on."

"Why?" said the strange man, who'd dwindled his speech lately to only simple questions, as if the effort to make sentences proved too much.

"Because I'll be damned if I'm going to be a failure," Svarde replied.

"It worked, then?"

"If you consider damning the woman you love to an early grave, it worked as best it could."

The man chuckled. Asked Svarde to tell the story again.

"A third time?" Svarde asked the dark. "How about something else? Much as I like talking about myself, there's different tales to tell."

"You won't find many."

Svarde frowned. He had stories aplenty, adventures ready for the telling. Whole taverns had been spellbound as Svarde relayed the story of how he'd slaughtered that . . . no, destroyed the . . . fought a . . . Svarde stumbled, rose, hit his head on the low ceiling and sat again, his gut tightening, mouth dry.

Little waited for his recall. Svarde could reach, oh yes he could reach, right to where the memories had always been. Only now, all that waited was fog. A mystery blankness. Svarde pushed against it, tried to come at the stories from different angles, from preludes and epilogues, from the action and the setting, and found nothing. He couldn't tell whether he'd lifted an axe against a fiend or a friend, a bandit or a beast.

Names, he had those. The truly special moments broke through, glimmers amid the shroud.

"You see now?" The man asked, breaking into another of his sad titters. "You have to keep telling the one story, because it's all you have left. When that's gone you'll be like me, no one and nothing."

Svarde shook his head, trying to dislodge the blocks. Nothing moved. Nothing changed. Just the drip, drip, drip of the water on the stone, its rivulets disappearing into the rock floor.

"This isn't natural," Svarde said. "Must be something making this happen."

"Oh yes. There is. It's feeding on us."

"It?"

"The thing that brought us here." Again the laugh. "I've been down here for so long, I think it's about used me up."

"What happens then?"

"I don't know. Maybe I forget to breathe? Does a heart forget to beat?"

Svarde felt for his axes, remembered they were gone. No quick way out for himself, then. Bashing his head on the rocks wouldn't do. Too risky, too brutal, even for him.

"Then we have to get out," Svarde announced.

"Try it. I wish you success."

No belief in that man's voice, but Svarde felt his way around the cavern anyway. The tight confines offered few options, save the one boulder at the tightest end. An imperfect seal, the stone resting against the cave's walls. Svarde ran his fingers along its edges. He'd tried to move it a couple times before, found it too heavy for his own strength alone, and the man in there with him offered no help.

Or, perhaps Svarde hadn't been asking in the right way.

"You want to hear the story again?" Svarde asked.

"I do," the man replied. "It fills me up. Food for the starving man."

"Then come over here. Help me, and I'll tell it as many times you want."

"It won't move, I tell you."

Svarde cursed under his own breath. Stupidity and its stubbornness. "Don't care whether it moves. You want the story or not?"

The carrot, well dangled, worked. The man's lithe form shifted on the stones, shoeless feet clicking on the rock where nails long overgrown scraped. The man's stale breath told Svarde he'd come near, so Svarde gave the man instructions, told him to place his hands on the boulder's right side.

"At my say, push up," Svarde said. "We'll roll it away."

"And then the story?"

"And then the story."

Svarde gave a quiet countdown, five to one, and at the final number he pushed his own end down, trying to get the boulder moving, dislodged from its spot on the rocks. The man laughed, said he hadn't used his arms in ages.

"Then make up for lost time," Svarde grumbled, heaving again.

The boulder, at least, respected their efforts. On Svarde's second push, something ground beneath the rock and its shape twisted in the dark. Svarde felt the coarse stone beneath his hands as it moved, an electric sensation, bringing with it both hope and, yes, fresher air.

"Keep at it," Svarde said. "Don't stop for anything."

"The story!" The man shouted. "The story or I stop!"

So Svarde launched into it again, pushing on the boulder all the while. He told about his friends, how they'd gone off at the Renewal's call, heading to the Great Forge for a chance at the skar and honor, and meaning beyond hacking away at a mine's crowded walls. Svarde dove into the terrible day, clawing at the memory even as its edges seemed to fade, the faces of his friend, the one Svarde was supposed to protect, rubbing into a blur.

"And the Great Forge? What happened there?" The man asked when Svarde faltered at the broken memory.

That, at least, held. Several Renewals arrived at almost the same time, rushing past the clueless Najahn guards for a go at the skar. The timing had been poor, the giant volcano growing restless, and it took their approach as an offense, blasting the earth and sky with ash, with lava and worse.

The boulder shifted again, rolled off to Svarde's left, not more than an arm's length before it struck another wall and stopped. The laughing man fell before Svarde, his push following with the boulder.

"Don't stop," the man said, lying there. "Please don't stop. Your story is all I have."

Svarde said nothing, instead stepping over the man into the wider tunnel. He couldn't see a damned thing, but his hands felt no resistance, the air moved through his hair. The stone ground held a slant, a way up and down. Which path led to Maena and the others? The wrong direction might send Svarde off on a long, pointless trip to nowhere, which—

"Please," the man said, his hands finding Svarde's leg and gripping it, though the fingers' hold was weak, frail. "I need your story."

"You need food and water, same as me." Svarde reached, pulled the man to his feet. "Can you tell which way to go?"

The man sniffed, "I'll tell you nothing, because I am nothing. Please."

A feeble ally was fast becoming an annoying drain. The man kept pleading, and Svarde tried to push the words away, tried to focus on the air. Which way it was moving.

Another tug on the leg. Svarde slipped on the floor, caught his balance, and shoved the smaller man away.

"Leave it!" Svarde snarled, his voice flying down the tunnel. "Either pull yourself together and take a chance at life, or stay down here and rot. I don't care."

Svarde tried to glare at the man, but the absolute black made it impossible to tell where he was, impossible too, to see the menace Svarde threw into his eyes, his frown. But the effort wasn't wholly wasted: a shout carried, weak and shrill, down the tunnel towards him.

Pennifer.

Leaving the whimpering man, Svarde stepped up the tunnel, moving fast but slowing every few steps to listen. Pennifer kept shouting and, behind him, the weak man seemed to be trying to follow, the scratches and kicks belying a four-limbed scurry up the cave.

Who knew if the man even had the strength to walk.

Pennifer's enclosure resembled Svarde's, with a rounded stone sealing her in. From the outside, with his shoulder and leaning in to the tunnel's natural slope, Svarde dislodged the rock without much effort. It trundled away, Svarde calling a warning to his follower, who squeaked. When the man resumed his whimpers, Svarde assumed he'd survived.

"You made it out?" Pennifer said, using her hands to

find Svarde's arm, brush his beard, and generally grab at him like the other man had. Svarde pushed her off with a growl.

"Took two of us," Svarde said. "You're hearing my partner, for what it's worth."

"I was alone. All alone."

"Not anymore. Heard anything that might be the others?"

"The others? What others?" Pennifer's voice dropped. "I don't know who you are." As if realizing what she said, Pennifer took a step back into the small cave she'd just left. "I . . . don't know who I am."

She started to break into a cry when Svarde grabbed her shoulders, gave Pennifer a single good shake. If he could've seen, he would've delivered the traditional Foti antidote to everything: a smack upside the head. As it was, the shake seemed to stun Pennifer, bring her back into reality.

"You're Pennifer," Svarde said. "Rana pirate, and a damn good one. I'm Svarde, your ally, and there's two more of us we need to find." Three, counting Kivi, but Svarde figured the ferrite would find them just fine. "Follow me. And watch the other one. He's a bit grabby."

"Can I trust you?"

The question came with such honest sincerity that Svarde stopped a moment, took a long breath. "Pennifer, right now, I'm the only one who can help you. Either you trust me, or you die down here."

Whether or not Svarde could get any of them out remained an open question, but the words did enough to steel Pennifer's nerves. She followed Svarde further up the tunnel, the whimpering man not far behind. As they went, Svarde kept his hands reaching to either side, feeling for more boulders.

They passed several more cells, opening each with a pushing of the boulder doors. Inside they found nothing, save for the last one, where a withered body offered no solace. Pennifer found the corpse, feeling with her hands and stifling a curse as her fingers touched old bone, the leather-like faded hide.

Rasslebeck waited in the fourth, the man muttering his own name, his family's names to himself.

"Glad to see you're still sane," Svarde said after they greeted one another. "Pennifer's on the edge, and the man behind us is right gone."

"Don't know that I'd say sane," Rasslebeck replied. "Sitting alone in that dark, wasn't much else to do but tell myself stories and hope for something better. At the least I'd die with my wife's name on my lips."

"You have a wife and you're down here?"

"She's long gone in those ways, Svarde, but I keep her where it matters."

Strange place to have a deep conversation, dangerous place to keep it going, so Svarde ended it with a grunt, kept them moving up. Hopefully Maena would be waiting in the next cell. Then they could figure out a plan to get their gear back.

Food and water too. Those'd be good to have.

And Svarde wouldn't mind having a word, a fist with the creature that stuck them here.

Marching up the cave further, those fists held ready, didn't get them Maena. The small boulder-blocked prisons petered out, the tunnel upward growing wider. Pennifer and Rasslebeck matched Svarde's reach outs, running their fingers along the walls to measure pace, to keep themselves grounded in the eternal dark.

During the walk down from the surface, there'd been all

manner of mushrooms and mosses, sparkling things giving off glows here and there, unnatural and natural auras to give the descending crew a chance at sight. Every wall, every cranny here seemed scrubbed clean.

"Even the sharper rocks are sanded off," Rasslebeck muttered. "Someone wanted to make sure nobody could find their way out."

"And that they didn't hurt themselves in the dark," Pennifer added. "Keeping their food fresh, this one."

Svarde didn't mention what the whimpering man had said, that their bodies might not matter all that much to this fiend.

Their trek upward ended when Svarde smacked his head on a rounded stone, one large enough to block the whole cave, more than twice Svarde's own wingspan across.

"No way we're moving that thing," Rasslebeck said. "Guess we could try going back down?"

The whimpering man caught up to them, moaned louder at the dire thought of backtracking.

"The air's coming 'round the boulder," Svarde replied. "This is the way we want. The creature brought us down here, didn't it? Either it's impossibly strong, or there's a way to shift this thing we're not seeing."

"Hey," Pennifer said, "maybe that's it. Seeing. You said you saw a different tunnel after we split up, right?"

"Did, yes."

"Then maybe what we're seeing now isn't right either."

"I'm seeing all black, Pennifer," Rasslebeck said. "You are too, unless you've been keeping one big secret."

"Hold on," Pennifer replied. "Svarde, you've got those Foti boots, don't you?"

"Always have."

"Big, strong iron?"

"Always been there."

"Then kick something," Pennifer said. "Let loose."

"Think she's lost it, Svarde," Rasslebeck muttered.

Svarde snorted in agreement, but when nothing made sense, sometimes you had to try the ridiculous. Clearing the other three for space, Svarde swung his leg at the blocking boulder, a stiff kick up angling to get his boots striking the rock hard.

The stiff iron smacked and shrieked, for an instant sparks flew into the dark. At their glow, shadows sprang out, Svarde winced, and nothing at all came clear save that their way did, indeed, appear blocked by more stone than the bunch of them could ever lift.

"Do it again," Pennifer said. "Think I saw something. Look to the left."

"I break my foot doing this, you'll be the one carrying me," Svarde said.

"You break your foot, it's your own fault for being care-less. Strike the metal, let's go."

Hard to resist an attitude like that. Svarde let his kick go again, striking the iron on the stone. He tried not to wince this time, looked left in the flash, and saw what Pennifer had: a gap in the upper left, about where Svarde's arm could reach if he stretched. The hole looked big enough to bring a body through, too, and explained the air.

"But how're we getting up there?" Rasslebeck said. "Unless either of you are a lot taller than I remember."

"A boost," Pennifer said. "That's how."

"You're the smallest, then," Svarde started.

"It's you who'll be going," Pennifer cut him off. "Rassle-beck and I barely know our own names. I can't remember what Maena looks like. You put us through that hole and we're liable to go off wandering and forget about you too."

"Speak for yourself," Rasslebeck said. "I've got my name memorized plenty fine."

"Shut it," Svarde said. "Pennifer's right. Boost me, then Rasslebeck, you and our friend here send Pennifer right after. We'll make a quick search, come back and rescue you."

"So I get left with the crazy one?"

"He's not crazy. He just likes stories. You've got a couple you can tell?"

"I've got my list of names, is all."

The whimpering man perked up at that, clinching the decision.

Pennifer and Svarde went through the hole, the bulkier man going first. Rasslebeck's cadence serenaded their first steps beyond, one name after another, followed by titles, a description, and random tidbits.

"Bigger family than any I've known," Svarde said, helping Pennifer to the ground.

"Then you've not spent much time on Rana," Pennifer replied, then stopped herself. "I've no idea why I just said that. Can't remember a thing about that Isle."

Again Svarde considered telling Pennifer what might've happened to her memories, and again he killed the thought. If Pennifer was going to be any good, he couldn't have her panicking. A good fighter might hold up well against a fiend, but who Pennifer was right then, Svarde couldn't say.

And anyway, their new cave presented better options. A single curling tunnel led to the left, and now the walls weren't scrubbed clean. Purple pink moss grew in clumps, nestled along the left side where a water trickle ran.

Possibly the same one that emptied through Svarde's former prison.

"Guess it's this way," Svarde said, leading off with a crunching walk.

Mere steps later the tunnel narrowed before emerging into a familiar room, one with three branches off it. To the right, an upward tunnel had a brighter pink glow. The quartz would be that way. Straight ahead was a mystery, and to the left lay the Dark Below and escape.

"Which way?" Pennifer asked.

"You don't remember?"

"Past these last minutes, Svarde, I don't remember anything. I don't know how I know what words to use, how to walk, anything. It's all blank, like trying to reach through one of these walls."

Svarde took a deep breath. "We're going right. That's where our gear's likely to be, which we'll need if we're going to get Rasslebeck free."

"Or we could run."

Svarde glanced back, gave Pennifer a once-over. Like him, she'd had her armor taken away, left only in the thin Rana robes. Her skin held scratches, her eyes tight, the slightest flush coming to her face at the ask.

"You remember, don't you?" Pennifer asked. "You're hesitating. You know where we are."

"I remember you, Pennifer. I remember you wouldn't run, not for anything."

"The old me, maybe. The new one? This one standing right here? I want to live, Svarde. I don't want to find whatever put us behind those rocks, whatever stole our memories. I just don't want to be here anymore."

"I understand. I really do. More times than I can count, I wanted to run from where I was." Svarde put a hand on

Pennifer's shoulder. "But running now will only get us killed later, by something just as nasty. You're a fighter, Pennifer. Trust me. Once you get a sword in your hand, you'll be as deadly as anything here."

Pennifer's eyes flicked back to the caves, her shoulders tensed, and for a moment Svarde wondered if she'd give it a shot anyway, break for freedom and take her chances in the dark, alone and unarmed.

"Please," Svarde said. "I'll need your help to save Maena and Rasslebeck."

And Kivi. Please let that damn Ferrite be all right.

Pennifer shuddered, gave Svarde a nod. "Okay. I'm with you. All the way."

Together, they broke right, up the tunnel towards the quartz, towards the gear. Svarde intended to take the walk slow, cautious, ears open. That plan died as soon as they entered the quartz tunnel, when stirring curses echoed off the rock, mixed in with what sounded like garbled speech, a loud conversation too indistinct to make out.

Those curses, though, came through plenty clear.

Svarde, whispering for Pennifer to speed up, broke into a dash up the tunnel, right into the quartz room. The gemstone's brilliance again shocked the sight, the action fading in slow, as if Svarde had just woken up.

The quartz itself jangled, the many garments and gear on its pink lines moving with the wind whipping around the cavern. The tornado centered to Svarde's right, landing on a miserable mess of wings, tiny limbs, and what seemed to be slate gray faces, their mouths alternating between blowing air and shouting, muttering nonsense. The fiend's focus seemed bent on Maena, the Rana pirate standing with her back against the cavern wall, saber slashing the air before her, trying to drive the thing back.

Struggling behind both, mashed into the corner, twitched Kivi. The Ferrite's stubby tail bounced off the floor, her claws scrabbled with half-hearted effort to bring her right-side up, a motion delayed, doomed by the constant wind.

"What is that thing?" Pennifer asked, frozen behind Svarde.

"Doesn't matter what it is," Svarde replied, breaking for the quartz, for two familiar axes hanging on the gem's left side. "We have to kill it."

Moving against the wind felt like pushing through a wall. Svarde lowered his shoulder, found himself growling against the grit as the whirling air picked up small rocks, dust and threw both against his face. Pennifer didn't join him, seemingly paralyzed there at the room's entrance.

To think stealing a person's memories could take all that they were, could render them useless, a shell and a shadow.

Svarde refused to wonder what might happen were this fiend to die and Pennifer's old self not come back, what such a scared creature might do down here in the dark.

Maena's yells were harder to ignore. She'd not yet called out to Svarde himself, not yet asked for aid. Instead, she seemed to, like Rasslebeck, be calling out her life. Friends, family, places on Rana and the Isles she'd sailed to. As Svarde reached his first axe and slid it off the gem, he looked back at the fiend, saw it wasn't trying to batter Maena, wasn't trying to strike her. Instead, the creature hovered just beyond her sword range, the winds keeping Maena pinned to the rock.

Those faces, then, howled at her, blew and sucked and whistled and spoke. Ate, Svarde realized, at the very pieces making Maena human.

Svarde snatched his second axe, drawing sparks from the quartz as the weapon's edge scraped the pink. He ignored the leather and furred armor, useless as it was against this monster.

"Pennifer, your crossbows," Svarde roared over the wind as he broke towards Maena and the fiend. "Now!"

The call shook Pennifer from her stupor, the woman stumbling back against the wind. She looked at Svarde, the gem behind him. Her crossbows were there, on the right, dangling. She gauged the distance. Svarde saw those eyes widen, saw them watch his steps and where they were heading, the fight to come.

Pennifer turned and ran without a word.

CHAPTER 18
A NEW LOOK

At least the view was nice. The afternoon was off to a beautiful start, golden waves lapping far below, broken by heavy ship traffic. The Renewal's call seemed to have spurred on the trade, everyone getting in their last profits before more fiends emerged and the isles hunkered down to survive.

This balcony wouldn't be a bad spot for such hunkering. Not very defensible, and the thin iron rails would get in the way of swinging Flamebreak at any winged fiends coming through, but the cool breeze whisked Ami's skin, the wine set on the table before her was a better vintage than any she'd had in a long time. The only downside came with the man sitting, all too smug, across from her.

Gladdring, repeating the morning's events, how he'd had one of the worthless scholars keep tabs on her after departing his room, gloated about her captured, tut-tutted her with a sausage finger about Ami's poor subterfuge, and asked just what Ami thought she was going to do down there.

"Walk out with our secrets? Kidnap one of our

researchers?" Gladdring asked, his noxious grin growing ever wider. "I'm so curious, Guardian. What was your plan?"

That Ami hadn't had one was a fact she'd never admit to this man. The mocking look that'd come over his face, the way his hands would twitch in smirking pleasure . . . Ami would have to get up and throw Gladdring off the balcony. Watching him splatter on the rocks below would be so satisfying.

Except tight ropes bound Ami's hands together at her front, with just enough give to allow her to grasp the wine glass, put it to her lips. Next to the balcony door, only a pace away, stood a Najahn guard too, voulge ready. Still, if she could get her hands free, Ami bet she could get Gladdring over the edge before the spear struck a fatal blow.

"Is that how you mean to help your friend, the Aegis? With random forays into places you don't belong?" Gladdring continued when Ami didn't reply. "Right now you could be at her side, protecting her from fiends. Prolonging our safety. Instead, you what? Became curious?"

"It's what I said in your office. I want to help."

Gladdring nodded, "Yes, yes. Do the impossible. Save the Aegis from her curse. I told you already, no such escape waits in our dark hollows. We have no miracles." Gladdring's voice drifted off, his eyes picked up a twinkle. "Yet."

Ami sighed. "Spit it out, Tenet. I'm not one for games."

"Not a game. A negotiation." Gladdring leaned forward, a move Ami was starting to think was a habit. "Look at this." Gladdring reached inside his purple-gold Najahn robe, decorated on the seams with the sloped swirls every Tenet earned. Gladdring's hand emerged with an orange-yellow stone, one small enough to hold between two fingers. "A Tamas skar."

"So you do keep them."

"Oh please. Don't act the idiot now, Ami." Gladdring drew his eyes to the stone. "What matters isn't that we have the stones, but what we can do with them."

Ami waited, Gladdring's tone suggested the man was about to launch into a speech he'd been preparing for some too long time. A secret finally getting to be divulged.

Gladdring, though, didn't speak. Instead he seemed to focus more on the skar, slipping it from his two fingers into a full grasp in his palm. The man seemed to shudder, his eyes closing, then snapping open. The smile returning now wasn't the mocking grin from before, but, if Ami believed the man capable of such an emotion, almost tender.

"You love her," Gladdring said, not a scolding, harsh note in his voice. "I'm sorry."

Ami squinted, "What? Love who?"

"Catya." Gladdring frowned. "Strange. I've never referred to an Aegis by their actual name before. There's a sadness too. As if the skar isn't just telling me, but—"

"The skar?" Ami chose to bull rush over the accusation about her feelings for Catya. If there was any person alive who she'd want to share those with, it sure wasn't Gladdring. "The skar did this?"

"They're the leavings of the gods, Ami," Gladdring said, slipping the Tamas skar back into his robe. "Every one carries a piece of their god within them, for a time at least. Some few of us have learned how to use them, in the way a child might pick up a stick and shake it."

"Use them how?"

Gladdring chuckled, "As toys, mostly. Take a Kance skar and make the wind blow through your room on a hot day. Use a Vis skar to make that paper cut heal in seconds."

"Paper cut? But, you could—"

"No, we couldn't," Gladdring's voice went iron. "These aren't miracles. A paper cut, I said, because a paper cut is what I meant. The skars aren't wishes made real. They are tools, and like any tool, the wielder must learn. Only, Ami, we are all apprentices in this art. There are no masters."

Nothing like getting her hopes up only to see them dashed, but then, Gladdring didn't seem the type to play in charity. Why tie her hands and drag her up here just to show off the skar?

"So what do you want with me, then?" Ami asked, bringing the wine back for another sip. The outside chance Gladdring was going to have his fun and then cast her over the edge made the wine taste sweeter.

What that said about Ami, about her outlook on life, better keep that buried beneath the deep red in her glass.

"Well, science requires research, and research requires subjects," Gladdring said. At Ami's scowl, he flipped his hands up, placating palms. "We are aligned in this, Ami. Noctia's goal with the skars is to stop the fiends, to keep us all safe."

"And chained to the Circle."

"Oh no. What a terrible yoke." Gladdring's turn, now, to roll his eyes. "Who complains when Noctia sends its aid to their isle? Who complains when we make it easy for every isle to trade with one another, when we mediate disputes for the benefit of all? The Circle is just a collection of people, Ami. That's all. They could come from any isle, just like the Aegis and their Guardians."

"You're not going to convince me this isn't a power play."

"Then I shan't try any further." Gladdring sat back. The interesting part of the conversation now over, things were headed towards negotiation, deal-making, persuasion and, yes, power plays. "There aren't many Najahn I can bring into something like this. Fewer still with your skill."

"Skill at what?"

"Destroying fiends, of course." Gladdring nodded at her tied hands. "Those hands and that sword back in your apartment have destroyed many a monster. With your help, with you showing us what these skars can do, we could design better weapons, better defenses. We could even, or win the battle with the fiends. Think what soldiers could do with skars at the ready? Wounds would heal, fear could be suppressed, and, if our guesses are right we could fly, could stab a spear with the strength of stone itself."

Gladdring started to spit as he spoke, excitement overrunning his manners. Despite the ugliness, Ami felt possibility's pull. Gladdring's hopes, if realized, would mean a massive change in how fiends were fought. It might even make an Aegis unnecessary.

Could render an expedition like Svarde's something other than a hopeless quest.

"If I say yes, what then?" Ami asked.

"Then the true adventure begins, Guardian." Gladdring finished his wine in a single gulp, wiped away the remnants with his sleeve. "I need not mention, if you refuse, we can't let you take what you know back to the streets."

Ami settled a dead look on the Tenet. He did seem a man accustomed to victory. Ami chewed on her lip for a long moment, wanting to delay the savoring he'd soon get. When a gull squawked overhead, though, Ami exhaled, nodded.

"What choice do I have?"

. . .

AT LEAST THEY freed her hands for the long walk down. A guard with a voulge handy followed Ami's steps as she followed Gladdring's. They descended again to the protected hallway, getting past the two Najahn stationed there with nothing more than a glance. Beyond, though, Gladdring took her left to a different hallway. This one held rooms on either side, a curling wing with every space bent towards . . . living?

"I have people cleaning out your apartment now," Gladdring said, stopping at the third doorway on the left. "Don't worry, they'll handle your sword with the utmost care."

"Why would they need to clean out my apartment?" Ami asked, though what lay in front of her made the answer clear enough.

A simple cot, a small table, and a back shelf laid up near the tiniest of windows looking out towards the ocean. Thin glass covered the narrowing arched opening, though at least the lower right corner looked to be open. Stale air made any prison unbearable.

Because this was a prison, Ami had no doubts about that.

"This is no idle project," Gladdring said. "Everything rests on your efforts. Morning, afternoon, night, you will be tasked with this. Do well enough, get us what we need, and you might see Catya with more than useless love to give her."

"You talk that way about Catya, about me again, and you can damn your skars."

Gladdring sniffed, "Yes, do get offended. When the histories look back on how the world went to ruin, I'm sure your vanity will cast you in a wonderful light."

Ami did what she'd been trained to do, what she'd learned as a Guardian and honed over all these awful years watching Catya suffer: she took her anger, molded it into a tiny ball, and placed it in the dark part of her mind. A crowded part, these days, and one begging for release. But not now, not yet.

"One thing," Ami said as Gladdring turned to leave. "Mattimo, the historian? Bring him down here with me."

"That wine-sotted fool? Why?"

"Because he knows more than you think, and I'm going to need help."

Gladdring shook his head, "Get us off to a good start first, then you'll get your requests. Rewards for good behavior, I believe they call it in the dungeons."

Ami's scowl only made Gladdring laugh, the man departing with a last word:

"Your first test begins tonight."

Three hours. They locked the door behind her when they left, leaving Ami sealed in her small room with little more than the window to stare out of, the walls to analyze. Not even wine to drink, food to eat. Just her own thoughts for misery.

And miserable they were. Ami never gave herself over to much introspection: a Guardian's life didn't encourage slow thinking, a questioning of one's motives and choices. No, instant action and a clear objective made much more agreeable company. As such, after a terrifying twenty minutes where Ami felt like she was going to descend into a dire rewind of her life and all its decisions, she stopped, shed her heavier cloak, and embarked instead on one exercise after another, the movements serving the dual purpose of calming her mind while excising her energy.

Though, given the rapid knocking on the door when those three hours ran out, Ami might regret working herself.

The knocking continued as Ami straightened up, made sure her latest lunges hadn't thrown her clothes in too much disarray. She eyed the door, the sturdy wood shuddering with every pound. Were they waiting for Ami to come open the door? What prison gave its prisoners this kind of courtesy?

The answer, when Ami tugged the portal open, came in the form of a smaller woman, though one covered in such a strange outfit Ami at first didn't realize what person could be inside.

"Hey there," the woman said, her voice a balance between boundless enthusiasm and reluctant restaint on the same. "Gladdring said to come get you when the next test was ready?"

Ami tilted her head, "Who are you?"

"Annalyse Everbrite," the woman said. "I might ask the same of you."

"Gladdring didn't tell you who I am?" And you don't know?

"Gladdring treats me like he treats every researcher down here," Annalyse shrugged, "like tools, like bugs, doesn't matter to him so long as he gets the credit."

Somehow, Ami didn't catch any malice in the words. A situation laid out as it was, facts on facts.

"So no," Annalyse continued, "he didn't tell me who you are." Beneath copper goggles, Annalyse gave Ami what looked like a sympathetic frown. "Then again, most of our subjects don't last very long, so maybe he didn't think I'd care."

"They die?"

"Die, go mad, lose too many limbs to continue. It's a whole range of maladies, really, but we're getting better." Annalyse glanced up at the ceiling, her voice trailing off.

"One week. that's how long it's been since the last, er, accident. A new record!"

"How do you recruit these . . . test subjects?"

"Gladdring doesn't tell us, and we don't ask," Annalyse replied. She folded her arms, each clad in a different silver bracer array, slots and notches awaiting tools. "I know that sounds horrible, I know it seems like we're doing the worst things in here—"

"I don't know what you're doing?"

"Right, I mean, I'm trying to say we have to make sacrifices. It's not easy on us either, right? We're pulling the triggers, we're taking the chances too. I live with those nightmares."

Ami took a step back into her room. Despite Gladdring's promise, nobody had come by with Flamebreak or her things. The sword would've been a comfort now: if nothing else, knowing she could try to hack her way out would've brought a warrior's solace. Instead Ami had her hands, her feet, and while it looked like Annalyse could get knocked over with a simple push with all that unsteady crap all over her, the guards beyond wouldn't be so easy.

"Scared you, didn't I?" Annalyse said.

"I don't understand you, is all," Ami answered. "What do you want?"

"Simple. Come with me."

Among the costs and benefits of exploring the Seven Isles during Catya's Renewal was the more neutral element of getting used to the unknown. After getting slapped with strange foods, stranger people, and the strangest places time and time again, Ami had learned to build up a stoic reserve, an ability to judge things as they came rather than dread, or delight, in their arrival.

So she followed Annalyse from her room with steady

steps. She listened to Annalyse babble on about the skar research, a topic interesting at the start but one that soon devolved into technical terms too obtuse and esoteric fro Ami to care about. Elemental wattage? Specific soul frequencies? Skar clarity?

These would no doubt matter to someone, and that someone, Foti willing, would not be her.

More interesting and more obvious was the place Annalyse took Ami. Not the stuffed cage and laboratory Ami had snuck into earlier, but a steeper stair, one whose lantern-lit, stone steps had their progress snared every other landing by strong iron gates. Walls closed in tight, eschewing the views from a wider space for the better defense offered by a tight corridor.

Annalyse didn't bother explaining the construction choice, and Ami didn't question it. Some things were obvious enough: this stair meant to keep something in, or keep everyone else out. For all that, not a single guard showed up, the walking deserted.

At least till the pair reached the bottom. The stair ended in a wide circle, stones ending in smoothed-over cave floor. The air gained a natural tinge, a wet salty taste. They'd gone down far enough to near the sea.

The change in air was matched by the change in surroundings: whereas above industrial design made things immaculate, down here rough hollowing out left burrows branching off their landing spot, the stair and its close walls a curling interruption to an otherwise open place. Torches, not lanterns, stood alight on metal posts jammed into the ground. The four burrows leading off the central room each had boards hanging from spikes nailed into the walls. Two had solid crimson sides showing, while the second pair looked splattered with grass-green dye. The room's walls held weapons racks, some actually holding weapons while others supported crates or things Ami couldn't identify, odd mismashes of metal. Several tables and chairs lay about the space, and a side cupboard looked to have fresh water and fruit atop it.

"A regular home down here," Ami muttered.

"It's a long walk," Annalyse replied. "The privy, should you need it, is through that last hole there."

The only unmarked tunnel. Ami hadn't even noticed it at first, yet a little concentration told her that opening brought the sea air. An opening to the beach, to a dock? For what?

"For tonight, can you use the spear?" Annalyse pointed to one on a rack. The weapon did indeed have a spear's pointed end, but the haft didn't match any Ami had seen before.

What should've been a straight wood or metal pole instead shone with pitted silver, the scalloped divots each overlaid with a copper top. Inside most sat nothing, but in the very top, a glittering orange-red ruby glistened. A stone Ami recognized well.

"A Foti skar," Ami said, going over and picking up the weapon. Heavier than a normal spear, but well-balanced. "What's it for?"

"You don't feel anything?" Annalyse asked, sounding somehow both unsurprised and disappointed.

"Should I?"

Annalyse, though, had whipped out a small book, was scribbling with a charcoal pencil. When Ami came closer, repeated her question, Annalyse glanced up, her grimace morphing into a calm smile.

"Should is an irrelevant question for us," Annalyse said.

"Either you do, or you don't. If you can follow me, I need you to try on these gloves."

Over on another rack, hanging on a peg jammed into the rack's wooden frame, sat a black-metal glove pair. Loose golden ringlets ran through the black, catching the light and blinking as Ami put them on.

"These are too thick for real fighting, if that's what you want," Ami said as she stretched her hands into the gloves. Too large, too puffy. She wouldn't be able to feel a blade or spear tell her what was coming.

"They're an experiment, like everything else." Annalyse stopped, tilted her head. "How bad are they for fighting, do you think?"

"I think anyone forced to fight a duelist would get their ass handed to them."

"And against a fiend?"

Ami raised an eyebrow, "Depends on the fiend."

Annalyse nodded, returned to her notebook and scribbled something short.

"You recording everything I say?" Ami asked.

"This is research. Nothing can be dismissed, Ami. Any little remark might be the key." Annalyse nodded towards the burrow with the green sign. "Okay, you ready for the main event?"

"After, do I get to eat?"

"Sure!"

"Then I'm ready."

The burrow didn't go far, a few seconds walk bringing them to a reinforced gate. Like the others on the stair, and one Annalyse again opened with a key. The same single key, Ami noted, that'd been used on all the gates so far.

Not so scared of thieves, then.

Beyond that gate, Annalyse told Ami to wait a moment

while she went to the wall's right side, pulled down on a small lever that Ami hadn't seen till that moment. Something seemed to sigh above their heads, tension releasing throughout the cave.

"What was that?" Ami asked, holding the spear tighter.

"Security," Annalyse replied. "You'll see why in a moment."

Ami kept her eyes open and looking during the next short stretch. Nothing seemed off about the torch-lit side walls, but up on that ceiling dark lines presented themselves, grooved and running almost the length of the way between the two gates.

Beyond the final barrier, though, Ami saw why security seemed so thorough: a snarling, flashing, green and blue fiend waited within. No taller than Ami's knee, the monster whipped itself around the enclosure with grasping noodle-like arms, each ending in two blunt fingers, ones nonetheless strong enough to dig into the rock and pull the thing about. As Ami watched, it snagged a grip and threw itself towards the gate, flying into the air and twisting so its stiff back could hammer the metal with reckless noise. The gate rung, but the metal posts held. The fiend bounced off, landed on its back, where Ami could count six nested arms emerging from the thing's underbelly. Those arms snapped around until, finding a grip on the gate, the fiend re-oriented itself and resumed its lurching about the arena.

"Should I even ask?" Ami said, seeing as Annalyse had kept quiet on their final approach. "Is this the horror you've been keeping down here?"

"Gladdring told you why we're doing this," Annalyse said. "The fiends have to be stopped. The Aegis is dying, and the next will die faster. That means we have to find another way."

"So you keep monsters down here for, what, tests?"

"You don't sound angry?"

Ami shook her head, "I was prepared to be. I expected to find something worse, some secret about how Noctia kept a way to save the Aegis under lock and key. Now I see you're trying to make it better."

Annalyse nodded, "Some of us, anyway." As if remembering she had her notebook in her hand, Annalyse straightened, her eyes sparkled. "Now, here's what we're trying to do. With those gloves on, you're going to hold the spear here and here." Annalyse pointed to a couple grip outlines on the spear. Both, Ami noticed, were laced with the same gold as her gloves. "If it works right, you'll feel the skar in the spear. Try it now."

Meanwhile, the fiend banged into the bars again. Annalyse flinched. Ami ignored it: despite its tentacles, the fiend seemed small enough to be an easy kill with a spear in hand.

A spear which, when Ami shifted the weapon in her hands, putting her gloved grip right in those grooves—a placement made for a man's broader stance—proved itself not just a spear.

Flamebreak's skar added flare, throwing sparks when the sword swished through the air, adding a burning touch if the sword thrust into its target. Accidental effects, done without Ami's thought, without her effort.

The skar in the spear spoke to her. Not in words, but Ami couldn't put another frame on what happened, on the sensation whispering in her ears, running along her spine, her arms, her hands all the way to the spear itself and the skar inside it. A hollow song, waiting for Ami to fill in the gaps, to twist and bend the sound before she sang it.

"I feel it," Ami said, drawing out the words. "What's happening?"

"Good. Another consistent link," Annalyse replied. "You're feeling the skar. We don't know what it is, exactly, that's coming from it, but we think it's what powers the Aegis's necklace and the shield. What Demion found."

"How?"

Annalyse shook her head, "Not important right now. For tonight, I need you to go in there."

"With the fiend?" Ami should've been more annoyed by the ask, but she had a hard time shaking the skar's whispers, those gaps in its conversation where she could, if she tried—

"Yes. I need you to take this spear and use the skar to kill the fiend."

That, at least, shook Ami back to the present. "Kill it?"

"Ami, that's the whole point. If you can wield the skar, you can show others how to do the same. That opens everything up. That saves the world. That makes an Aegis unnecessary."

Ami looked at the spear, the red skar at its front, glimmering in the torchlight. Could something so little do so much?

Yes, the skar seemed to whisper. Yes it could.

CHAPTER 19

LAVA ROLLING

The river gave itself away through the air. Before Wax the world seemed to shimmer, heat folding in upon itself to distort the rippling mountains in the distance. Behind those, so Sledge said, they'd find the western ocean, a place too empty for sailing ships and the perfect spot to hold pesky Renewals till their time was up.

Sledge kept Wax up by her, at the small column's head. Quik and the other bandits shuffled a few steps behind, while Bliss and the girl keeping eyes on her seemed to ramble off and on into off-shoots and distractions.

"Don't worry about them," Sledge said once during the walk, a barren hike through scrub and dust. "First time for Torny, and I think your friend's smart enough to know dashing off alone here's a quick way to die."

"She's not my friend," Wax muttered.

"Guardian, then."

Wax stopped his rebuttal short. The less these morons knew about him and his family, the better. Not that Wax had much experience with these kinds of people—bandits on Vis had a habit of getting hunted down, violently, by the Lira—but Sledge always had a hungry look about her, a narrow stare and big eyes wanting to suck up information.

Sledge looked like a hanoko wanting its next meal.

Wax himself wouldn't have minded lunch, but Sledge barred any breaks till they'd made it to the river's other side. When Quik had asked why, given his rumbling stomach, Sledge replied that it was better not to waste food on someone who was going to die.

The macabre mood hovered over the troop as Sledge led their descent into a narrow gorge, a cut down path just smooth enough to argue for human intervention. The heat grew, stifling enough that everyone tossed off extra clothes, stuffing them into satchels or tying them around waists.

"Won't help you anyway," Sledge said. "You fall off the rocks, it's over."

"Tell me again why we're doing this?" Wax asked. "You said you wanted us alive?"

"Because walking all that way's going to kill us as sure as the lava will. It's all desert between here and the coast."

"What I don't get," Wax said as he and Sledge picked their way down the stones, black lava rock mounds rising on either side, "is that every river I've ever seen only flows one way. If the walk's going to kill us, how're we ever getting back?"

"Long ways in the future to think of, boy," Sledge replied. "Focus on what's in front of you and maybe you'll live to see it."

"Is everything death with you?"

"Live in this part of Foti long enough and you'll start talking like this too."

"No thanks."

Sledge threw a snort back his way, "You think people

here choose this? The isles need somewhere to put their trash, and you're walking through it right now."

As trash went, Wax had to agree with Sledge: the lava flow was a pretty good place for it. Wider than the lava tube they'd walked through, the flow moved at a good clip from the higher hills back east through the narrowing valley towards the far-off coast. Oranges and red ripples, darker chunks coasting over brighter patches in the lava, looking more alive than any river Wax had ever seen. Along the edges, embers splashed up against the black rock mounts, leaving glowing patches wherever they struck. Spitting and hissing noises dwarfed the conversation, sizzling smoke rising wherever some poor thing came close enough to ignite.

Sledge dropped her pack a few long strides from the flow, where their path down sprawled out into a shallow entry, the flow lapping its crusted edge like a friendly creek might back on Vis.

"You can't be serious," Wax said, staying further back than the bandit leader. "We'll all die riding that."

"I've done it three times," Sledge countered. "Everyone here save you three and Torny has done it at least once." Sledge patted the new sheathe on her waist where Wax's Foti blade rested. "Besides, not like you have a choice."

"But how? Don't know if you noticed, but we're not wearing anything for this. We'll burn up."

"Not with these," Sledge replied.

Wax was about to ask what 'these' were, when Sledge turned to her right and pushed against a leaning rock. The tall, thin slate shifted aside easily enough, revealing a hollowed out hole and, inside, more than enough thick boots for everyone.

With a couple other bandits helping her, Sledge soon

had enough pairs laid out, the lava waders a study in Foti practicality. Splattered iron plated the boots along the outside, giving way to a rough-fashioned rubber-like material on the inside. When Wax asked what it all was, Sledge only grinned and said he'd have to trust Foti talent.

"What if I don't?" Wax asked.

"Then don't," Sledge replied. "You're going either way. I suggest you wear the boots."

Not only did the boots come up over Wax's knees, nearly to his waist, he found putting them on—a difficult endeavor—that their soles held small, diamond-sharp treads.

"That'll keep you on the rocks or anywhere else you choose to step, so long as you're not stupid." Sledge finished her boots first, then reached back inside the hollow, pulled out, one by one, a series of sticks half as long as Bliss's staff. Each one ended in another forged metal point, and each had a scraping plate along one side, sticking out like a square fan.

"Any lava lands on your boots, you scrape it off with this," Sledge said, demonstrating by slapping the end against her booted shin. "Then you jam this end into the rock fast to keep your hold."

"How long are we doing this for?" Quik asked, Wax's brother on the ground trying to get his leg into the largest boots the Foti had.

"Till we get to the coast," Sledge replied. "If the flow's fast, only a few days. We'll step off to rest."

Wax turned back to his siblings, read a daunted fear in their eyes, "Just like swinging back home. It'll be fun."

Inspiring stuff. Just what the Renewal was supposed to say, right?

Their boats down were, as Sledge kept saying, rocks.

Wax had assumed up to this point that she'd been speaking in some metaphor, that there were indeed some real craft here that'd ride along the lava's surface and bear them to the coast in comfort. But no, once the boots were on, the poles in prime position, Sledge brought Wax up to the lava's edge with her.

"Look right," Sledge said. "We wait for a big one to come by, then hop on board."

"No boats? Seriously?"

"I already said the walk up this way from the coast was a desolate one," Sledge replied. "Hard to survive with nothing but the food and these boots on your back. Nobody's carrying a boat that far."

Argument made, Sledge again pointed down the flow. His face running in sweat—regular pulls from the warm waterskin kept Wax from collapsing—meant he couldn't be sure, but Wax thought he saw tumbling chunks poking up above the lava. The rocks, some wide and others tiny, coasted down the flow.

"Foti's not a restful Isle," Sledge said, gripping her pole in both hands. She had her bow and quiver over her back, along with her satchel, a stuffed combination the bandit bore without discomfort. "The volcanoes are breaking the lava rock all the time. Wait, and we'll find a good one."

"How long?"

"We'll find out."

Behind them, the other bandits broke out food for a lunch break, something Wax wouldn't mind sharing, something Sledge told him to get over. First ones on meant first ones off, and Wax could survive.

Their ride didn't take long to show, a slow-spinning crescent stone with a jutting spike at its front end. As it came into view around an upflow bend, the rock bounced off the far bank with a spark-scattering wave and circled to their side.

"This is it," Sledge said, then whistled. "Next pair, get ready!"

"Assuming we'll get on this one?" Wax asked, firming up his grip.

"We'll get on it or die trying, Vis. Try not to be the latter." Sledge moved herself to Wax's right, further down the bank. "I'll go first. You follow." She threw a nasty grin at Wax. "Don't try anything stupid now, or my friends will gut you before they follow me."

Noted, but Wax had his eyes on the slow-spinning rock. Running the distance, the angle, the speed he'd need to hit with these big boots. Not like the barefoot runs back on Vis, but if the rock kept on its current course, he wouldn't need to—

Sledge jerked, slapping her pole into the ground and taking a running lunge. Her left foot, planted farthest, took a lava lick. Sledge's right crossed the gap, planted on the rock. Her trailing arms yanked the pole free as she picked up her left foot, an ember splash accompanying her arrival on the stone.

"Now, Wax!" Sledge yelled, jamming her pole into the rock to steady herself.

Leading with his left, just like Sledge, Wax launched over the orange. The boots weighed him down, his own lunge not getting far above the orange death. Wax reached forward with his pole, the spike hitting the crescent rock raft at the same time as his right foot struck stone. The hit made Wax wobble, his left knee dipping towards the lava. Panic served its purpose, pushing Wax to drag up his left foot even as his right slipped, those diamond treads scraping on the black rock. The pole, at least, held, Wax leaning backward over the lava flow as the rock continued on. Both his boots clamped into the crescent's sloping side, Wax's heels getting hot as lava brushed up close.

"Hold on," Sledge growled, stamping her pole and walking the two strides over to Wax. Keeping one hand on her pole, Sledge reached out, gripped Wax's right forearm, and pulled him forward. "Keep yourself level, roll your knees with the stone."

Wax figured he'd start with something simpler, like breathing. He kept both hands on the pole, started to kneel on the rock before Sledge caught him.

"The stone's too hot to touch. Keep your hands on the pole and nothing else." Sledge gave Wax a hard pat on the shoulder. "Be proud, Vis. You've just done something few in the Isles could ever manage."

"With good reason," Wax muttered, looking back towards the bank.

Quik and another bandit took Wax's place now, already getting ready for their ride, a flat square bobbing their way. His brother met Wax's eyes, gave the younger man a nod. Not what they expected, perhaps, but they'd see this one through.

Riding on a lava flow, after the first few moments thinking every second would result in a terrible death, proved to be exactly as harrowing as those first few seconds. Flying through the trees on Vis certainly put Wax close, with a mistaken swoop liable to land you right in a hanoko's lap or impaled on a sana thorn. The lava, though, had a certain immediacy, its sizzling bits landing up on the rock, splattering Wax's boots and forcing him to unstick his pole and swipe the goop off.

"Do it fast or it'll cool and stick to you," Sledge warned after the first splash. "Every bit'll weigh you down, make it harder to move. And you won't want to be stuck on this thing near the end."

"Why's that?"

Sledge coughed, the harsh air getting to them both, and grinned, "Spoil the surprise? Why would I do that?"

They'd been on the flow for a couple hours now, winding their way as the lava twisted and turned through fast chutes and lazy curls. Behind them, the bandit crew with Wax's brother and sister spaced out on their own rock rafts. Even without the lava sprays, the travel wasn't easy: the rocks weren't level things, and Wax had to push off the lava flow's hard banks often to keep their crescent boat from tipping over.

An ask made harder with the sweat covering his skin, pooling in his boots. A couple times he'd slipped, the pole sliding in his hands, only caught by a panicked grab. Sledge made clear losing it meant losing his life.

Yet, as the flow filtered into yet another valley, lava rock bulking out and up on either side in its layered mass, Sledge called out a different sort of warning.

"Stay sharp," Sledge shouted, her call ranging back towards the other rocks. "Ferrite territory."

Wax laughed, "Ferrites? We've met a little tamed one. The nice rock lizards?"

"Hardly nice," Sledge replied, then cocked her head Wax's way. "You mean you met someone with a tamed Ferrite? Not for hauling ore?"

"Yeah?"

"Lucky man," Sledge muttered. "Have to get an egg, raise it right from birth. Keep it from growing too large, else those lizards start getting other ideas."

What those ideas might be grew clearer around the next bend. The lava rock lost its smooth contours, deep divots and cuts lashing their sides. The cause wasn't hard to find either, as the ferrites lay right out in the open, soaking up the noonday sun. Wax could do little save gape: these rock lizards were more than triple Kivi's size, their stone shells battered, clawed, and clumped over with dried lava. Their sapphire eyes shone just fine, though, as the fifteen or more turned their heads to watch the newcomers float on through.

"They want rocks, right?" Wax asked, watching as the ferrites vented steam overhead, making a thin cloud. "What would they want with us?"

"What're we standing on, Wax?"

"But they're sitting on lava rock right now. It—"

"Eat your home, or go for a swim and get something fresh?" Sledge snapped. "Keep quiet, Vis, and let me focus."

Focusing, at least to Sledge, seemed to mean putting one hand on the pole and using the other to draw Wax's Foti blade. The blue metal made a sparkling difference in the light, but seemed to do little to intimidate the ferrites. The lizards, Wax and Sledge nearing the middle of their domain with the other bandit rocks coming up behind, began creeping lower. Their claws bit in slow with every step, the heads and their slipping tongues flicking between the targets.

"Thought you said this was the safer way," Wax asked, adjusting his grip on the pole.

Sledge said nothing, instead whistled again.

"What's that mean?" Wax asked as Sledge yanked her pole from the rock, steadied it in both hands as the crescent raft they rode on drifted towards the rightward bank.

"Means we need to get closer together," Sledge replied. "Those ferrites won't tangle with too many people."

Getting closer together on a lava flow meant, apparently, using their poles to push against the current by jamming them into the rocky banks and pushing back. A slight delay, and one Wax didn't much like, seeing as it had him swaying over the orange stuff, but the bandits and his siblings did the opposite, swiping with their poles and using them like makeshift oars to bring the various platforms together. The ferrites watched as the rock rafts bashed into onto another, forming a clunky chain.

"Quik, Bliss, you okay?" Wax asked, his siblings within shouting distance for the first time in hours.

Quik seemed as sweaty as Wax, his skin shining, his face taut and tired, the pole held tight. Not his brother's favorite day. Bliss seemed better, holding the back with Torny and keeping her eyes up on the lava lizards. A snappy hand signal said she was doing fine, said to stay sharp.

That was Bliss, always on the important things.

"Now we see if they're cowards," Sledge said, Foti blade once again drawn and pointing towards the lizards.

Maybe the ferrites heard Sledge's words, maybe they decided they were too hungry to let such a meal go by, but the creatures came on at once, all scrambling as if some flare had fired. The beasts ran down the rock walls, some straight leaping for the rafts. One missed ahead of Wax, splashing into the lava and looking none the worse for wear.

"Use the poles," Sledge shouted. "Keep them in the lava long enough and they'll overheat."

Wax spread his legs, getting an even footing as he pulled up his pole, looked for something to jab. The crescent's upturned front lay before him, a leading spike down the flow's broad way forward.

And, peeking its head over that spike, came the ferrite that'd missed its diving ambush.

"Stay off," Wax said, smacking at the thing with his pole.

The hit wasn't Wax's finest work, less a brawny shove than a light slap. The ferrite took the strike on its stony brow, the pole slipping off with a spark. Sapphire eyes narrowed at Wax, and the ferrite brought its two front claws up to join its snout.

Wax hit it again, harder this time. Driving the point in at the ferrite's right claw. Having met Kivi, Wax didn't exactly want to kill the ferrite, even hurt it all that badly, but that kindness faded fast against the prospect of getting tossed into the burning river.

Yet this hit too glanced off the ferrite's rock hide. The pole slid to the right, Wax over-balancing, feet sliding till he felt a tug on his back, yanking Wax into a better spot.

"Fight smart and you'll survive," Sledge said, her own pole jabbed into the stone and standing free.

Wax saw her swipe with his Foti blade at a second ferrite, cutting into the lizard's reaching claw. Unlike the pole, the blue sword cleaved the stone skin, melting it away. The ferrite hissed and jumped away, barely making the near bank.

Wax's own lizard wasn't done. Half its body lay on the crescent rock now, its bottom half glowing from the lava's heat. Those spindly claws made swipes at Wax, ones he deflected with the pole. Each hit forced Wax to dance his feet, steady himself, offered no chance at a comeback.

Not a fight he would win.

"Help?" Wax called.

Another tug and Sledge pulled herself by Wax, raising the sword. The ferrite saw the blue and didn't risk it, pushing back off into the lava and swimming away.

"Thanks," Wax said as Sledge reversed spots with him

again, where she could help the bandits behind her cover themselves.

And did they need the help. Sledge and Wax had dealt with two ferrites, but the rafts behind them were overrun. Quik, using his pole less to stab than to sweep, launched one, then a second lizard off his rock in a single long swoop. The motion had him losing his footing, putting Quik onto one knee, barely dodging flying lava embers.

The closest raft to Wax, one with two bandits on it, looked in the most trouble. Slammed on both sides by a ferrite trio, one bandit already lay on his back, knives drawn but making little headway on those hard carapaces. The other, a woman, had picked up her friends pole and used them both to keep the ferrites away from her in a slow retreat towards Sledge and Wax's crescent. She had a few steps of rock left to walk, steps that disappeared when a ferrite lunged up from the lava and bit away the rock behind the bandit.

Sledge, charging as best one could towards the knife man, didn't notice. Wax flashed a moment's doubt: the bandits were their enemies, one fewer would mean an easier escape.

But Wax remembered that seafarer on the great sana, how much he'd been sickened by the thought that he'd killed her. He had a chance, here, to do something different, something better.

"Stop!" Wax shouted, kicking off the stone towards the backpedaling bandit.

She either didn't hear him or realize the words were for her. Swinging again with both poles, the bandit saw her weapons batted aside by a huge, pursuing ferrite. The thing followed the deflection with a scurry, the bandit making one step back too many to get away.

Only for Wax, leaning off his rock's end, to catch her backwards spill. Wax fell back too, the bandit's boots skipping across the lava as they both hit the rock raft hard.

Through Wax's weave, the rock burned. Both he and the bandit scrambled up, the bandit muttering a quick thank you, then grabbing on to Wax as they both tried to find their footing.

Sledge, Foti blade flying, scared the ferrites off the knife-wielder, the lizards diving back into the lava and away. The creatures seemed to be in retreat now, the flow pushing past their hollowed holes and nests.

"Made it," Wax said, grabbing his pole and setting it in the stone where both he and the bandit could grab it. "Outlasted them."

"No," the bandit said. "They took their prize."

Quik, on his raft, stood alone. His bandit escort vanished. Wax's brother didn't look to have noticed, as the man was shouting back down the floe, towards the last raft. A raft floating, now, on its side, empty.

Bliss, gone.

CHAPTER 20

REMNANTS

Ami with Flamebreak, cutting a burning edge through the air while Catya threw her knives, the braces running over both shoulders. Their distractions letting Svarde get into a killer's position, diving down on the fiend, the bandit, the creature with murderous glory. A team, that's what they'd been.

One Svarde sorely lacked now, trapped in a gale alone. Well, not alone, but Kivi still lay on her side, evidently stunned or wounded. Maena, trapped against the wall, cowering now as the fiend devoured her will, wouldn't be helping either.

And Svarde, with nothing more than his axes and a scraggly shirt, dirty undershorts, had to once again go for the rescue.

The wind tested that idea, pressing against Svarde as he tried to push towards the fiend. Lifting his foot strained Svarde's thighs, while keeping his axes pointed at the enemy cramped his hands. Svarde's eyes watered as grit blew in. Ahead, those howling faces, those awful hands sang.

One step, two, and Svarde remained well outside swinging range. Maena crumpled further, the fiend now spreading over her, looming. The faces whirled faster, the wind growing stronger, the hurricane reaching its apex.

The plan wouldn't work. Svarde couldn't force his way through. He needed another plan, and that plan began and ended with his favorite rock lizard.

Kivi, her back against the quartz and claws scrabbling, losing to the gale, remained on her side. Dropping his axes, Svarde cut hard left, the gale battering him on the gemstone. His shoulder took the strike, his legs earned small cuts on crystal spears, but Svarde could move, could walk when he didn't have to charge at the wind.

Nearing Kivi, Svarde pushed out from the quartz just enough to put himself between the wind and the ferrite, blocking the gust. Kivi, her sapphire eyes lighting up as Svarde came into view, used the reprieve and threw herself onto her stomach, all four claws digging into the stone.

"Go get her," Svarde shouted over the noise.

Kivi obliged.

The ferrite stayed low, pressing her belly to the stone floor, herits claws biting in with every scuttle. Svarde twisted, the wind blowing his back against the same pink wall Kivi had been stuck on. He watched as the ferrite, doing her best to shrink her profile, snuck up on the siphoning fiend.

Watched as Kivi made her way beneath the monster, jerked up her head and took a bite.

The wind snapped, died as the fiend flew up and away from Kivi's rock jaws, flattening itself against the ceiling. Those pallid, formless faces pressed against the stone, blending in enough to make Svarde wonder if the monster had been watching them the whole time.

A question better to ponder after he'd cut the thing apart with his axes.

Svarde darted back to his arms as Kivi jumped on the wall, scurried towards the fiend. The ferrite's slats split, burst steam. Kivi was angry, then, and ready to enact some brutal vengeance on the creature.

Good.

Svarde scooped up his axes, saw a flash as the fiend slid away from Kivi, those faces howling hard enough to push the fiend's airy body off the wall and glide it across the room to the far side.

Not too far, though, for a throw. Svarde lifted the axe, took aim—

"Help me," Maena whimpered, the shattered voice stalling Svarde's move.

She'd broken from her shell, leaned back against the room's wall. Maena's face looked bloodless, her eyes almost all white. She shivered, so violent Svarde at first mistook it for some sort of attack. Her breath came in quick, shallow gasps.

"Kivi, keep that thing occupied," Svarde ordered and the ferrite obeyed, using the ceiling as a floor to chase the monster.

Svarde settled before Maena, looking her over. Aside from some scratches gained bashing against the walls, Maena didn't look worse for wear. Svarde himself likely had more bruises from the blind run up the tunnel in the beast's back room.

"You're okay," Svarde said. "We've got it on the run now."

"Svarde?" Maena asked. "You're here?"

"Through no small effort." Svarde looked right, saw Kivi again approach the fiend, saw the monster again glide away, floating to a perch on the quartz's highest point. Those faces turned, eyeless holes staring at the two humans. "Can you stand?"

"Svarde," Maena said again, repeating his name. "That's the only name I know. Yours."

Svarde shoved away the chill her words threatened. He stood straight, dropped an axe to pull Maena to her feet.

"Worry about names later," Svarde said. "What matters now is skill and instinct. The fiend doesn't seem to take those. Can you wield a weapon?"

Maena blinked, "I don't know. Are you a friend?"

"As good a friend as you'll find down here," Svarde said. Kivi snorted and the Guardian whirled, bringing his one axe up in a swipe across his chest. The fiend, closing in, howled and blew itself to the right, flattening against the ceiling. "We have to get this thing pinned down, and I know how we're going to do it. Kivi, keep it there."

"Who's Kivi?" Maena asked.

"A question for another time." Svarde pulled her along, towards the quartz's left side, where Pennifer's gear dangled from the gemstone's spikes. "Take one of these. A crossbow."

The first test came when Svarde handed Maena the weapon, and she passed it, gripping the haft like an archer would, immediately whipping the weapon right-side up and checking to see if a quarrel was loaded.

"You can use it?" Svarde asked, daring to hope.

"I think so?"

"Then shoot that fiend," Svarde said. "After you fire, grab this other one here and do the same. We'll take this thing down yet."

Trusting someone who'd just lost their memory seemed a bit foolhardy, but Svarde figured he didn't have much to lose. That he still had his own mind seemed to be a stroke of luck, and if the fiend managed to win out here, it'd be a fast descent into the blind nothingness of the void.

"Kivi, hold it steady," Svarde called, shuffling back to pick up his dropped axe.

The monster and its faces seemed content to hang there, watching for their next move. Those misshapen hands twitched beneath its dark cloak, as if wanting to reach out and grab something but getting called back at the last moment by better instincts.

"What kind of awful spawned you?" Svarde muttered, then glanced back at Maena, who had the crossbow up and aimed. "Give it a shot!"

Maena lifted, aimed, and fired. The quarrel blasted out, zipping across the cavern and right into the static fiend. Not a sound echoed when the quarrel struck, no deadened hit to flesh or bright clink of metal on metal. At least at first.

Those faces all widened, their mouths stretching to the very edges, the pale gray thinning out. The howls came then, rolling over one another, loud and frightened, sharp and high. Svarde winced, yelled at Kivi to charge the thing, and ran in himself.

The fiend began to squirm, folding in around itself at the point where Maena's quarrel struck, as if the dart had the monster pinned against the stone wall. The faces turned and swam, their eyeless sockets looking everywhere, nowhere. The hands thrashed. Svarde raised his axes, Kivi barreling in across the ceiling, and Maena sent another quarrel lancing in, this one pegging the fiend's left side.

The howls squealed up higher, the noise piercing Svarde's ears and setting his mind aflame, as if he'd stuck his head into fire. His own eyes watered, his teeth clenched, but Svarde did what he'd done so many times before: he focused on his grip, the solid hafts on his axes, and kept going.

Two strides away and the fiend summoned its winds, the howls gusting up and over Svarde's head, buffeting his hair and blowing Kivi way, dislodging the ferrite from the ceiling and sending its too-wild charge into the rocky floor below. A third quarrel had its flight spun off, bouncing away.

But the wind swirled behind Svarde, pushed him towards the fiend with more speed than the Guardian expected. He stumbled, the double-high swing he'd been planning coming down early so Svarde could plant his hands on the ground, keep himself from sprawling.

The fiend took its chance.

The water's slow drip in the cave below seemed like a disease, a slow siphoning away of Svarde's memories, sensations, sanity. When the fiend struck, that disease became a disaster, a full on stripping. Svarde felt his connections to his old life fall away, faces and names flashing by as if saying goodbye before vanishing, swept away by those howling faces.

His life growing up on Foti, sweating in the mines alongside his father and uncle. Siblings all clustered together to eat what they could spare from the dismal gardens in the wastes, the brilliant lucky days when a trader happened through who'd want some of their ore for a new toy, a new chance. The Renewal, the desperate call for healthy young try-outs. The first time Svarde wielded an axe in anger.

And Catya. There in the Great Forge, accepting Svarde in his most desperate state and giving him a second life.

She faded, her features smearing there in that cave.

Catya had brought Svarde on for his axe, and he would not let her down, not again.

Did he howl himself? Did he roar? Svarde didn't know, couldn't tell anything save for his hand on the haft and the gray faces before him.

Svarde threw the axe, the weapon catching the fiend's own gust and spinning end over end to smash into the nearest face, its edge breaking the mask and shattering the broad mouth, those eyeless eyes. The face split apart, its halves falling to the ground and breaking like so much pottery. Behind it lay only dark and the barest hint of sparkles, like stars on the deepest night.

The howling stopped, the sucking clipped, memories crashing back into Svarde like an hourglass reversed. His thrown axe fell to the floor and the fiend fled, ripping itself off the wall and disappearing down a side tunnel. Left behind, dangling on the quarrels near the stone, were dark shreds, a cloak made not of fabric but more devilish stuff. As Svarde found his feet, the remnants shriveled and vanished into thin gray smoke.

Kivi bumped into his leg first, snorting fast.

"I'm okay," Svarde replied to the ferrite's question. "I think, I think it hadn't swallowed me yet."

The word tilted Svarde. He'd been so close, so close to losing everything. One lucky throw, or he'd have been worse than dead.

"Svarde?" Maena called from across the room. "Do we chase it?"

"No," Svarde turned, nodded at the quartz. "Grab what you can, quick. Then we leave before it comes back."

Svarde acted on his own order, snagging his armor from the gemstone's branches and throwing it on. His satchel, and Rasslebeck's too. Maena picked up and put down a few things, looking at them with a blank face, until Kivi helped her out, the ferrite guiding the lost woman to her satchel, her saber.

"Come on," Svarde said once they were put together. "Let's get Rasslebeck and leave. We hurt that bastard, but it's not dead, and I'll not chance my luck with it again."

Svarde's luck held long enough for the trio to duck down the tunnel away from the quartz, then cut left back to the big boulder sealing in Rasslebeck and the broken man. Rasslebeck's recital had continued the whole time Svarde had been gone, a constant replaying of names and lives to satisfy the other man's desire for stories.

"Please, Svarde," Rasslebeck said after the latter announced their return, "you've gotta get me out of here. I'm going to kill this one soon."

Rasslebeck's rasp proved motivating enough, but the three didn't have the strength to move the boulder. The small man on the other side could've boosted Rasslebeck up and through, but that would leave him trapped, doomed in a way Svarde didn't want to think about.

And yet.

The fiend still lived. The minutes they burned here before this damn boulder trying to plot out a path—Kivi had even taken some bites from the big stone, but the small lizard couldn't devour an entire escape from the rock —only let the fiend recover, find some new way to hurt them.

"Can you lift him out?" Svarde asked.

"Me, lift him?" Rasslebeck replied.

"Not you. I don't know your name, my friend, and I'm sorry for that, but I need to know. Can you lift Rasslebeck free?"

The whimpering man said nothing for a long moment,

then Svarde heard scuffling on the stone's other side. Hands moving, boots lifting.

"He's trying," Rasslebeck said. "I think we can just about make it."

Svarde glanced at Maena, tried to see if she had an opinion. The old Maena, the one with raiding baked into her blood, seemed like she would've made the cutting call. Save the crew member, forget the broken man.

Would that Svarde didn't have to damn someone.

"I can reach the hole,' Rasslebeck said. "Should I come through?"

"If he leaves," the whimpering man said, "then I'm alone, aren't I?"

"There's got to be a way," Maena said. "A rope somewhere? Maybe our shirts, we can tie them together?"

"Even if the rags we're wearing now would hold his weight, we haven't the time," Svarde said. "The fiend's going to come back."

"Hold on," Rasslebeck said. "I've an idea."

Svarde watched, the slim silver light showing little more than shadows in the tunnel. Up above, just over Svarde's bushy hair, a foot showed through, then another. Rasslebeck's bare feet, scratched and dirty.

"We've got your gear here," Svarde said.

"Good, because if I have to walk another minute on these rocks without my shoes, I'd just lay down and take it," Rasslebeck replied. "Now, sir, I don't know your name, but I'm going to reach down. You'll have to take my hand."

"I can do that."

"Okay, I've got his arms," Rasslebeck announced, his bottom half the only things showing in the tunnel. "You'll have to help pull me through. I'll lift him along."

Buffed with vigor at not having to leave the poor man to

an awful fate, Svarde boosted Maena, letting the woman get a grip on Rasslebeck's legs. Together the whole crew worked in concert to pull Rasslebeck through, dragging the skinny man along with them.

As Rasslebeck settled to the ground, grabbing for the few scraps Svarde had brought along, he took a look at the trio that'd come back for him.

"Where's Pennifer?"

SHE'D GONE the wrong way. Svarde led the group outside the fiend's domain, cutting back through the caves into the Dark Below. They'd gone the whole way back up, by the sealed entries the fiend had made to guide unsuspecting creatures, explorers, food to its lair. The next fork offered a choice, up and to the right, the long journey back to the Whent surface.

To the left, another descent, sharp and jagged, but better lit and treated with the sound of rushing water. When the crew had first come to this choice, Svarde and the others had opted for the more gradual tunnel rather than the one needing a stiff climb, but Pennifer apparently had no such qualms now.

Her footprints, slicked with blood earned by passing rocks, gave a clear marker for her path.

"She was one of us?" Maena asked as they stared at the choice.

"Is one of us," Rasslebeck replied. "Just because she doesn't know it right now doesn't mean we give up on her."

The whole walk up this far, Rasslebeck, voice refreshed with the recovered satchels and their waterskins, had detailed the journey back to Maena and the other man. At first, Svarde had been reluctant to use the water, seeing as it came from the fiend's nefarious pool, but the effects on memory seemed to falter beyond the fiend's borders, or perhaps the storage in the skins slowly sapped the water of its power.

Either way, after Rasslebeck took several gulps without ill effects, the whole group found themselves indulging.

"The question is whether we can follow her," Svarde grumbled. "Maena barely knows who she is. We have another who's totally lost. You and I are drained, our gear battered or destroyed. Whatever's down there is sure to be just as bad as what we've left behind."

"You're the captain," Rasslebeck snapped back. "Whether you want to be or not, with Maena down, you're up. You can order us topside and I'll follow, because I don't want to die, but I know this. I'll regret leaving her for the rest of my life."

Again Svarde found himself turning to Maena, just as he had to Ami and Catya all those days marching around the isles. He was a weapon, not the captain. A breaker of men, not a leader of them.

"We go after her," Svarde said. "A half day only, till we have to rest. If we find her, if we're close, then we'll have our reward. If we don't, if she's still gone, then we turn back."

"A fair deal," Rasslebeck nodded.

"DO I get a say?" Maena asked.

"Or me?" The other man added. "I'd like to go to the surface. Please. I thought I was going to die in there, and now I'm not? I have a chance?"

"We're going after Pennifer," Svarde snarled. "You'll have some chance staying with us. You'll have no chance on your own. Make your choice."

After that, there was no dissent.

CHAPTER 21

RAFT

By the third hour, Bliss and Torny had exchanged names. By the time they'd reached the lava flow and watched Wax and Sledge mount their crescent raft, the two had an understanding: Bliss wouldn't try to run, and Torny wouldn't keep asking probing questions. The two had gone on in a respectable silence ever since, which had given Bliss all the time and focus she'd needed to keep tabs on her brother, and figure out how the bandits worked.

First and foremost, the crew seemed bedraggled. Their equipment lacked care, was coated in soot, damaged by heat and rocks. Their weapons were about the only thing that seemed in decent condition, the metal edges gleaming. Focus on the priorities, Bliss supposed.

They also spoke little. Nothing like the songs, the banter buzzing around the hunting companies on Vis. Bliss couldn't quite pin down why, except desperation. These weren't on some honorable mission to save their friends, pursue a noble goal. They needed Wax's skar and any profits from it to survive.

Miserable creatures, these.

Except, oddly enough, Torny. The younger woman had the brightest eyes in the group, even though she didn't talk much with the other bandits. Her outfit seemed the least tarnished, her face not so grim. Adventure still seemed to have some excitement for her.

That excitement found a new test on the slim oval Bliss and Torny picked for their lava raft. Or, rather, Torny picked, pushing Bliss forward to the burning river and pointing, saying they couldn't get too far behind. When Bliss shook her head, Torny frowned, repeated her ask and moved her hand to the knife at her waist.

With her pole in hand, Bliss figured she could whip it up, smack Torny into the lava before the bandit could do a damn thing to stop her. What that'd mean for Wax and Quik, though . . .

So when the rock floated near, Bliss took a single vault, landed on the rock steady in those boots—ugly, uncomfortable, but useful—and planted her pole. Torny came behind, her leap too long for the oval's small size. She over-balanced, her landed foot sliding on some loose stone. Torny jammed her pole down, grabbing it with both hands even as her feet slid out from under her. Boots licked lava, the black stone swayed, and Bliss went to a crouch, reached over and snagged Torny's tunic and pulled her up.

"Thanks," Torny said, getting stable and brushing, with the pole, some drying lava off her boots. "Not my finest moment."

Bliss leveled a single raised eyebrow at Torny, then went back to watching Quik and Wax. The two seemed settled enough on their rocks, and they were too far away for Bliss to help if something went wrong. For the next few hours, at least, Bliss the Guardian would only be responsible for Bliss herself.

"Sledge said this wasn't going to be hard," Torny muttered, holding her pole with both hands, the stick properly jammed in now. "Would be an easy ride down to the coast, she said."

Bliss didn't look at her raft partner, but rolled her eyes anyway. Sledge seemed like the kind of leader that'd drag her team through anything to get what she wanted. Not one to trust.

"You're pretty comfortable," Torny said, the lava flow bringing them around one lazy curve after another. "You ever done this before?"

Bliss shook her head.

"Of course not. Why would you, being from Vis and all?" Torny chuckled. "It's me, sorry. I tend to talk a lot when I'm nervous."

Bliss nodded.

"That obvious?"

Bliss nodded again.

"It's kind of nice that you can't talk, know that?"

Now Bliss gave the bandit a solid glare. Torny tried to contort her mouth, her bright eyes into something apologetic. It might've worked, were she not clinging to her pole as lava sparked and popped around them.

"Look, I'm not meaning any offense, okay, it's just most people tend to ignore me," Torny continued. "I mean, you're free to, and I guess I'm not sure if you are, but at least you're not talking over me, right?"

Bliss squinted an eye. Was this self-pity or just babble, a nervous person trying to distract herself from the situation?

"It's strange how you wind up in places like these,"

Torny kept on. "Not like I planned to, you know, but things kept piling up. Almost without my control. Except, I mean, the obvious ones, but still. You don't wake up one morning planning to be riding a rock down a lava river."

Bliss shrugged. Really, this wasn't too far from some of the adventures she'd had back on Vis. The Isles had strange and wondrous things aplenty, and Bliss had to count herself lucky she'd seen so much in her young years. Though, the lava flow might be a bit on the dangerous side.

Especially now that ferrites loomed on the rocks above them, sapphire eyes glinting. Sledge shouted something about being on guard, staying cautious.

"Don't like this," Torny said, for once managing to take a hand off the pole and bring it to her knife. The bandit's short spear might've been more useful, but it'd snapped back in the fight. And Bliss's staff on Torny's back? Better still, but Torny didn't seem to know how to use it. "If these lizards decide to jump us, stay close, okay?"

As if Bliss could go anywhere else. Their oval raft seemed to be taking the slowest route, and they had distance aplenty between their rock and Quik's. Her older brother seemed to be splitting his glances between Bliss and Wax, though no fear showed on the man's face.

Confident he'd make it through. Bliss could be the same, would be the same.

Confidence, though, did nothing to deter the lizards. Torny's curse added flavor to what Bliss saw, the rapid breaking as all the ferrite jumped, ran, and splashed into the lava to come at the four rafts. There hadn't been any command, any whistle like the birds back home, just a couple popping their steam vents and the whole batch was on them.

The first ferrite hit their raft from the air, plopping onto the small oval and spinning towards Bliss, the lizard's tale smacking Torny and sending her to ground, her knees hitting the rock hard as both hands kept their death grip on her pole.

Bliss yanked hers from the rock, bringing it up to ward off the ferrite's snapping, stubby jaws. The lizard kept its claws locked into the rock, making those teeth its only weapon. Not that, given how many gritty points lingered in that mouth, the ferrite needed another.

The ferrite, though, was grey. Just like a hanoko whose thoughts were on the future dinner rather than catching the prey that'd make it. After a couple of failed snaps, Bliss feinting to either side without shuffling her feet—just like playing games with Wax on the tree branches back home— the ferrite lunged right for her.

Bliss swung her pole up, bending her back as she did so. The sweeping blade on the pole caught the ferrite's body as it came in, Bliss's arms buckling under the weight. The ferrite toppled her to the rock, but kept on going, its own momentum boosted by Bliss's swing. With a surprised snort, the lizard rolled off the raft's front and into the lava, leaving Bliss scratched and burned on the stone.

"Are you all right?" Torny asked over the shouts from ahead. Sledge was saying something Bliss couldn't hear. "That thing came out of nowhere."

They're all coming out of nowhere, Bliss wanted to say, but instead she rose, sticking her pole back into the oval to help her stand. Torny had herself up too, and she'd moved from her end of the oval towards Bliss. A strange move, given how—

"Our boat's being eaten," Torny noted as she moved. "Look."

Bliss didn't have to look hard, as the oval had lost its

back end, the rounded off rock now a spiked edge as a ferrite chomped, head emerging from the lava to take a bite before diving back beneath the hot orange.

"Really not a fair tactic," Torny said, backing up near Bliss. Behind them, shouts and struggles continued, enough to suggest help, even if it were possible, wouldn't be coming. "Any ideas?"

The ferrite's chomping and the swirl from the fighting had pushed their breaking raft closer to the north bank, an intimidating slope that nonetheless looked to have more handholds than the average sana stalk. And attempting to climb still had falling into lava beat on just about every count.

Bliss tapped Torny's shoulder and pointed.

"What, jump?" Torny gave a dire laugh. "We'd lose the rest of the crew."

Again, better than death. Bliss had no time to write the comeback on her little tablet, a move she wouldn't risk anyway on the listing rock raft. The ferrite took off another chunk, breaking back towards the center. The lizard's weight pushed the raft deeper into the lava, the gooey orange flickering towards their boots.

"There's got to be another way," Torny said, poking at the ferrite with the pole.

And she could take the time to find one. Bliss wasn't going to wait. Sliding on her toes, and turned northward, kicked off while planting the pole in the raft's side. Bliss took the boost, left the pole behind as she flew, striking the cliffside less than an arm's length over the spitting river.

Bliss's fingers felt for handholds, the cliff's heat little less than their raft's this close to the lava. Every touch burned, but Bliss had ignored pain before, could do it again.

She kicked her boots at the black rock, felt the soles bite in as Bliss pressed herself against the cliff. Torny yelled something behind her.

Didn't matter. What did, was climbing up.

Bliss flicked her eyes skyward as her fingers found lips in the rock folds. Like she'd done countless times with the sanas, a path peeked out to her eyes, lines within leaping distance running from handholds and footholds to the next.

She kicked off, boots and hands on either side moving in tandem. The weight on her feet didn't help Bliss move, but given the pain in her hands, on her shoulders and arms where the sparse weave hit the hot rock, Bliss would make do.

A hard vibration bubbled up, and Bliss risked a break in her climb to look down, see Torny, face screwed up in a wide-eyed panic, hugging the cliff beneath her. Bliss's staff still hung on the bandit's back, the Foti knife bouncing off the cliff at Torny's waist.

The bandit looked unsteady enough. Bliss eyed her staff. She could scoot down a couple holds, try to lean and grab her weapon, then kick Torny into the river.

No, too risky. Torny might panic, fall. Then Bliss would never get her staff back.

Besides, the ferrites had noticed their escape. Two lizards scurried Bliss's way on her left, those stone-munching maws ready to deal some serious damage if she remained on the cliff.

Pushing, Bliss took what Vis gave her and scaled the black rock at a speed Wax would've admired. Every kick brought Bliss up two handholds, every reach with an arm parlayed the momentum into another push off with her legs. The stones cooled with every rise, the air even picking up breeze that didn't stink of lava's sulfurous offal.

As the first ferrite took a nip at her boot, Bliss reached a break, the steep side leveling out into a small hill before resuming its upward slice. Heaving, Bliss pulled herself onto the fold, kicked out with her boot and smacked the ferrite in its biting mouth. The lizard snorted, took a long look at Bliss, before turning and darting down.

Down, no doubt, towards Torny.

Turning around on her hands and knees, Bliss crawled towards the cliff's edge. Looking down, she saw Torny stuck, her right hand and feet clinging to solid handholds while her left hand waved the long knife at the patient ferrites. The lizard pair studied the bandit, staying resolute between Torny and the pocketed cliffs where, Bliss assumed, the things made their homes.

The sight sparked an inspiration, an answer to a question Bliss had been bubbling over since the lizards made their move: if the ferrites ate rock and stone, why bother with a bunch of humans?

Why, unless the lizards wanted to protect their home, their nests, their young from intruders. If Torny moved away from those holes, she might escape the ferrite's wrath.

But how to communicate that?

Bliss looked around her. Loose rocks abounded, small and large. Bliss grabbed one, Took aim, and sent it flying. The stone clipped the cliff between Torny and the ferrites, causing the bandit to look up. Bliss waved left, back away from the ferrite nests.

"What do you mean?" Torny asked, tight and strained.

Bliss pressed her lips together. The ferrites moved, one going down and the other scaling up the cliff. If they split

Torny, that long knife wasn't going to help any. With that blade drawn, too, Torny couldn't move all that well.

Guess Bliss would have to get aggressive.

Casting about for another palm-sized stone, Bliss threw it down at the higher ferrite. The rock broke against the lizard's hard shell, causing precisely no damage and drawing only a snapping glare.

Torny tried a swing at the lower ferrite, a misguided strike the ferrite saw coming. The lizard shied away from the initial swipe before lunging after the knife, catching it on Torny's backswing. With a curse, the bandit let the blade go as the ferrite put its jaws on the slender metal, yanking it away and flinging the knife into the river.

Now the bandit had no choice but to run.

Bliss launched another stone as Torny made to scale the cliff, the rock whacking the upper ferrite's squat neck as the lizard tried to take advantage. Its bite swung just wide, getting Torny's hair in its teeth. Some strands snapped off as the bandit scrambled by, the ferrite coughing as Torny's wirey locks snagged in its teeth.

Torny kept up the curses, kept on climbing. The lower ferrite chased, biting at and breaking off the metal heel on Torny's left boot. The other, ignoring another Bliss thrown rock, snapped and tore away Torny's satchel, the food and gear tumbling away. Yet the bandit kept on moving, kept those fingers stretching, those booted toes kicking into new handholds.

Bliss reached out, caught Torny's hand as she came near and tugged her over onto the shallow slope. The ferrites poked their heads over, received kicks for their efforts, and vanished. Torny crawled away, knees and elbows pushing her up the slope, while Bliss waited, watched fro any more lizard incursions.

None came, and along the cliffs, Bliss watched as the lizards returned to their burrows. In the distance, the bandit rafts continued on. Bliss could make out Quik, standing tall and alone on his raft, then the three bandits and her brother all adjusting. As for Bliss's old raft, the oval seemed gone entirely, or broken up into pieces too small to see.

Gratifying, at least, to know they'd made the right move.

"We're dead," Torny said, coming up beside Bliss. "They're gone. We're stuck here, in the wastes. I've got my waterskin and that's it."

Bliss nodded at the staff on Torny's back, the thin ties keeping it on the bandit's shoulder's fraying but still intact.

"What, your stick? Yeah, that'll save us," Torny muttered, her eyes tracking the departing bandits. "Can it find food, water? How about teleport us to the coast, because that's where we need to go."

Bliss shook her head. Judged Torny's hunched form. Burns marred the bandit too. They'd need medicine, ointments if they wanted to make it through the next couple days without infection or worse.

Torny wasn't wrong either, food and water would be necessary. Bliss flicked her eyes skyward. Mid-afternoon. It'd be dark in a few hours, and while she didn't know what predators roamed Foti's wastes, getting caught out at night in the open seemed a poor plan.

Bliss moved without warning, diving at Torny and wrestling at the staff on the bandit's back. Torny tried to fight Bliss off, but without her knives, without the bandits backing her up, Bliss had the scrappier hand. She had Torny pushed over to the cliff's edge, looking down into that lava in two quick heartbeats, a dire enough view that the bandit gave up the fight with nothing more than a shrug.

"Okay, you win," Torny said. "Hurrah for you."

Bliss slid the staff from its carriage, gave it a once-over. A few small lava burns on one metal cap, but otherwise ready to go. A slight blessing.

Bliss stood, the boots giving her a good grip on the rough rock, and practiced a swing, swhishing the staff across her body. Torny sat up, watched the bamboo fly over her head. Kept watching as Bliss moved through a simple routine, ignoring the progressing pain from the burns.

"Okay, so you know how to use that thing," Torny said, crossing her arms on her lap. "Great."

What a tone. Bliss would've guessed Torny didn't take well to being cast out of power, but the bandit seemed less concerned about Bliss having the upper hand and more worried about, well, supplies. Torny's eyes went to her waterskin, to Bliss's own tied along her thigh.

"Done showing off?" Torny asked as Bliss moved the staff to one hand, looked upward. "Maybe we can figure out what we're going to do?"

The cliff didn't offer immediate solutions, only more climbing, but going back to the ferrites wasn't an answer, neither was the lava flow. Even if they went back down, tried to wait for another rock raft, they'd have to brave the lizards again.

Bliss pointed the staff towards the cliff, stepped off that way.

"Oh, I see, this is a dictatorship," Torny said to Bliss's back, but she stood, started walking. "You get to make the decisions because you have a big stick."

Bliss nodded without turning her head. Reached the

cliff, glanced back to Torny and gestured for the bandit to take off the straps to hold the staff.

"Now you're taking my stuff too?" Torny asked, but she did as Bliss asked.

Staff secured, Bliss climbed. Grumbling, Torny followed, and the sun fell further towards the night.

CHAPTER 22

PRISONER

The tentacle turtle—Annalyse's name for the thing —regarded Ami as the warrior entered the cage. At least, that's what Ami supposed, seeing as the fiend had no eyes whatsoever. With its tentacles quivering beneath the shell, the monster twisted itself to match Ami's entry, as if plotting the best time to launch her way.

If only it would. Then Ami could skewer the thing, declare the experiment over, and go see what Gladdring offered for dinner in his prison. The wonder of the skars was just that, a wonder, but handing Ami a spear and telling her to make some magic was . . . annoying.

"Remember to keep your hands on the grooves," Annalyse said, safely outside the bars. She had a charcoal pencil at the ready, her paper pad pressed up against the cave wall. "The goal isn't to kill the fiend, it's to use the skar."

"Thanks for the reminder." Ami leveled the spear at the fiend, tried to keep her gloved fingers in the shallow grooves. "Any other requirements? Do I need to let it take a chunk out of me first?"

Before Annalyse could answer, the fiend lurched forward, those tentacles slapping the stone ground and pushing the turtle at Ami. A slow charge, one Ami might've fallen for if she hadn't seen the monster's earlier cage-crossing moves.

Baiting into a reaction. Hardly the stuff of stupid creatures.

Ami feinted in, trying to bluff the fiend into thinking its own plan had succeeded. The turtle took it, proving its intelligence placed somewhere short of tactical genius. Two tentacles around the turtle's back whipped up and over, slapping where Ami would've been had she committed to the frontal stab. Instead they whacked stone, bouncing out wide.

"Tricky, tricky," Ami muttered.

"The skar, Ami," Annalyse reminded.

Sure, the Foti gem's heat coursed through the spear, concentrating on those scalloped insets. The skar's whisper, distorted, as if howled from a long distance, wanted an answer.

"Burn it, then," Ami muttered to the spear.

The skar didn't react.

The fiend scuttled forward and Ami back-stepped, giving up the ground before the cage door. The monster had her cut off from an easy exit now, but Ami refused to be fazed. Even if she wasn't a master spear-wielder, this thing ought to be an easy kill should circumstances arrive.

Okay, if words wouldn't work . . . Ami tried thinking at the skar, keeping her mouth shut and simply yelling, in her head, for the Foti stone to spit fire from the spear and turn the fiend to ash.

Again, nothing. The fiend seemed as confused as Ami, but when the attack didn't come, the monster tried another forward scuttle, its tentacles whacking into the stone floor to launch the turtle creature into the air, a living missile gunning right for Ami's chest.

"Watch out!" Annalyse called.

Ami sidestepped, ducking as she went and holding the skar spear into her chest. That would've been the perfect time for a skewering, but apparently there were rules here.

The skar kept whispering as the fiend shot past, tentacles reaching out to smack Ami's shoulder. The hits seemed like they should've been light things, mild brushes, but each one thudded like a bad bar punch, a bit wild and indirect, but together enough to knock Ami into a backward stumble. Only the cave's wall kept her from an unfortunate landing on the ground.

So no spoken words, no thoughts. How did the skar want to work?

"You have any tips?" Ami called out, the fiend rolling over its landing and sighting on her again.

"Listen to it," Annalyse replied. "The skar will tell you how to use it."

Listen to what? Those insane mutterings coming into her mind, a conversation half heard and little remembered? Ami centered herself, planted her feet and pointed the spear towards the fiend.

If it jumped at her again, Annalyse or no, Ami was going to spit the fiend.

As she leveled the spear, the skar's whispers changed. The voice, if you could call it that, went up an octave, spitting the nonsense out at a faster pace, like a barkeep calling out orders.

Interesting.

Ami tried waving the spear around, feeling a tad ridiculous, but as she moved with the weapon, the skar changed its response. Pointing the spear straight ahead led the skar to a high speed stutter, while raising the weapon into a guard's stance dropped the skar's mutters to a sluggish slur. When Ami jabbed at the fiend to drive it back, the skar piped up, almost yelling in Ami's head.

"What's it telling you?" Annalyse asked. "You have to let me know. For the research."

Ami, though, barely heard the scientist. Instead, she danced with the skar, listening to its changing tone as she back-stepped, dodged, struck and shielded with the spear. Every move seemed to reveal something new, a cadence to the skar, a beat to its language.

The fiend, either confused or plotting something new, put distance between itself and Ami. Tentacles wrapped around the cage's bars, lifting the fiend up near Ami's height. The warrior watched, giving the spear a twirl over her head and listening to the skar's excitement. Every time the spear's point whirled over Ami's head, the skar pulsed, like a happy shout in her mind.

Those were the points, the rush, the moment the skar could work. And, as Ami lowered the spear back to her side, she could still catch them out, the shouts more muted but still there. Points where the spear, the skar seemed open to something special.

The fiend jumped. The leap fell short of Ami's bulk, but the turtle thing rolled on the ground, putting its shell down and lashing a full tentacle forest towards Ami's face.

Timing the move with a shout, Ami swept the spear before her, stamping the base into the ground and hoping, hoping the skar would react.

If not, those tentacles were going to leave some hard bruises.

The spear glowed, a flash flying from the skar and

wrapping the weapon, the space around it in hot fire. The fiend's tentacles struck the sudden barrier, sizzled and bounced off.

"Amazing!" Annalyse shouted.

Ami didn't quite know, as she'd fallen back, patting hard at her arms, her hair where the spear's fire found something to catch. The weapon teetered as the fire vanished, falling to the ground with a hard thunk.

The fiend writhed, burnt tentacles flailing, While Ami picked herself up. Stared at the spear.

"It nearly killed me," Ami said over Annalyse's continued amazement. "Hardly an innovation."

"But you don't know what you're doing! Imagine someone who did?"

"I'll try that when I'm out of this cage," Ami said, reaching for the spear.

And drawing her hand back quick. The weapon radiated heat, as hot as any Foti forge. Annalyse's gloves seemed to have survived the initial burst, but picking up a white-hot weapon wasn't something Ami wanted to risk.

The fiend noticed. Getting over its tentacle troubles, the turtle flipped itself, dragging its limbs out and scuttling towards Ami.

"Grab the spear!" Annalyse shouted.

"It's too hot." Ami shifted left, trying to get back to the cage bars and the door. A chance to run. "Your experiment worked too well."

The fiend apparently caught Ami's intention, lashing its way through the room's center and cutting the Guardian off as she made her getaway. The fiend reached out, snared the cage bars and yanked itself to the metal, prepping for another toss and slam.

If getting out wasn't in the game, Ami could try something different.

She spread her feet, set her hands out before her, and told the fiend to come and get some.

The monster did, launching off the bars and flying towards Ami. The Guardian saw the angle, slid her left foot, ducked and swung up her right arm. Tentacles lashed like small clubs, battering her shoulder, but Ami's gloved hand caught the fiend's middle on its fly-by. Kicking off with her feet, Ami's right fist clenching the monster's tentacle mass, Ami ran with the fiend's momentum, dipping the fiend with its own weight and ramming it right into the rock wall, shell first.

The monster's barrier didn't break, no, but Ami felt her fist move through plenty more squishy bits, taking the fiend's soft center and mashing it to nothing. Those bashing tentacles fell limp, leaving Ami with nothing more than a spray of guts and bile all over her gear, her face, her hair. She pulled back, let the corpse fall to the floor.

"You okay?" Annalyse asked, opening the cage door.

"Tell the guards I'll be needing a bath."

If there was an advantage to Gladdring's luxury prison, it came with the Tenet's own bath. Noctia's desert demanded citizens share public baths, great big pools mixed with sea water and rain run-off, refreshed when nature or absolute filth demanded it. Ami, along with everyone else, grew used to it over time. Your only other option was a swim in an ocean flush with predators and, now, fiends.

The Tenet bath waited at the bottom of the Circle's central tower, a place Ami had no right to without two Gladdring guards by her side. Whenever they passed some official, some other Najahn soldier, the guards flashed a token, one Ami kept trying to sneak a look at but never managed, and the trio was waved on through.

A steaming pool larger than any room Ami had ever stayed in greeted them past the last gate. Thin wood slats sectioned the pool off, making eight separate bathing births. Each slat could be pulled aside, so Ami noticed, allowing Tenets to talk with whomever they chose while soaking their soft hands and feet.

The hour creeping towards dinner meant the baths had but two occupants, both with their slats up, both quiet. Ami picked her own spot, one well separated, and checked to see both guards had retreated outside the room. Not that she was much of a risk: the stone chamber offered no other exits, and besides her Najahn robe and the fiend's remnants —Annalyse wiped the worst off with a scrap rag—the Guardian had nothing to effect any escape.

Instead, she slipped into the burbling pool, fired by a boiler beneath, and gasped. Hot water alone was a rarity, reserved for teas, not commoner baths, and sharing a pool not with a hundred others made for something nearing magic. Smoke rose up around her, the slats dripping, and as Ami lowered herself up to her chin, a waiting cloth already used to wipe her clean, the long years of her life burned on the road, in battle, fell away.

"You're a hard woman to find," said a voice on her right, through the slat. Ami started, sitting up, the doze slipping away. Her skin looked shriveled, her breathing shallow.

How long had she been laying there in the bath?

"Are you going to open the slat, or am I going to talk through the wood?" The voice again, one she recognized, though this time wine hadn't made its mark. "If it's modesty you're concerned about, fear not. I'll keep my eyes to myself."

Ami reached over, pulled the slat ahead just enough to show her face, and Mattimo's puffy mug. The man seemed to be enjoying the bath as much as she'd been, his eyes closed despite his words, his shoulders relaxed.

"Modesty dies the minute you see someone carved up by a fiend," Ami said. "What do you want?"

"I thought the question was, what does Ami want?"

"No more riddles, that's what."

Mattimo cracked open an eye. "Riddles? This is no riddle. You came to me looking for information, I gave you the price, and then you disappeared. Hardly a fair play."

"I found what I was looking for."

Mattimo shook his head, "You found what Gladdring wanted to show you, no doubt. Not what you were looking for."

"I've seen the skars. I know what he's doing with them."

Now both eyes shot open. Mattimo turned, looked through the steam at Ami. "You're lucky the other two have cleared out. The Najahn keep strict dinner hours and there's not another soul in here. Otherwise, you might be dead before you return to your room."

"I'd like to see them try."

Mattimo chuckled, "That's just it, Ami. You wouldn't. Don't mention the skars. Ever, unless you're in Gladdring's little dungeon."

"If you knew what he was doing, why did you want me to find a way in?"

"It's not what he's doing that interests me," Mattimo replied. "It's what he's not doing. What he doesn't know and refuses to learn."

Ami sighed, closed her own eyes. "I said no more riddles, Mattimo."

"Then help me, Ami."

"You want in, ask Gladdring yourself."

Mattimo splashed the water, a light pitter patter against the wood. Playful, like a man imagining throwing a punch at an enemy.

"I don't need to get in anymore," Mattimo said. "Now that you're there."

"I'm not doing anything for you."

"Then how about for Catya?" Mattimo asked.

That earned him Ami's eyes, her attention.

"Gladdring told you there's no hope for her, right?" Mattimo rubbed his hands together. "He's wrong. The skars have power we don't understand, not today, but that some used to know."

"Power like what?"

"That, dear Guardian, is the mystery, and the key to my request. Bring me a skar. A Vis skar, and I will find a way to save your Aegis."

Another bath in three days time. That's when Ami, dried off and walking, escorted, back to Gladdring's tower, would deliver the skar to Mattimo. Some time after that, again in the Tenet's pool, the historian would pass back what they'd found, the supposed key to Catya's survival.

Again she'd be donning the thief's robes. Again Ami would be stepping beyond her bounds. Yet, who would be there to stop her?

As Ami went through the last guarded door, once more to the bland corridor to her dull room, the only sound she heard came from ahead and below, laughter, a gasp, and an excited shout.

All from one person, the only obstacle in Ami's way. But what risk did a scientist pose to a soldier?

CHAPTER 23
HOSTAGES

Wax threw the gruel at Sledge. The small wood bowl smacked the bandit leader across her forehead, the gunk splattering all across her battered gear, since restored to her person after the crew left the lava flow behind not long after the ferrites.

They'd be returning to the lava soon enough, according to Sledge, but for now a regroup, a reassess, and, perhaps, a chance for Torny and Bliss to catch up.

The wait put the numbers at three against two, with Quik's former captor being tossed into the burning river. Sledge along with another man and woman, whose names she gave but Wax promptly forgot, given that his mind turned on more important matters, like how to deliver the late lunch to the bandit leader with force.

Sledge reacted like most people would, falling back off the lumpy black rock she'd claimed for a seat, cursing. Wax jumped up, speeding towards the set down satchels, among them his Foti blade. He'd formed the plan the moment Sledge removed the sword, a fatal error brought about by her chosen stone's lack' of accommodation to hanging weaponry.

The other two bandits shouted, words muffled as Quik rose to do what Wax assumed any Guardian would: protect the Renewal, with fists and fury.

The five chose an ugly bluff for their break, far enough up from the lava flow to make fresh air a viable concept, if not far enough to dispel the heat, the acrid sulphur smell. Black rock and some brave scrub brush completed the place, one that'd already claimed a spot among the most loathed in Wax's heart.

That loathing found new vigor as Wax reached the piled gear only to find the brittle stone a cutting surface to brush when grabbing wildly for a weapon. His scuffed knuckles found the sheath, yanked the cerulean blade free. Wax held the sword up in a kind of triumph, the edge catching the sunlight and putting a momentary stop to the scuffle.

"Hurt my brother and I'll kill you," Wax said, leveling the blade at the two bandits, though both looked boxed up by Quik's clenched fists. "This whole thing ends here."

"Does it?" Sledge asked, standing up behind her stone, goop dripping from her hair. "What're you going to do, Renewal? Hike all the way back to Jarl's Tooth? You'll starve before you make it there, or melt on these cursed wastes." As she spoke, Sledge crossed her arms, glaring at Wax like his own mother might've. "Ride the river and you'll come to our camp, where you'll find nothing friendly waiting for you. Death either way without us."

Sledge's words threw Wax sideways for a second. Camp? Nobody had mentioned a camp. Wax had built up some beach nightmare, whereby he'd spend the next year eating bugs and fish on the sand under Sledge's watchful eye. A camp implied something larger, something worse.

"Think we're the only crew out hunting Renewals and any other foreigner not following the rules?" Sledge laughed. "Naivety will get you killed, boy."

Wax glanced at Quik, looking for an answer and found little in his brother's frowning face. A different answer, though, lay at Wax's feet, around his legs. The bandits had enough food, so Sledge promised, to get their whole team to the coast. Split that food among just Wax and Quik, and Jarl's Tooth should be in reach.

Even better, that'd be going up-river, towards where Bliss and Torny jumped their rock. Quik had seen the pair make the leap, swore they lived, which means they needed to be found.

"Think I'll take my chances," Wax said. "You and your two friends can take a walk. Go out there, to the lava. Wherever you want."

Sledge narrowed her eyes. The other two bandits watched her. "You mean to keep the satchels?"

"I mean for you to take a walk. You can keep what you're wearing."

Sledge laughed again. "Then you're killing us. That won't do. What will, though, is keeping on our road. So put that blade down and let's find ourselves some new rafts. Daylight's burning."

Wax felt a flush coming on, pushed it away. Not a chance he'd get pushed around by Sledge, not after what he'd seen, what he'd done.

"You heard me," Wax said. "Go."

Wearing her infuriating half smile, Sledge stepped around the rock, walked right at Wax, her arms falling loose to her side.

"You willing to kill me now, boy?" Sledge asked as she approached. "That's what you'll have to do. Stick that sword right here." Sledge pointed to her own heart with her right hand. "Make it a strong thrust, mind, because even though this leather's hot and seen too many years, it'll still turn a coward's stab."

"I'm no coward."

Wax gripped the blade with both hands. Angled the point towards Sledge. What'd they say on the Kance ship? Don't wait to strike. Surprise and speed wins more fights than skill.

"Then prove it."

As Sledge finished the words, Wax kicked off his feet, thrusting the Foti blade ahead more like a spear than a sword, going for that stab right where Sledge told him to. Right where she expected him to be.

Raising her arm, shifting on feet lighter without the heavy lava boots on, Sledge let Wax's blade slip by her left side. She clamped her arm down on the sword, cocked her right fist and smashed Wax's face, splitting stars across his skull and sending him into a backward stumble.

Sledge ripped the blade free from Wax's half-hearted hands, finding the hilt and turning the point on its owner.

"Not a coward," Sledge said. "I'll give you that much."

Wax steadied himself, shook his head to clear the buzzing, and watched the sword. The provisions and possibly other weapons lay to his left, an impossible distance. Behind him sat the bluff's edge and a long fall to a grim death. Quik and the others lay the only other way, a route Sledge could also cut with a swift strike.

Trapped, and in trouble. Not exactly an unusual situation for Wax, a fact he'd reckon with later.

"What's your choice?" Sledge advanced another step. "Die now, along with your brother, or live."

"Do you always talk like that?" Wax countered, letting his hands fall to his side.

"Talk like what?"

"A Najahn who needs a vacation," Wax said. Sledge took another step forward, frowning now. The needling making its magic. "I mean, c'mon. We're on some desolate rocks, you've lost half your crew. Not exactly the work of a genius, am I right?"

"You'll be little more than a corpse in a minute," Sledge growled, bringing the blade within a hair of Wax's chest.

If Wax had learned one thing from the Kance duelists, it was that stance told you more than where the sword, the spear happened to be. How Sledge stood, how she gripped the blade said what she'd be doing with it, and right now Sledge's single-handed point said threaten, not kill, not stab.

So Wax kicked off the rock and ran, right towards the only ally he had.

"Now Quik!" The shout didn't quite ring with triumph, but Quik used the opening anyway, elbowing the bandit on his left while pushing the other forward, tripping them into the rock.

"What's the plan?" Quik said as Wax closed, delivering a second punch to the elbowed bandit and leveling her. "Run?"

"Or win," Wax kicked the tripped bandit, sending their head lolling to the side. He reached down, pulled a knife from the bandit's belt. "We've got'em now."

"You've got nothing," Sledge announced, frigid iron on her words.

"Wax," Quik muttered.

"What, sword or no, she—" Wax turned, knife at the ready.

Sledge, the Foti blade on the rocks at her feet, had her bow drawn, arrow ready to fire. The distance long enough to give her a clear shot well before either Wax or Quik could close.

"Drop the knife," Sledge said. "Apologize. And maybe I don't kill you right away."

Why did this woman seem to have a counter for every one of Wax's tricks? Frustrating, and for the first time, Wax found himself drawing blanks.

"Run," Quik whispered. "I can buy you time."

Wax started to refuse out of hand as Sledge demanded again that he drop the knife. Sacrificing Quik to give Wax a random run into the wilderness wasn't an option. But the suggestion gave rise to a better idea.

Wax started a slow crouch, reaching with the knife as if to set it down. Just before Wax touched it to the stone, he darted to the right, wrapping his left hand around the knocked-out bandit and putting the knife to the man's throat.

"New deal," Wax said as Sledge swung the bow, her arrow tracking to Quik's unguarded form. "You let my Guardian go, and I'll come with you. No tricks, no fights, no fuss."

"Wax, what—" Quik started.

"Go?" Sledge shook her head. "There's nowhere to go. The closest town I know about is days to the north. He'll die before he gets close."

"He'll take that risk," Wax said.

He threw a look Quik's way, a firm set. His brother had to understand that the only thing they'd get with these bandits would be a slow death. Whatever Sledge said about past Renewals, letting Wax and Quik live after who knew how long had passed seemed unlikely. Stupid. A vain hope like the one Wax had before Pan had a thorn shoved in his side.

Quik's odds in the wastes would be better. And maybe, just maybe, his brother could find some help out there.

"Wax's right. I'll take my chances," Quik said. "Give your friend his life. Let me go."

Sledge weighed the options, her arm keeping the arrow ready. Wax figured the strain had to be tough, hard to keep ready to fire. And Sledge proved him right, letting the arrow relax with a shrug.

"Then go. Take your waterskin and run, Vis. If I see you coming back, your brother dies first."

Quik nodded, put a hand on Wax's shoulder. "I won't forsake you, brother," he whispered. "Hold on."

"What, I'm just going to be spending some lovely time with these people. You're in the hard spot."

Quik laughed, looked to the north.

"Go," Sledge ordered. "Or I'll shoot you now."

Without a last glance Wax's way, his brother ran, huffing up the black rock and over the hill, vanishing as the sun crept lower in the sky.

Getting back on the lava flow went easier the second time around, the ride thankfully ferrite free. With Sledge in front and the other two bandits behind, Wax took his victory and rode in the middle, holding his pole on the large stone they'd secured.

No Guardians with him now. Quik, a Vis hunter, could survive just about anywhere. Bliss wasn't far off either, so long as the other bandit didn't get desperate and stabby. Still, Wax had to favor his sister in any fight.

Sledge seemed to feel the same desperation. With one hand on the pole, the other on Wax's Foti blade, the bandit leader kept looking back, as if to confirm her prisoner and couple remaining members were still there. Creases lined her face, now kept in a permanent frown. No more anecdotes about Foti, about life amid the wastes came tumbling from bored lips. This was someone, Wax figured, who realized this attempt had gone badly wrong.

Who would be waiting at the end to judge her for it?

The other two bandits kept to themselves, save from taking back their weapons from Wax's grabby hands. They muttered nothing more than necessary navigation, their eyes hooded and lips tight. Hands gripped the poles. Sighs came often, audible over the lava's endless pops and sizzles.

When they stepped off the rafts, darkness had set in, the lava's orange yellow glow providing enough light for a scramble up a softer hill, this one speckled with more life. When Wax asked why, Sledge didn't answer, but a bandit behind him offered a solution:

"Closer to the coast, more rain," the other woman said. "You can smell the salt."

Wax sniffed. Every breath still came with more sulfur, more noxiousness than anything, but the bandit had a point: beneath it all, the ocean left a tang.

"Don't talk to him," Sledge said as they dropped the satchels. "Not till we reach the camp. I've heard enough out of his mouth."

"Sorry," Wax said, throwing up his natural, cocky grin. "Not like me to be quiet."

Sledge shook her head, nodded over Wax's shoulder. "Shut him up, would you?"

Wax held his smile as he turned back, held it long enough to see the knife coming, hilt first into a strike against his forehead.

Nobody caught his fall onto the rock.

CHAPTER 24

RESCUE MISSION

Svarde told the tales as he walked, with Rasslebeck jumping in from time to time with his own whenever the Guardian's throat grew too parched. The caves around them blurred in their endless dark rock at the telling, turning into sailing ships under Maena's watch or narrow battlefields where Svarde, Ami, and Catya faced fiend after fiend en route to another skar. Through it all, Maena and the whimpering man listened and asked for more.

At a break, eating what mosses and spring water they could find, Svarde asked the torn pair what they were hoping for.

"To find ourselves, obviously," Maena replied. "I want to remember who I am."

"You'll know what we tell you, nothing more," Svarde answered. "The shell, not what's inside."

"Then the shell is what I'll have."

Svarde nodded, looked to the shriveled man. He'd been quieter lately, spending more time looking at the stones. "And you? We know nothing of who you are. What will you do?"

The man scratched at his chin. He had a habit, Svarde noticed, of running his hands along his own body, as if exploring his own skin. Perhaps reminding himself what he looked like, what his body was.

"An empty vessel looking to be filled," the man replied. "These stories you're telling, it's scaffolding for me. Pieces to cling to, memories to recall even if they're not my own."

"You're holding on to them now?"

The man nodded, "With every step away from that creature's lair, I feel myself returning. Not the memories, no, but my sense of . . . myself."

"Anything useful in that sense?" Svarde gestured a half-eaten mushroom at Maena's crossbow and saber pairing. "Think you could use one of those?"

The man shook his head. "I don't think I was ever much of a martial man."

Rasslebeck snorted, "Then why were you down here at all?"

"I think," the man said, fumbling and slow, "I think I've always been down here."

Rasslebeck rolled his eyes, looked at Svarde. "Guess he'll serve as bait, if nothing else."

PENNIFER'S bloody footprints ran out after several hours walk, their smears tracked sometimes by feel, sometimes by smell, and, rarest of all, by the occasional moss-given glows down deep. Without torches, the foursome went forward with careful caution, leaning on Kivi to guide the passage. Her snorts warned of steep slops, sudden drops, or jagged walls. If need be, the ferrite would split her shell, eject steam and give a low orange glow for a few strides, letting the group pass over streams or beneath spear-like growths dropping down from the ceiling.

"A miracle she's kept running this long," Rasslebeck noted as they reached the latest print. Pennifer's blood, now, looked black and brackish, mingling with worse things. "We don't catch her soon, I'm thinking there won't be much to save."

As if to defy his words, a shout echoed along the corridor, a crystal clear cry of shock. Rassleback and Maena jolted forward only for Svarde to hold out an arm, stop them from running past into the gloom.

"Kivi leads. We're no help to her if we fall apart on the way."

The ferrite took Svarde's command and snorted her way on, clearing her vents and lighting the cave, a narrow, purple stretch. Claw marks scarred the walls here and had for a while, old and new slashes exposing glittering minerals. Svarde used to assume every fiend made its journey up to an inevitable end against the Aegis's shield or a warrior's blade. Now . . . now it seemed like some monsters chose to stay down here, making their home in the dark.

Had Pennifer found another lair, or ran into a roaming fiend no more at home here than she?

The tunnel leveled out, a stream cutting into the path and running into a deeper pool. Svarde and the others splashed in as Kivi took to the dryer walls. Pennifer hollered again, less panic and more anger this time. She wasn't dead, perhaps the biggest achievement for someone without a weapon this deep.

"Hold on," Svarde replied to the noise. "We're nearly to you."

A click behind said Maena had her crossbow up and ready. Svarde drew his axes as he waded through the chilly water. The wet almost felt good on his sore feet, those rough callouses, but its effects would turn against him after. The blisters, the disintegrating footwear, too many times had—

A body splashed into the water before him, hands flying up along with the water. Rather than reaching for the form—Svarde assumed Pennifer, but Kivi's vents couldn't pierce the water with their glow—Svarde stepped on by the splashing form, assuming it was Pennifer. If it wasn't, Rasslebeck had a knife that'd make a quick kill.

The real fun lay ahead, the pool growing deeper as Svarde waded forward, sodden shoes slipping on smoothed stone. In the water, burbling shoots sprayed upward, their bubbling geysers catching Kivi's vented gasses and glowing with their reflection.

So did, thankfully, the eyes. Two large perfect circles, their pupils black and as large as Svarde's head, fixed the warrior in their glares. Each sat on its own side of the cavern, distant enough to make Svarde reconsider his chances of wading all the way across to them without taking a fatal smack or two.

Though, a smack from what? Svarde hadn't seen anything yet. No claw, no tentacle. The eyes tracked him as Svarde stopped near the geysers, enduring the warm water splash as he considered.

"Don't look at them!" Pennifer, her voice sputtering, shouted from behind. "That's how they get you."

Svarde snapped his look straight ahead, towards the faded far wall across the rippling water. Eyes as a weapon was a rare quality. Rarer still was the quiet, the absolute silence coming from these fiends. Svarde guessed there were two, each taking half of the cavern.

"Get you how?" Rasslebeck asked. "I don't see any weapons."

"Don't need'em," Svarde answered for the man. "You saw the last fiend. Some things don't need an edge."

Maena splashed up near Svarde, holding her look ahead just like he was. "Then what do we do? They're just watching us."

"We've found Pennifer," Svarde said. "Let's go back. There's nothing gained in a fight."

"You sure?"

"Fight enough, you know when not to swing the axe. Let's go."

In a single move, Svarde turned his back on the eyes, their unblinking stares. He reached out, turned Maena too. Kivi, waiting on the cavern wall near the room's entrance, snorted.

"Nobody likes running, Kivi," Svarde said, starting the way back. "We're not in any shape for a fight, especially not with the walk back we've got coming."

The plan seemed a good one, the eye-fiends doing precisely nothing as Svarde and Maena waded back to the tunnel, to where Rasslebeck held Pennifer. The woman struggled, arms and legs kicking at the water.

"You can't leave them alive," Pennifer said. "You can't."

As Kivi matched Svarde's return, the glow gave him a good look at Pennifer's situation, at the cuts and welts laying over her body. What rags she still wore seemed to split and disintegrate there in the water, save for the sturdy leathers. Those would be heavy, cold, and uncomfortable companions during the walk up, but the woman had no other choice.

"We're not risking—" Svarde started.

"They have our friends," Pennifer said, and Svarde

couldn't be sure the water staining her cheeks wasn't tears. "They have them and they won't give them back."

"What friends?" Rasslebeck asked, starting to pull Pennifer back down the tunnel. Behind them both, the whimpering man only held himself and shivered. "All our friends are topside, Pennifer."

"Not these," Pennifer said, her burbling fading to a whisper. "These are all the friends I have left. Please."

"She's lost it, Svarde," Rasslebeck said, then tightened his grip on his captive. "Stay still, damn you."

Fiends came in all types, all possibilities. Who knew what friends Pennifer was talking about, what they meant to her, whether Svarde would find his own 'friends' stolen if he went back to those monstrous eyes. A mystery he'd be content not finding out.

"They're moving," Maena whispered, tugging on Svarde's arm and forcing the warrior to turn around.

Where there'd been a straight shot to the cavern's dark end there now sat one of those eyes, its pupil larger now, canceling out the whole white. Just orange and purple filaments blazing Svarde's way. A fascinating dance, even at this distance.

Why, if he looked hard enough, Svarde could even see himself in those lines. The eye seemed to grow larger, the pupil splitting like a pie into sections, each one reflecting Svarde, a part of him, a past him.

Svarde?

There, on the left, he stood with Ami and Catya near the great Rana whirlpool, waiting for the boat to take them to the center, to the skar. Near the eye's top, Svarde sat in his family's home, a small house in Smythe. He had a child's hammer in his hand, banging on a bit of ore while his older brother watched. On the right, the Rat's Fang and Svarde lifting a pint with Che-Ri. And at the bottom? Svarde with Kivi in their mountain cabin on Vis, putting the finishing touches on the outer deck.

At first every memory appeared as it should, a fragment vague at the edges but clear in the action. Clear enough for Svarde to see the one difference: in every memory, every shard, lingering behind the scene sat that same eye, and in it, the details too fine for Svarde to parse, seemed to be more shards, more memories.

Water struck his face as Svarde fell into the pool, Maena's push doing its work. The chill woke Svarde's nerves, his muscles twitching back to life, breaking from some phantasmal chains that'd held him in an unseen, unfelt paralysis. Using his axe handles to push himself up above the water, Svarde reeled from the giant eye to see the backs of his friends. Even Kivi swished her stubby tail nearby, her sapphire stare pointing forward.

"You with us, warrior?" Maena asked, reaching one hand back without turning.

"You saw it, didn't you?" Pennifer yelled from farther up the tunnel, where Rasslebeck dragged her free from the water. "You see why we have to destroy it?"

A terror. The fiend certainly qualified as deserving an axe to its eye, but Svarde heard no battle call, felt no great desire to turn around and brave the stare again. Two fiends making a meal of his mind in too short a time had him stumbling forward, sheathing an axe and accepting Maena's help.

"We're leaving," Svarde said as the water ran off his beard. "Leaving, and damn sure never coming back. These things can rot in this hole."

"Snaring more of their own kind, likely," Maena added.

"A favor then, for us."

Pennifer's fury calmed after she dried, after they all did among the dusty stones. Walking back towards the surface seemed to rekindle a shared purpose, a fired goal that kept their legs moving, their spirits, if not soaring, then staying away from despair.

Rasslebeck and Svarde took turns telling tales, the stories sucked up by the other three. Pennifer, for her part, explained her escape from the eyes on simple chance:

"I had no shoes. I slipped, is all."

At the first break, taken in a small side alcove overgrown with purplish glowing mushrooms, the group ran out their soaked clothes, assembled what gear they had, and tried to pull together a way forward. A task made all the harder when Rasslebeck, perhaps carrying some grudge after having to haul Pennifer free from the pool, accosted the woman.

"Now that we can breathe, maybe you can give us all an apology?" Rasslebeck asked.

Slightly less soaked but no less ruined, Pennifer shrank back at the words. A motion the old Pennifer would never have made. Svarde glanced at Maena, wanting to see if she'd made the same observation, but the Rana captain watched the confrontation in wide-eyed curiosity.

"An apology for what?" Pennifer squeaked.

"For running off, that's what."

The whimpering man stepped between the pair, thin arms reaching for Rasslebeck, who shoved them aside.

"Please," the man said, "she doesn't know anything."

"You don't either, but you didn't go running away." Rasslebeck spat off to the side, loomed over Pennifer. She squeezed against the rock, the stones biting into her back. Svarde almost started forward then—the last thing their party could afford was unnecessary wounds—but Rasslebeck rocked back on his heels, his chin falling low in the magenta glow. "Sorry. I don't know what it's like, where you are. What you're feeling. I just know my damn feet hurt, my stomach's rumbling, and we've got too many days to walk until we reach the surface."

"Been thinking about that," Svarde said, drawing the attention back his way. "We don't have enough supplies to make it back. Our waterskins are low, we have few satchels to store any food we find. A straight break for the surface will leave us more than likely to starve."

"What're you saying?" Maena asked, though her tone said she already guessed.

"We've got to go back. Find that fiend, and finish it."

CHAPTER 25

THE WASTES

The Wastes were true to their name. Bliss hadn't ever seen a more desolate stretch than the black ripples heading to the horizon in every direction. Brave scrub brush poked up here and there, lone buzzards flirted with the sky, but otherwise little broke up the monotony.

Save Torny's endless, colorful cursing.

The bandit seemed to have a vocabulary crossing the Seven Isles, and she employed it liberally, bouncing between lighter insults to the gods when a toe—they'd left the heavy lava boots behind—stubbed on a rock to grittier diatribes against fate itself when a wrong step led to a skinned knee or when the waterskins ran dry.

The evening stretched on by the time Bliss wrangled her last drop from the weathered skin, its sun-bleached brown wrinkling up in her hands, withering much like herself. The early cocky confidence after escaping the ferrite had evaporated, leaving only a muted apathy.

Torny claimed they'd never reach shelter before starving, dying of thirst, and Bliss was beginning to suspect the bandit had it right.

So she stopped atop a slight mound, its pocked black height giving enough vantage to confirm a beautiful sunset and little else.

"At least our bones will stick out," Torny muttered, trudging up alongside Bliss. "The buzzards will eat every-thing else, but they'll leave the bones."

"And our clothes?"

"Any idiot lost like us won't use'em," Torny sniffed. Sulphur poked through the breeze, a rotten egg experience all day long. "My guess, they wear away just like us."

Bliss nodded. During their breaks, she'd started giving Torny the first lessons in signing. Simple things, like her name, where to look, danger, and so on. The bandit took to it quick, noting she'd used hand signals before.

When, where that before was Bliss didn't bother to ask. Torny wouldn't know the signs, and chipping it out on the tiny tablet would take too long. Besides, not like the past mattered when the future would be ending soon.

"I've never even been to the coast before," Torny said, her voice scratchy, dry. "I joined up with Sledge way back in Smythe. Needed the pay. Desperation making you just more desperate."

Bliss nodded, though she didn't have a clue what Torny meant. Vis wasn't an isle for desperation. Wasn't a place to force these kinds of choices on you. Maybe that's why Torny seemed so twitchy, prone to staring off at nothing as they walked, her mind so far away.

Far away enough, anyway, that Torny said nothing when the obvious route opened up. Courtesy of those buzzards, the isolated birds coming together some distance north and west, at least seven or eight swirling around something.

Bliss pointed with her staff, Torny picking up then there was something more than self-pity in the world.

"What, the birds? Who cares?"

Bliss sighed, kept herself from grabbing Torny's shoulders and shaking the bandit. Anywhere there happened to be buzzards circling, there'd be resources. Food, water, maybe just a body with something they could use. A dead animal could be cleaned and cooked, its blood, if necessary, something to drink.

A Vis hunter always needed to be prepared. A Lira, doubly-so.

Bliss took off down the hill. Torny, thankfully, followed.

Night fell on the walk, making the path through the lava rocks treacherous. At least for someone not used to wandering nature without sunlight, as Torny apparently was. Bliss slowed her pace, sometimes reaching out, holding Torny's hand to help her navigate narrow stretches, dodge large holes and keep on moving.

Were they well equipped, Bliss would've given up at the first time Torny tripped and dashed herself on a boulder, drawing a red line up the bandit's arm, tearing the already-ragged clothes they'd kept on from the lava flow. Bliss herself moved on instinct, but close calls were legion. Her eyes often blurred, her legs a hitch slower than they should've as she walked.

Fatigue.

Quik had told stories about this. The slow wasting as a hunter pushed their bodies to an extreme. You could pursue, could fight, could survive for a long time in a single bout, but the time and effort would catch up eventually.

More than a few Vis had been found, food for hanoko after failing to stretch a journey from one day into two or three.

And those hunters started with provisions, had a plan. Bliss had neither, save pressing forward towards those birds, still circling, still squawking now, pink shadows in Sichi's slim light.

The scrub brush thickened as the pair neared the place, Bliss holding up Torny and slowing their pace to a creep. Buzzards might mark the dead, but who knew if they were the only two out hunting tonight?

Torny, at least, seemed to grasp the moment and shut up. A blessing to be freed of her curses for even a minute.

Deep into a crouch, Bliss pushed aside thin dry stalks, each one topped with a sparse ash-white thistle. Beyond, the buzzard's target lay sprawled on the stone.

"No way," Torny muttered. "You never see tolkets outside the forges."

Bliss applied the word to the thing before her, a rolling mammoth beast. If ferrites had rocky scales made for lava, the tolket looked to be built of red-and-black netting, the gridded skin plastering a legless form. The tolket's head—if it was the creature's head—appeared to end in a several antennae, each as long as Bliss's arms and crusted over with hardened lava. The tail split into two fins, each looking as hard as the rock Bliss stood on.

The creature didn't look like it belonged on the dry land like this. Looked like, instead, it ought to be swimming the lava where those ferrite had been before.

Bliss swept a look 'round, trying to see if someone, something else beat them to the mark. The first thing she saw was Torny brushing past her, the bandit heading right for the tolket, still shaking her head.

"These things are rare, Bliss," Torny said, her whisper

dying. The buzzards chirped, flew away as Torny approached, angry at their interrupted meal. "So far as I know, they stay real deep in the earth, down in the lava pools." Torny reached out, touched the tolket and drew her hand back with a hiss. "It's still hot too."

Bliss matched Torny's walk up, confirming no evil lurked nearby. She didn't need to touch the tolket to confirm the creature seemed very dead. Nothing moved. No breathing, no twitching like a fish might when yanked from its watery home.

"I'm not, like, an expert," Torny continued, massaging her hand as they continued around the tolket. "Not sure anyone is, really. But you'd hear about them from time to time. Good luck if you see one when you're smithing."

Would they grant the same luck to two hapless explorers?

On the tolket's other side, a walk taking more strides than Bliss would've expected, a hint to where the creature had come from lay hissing and spitting.

As if the black rock had simply melted away, a bubbling black-and-orange pool sputtered. Bliss frowned at herself. She should've been able to recognize that glow in the night, know lava waited. But then, she'd never spent a night in the Wastes before.

"Look at those things," Torny said, and Bliss turned back to see the bandit getting up close with what looked like a million inty fins, each about as big as Bliss's finger and glittering. "There's so many. They'll harden when they dry out, too. We could cut'em off, make a fortune back in Smythe." Torny glanced at Bliss. "Or wherever we're going."

Bliss flicked her fingers, a sign she'd taught Torny.

"Yeah, we," Torny flicked up a half-smile. "I'm not stupid. You could kill me with that staff any time you wanted. Or hit me on the head and leave me behind. You're not, which means we're together in this."

Bliss pointed at Torny and waved off into the dark distance.

"Oh, what, you mean I can just walk away?" Torny laughed. "No thanks. Did you not just spend a few hours with me back there? I'm a city girl. I'd be deader than this thing out here on my own."

Bliss couldn't disagree with that.

Instead she focused on the lava pool while Torny investigated the beast. The pool itself seemed large enough, if barely, for the tolket to use as a way to splash on up to the surface. The question, though, was why?

Animals could be strange, but Bliss had yet to see one intentionally launch itself into deadly peril for no reason. Was the tolket sick? Had it been confused?

"Hey," Torny said, pulling Bliss back to her. The bandit had her knife out, was pointing the blade at the creature. "You know how to carve this up? I'm getting hungry, and while this thing doesn't look delicious, it beats eating rocks."

Sichi was high above by the time Bliss and Torny carved enough tolket blubber and muscle away to get to the good stuff. The lava pool made a convenient cook fire, with Bliss's staff serving to stick newfound tolket steak over the bubbling pit till it browned over inside and out. Even better, the two large blisters beneath the tolket's head proved to be water bladders, storing fluid to keep the thing alive. Torny made a small cut with her knife and the pair refilled their waterskins with what was, admittedly, the foulest water Bliss had ever drank.

But water it was.

After they ate, Torny changed her cursing for a lilting

tune, an almost spoken-word song tale of a smith who'd lost everything chasing after some mystical ore. The tale would've been depressing save for the last verse, where the smith, having strived for so long, gone so far, found that ore and used its brilliance to better the family he'd all but abandoned.

"That last bit?" Torny said, bowing after her finish as Bliss dished a polite clap. "We all added that before the last Renewal started. Too grim otherwise, you know?"

Bliss pointed at her own chest. She couldn't sing, but Vis had other ways to spend a good night. The young woman stood, leaving her staff on the ground, backed up a couple steps and steadied her feet.

"Oh, what's this? A taste of Vis's culture?" Torny asked.

Letting Kitaye's drums, its singing voices find a groove in her mind, Bliss closed her eyes for a long several seconds, bringing her hands together. Her left foot began to tap to the silent beat, a count beginning in Bliss's head. On the sixth tap, she snapped forward, leaning into a lunge almost all the way to Torny, who jerked back with wide eyes. That reaction alone, from someone who'd never seen this dance, almost had Bliss stopping, laughing.

Instead she rebounded, followed the next beat into an arched retreat, her arms flying out overhead in respect to the great sana. Bending her knees, her calves, Bliss finished the arch in a tight backflip, landing on her hands and toes, face drawn in a tight growl.

The hanoko.

Torny, catching the drift, gave Bliss a whistle. Started clapping her hands, close enough to Bliss's actual beat, while the dance continued, making its way through Vis's major creatures, its places, its people.

With a final spinning flurry, Bliss concluded with a deep

bow, one that should've been pointing out towards the ocean, one that now aimed right at the lava pool.

A very, very active lava pool.

Torny's claps died as fast as the dance, both women staring as the lava spawned one bubble after the next, each one growing up and out before bursting in a sizzle. The pool's edges expanded too, reaching over the rock towards them.

"Time to back up," Torny said, grabbing her waterskin, scooping up the meat they'd saved. "Something's made Foti angry."

Grabbing her staff, her own waterskin, Bliss followed Torny around the tolket. Overhead, the buzzards gave another annoyed squawk before scattering off in their own directions. Strange, that, leaving a good meal behind.

The lava, though, made the buzzard's call the right one, sending a sudden geyser upwards, high enough for drops to land on the tolket, burn on the dark netted skin.

Another Torny curse. Bliss flipped the staff, gripping it in her hands.

When the geyser faded, four obsidian legs straddled the pool, all heading up to a clam-shell body, the front facing them with warped, crusted teeth going jagged in every direction. Steam poured off holes marking the monster's shell, the whole thing brilliant orange.

"Guess we know why the tolket's here," Torny muttered, knife in hand. "Bet it was running away from that thing."

Just like they should be.

CHAPTER 26
A TEST OF LOYALTY

The arrow flew sharp, stabbing into the target's left side, well off the bullseye. Ami lowered the bow, frowned. She'd never been a great shot, the accuracy wasn't the issue, but she'd not heard a whisper from the silver-blue skar embedded in the bow's middle, right near where her left hand gripped the curving wood.

"Still nothing?" Annalyse asked.

"It's faint," Ami replied. "As if I'm trying to listen to someone talk on the other side of the room.

The surf made the skar's quiet voice harder to hear too. Annalyse had abandoned Gladdring's tower for the day, leading Ami through another direction from the bottomed-out stairs, this one leading to the secretive inlet where the Tenet's experiments could come in by the sea. The scientist had set up several targets along the sand, each one at a different range, with the last bobbing out in the waves.

Near it, caged beneath the water, was an ill-tempered fiend. The ribbon-like creature, its furred skin an ochre color, flashed as it swam up to and against the cage's bars, making concentrating on things like Ami's arrows more difficult.

"With the spear, I could hear the skar clear. Just had to figure out what it wanted. This, it's muddled." Ami turned the bow over, confirmed she had her fingers placed in the narrow divots. Just so. "The words are different too. The skar's not talking like the Foti one."

Annalyse nodded, "That matches what I've found. Every isle seems to need its own solution."

"Can we try putting this one in the spear? Maybe that would give us something—"

"It works there, Annalyse interrupted, tapping her chin with the charcoal pencil. A permanent black smudge lived there. "The spear is our baseline. It's the easiest one so far."

"The easiest one?"

In the cage, the fiend rattled the bars again, sending a spray over the slow waves. Outside, a gray morning continued to herald the coming winter. Both Ami and Annalyse wore thick leathers, the former's gloves stuffed with Whent furs. Behind, some invisible servants left a stocked table with fresh water, now-cool coffee, and breads, cheese for breakfast. All in all, Gladdring ensured the work could continue with minimal fuss.

"The skars seem to react to where they are," Annalyse said. "As if they pick up the properties. They say 'I'm in a spear, now, so this is what I can do'."

"You're saying they're smart?"

Annalyse shrugged, "They're malleable, at least. What we've never been able to do, though, is get one to work with a bow."

Ami didn't have to ask why that'd be valuable. Not everyone wanted to get up close with a fiend.

"Sorry to disappoint." Ami went over to the weapon

rack, put the bow back in its place. "Anything else we're doing this morning?"

"You don't want to try another shot?"

"I'm not going to waste my time," Ami said. "You want to try something different, I'm game."

Annalyse flicked a glance back towards the cave leading into the tower's basement. She'd been doing that a lot this morning, distracted from the testing. Ami had chalked it up to the bow's failure, an expected result prompting a turn towards more interesting possibilities.

Now?

"Look," Annalyse said, "why don't you try again? Just one more time?"

"Why?"

"Because I'm asking you."

Annalyse was about as scary as a mouse, and her putting on a demanding tone didn't help her out. Ami raised an eyebrow, thought about folding her arms and saying no. But then, what was the harm in one more arrow?

Hefting the bow back up, Ami took another black-feathered arrow from the quiver down in the sand. She went to the line marked by her own feet and took aim, this time at the closest target. The easiest shot at a bullseye. Might as well leave with a good mark.

Placing her fingers on the divots, Ami again heard the faint whisper. With the spear, she'd learned to hear the beat, to thrust and dodge, block and stab with the skar's intention. Here, even with the arrow nocked, the bowstring drawn back, the skar seemed to have no focus, like someone telling a story and switching focus every other sentence to something new.

Ami took a deep breath. Focused in. Her arm, already tired from the dozen arrows she'd shot, strained in a position it didn't find itself often. Tired muscles, a cramp coming. Ami tried to adjust, get her angle just right and relieve the tension just a bit.

The skar responded. A sharp rise, the whispers speeding up into a rapid staccato, like someone clicking their tongue. Ami held her position, went back to aiming the arrow. Maybe now the—

The skar faded as Ami looked down her arm, aiming the shot. Hmm.

Back to her arm, focusing on the pain, the strain. The skar reacted like it did before, bubbling up to life. Okay, so it read the tensing, but how could Ami use that?

She tried following her arm, feeling the pulled muscle all the way down to her fingers, to the bowstring and all the way across her chest to her left arm as it held the bow itself straight. As Ami held the focus, the skar picked up speed, until it became an uninterrupted popping stream.

The connection came when Ami finished tying her muscles together, following the line from the fingers of one hand to the other. The skar went solid, and a lightning rush ran through Ami's body. Her right hand released, the bow string snapped, and with a bang the arrow shot towards the target. The tiny missile struck, bursting the simple wood into splinters, the arrow itself breaking too, flying in all directions.

"How did you do that?" Annalyse asked, after she'd picked herself up off the sand, where she'd dove as the target exploded. "What did it feel like?"

Ami hadn't stopped staring at the bow, the Kanse stone inside it. Every skar had its own language, and more than that, they needed to match their surroundings. Work, but if it could turn a simple arrow into a force like that?

Ami turned to Annalyse, ready to answer her question,

but the words died on her lips. Gladdring, hands clapping, emerged from the cavern. Behind him, with two familiar Najahn guards pushing him along, stumbled a bloodied Mattimo.

The historian bored his battered look with an aristocratic flare, casting verbose insults at his guards and Gladdring in equal measure, their syllables interrupted often by bloody coughs. His Najahn robes were torn, stained, as if Mattimo had been pulled from a meal and dragged along before finding his footing. When his eyes found Ami, the historian played a smarter game than Ami expected, betraying no recognition and offering up a fresh sneer.

"This is who you have doing your work, Gladdring?" Mattimo asked. "The Aegis's used up Guardian?"

Gladdring held a single hand towards Ami, as if to apologize for the man's outbursts. The Tenet seemed a bit uncomfortable on the sand, his balance wobbling with his steps. Together, the two dispelled Gladdring's usual imperial presence, instead rendering both him and Mattimo into something less than threats, something less than serious.

The two Najahn guards, at least, preserved their roles. Neither erred in their steps onto the beach, both held to straight looks, one hand apiece on Mattimo's robes and the other, always, drifting to the voulge strapped across their back shoulders.

No chakrams, these. Apparently they didn't fear Mattimo running away.

"A new test subject," Gladdring announced to Annalyse, who regarded the whole party with her normal wide-eyed, dry observation. "This one has proved to be a pest, so let's at least make him a useful one."

"How?" Annalyse asked.

"By letting me go," Mattimo answered before Gladdring

could speak. "I'm not some prisoner scooped off the streets, girl. I'm—"

"Nobody of consequence," Gladdring interrupted. He shot a toothy glare Mattimo's way. "For all your research, Mattimo, not a soul will remember you. Those awful parties will carry on, you r sycophants and suppliants pausing only long enough to find a new source for wine. You are a miserable soul, fascinated in your twilight with things far beyond you. You should've stayed with your books and remained the footnote you are."

Mattimo's face had gone red, his inhale a sign some equal bluster was preparing to spew forth when Gladdring made a sharp cut with one hand. The guard on the left pushed Mattimo forward, cutting off any rejoinder with a face filled with sand.

"You said you planned to work with a fiend today?" Gladdring asked quick, turning back to Annalyse. "Is that it, there? Ami's not killed it yet?"

"Not yet," Annalyse answered.

"What's the skar today?"

"Kance. Ami may have had a breakthrough."

Gladdring nodded, his eyes flicking Ami's way for the barest fraction before returning to his scientist. "Perfect. Here is a chance to replicate the success. Give Mattimo the skar and throw him in. If the man masters what he's been seeking, he might live. If he doesn't, then the fiend might offer him the oblivion he deserves."

Ami, still holding the bow, heard Annalyse ask her to remove the skar. The scientist didn't seem to be pushing back. Executions, trials with likely deaths weren't exactly uncommon in the isles, but this seemed obscene. That, and if Mattimo wound up dying at the fiend's hand, he'd never get to fulfill his end of the deal.

"Why?" Ami asked, Mattimo before her trying to spit sand from his mouth. "What'd he do?"

"That, Guardian, is not your concern," Gladdring said. "Remove the skar. Now."

Catya. That's who Ami had to think about here. Not the wine-sotted historian, not the injustice. This wasn't some child being thrown off a cliff, some innocent being given to the sword. Everyone here played in Najahn's politics, and Mattimo had lost the game.

What such rationales were doing to her soul, Ami tried not to think about. She popped the skar, sliding her thumb beneath the stone in its slot, and handed it—the whispers intense at the touch—to Annalyse's waiting hand.

"Mattimo," Gladdring said, kneeling next to the historian, "do you even know how to use a weapon? Not counting a wine bottle, of course."

Mattimo coughed. "Damn you, Gladdring."

"I take that as a no." The Tenet stood. "Give him the skar, Annalyse."

The scientist went to Mattimo's side, held the skar out. The historian took it with one shaking hand. Gave Annalyse a look blending hope, fear, and wonder. Open mouth, narrowed eyes, sweating skin.

"This is a Kance skar," Annalyse said. "You'll feel it talking to you. Use it right, and you'll be able, we think, to do what Kance could. At least somewhat." Her face lit up as she spoke, as if the circumstances no longer mattered once possibility entered the play. "You could even fly, I think."

"How?" Mattimo asked.

"A mystery we are all depending on you to solve," Gladdring said. "Enough chatter, Annalyse. Send him in."

The guards picked up on the order, lifted Mattimo and dragged him down towards the surf.

"Ami, if you would be so kind as to take another arrow and reload your bow," Gladdring said.

Annalyse followed the guards and Mattimo down to the waves, talking all the while about how Mattimo might connect to the skar.

"For the fiend?" Ami asked, knowing it wasn't.

"If by some miracle our friend finds the secret to the skar and begins to fly away," Gladdring said, "you will bring him down."

"I'm not your executioner."

"Wrong, Ami. You are anything I ask you to be."

Ami's grip could've broken a man's neck in that moment, but the bow held. Mattimo, when the guards pulled him through the sea to the fiend's cage, did not.

From the first splash into the ocean, the historian floundered, his robes dragging him fast beneath the waves. For a soft moment, the only thing above the water was the man's hand, the Kance skar glittering.

Then it, too, vanished.

"Ah well," Gladdring said, the water turning red as the fiend found its next meal. "It's never so easy, is it?"

CHAPTER 27

ROCK RUN

Which was worse, abandoning your duties as a Guardian or a brother?

Quik, in the hours since leaving Wax and the bandits, hadn't come to a firm conclusion. What he did know, now, was that he would likely die out here. His hunters instincts kept his feet moving light over the stones, Sichi's glow giving just enough to keep him from a bad fall, a broken ankle, or complete despair. The concentration helped him, a focal point that wasn't the chain that'd led to the lava floe, the ferrites, the bandits.

A chain that'd started with him.

Water. That was all. A late night attempt to quench some thirst and Quik gave it all away to the wrong people. His hesitation, too, when Bliss attacked back in the narrow canyon. Sure, Sledge had them under an arrow's line, but Quik's sister had it right: she wouldn't risk her quarry. He could've taken the skinflint thieves, their ragged gear and bodies showcasing a hardscrabble life. Nothing to a Vis hunter.

A bloom caught Quik's eye as he crested another lava

mound. The hills were dwindling some now, getting less ragged as Quik moved north, giving him better sight lines to see how far he'd walk to nowhere.

The bloom, though, promised something else. Something interesting. Orange and red, lava's color. Perhaps a pool, but, if nothing else, warmth. The Foti night up here grew chilly, the wind snapping at his loose clothes. They'd ditched their warmth before riding the lava, a choice Quik would've regretted except there'd been no real, well, choice. Riding the lava in full gear would've only meant drowning in his own sweat.

Buzzards erupted over Quik's head, flying south. A group, strange enough, stranger still to be seen in the air at night. That they were here at all meant something more than lava lay ahead, though their flight suggested worse things besides.

Worse for the buzzards, anyway. Quik's stomach jumped at the idea that something tasty might be in the offing, the continual slap of his waterskin against his thigh a reminder he'd had nothing save a few drops in the hours since fleeing Sledge.

A meal, properly cooked over some warm lava, would be worth almost any risk.

The ground leveled out down the hill, letting Quik break into a full run towards the bloom. Charging headlong might not be the most hunter-like choice, but the fleeing buzzards meant something had to be active, could be destroying Quik's potential prize.

Besides, odds suggested the creature in question was another ferrite, a lizard Quik figured he could scare off with his hands alone. Even so, as he ran, Quik bent down and scooped a palm-sized stone off the ground. The brittle lava rock might not hold up much in a fight, but animals could be intimidated with a well-placed toss.

The sprint brought Quik into another kind of life as well, rising up a dormant vigor, the cold night a balm on his lava-scarred lungs. Blood pumped, his muscles sang like they hadn't since departing Vis. Thus far, Foti hadn't offered a chance to get out and run.

Thus far, Foti had been a miserable place.

The voices carried on the wind didn't sound so miserable, though. Two, if Quik heard them right, and coming from the bloom. Their shouts came with fear's tinge, with a fight's edge. Short barks. No, a single voice, one changing its tune.

Why?

Quik slowed up, nearing the bloom and noticing now the source lay hidden behind some large bulk. Sichi's light made the lumpy worm a shimmering black and red, a bold skin made more fantastic as Quik neared, crouching now, and noticed the latticed design. The creature seemed dead, though with its back facing Quik, the hunter couldn't be sure.

As for that voice, it yelped again, then rose up higher into a singsong tune. Something rumbled after it, digging into the dirt with the sledge-like sound of a dragging sled.

Not a ferrite then.

Quik crept up against the red-black bulk, confirmed the dragging noise chasing the yelps was heading away before popping his eyes over for a look.

The creature—Quik would've called it a fiend, but who knew what horrors might lurk on Foti's blasted isle—drew his eyes first, because how could it not? The great shell, bristling with haphazard fangs, dragged itself along the dirt with scraggly fins. In the lava's glow, the monster appeared more shadow and flame than living thing, a surreal beast belonging in nightmares.

Not so the person it chased. The bandit girl danced back from the fiend, her hand flittering over her mouth, changing her voice as she moved, outpacing the monster without much difficulty.

Why didn't she turn and run?

Both the fiend and the bandit were on the lava pool's far side, putting its brilliance in the way of seeing anything else. At least, anything beyond his fingers.

The skin beneath his hands had death's chill, but life had once been there, which meant meat. The bandit might've gone hunting, found a problem.

But then, the bandit had also been the one with Quik's sister. If anyone knew where she'd gone, it'd be the girl facing off with the fiend.

A girl now yelping for real. Quik found her, saw she'd stumbled and hit the ground. Poise crumbled quick, the bandit's feet slipping on the rocks while her hands tried to push her back up. The creature, sensing some victory, rushed its fins.

Quik made his move, vaulting over the dead creature's bulk. The snatched rock in his hand, Quik flung the stone as he landed. The rock smacked the creature's shell, bursting. The strike couldn't have hurt the thing, yet the fiend shivered to a halt. If it had eyes, Quik would've expected the things to turn his way, but none did.

"It's sound!" the bandit shouted, recovering her footing and getting distance. "That's how it'll find you."

Swift to mark him as an ally, and right about her guess, as the creature heard her voice and kicked off its pursuit once more, black rock flying up as it hustled forward.

A tapping, much closer to his feet, drew Quik's attention from the chase down tot he ground, where, lying and favoring a gashed leg, lay his sister. Her staff rested by her side, and behind it, near the dead mammoth, sat the first carved pieces of what would make a good many dinners.

"Bliss!" Quik started the name as a shout, shrank it to a whisper as he knelt at her side. "How bad is it?"

Bliss shook her head, her signs flashing in the lava light. 'Looks worse than it is. Help her.'

If Quik had his gauntlets, helping the bandit would've been easy: a running jump up behind the shelled creature, a battering on the top to drive it into the ground, and then keep whaling away till the monster gave up.

Without his usual tactics, Quik was going to need something new.

That something looked to be Bliss's staff.

"Can I borrow this?"

'You break it, I break you.'

Quik chuckled. Good to see his sister still had her heart.

Bliss's upgraded staff had metal on either end, metal that glowed bright as Quik stuck the edge into the lava pool. Beyond, the bandit continued kiting the monster around in large circles, following Quik's shouted call to keep it close.

But not too close.

"Getting tired over here!" The bandit called.

"Ready!" Quik replied.

The fiend, according to Bliss, had emerged from the lava. That meant the thing's shell, its fins would take the heated staff without a problem. But how about the monster's insides?

Hefting the staff in both hands, Quik went around the pit's left, dragging the meta end in the lava to keep it hot. The bandit cut across the pit's front, the shelled fiend hustling after her. While the bandit breathed hard, sweat everywhere, scratches and their blood glistening in the lava's light, the fiend showed no such exhaustion. The fins worked as they had when Quik first arrived, hustling along the ground.

"Keep going past me," Quik said, drawing the hot end from the pit.

"It's all yours," the bandit said, running right by the hunter.

The fiend closed. Quik took a breath, aimed the hot end right where he hoped that giant mouth would open.

"Right here!" Quik shouted as the fiend crossed before him, trailing the bandit.

The creature lurched to a stop, its fins scuttling on the rock to turn Quik's way. Those gnarled teeth pitted and charred, coated over with dried lava. The shell looked much the same this close, and Quik couldn't imagine how heavy all that dried rock had to be.

The fiend didn't give him much time either, jerking forward in a head snapping bite. Its jaw eclipsed the hunter, blocked Sichi's light behind. But Quik had a hot-glowing guide, and he jammed it forward.

The staff struck something soft. Quik pressed, felt the monster recoil, those fiends struggling to reverse. Those teeth quivered, but didn't shut.

A monster smart enough not to swallow its own death. Not good. Quik danced back on his toes, bought space while the fiend coughed, a dry spasm. The staff left the monster's mouth, but the beast kept it open, perhaps airing out the wound, perhaps displaying all its teeth in some frightening dance.

Eitehr way, the bandit took the opening.

Quik expected the girl to retreat, maybe vanish in the

night given the chance. Instead, her feet light and silent on the stone, the bandit came up alongside the fiend with Wax's old Foti knife drawn. She stabbed the weapon inside the mouth's corner, prompting the fiend to jerk away. The bandit bounced back too, twirling the knife in her hand.

"Got you, you ugly bastard," the bandit said.

"Don't think that killed it," Quik muttered as the fiend again changed its target, chose the bandit and surged forward.

This time, though, the bandit didn't retreat, didn't move. The big mouth came closer. She'd be eaten, slaughtered. Quik swore, dropped Bliss's staff and burst into a headlong run.

Those gnarled teeth closed in. The bandit grinned. Quik leapt.

He tackled the bandit, didn't feel the teeth strike, and curled in around the bandit's smaller form as they hit the stones. Quik's ragged clothes tore further, new bruises and cuts adding themselves to his collection. His head knocked hard on a stone, sending the world sideways, his ears ringing.

Hard enough so he couldn't understand what the bandit said as she forced herself from his arms, stood up over him.

Though he understood her kick well enough.

Quik shook off the mild blow, brought his focus back into line, and sat up. Saw the bandit go back towards the fiend, those teeth held high.

So high, it was like they hadn't even come down, gone in for the bite.

The bandit neared the fiend, took in a breath, and spat on the monster, before continuing right on past the thing towards the lava, towards Bliss.

Quik scratched his head, stared. Mystery upon mystery.

"No mystery," Torny, the bandit, said as they ate cooked toleket and a few fired weeds they found growing between the stones. "Want to kill something bigger than you? Poison's the way to do it."

Quik frowned. "An unclean way."

Bliss flicked her eyes between the two. Torny laughed at Quik's response.

"Unclean? You look at yourself lately? You're probably the dirtiest person on the isle."

Quik ignored the flush. The dirt probably hid it anyway.

"I mean, it lacks spirit. Fairness. You didn't earn the kill."

"Sure I did. I killed it, didn't I? It's dead, isn't it?"

'Stop it, Quik,' Bliss signed. 'She won't understand.'

Now Torny's look flitted between the siblings, the smug smile never leaving her face. "Look, I don't right care what you think. I saved your damn lives, and that makes us even."

'I could shove her in the lava pit now,' Quik signed to Bliss, then turned to Torny, who'd stuffed her face with more charred toleket. "We wouldn't have been here save for you and your friends. This is your fault."

Torny rolled her eyes. "Already explained this to your sister, who's way cooler than you, by the way, but they're not my friends. They're an opportunity. Just like you."

Quik snorted, "An opportunity for what?"

"To stay alive. What else is there?"

CHAPTER 28

RETURN

Familiar and alien. The tunnel stretch, the blocked off splits, looked the same as before, lit up in the dim fungal glow. Lightning blue, new leaf green. The air stank as it always did, moldering on Svarde's tongue with every breath.

Those things were the same, had been the same for days, weeks, however long he'd been beneath the surface.

Now, though, Svarde treaded the stones not as a wanderer, an explorer searching for answers, but as something he'd never been before: a killer.

Kivi took to the mindset change with more gusto, the ferrite scrambling before Svarde, busting open her vents with happy regularity. The steam, the orange glow beneath led the party onward, let Svarde focus on his steps, his strategy.

Maena and Rasslebeck were willing enough to engage the fiend again. Armed, albeit without much defense, the two chattered on about tactics, Rasslebeck doing more educating of his former commander. Rana raiders had, it seemed, a long list of combat techniques with those crossbows, with Rasslebeck's scavenged stones.

Pennifer and the whimpering man straggled on behind, both reluctant in their approach, yanked along through an invisible chain promising a slow starving death in the dark should any steps lead them astray. Maena, Rasslebeck offered up the occasional word of comfort to them, a hope that memory might be restored, that the fiend, without surprise, would fall quickly to their combined arms.

Svarde had neither that confidence nor that expectation.

He did, though, have two axes eager to sink their sharp edges into the fiend's flesh.

The long march down the fiend's tunnel wore out the conversation, the mood. Anxiety, anticipation died along those steps, slow enough that Svarde considered calling a halt, even setting up a watch and getting sleep. A battle on rest, on a full stomach would be better than one without either. Yet the fiend had pounced on them before, and now, Svarde felt, they were close enough again.

"We're nearly there," Svarde said when Maena asked about the same. "You'll get your energy back when the monster appears. Don't doubt it."

"That's what you're hoping for?" Rasslebeck asked. "Our ragged asses will pull it together in the end?"

"It's not hope. It's fact. We sleep here, we won't be waking up."

"Some of us might not mind that so much," Pennifer added.

"The old you wouldn't have said that," Rasslebeck countered, flipping sides. "The old you would've been wondering why we didn't stick the bastard the first time around."

"The old me lost."

"Then get some revenge," Svarde snarled, his feet never stopping, always going down, down, down.

The fiend's lair looked much like Svarde remembered: the three-pronged entry branching off the prisons, the quartz in the center, and a leftward path they'd never explored.

Now wasn't the time for new directions.

The soft breeze returned with them, a change not unwelcome even knowing its source. At least the air moved away their collective stink.

"The middle," Svarde said. "If the fiend's home, it'll be there. If it's not, we get our gear back. Be ready."

"Thanks for the warning," Rasslebeck muttered.

In the back, the whimpering man continued doing as he had for the last hour, repeating Rasslebeck's story, the names on the Rana raider's list. It could've been annoying, but instead came through as a comfort, a sort of cadence to their damned march.

Kivi led them through the middle tunnel, up its sharp bend to the quartz chamber. Again the pink light blew away the dark, forcing a squint as Svarde made the entry. The gemstone remained as he'd left it last, with armor and clothes, weapons and satchels hanging from the spearing prongs.

The fiend seemed absent. Kivi centered the room, spinning around on her stubby legs and snorting. No immediate threat.

"Get in and get armed," Svarde said, leading with his axes. "No telling when it'll realize we're here."

Rasslebeck and Maena moved past the Guardian, angling towards the gemstone. The whimpering man followed, eyes and mouth agog at what he saw.

"Any of it yours?" Svarde asked at the man's expression.

"If it was, I wouldn't know."

What the man also didn't know, when Svarde pressed him a moment later, was where Pennifer had gone. When the whimpering man claimed ignorance, Svarde whistled the crew back to action. The Guardian wanted to go rushing off down the tunnel, find Pennifer and either drag her back with them or slaughter the demon sucking her soul dry.

But he didn't move.

"We're not going after her?" Rasslebeck asked, sabers now in both hands. "Isn't that the point?"

"The point is not to die," Svarde said. "If the fiend's found her, there's little we can do. Rushing into those dark tunnels gives it every advantage. Instead, we set up. Wait."

"And Pennifer?"

"We'll find her after."

That she'd be dead, a husk, Svarde didn't say, didn't need to say. His body gave that edict for him, and the other three didn't push back. Kivi, making her way up to the ceiling, gave a soft, agreeing snort.

"We tried to save her, went all that damn way, and now you're throwing her life away?" Rasslebeck spat on the dusty rock. "Some leader you are."

"Never wanted to be a leader," Svarde replied. "Get back near the quartz."

Svarde drew up the hasty strategy. Maena and Rasslebeck would hold the room's center, with Maena ready to fire her crossbow—a second, loaded and ready, sat at her feet—the moment the fiend appeared. Rasslebeck would defend her as he could, draw the fiend's attention so Svarde, crouching near the middle tunnel's exit, could spring. Kivi, above, played the surprise, a second trap or a chase down clawing as needed.

The whimpering man stayed off to the side, a Rana long knife in his hand. Svarde wouldn't trust the man to stab anything more than himself, but everyone had the chance to get lucky.

The wind proved the clue, picking up its gentle breeze to rapid gusts, much like it had before. Svarde met eyes, received nods in turn. The whimpering man continued running through his list.

As ready as they could be.

Stone's crunch sounded to Svarde's right, where the middle tunnel opened into the quartz. Maena raised the crossbow, only for Rasslebeck to slap it down.

"Pennifer," Rasslebeck said. "Get over here!"

If she'd seemed half-dead before, a ragged scoundrel alive through desperation and a failure to die, Pennifer now ranked among the least things Svarde had ever seen. She shuffled into the chamber, her eyes glistening and locked straight ahead. Her teeth, her mouth made a slow whistle with every breath, as if not sure how to open, how to inhale. Her hands hung limp, her short hair scattered. Fresh cuts littered her legs, as if Pennifer had been dragged along the ground.

Or thrown herself on the rocks in terror.

Kivi's snort snapped Svarde away from Pennifer's wreck. The fiend, taking the distraction and blowing in from the left tunnel. The gray faces, the black cloak, the many spindly arms reaching for Maena, for Rasslebeck.

Neither were ready.

The Rana captain turned, bringing up the crossbow, and pulled the trigger into lashing wind. The bolt bounced off the rock beneath the demon, a hasty miss, and one that'd see no follow. Maena sank down as a gray face found her, the fiend rotating its masks until a gaping maw began to suck upon her soul.

Rasslebeck howled a Rana charge as Svarde kicked himself off the wall, angling left to get behind the demon. Kivi seemed to be doing the same along the top, getting ready for a drop. Both advances came slow, the wind shoving against their every move.

To Svarde's right, the gust blew Pennifer into the waiting, weak hold of the whimpering man, the pair crumpling against the stones. Out of the fight, at least, and therefore barred from Svarde's worry.

Rasslebeck's opening swing seemed destined to break a gray face, destined until an arm rose to meet it. The thin limb blocked the saber like any club, the fiend issuing a pale cry as the blade bit into its dark skin. Something white and writhing oozed forth from the wound, vanishing into vapor before it hit the ground.

With it came speech, conversation, several seconds bearing voices Svarde had never heard before, an accent he couldn't identify.

Talking about home, and the dark within it.

Another time. Focus.

Svarde planted each foot after the next, his shredded shoes, the blisters on his souls nothing as the battle lust found its foothold.

This wouldn't be a fight to flee.

Rasslebeck cursed as he swung the saber again, a different arm blocking the blow. Another mystery conversation. Still the fiend inhaled Maena, who added her own cries to the blowing wind's rush.

Kivi dropped. The ferrite landed on the fiend, twisting in the air to strike the black-cloaked, faced body and drive it to the ground. At once Maena broke away, leaning back against the quartz and sobbing. Rasslebeck went for a crossing slash, stopping as the thrashing monster swung a gray face to meet him. Rasslebeck shivered, the saber falling from his grip and bouncing on the rock.

"Fight it!" Svarde shouted, giving up any surprise and rushing the last few paces.

The wind blew him off course, bringing Svarde closer to Rasslebeck than intended, and so his opening blow, coming as the fiend struggled with Kivi, snared only the fiend's right edge, tearing at the black.

Words erupted. Sounds. Clapping, cheers, crying, conversation and the rolling thunder of a storm. The noise filled the room, stunning Svarde with both its volume and randomness. The wind took advantage, stumbling him past Rasslebeck.

The fighter fell to his knees, his mouth moving in a familiar cadence even as so much chaos continued. Repeating his list, holding to himself.

An effort Svarde would not let die in vain.

The Guardian's foot struck something softer than crystal, something familiar, and Svarde dropped his axes, exchanging them for a chance.

Before him, the fiend managed to snare Kivi with its arms, throwing the ferrite into the wall near the middle tunnel. Kivi struck hard, cracking against the stone, claws already searching for purpose to make another run.

His ferrite friend, so loyal, so strong. Another Svarde couldn't let down.

The wind swirled, the gusts changing direction as the fiend pulled itself together, rising. White memories—for that's what they had to be—streamed from myriad wounds covering the beast, dissipating as they struck the ground. A gray face spun fractured, but the other seemed whole.

As Svarde raised the crossbow, the fiend noticed. It swept aside Rasslebeck and rose up before Svarde, its great, torn mass writhing faces, limbs, blotting out the world.

Svarde sighted on the monster, had his hand slip to the crossbow's trigger, and found himself elsewhere. Nowhere.

If the great eye down below had pulled Svarde into several moments at once, cast them in a warped light, this fiend felt as though Svarde were stretched across his entire being. Thoughts, feelings, emotions collided upon him, banishing anything real in favor of what had been in an impossible slurry, one beginning to drain as the gray-faced fiend found its hook.

As soon as it started, as soon as Svarde lost himself within himself, he snapped back. Right to the room, the quartz, the fiend. And before him, hand outstretched in a futile stab at the monster, stood the whimpering man. The fiend took the stab, gripped the man with its wounded arms, and pulled the poor soul towards its middle, blank gray face.

The wind assisted, pushing Svarde, the man towards the fiend.

Giving Svarde a perfect target.

The Guardian pulled the trigger. The crossbow jerked. The loaded bolt flew over the whimpering man's head, right into the fiend's circular, sucking mouth.

The wind died first, the faces cracked second, but the conversations, the spent memories of who knew how many, those kept on going as Svarde fell to his knees, hands reaching for the whimpering man, not knowing if there was anything left to find.

CHAPTER 29
BANDIT CAMP

The lava flow brought them through a misted wall, chill droplets gathering on Wax as he gripped his pole. Sledge again in front, the two other bandits behind. Between them, on the large stone serving as their raft, lay their possessions, the meager remnants after several more days spent riding the heat.

The raft came to a stop of its own accord, the gray-white fog blotting out everything save Sledge's shadowed form. The rock shook, a grinding crunch rattled Wax's bones. Their ride coming to an end.

"Gather the satchels, follow me," Sledge ordered. "We're here."

The three bandits had barely spoken to Wax on the ride, and he'd been happy to oblige them. Instead, Wax turned to the skar, keeping at all possible times one hand on the necklace, on the warm Vis gem. When he touched the emerald, it seemed to speak to him, a soft whisper in a language he couldn't make out, if it was even words at all. Nevertheless, the tone didn't hold the hate, the loathing, the frustration baked into Sledge's every word.

Wax wouldn't call himself a fragile soul, but day after day treated like an animal could beat a man down. Before the ferrites, before the escape, Sledge had seemed an honorable thief.

Death and failure, it seemed, could break her.

The lava's end seemed to restore her spirit, though. She even reached back to help Wax off the rock into the fog, warned him to take the pole with, use it to steady his feet on the shifting ground below.

"The lava's growing the land here, but it takes time," Sledge said as Wax took his first steps free from the floe. "It's temperamental, prone to breaking. Test every footfall before you make it."

"How long?" Wax asked.

"You'll find out when we make it," Sledge replied. "Though we'll not see another night in the wilds."

That prediction proved wildly off. Their slow walk lasted only minutes till the fog thinned, the rocks hardening. Before the mist, Sledge said the ocean neared, its chill waters clashing with the lava to form the wall.

Now, as the mist's last curtain parted, Wax followed Sledge onto a rugged lava rock peninsula, one jutting out into crashing waves. On either side, a broad beach overrun with scurrying critters and brown sand sprawled. Gulls speckled the sky, their white forms whirling and diving at those same critters, their calls a welcome change from the lava's incessant, lethal pops.

Below the birds, to the south, came other noises, civilization's song. Wax followed Sledge's turn that way, though he didn't copy her relieved sigh.

Their target looked to be built up along the beach and bleeding back into the rocky land behind it. Thatched shelters, dredged up dirt walls circling brush-covered roofs.

Campfires burned, the smoke climbing into the clear afternoon sky. Laughter coasted over the waves, mingling with some song.

"Home," Sledge said, nodding. "Always good to find it where we left it."

"Your house moves often?"

Sledge flashed a grin as the other two bandits emerged, satchels loaded on their backs and shoulders. "Do what I do, and you'll learn to always be restless."

The bandit camp did have a nervous energy, even though the singsong vibe, the clashing as ale mugs clattered against one another, did what they could to dispel it. Wax, now carrying his own share of the satchels, saw speed's necessity with every look. Weapons lingered on easily-snagged racks, hilts up and blades gleaming. Salted fish and harvested vegetables—garden plots dotted the rocky hillside above the camp—lay in clumps, satchels nearby for ready packing. The eyes he saw, when Wax didn't draw their attention, seemed to always circle back to the horizon, waiting for something to appear.

"We're not all so cozy as you," announced Eggrad, the camp's captain after swapping introductions. "Permanence is a luxury for us."

The bandit chief didn't hold much with pomp, but the hall where Wax found himself did ornament its spare stone and sand with captured goods. Foti-made jewelry lay on one side, piled atop a flat rock. Nearby, on the ground, lay collected gear. Quik's wooden gauntlets made the newest editions to the pile. Past that, continuing on the northward side, lay random valuables. A book, some odd device Wax didn't recognize, and several bottles of Tamas red wine.

Eggrad kept himself in the room's center, flanked by two guards who didn't seem to take their roles all that seriously. The woman on the right tossed a single knife up over and over, always catching it by the hilt. The other seemed asleep on his feet, both eyes closed with his hands hooked into a ragged belt.

"Permanence and quality," Wax said. Eggrad, like so many other bandits, wore a mismatched, used linen and leather collection. "I'm not impressed."

Eggrad chuckled. "Vis picked a feisty Renewal this time." He nodded at Sledge. "I see you found something on the journey?"

"What do you mean?" Sledge asked.

"I mean that new sword on your hip, or am I mistaking what you left here with?"

"Not her sword," Wax said. "It's mine."

"Nothing's yours anymore, boy." Eggrad pointed towards the gear pile. "Give it, Sledge. Consider it your price to pay for the ones you lost."

Sledge folded her arms, "Every mouth we don't have to feed makes more for the rest of us."

Wax blinked. Was Sledge saying she'd set up the casualties? Were the ferrites planned?

"You're making my argument for me," Eggrad countered. Unlike Sledge, the man kept his hands on his waist. "Us, you say. The blade belongs in the pile. We'll divvy it up at the season's end, just as always."

"Where it'll wind up with you," Sledge countered.

"Is that a challenge?" Eggrad bared his teeth, mottled and mangy though they were.

Sledge tensed. Would she take Eggrad on right now? Wax hadn't been in the camp an hour yet, but what would a fight like that mean? A possibility of escape?

"It might be, someday," Sledge muttered, hand moving towards the Foti blade. She drew the weapon, tossed it past

Wax to the gear pile where it landed with a stiff clank. "You're going to push someone too far, Eggrad, and they'll kill you for it."

"I have no doubt you're right," Eggrad said. "That day, however, is not today." He turned back to Wax, a new light in his eyes. "Well then, Renewal. Let's see it."

"See what?"

"You're not dumb enough to pull off an idiotic question, boy. The skar."

"Stop calling me boy."

Eggrad tilted his head, brought a hand up to the flimsy gray-and-red goatee on his chin. "What should I call you, then? Your name? No. You haven't earned that yet. Are you a man? Hardly. Sledge captured you, dragged you all the way here. No man I know would suffer such an embarrassment."

Sledge flushed. Wax clenched his right hand. Eggrad was near enough Wax might be able to get off a step and a swing, deliver a socking blow to the man's jaw before the guards reacted.

That, though, wouldn't earn him anything save a beating. Pan would counsel caution. Find the right path and take it.

"What do you want it for?" Wax asked, his left hand moving to the skar, finding it beneath his torn canvas shirt.

"I don't, but our clients dearly do," Eggrad said. "I'm asking you for it, because I would like to feed my people, their families through the coming winter. A donation, and one we'd thank you for."

"That's nothing against the lives an Aegis would save."

Eggrad laughed. "You? An Aegis? Too scraggly, too snappy. This is serious business, boy. Best leave it—"

Wax jumped, not at Eggrad but left, towards the gear

pile and one shining hilt in particular. His hand closed on the Foti blade, and Wax whipped it up and around, angling for the face, the body he knew had to be there.

The sword struck iron, the gauntleted wrist of the sleeping guard, who'd snapped to his senses fast enough to block Wax's strike. With the Foti blade knocked out wide, Wax had no defense for what came next: the guard's other hand, balled into a fist and crashing into Wax's temple.

THE CHILL WOKE HIM, the wind slicing through Wax's thin clothes. At his feet, a wave tickled his toes, sliding in beneath him. Wax blinked, tried to shake off the headache, and felt dried blood caked to his left eye. When he reached to brush it off, Wax's hands wouldn't move. Bound, along with his legs. Wax traced the feeling, saw the wood set deep in the sand on either side.

"Awake?" asked Sledge. She sat in the sand before him, her bow resting on the grains beside her. "Or just another twitch?"

"What's going on?"

With an arrow, Sledge drew an idle pattern in the sand. Behind her, the day leaked away. The bandit camp's fires stood out now, the rocks a leering silhouette behind the shelters.

"Eggrad's happy to play word games all day," Sledge said, "but if you try something physical, he takes it personally."

"So I should've let him walk all over me?"

"You want to live, you do as he asks."

"Is that what you do?"

Sledge shook her head, "You're not smart enough to rile me up, Wax." She picked the arrow from the dirt, pointed it at the Vis man. "He took the skar from you. He'll take your life too unless you make a promise."

Wax didn't have to free his hands to confirm the truth. The skar's warmth had vanished, its whispers silent. His mouth went dry, his muscles shivering not from the cold.

"What promise?"

"To stay. To join us."

Sledge didn't seem interested in the words as she spoke them, as if a request for Wax to give up his livelihood was a simple thing.

"Why would I do that?"

"Because you'll stay out here, tied to these beams, until you do. When high tide comes in, you'll either freeze to death or some curious fish will take a nibble."

"Doesn't sound like I have much choice."

"You don't. And when you say yes, you'll be watched every minute for months until Eggrad's convinced you this is the only way to live." Sledge took a deep breath. "Every second of your every day will be steeped in this life until it's the only one you can imagine."

"You don't seem sold."

"I'm here, aren't I?" Sledge asked, standing up. "It's not a perfect life, but it's a damn sight better than dying down in those mines. On Foti, you can't ask for much more." She turned towards the bandit camp, made to leave. "I'll be back in a few hours. Make up your mind by then. No use dying for nothing, Wax."

"My brother and sister will come back for me."

Sledge laughed as she trudged up the sand, "Your brother and sister are dead. And even if they're not, nobody on this isle will help them."

Wax wanted to call out another spicy retort, but there wasn't one to find. His wrists and ankles hurt where the rope bound him to the wood. The cold stole his breath, peppering his skin with bumps. Hunger gnawed, thirst scratched. Not once in all his time on Vis had he felt so miserable, not one time.

This is what Pan had given him. No grand adventure, no heralded journey. Just a struggle, one ending with nothing, nothing save the cold, the dark, and the sea.

CHAPTER 30

A GUARDIAN AGAIN

The lelune bloomed again tonight. Ami walked past them, down the crater towards the familiar prison. No Najahn guard paced her steps for the first time in days, yet their chains weighed on her almost as heavy as her sword, her Foti armor. Gladdring's declaration, before Mattimo even stopped struggling in the sea, naming Ami as his tool and little else.

"You will work for me, with me, and as I say, with no lies, tricks, or deception," Gladdring said there on that beach, half-turned back to the cave and his tower. "Mattimo's death will cost me, but yours, not a soul will notice or care."

Catya would.

Though, as she trudged towards the Aegis and the Wound, Ami faltered in that thought. How long before Catya's mind withered like her body already had? Would she even recognize Ami now, or had the stress ruined Catya?

The word came as the day's experiments—another fiend, another skar, another small success—wound to a close: fiends poured from the Wound, the Wards were being overwhelmed, and the Aegis needed her Guardian.

Gladdring gave Ami up to the shieldwarden, blathering about the cost to Noctia, about how he was still glad to make this sacrifice for the good of all.

Though they' d been on the tower's doorstep, scholars and Najahn all around, Ami had sorely wanted to break Gladdring's neck in that moment. A simple reach and twist would've done it.

Again she'd held for Catya.

"How many lives you've saved," Ami muttered.

"What's that?" asked the lone Ward standing outside the Aegis's home, the bone-white canvas stretching up and over a gash in the ground. That gash, the Wound, supposedly led straight to Noctia's heart, or where one had been when the goddess still lived. "Are you the Guardian?"

Ami read the clean armor, the unscarred voulge, and a fresh chakram riding the purple-black ensemble. The young face behind it all wasn't a shock, more that someone so new could be standing here, in this place.

"It's worse than I thought," Ami said, straightening. "How many years, Ward? Or should I say days?"

The man flinched. Another bad sign. Wards had to be confident, ready to face anything because anything could face them.

"It's quiet now," the man said. "The fiends fight each other as much as us. It's a good time to visit."

"Not a visit. I'm staying."

At least till Gladdring tugged on her leash.

The Aegis, for all her stature, all her importance to the isles lived a pauper's life. Food and drink came carried, yes, and for the first few years when Catya was well enough to make her own orders, there were happy times shared among the hard stone beneath the canvas. Entertainment would visit, musicians, writers, even politicians from around the isles paying respects and giving gifts.

Those dwindled as Catya did, and now she lingered, barely a wisp, on her stone throne. Blankets cloaked her as winter's onset turned the Noctia nights chill, though Ami thought the standing torches around the space kept things warm enough.

The Wound filled the room's center, a jagged cut unbent by so many years. Ami looked to it first when she came in, expecting a fiend to emerge right then, crawling forth with a spider's legs or a bat's wings and demanding their blood, their souls, or something somehow worse.

Instead, she saw Wards. Nearly a dozen, though most were either tending mild wounds, polishing equipment, or indulging in the stacked and set food and drink on the lone dark wood table near the entry. A calm time indeed.

Only two seemed on watch duty, both armed with their charkams and standing at the Wound's edge, staring down into the black like Ami used to stare at the stars from her Noctia balcony, looking for some reason to care.

"Guardian, we're glad you're here," came Terrevin's voice, its owner standing up from a new desk just inside the door.

A tablet lay across the desk's surface, coated in smudges from lines erased many times over. Fresh markings looked like days, names in a long table. Terrevin loomed over them, giving Ami a respectful nod at far odds from the cocky attitude she'd first expressed back at the Guardian's apartment.

How long ago that seemed.

Terrevin's one-time confidence had bled away to wariness, her left hand tapping idly on the table while wrinkles creased a forehead still in thought about something other than the new arrival's sword. Nevertheless, when Ami returned the greeting, Terrevin settled into a smile as she returned to the stiff chair.

"But a moment, then you can go to Catya as long as you like," Terrevin said.

Catya didn't seem to notice Ami had arrived, so the Guardian did as the shieldwarden asked, making sure to fold her arms, keep her face stern. Respect or no, Ami wasn't going to be Terrevin's lackey.

She'd already given enough ground to Gladdring on that score, and there were limits to the damage her dignity could take.

"You know why you're here?" Terrevin asked.

"Your Wards can't keep Catya safe."

Terrevin sniffed, shifted her tapping hand to the tablet and ran a single finger along the names on the left side.

"It's because we *are* keeping her safe, Ami," Terrevin said. "We're doing everything we can so your friend stays alive. The fiends are doing their best to make it difficult, and our body count, both injured and worse, is razing our numbers."

"So you weren't prepared."

Terrevin breathed deep, closed her eyes. Deflecting Ami's needles then. Ami readied a harsher barb, aware her annoyance came less about Catya's safety and more at being stuffed in Gladdring's box for days upon days. Realizing that only annoyed Ami further.

Catya's cough killed it all.

The cough itself came as a weak thing, a dying animals gas. Ami's head snapped around, sighted on the Aegis as Catya's eyes opened and found hers.

"Ami," Catya said, a whisper but one that found its target. "You're here."

Terrevin could keep her breath and her excuses. Ami ignored the Wards looks as she walked to Catya's side, knelt by the Aegis and took up a hand more bone than skin.

"They kept me from you for too long," Ami said.

"For a reason, or were they jealous?" Catya's eyes, damn them, still had her sparkle.

"Jealous." Ami took her own deep breath now. Always a war being this close to Catya, a melding as possibilities lost collided with continuing hope. "I haven't been idle."

"So I've heard," Catya said, and Ami started. "Don't look so surprised, Ami. I've lived here for more than a decade. You aren't my only friend."

"Then what?"

"Tell me first, is there a chance?"

Oh, that sparkle. A life that'd suffused Catya's every moment, a leaping light. Could Ami crush it with the truth? That the skars offered some chance to future Najahn fighters, but nothing so far for the Aegis?

"Maybe," Ami said.

Catya tilted her head, "Are you lying to me, Guardian?"

"I can't. Not to you."

"No. I believe you still owe me from our games on the road." Catya tried a laugh, coughed again instead. Shook it off, bent closer to Ami's ear. "Be careful. This isn't what it seems."

Ami fought to keep herself still, "What?"

"Not everyone wants you, or I, to survive."

"Who?"

"That much I don't know. Only that their weapons aren't quite as loyal as their masters believe." Catya's grip tightened, like a feather's touch. "Just keep yourself safe, Ami. You're the one I worry about."

"It's yourself—"

"It's you, and only you." Catya's eyes went towards the drinks, the food. "Think you could fetch me some of that Kance tea? It really is the best."

Terrevin met Ami at the refreshments. Filled up her own earthen mug, stuffing a small metal ball with the loose tea leaves and settling it into hot water, maintained by a low cooking brazier nearby.

"We didn't finish our conversation," Terrevin said.

"Really? I thought we did. You can't keep up, so you need my sword."

"I need more than your sword," Terrevin replied. "I need what you're working on with Gladdring."

Ami stopped, Catya's mug steeping in her hands. "The last person to dig into his business wound up dead."

"Gladdring's going to die if the Wound breaks," Terrevin replied, looking not the least concerned. "You'll ask him. If he refuses, then—"

"It's not ready," Ami said. "No matter how much you want it to be, what he's doing will only get your people killed."

Ami herself could barely get the skars to respond. Some Ward not knowing what to do would only let a fiend tear them from head to toe while trying to parse a skar's whispering madness.

"Then what other miracles can you offer?" Terrevin asked. "Because I am trying to keep my people alive, and I am running out of options."

Of all things, Svarde's reckless mission to the Dark Below tickled Ami's memory.

"Maybe we attack instead of defend?" Ami suggested.

"Go at the fiends rather than waiting for them to come to us?"

"Going beyond the Aegis's protection invites death," Terrevin countered.

"Death is coming for us whether we invite it or not, shieldwarden. I'm thinking we might be better off trying to fight it first."

"We only need to hold out till the next Renewal completes." Terrevin backed off from the table. "You forget, Ami, that my Wards have families, lives beyond these duties. I can't ask them to accept suicide, not even a desperate one."

Ami watched Terrevin return to her desk before going back to Catya's side. Suicide. A hard word for a mission to save the seven isles. Then again, that's what the Circle had deemed Svarde's efforts. Suicide, and nothing more.

As Catya took the steaming mug from Ami's hands, a Ward overlooking the Wound whistled. The man's second echoed the noise, bringing his hands to his mouth and calling out a readying shout.

"How many?" Terrevin asked, picking up her voulge from its lean against the desk.

"One," replied the first Ward. "A big one, and angry."

"Aren't you glad you came?" Catya said as the Wards burst into a frenzy. "How bored were you?"

At Terrevin's direction, Wards began dropping Foti fire-bombs down the wound. Others picked up Whent throwing stones, launching them into the breached ground. Still more moved small palisades up to the Wound's edge, their metal tips holding Vis-crafted natural poisons, meant to turn any beast into a paralyzed, sickened, sloth.

"Ready arms!" Terrevin called, the Ward defenders

dropping back, half taking the closer ranks with their voulges ready while the others unslung their chakrams.

Ami stood, drew Flamebreak and held it clasped before her. She planted herself between the Wound and Catya. Flamebreak's skar glowed an orange fire, ready. Now, listening for it, Ami could hear its whispers, its eagerness to lunge forward and find a foe.

Don't worry, Ami thought, it'll be here soon enough.

The fiend didn't announce its arrival with a roar, didn't shriek or spew bile up from the Wound in an acid rain. Instead, the creature erupted, leaping from the opening straight towards the shelter's roof. Its rise tore through the canvas canopy, exposing the night sky. Into it rose a bleeding, burning, misshapen monster whose flailing, dripping wings coated a body that kept coming, rising and writhing into the air. A furred serpent, a cat stretched too long and with a bat's wings, the parallels blurred as the fiend's charge faded, its wings, beating like a hummingbirds, failing to keep it aloft.

"Here it comes!" Terrevin called.

And the monster, blotting out the stars above, came crashing down upon them.

CHAPTER 31

A SHIP, A SHOT

Quik kept them alive with tricks Bliss had never seen, never imagined. The hunter led their trek over the wastes north with narrow guidance, strict rules. Movement and moments couldn't be wasted, even with the toleket's plentiful protein stuffing makeshift satchels carved from its netting skin. Over that first night, Quik tore apart the dead fiend too, using its broken teeth to fashion crude knives, battering its shell with rocks to get at gooier insides, including more water sacs.

"He's real gross," Torny said more than once as the days crawled by and Quik suggested slathering themselves with mud to keep the sun and the flies at bay. "He's really your brother?"

Bliss nodded and did as Quik suggested. Vis custom demanded deferring to the most experienced hunter on an expedition, and this was nothing if not a journey through harsh lands unfamiliar to them all. Even Torny, supposedly a Foti native, claimed she'd never ventured beyond the cities until Sledge scooped her up on this latest trip.

"How could I say no?" Torny quipped one night by another campfire, a quick thing burning scrub brush and sticks just long enough to heat their lava-cooked dinner. "A chance to leave behind the ash and ore for a life of scintillating banditry? Exciting stuff."

Quik had been gone for that conversation, had been quiet most other times as well. After the initial shock of seeing his sister and Torny alive at all, he'd fallen into a frowning sulk whenever he wasn't giving orders, advice to follow.

Bliss could guess as to why, because the same feeling threatened to tug her under too. Would've, if not for Torny's incessant conversation.

They'd not only failed as Guardians, they'd failed their family. Simple, devastating, as that.

'You have to push it away,' Bliss signed to Quik, walking beside him on their fifth day. 'We haven't abandoned him. We didn't have a choice.'

'You, maybe,' Quik replied using the signs, keeping the trailing Torny out of the conversation. 'I chose to leave. I could've turned back, tried to ambush them. Fight.'

'Why didn't you?'

Less an accusation, more a push to get Quik to stop hating himself. Hopefully her brother would catch the meaning. Quik, though, just sighed and turned his eyes forward. The rising dawn broke over something new today: a land not all shaped over by black rock, that instead offered long grasses and spindly trees rising up in narrow groves. Birds, more than just buzzards, alighted from the tall grasses and dove back in among them.

A good sign: food must wait in those stalks.

"Amazing," Torny said when they all stood at the lava

rock's edge, taking a break before venturing into the long grasses. "I didn't think we'd actually make it to the end."

"You wouldn't have," Quik said.

Torny laughed, "Absolutely not. My thanks to you, oh hunter of the wilds. Your ways with the mud and the guts are truly remarkable."

Quik narrowed his eyes.

'She's joking,' Bliss signed at him.

"I know she's joking," Quik replied. "She's still a bandit, and she's lucky we didn't leave her back there."

"Oh, you could've tried, but I would've followed you."

"You would've failed."

"Maybe. Guess we'll never know."

Bliss stood up, put herself between the two. Her brother's face kept getting more furrowed, a slight flush rising in its depths. A mood she knew well enough: Quik would suggest something stupid soon, something not easily taken back.

Torny, too, would be cocky enough to call him on it.

Instead, holding her staff, Bliss pointed northward. With her left hand, she flashed signs Torny knew by now.

'Let's go.'

Smoke and civilized smells hit the air by mid-day, along with salt and a sea breeze. Torny noted Foti's aisle narrowed as it climbed north, ending in a point. They weren't quite to that edge yet, but the Great Forge and its attendant towns would be close.

"Which means we can get a bath," Torny said as they wandered through the tall grasses, scattering vermin and birds with every step. "The hot springs up here are supposed to be amazing."

"Not till we get my brother back," Quik said from the front.

"Yeah, sure, but unless you're planning to hike back the whole way—"

"I will. Once we get some supplies."

"And how're you planning to do that? Beg? Sell some of this rancid toleket meat we've been carrying almost a week?"

Bliss whirled, put her staff's end against Torny's chest. The bandit shrugged, kept her wide grin up and open.

"What?" Torny whispered. "Your brother's so serious. If Wax isn't dead by now, then he's either made a deal or joined up with Sledge's crew."

Bliss blinked, 'What?'

"It's what they do. Take all you've got, leave you desperate, then let you join to earn it all back," Torny reached up, moved Bliss's staff out of the way. "How do you think they keep growing? You've gotta be almost dead to want to take up with them."

Bliss nodded at Torny, letting her eyebrows ask the question.

"Oh yeah. I was. Still am, I guess." Torny laughed again. "I made some real bad choices, but hey, who hasn't?"

Quik's shout called an end to the conversation, especially when his follow-up proved so enticing: "We're here."

If Kitaye, the Vis city, built itself within the trees marking its inlet, the Foti town ran rough over the land to make its own. The long grasses and thin trees vanished at the town's outskirts, giving way to plowed fields laid over with harvested crops. Stone and sand-blasted bricks framed shallow single-story homes, a far cry from Smythe's taller, dominating structures. Cleared paths blew with seaside sand making the migration up from the nearby beach and the spiderwebbing port jutting out from the town's westward point. The people occupying the place glanced in startled surprise at the trio as they made their way into town, a look Torny put down to their bedraggled appearance, not the fact that they existed at all.

"Down south, it's Smythe and that's it," Torny said as they walked past the town's outskirts. "You've got places like Jarl's Tooth running mines in the lava tubes, but otherwise nobody goes anywhere. Up here, it's ports, it's trading between Rana and Whent. There's action."

"You've been here before?" Quik asked, curiosity seeming, for the moment, to override his loathing of the bandit.

"'Course not. Why would I come to a place like this?"

Quik caught Bliss's attention, rolled his eyes. Torny didn't always make sense, Bliss could admit that, but she seemed less dismal than her brother, so Bliss would put up with her.

The town's center offered an inn, several shops, and the usual standbys required for civilized living: butchers, builders, grocers and the like. If not for the different architecture, the windswept vibes and linen clothes, Bliss could've said it felt like home.

Especially once they caught a clear view of the port, sprawling out before them on a downward slope from the town's middle. Much like Smythe, the people around them all seemed to be going to or coming from the seaside center. The reason rose up from the water: two ships, a heavy Foti galleon taking on crate after crate in cargo, and another swifter craft flying purple and black sails.

"A Najahn ship in a town like this?" Torny mused. "Bit odd. We're not far from the Great Forge, but there's closer ports."

"They're the help we need," Quik said. "For once, a bit of luck goes our way."

The hunter squared his shoulders, started off only for Bliss to grab him, pull Quik to a standstill.

'We'll get no help looking like this,' Bliss signed. 'And I bet we smell worse.' Torny's point about Wax's existence buttressed the feeling. 'A few hours won't make the difference now.'

Quik's own stomach echoed Bliss's sentiments, growling above the town's quiet bustle as the hunter opened his mouth. Quik shut it, grimaced, and looked towards the inn.

"A meal and a bath, then, but we wan't take long."

The inn proved its location wasn't an accident. Several hot springs, a merging between sea and underground lava, bubbled up in its back. The trio had to give up all their harvested fiend teeth, their makeshift satchels, and their leftover toleket meat—good for bait, so the innkeeper said—but the payment earned them a fresh fish meal, bread, and, yes, that most coveted item: a bath.

Waiting for each of them after their dip was a refreshed, albeit thin, set of linen slops. Good enough to wear, too little to keep anyone warm in the wind, the three nonetheless didn't have anything else. Even Torny's leathers were little more than scraps after the long walk without any oils, any care to give them.

"Still, at least we look like people and not especially ugly fiends," Torny said as they left the inn, the day crawling towards dinner. "Don't know about you two, but I'm a big fan of not having grit between my teeth and my toes."

Quik stopped at her words, the three of them on the street's side heading towards the port. Crusted sand and short lava-and-limestone cliffs rose about them. Gulls dominated the skies now, and the day's catch overpowered the sea smell on the air.

"Why are you still here?" Quik asked. "We made it to the town. Shouldn't you be off finding someone else to rob?"

For once, Torny's glibness failed her. She folded her arms, looked at Bliss.

"Honest, I don't really have anywhere to go," Torny said. "Figured if you're going back to the bandits to get your brother, I could ride along."

"And what, rejoin them? Take the first chance with that knife and stab us in the back?"

'She wouldn't do that,' Bliss signed fast. 'Not after all this.'

"Why do you trust her?" Quik rounded on Bliss now. "You've been defending her all this time, as if she didn't help cause all this."

'Because without her I'd be dead.'

When Bliss's first attack against the fiend around the lava pit resulted in a battered staff, a tooth scraping up her ankle, it'd been Torny hooting and hollering, throwing rocks and drawing the fiend away.

'She could've left, could've backed off and let me die, but she didn't,' Bliss signed. 'You weren't there.'

Quik rocked back on his feet at that, a punch Bliss didn't realize she'd thrown until that moment. The hunter, though, rebounded fast, uncoiling that same protector's rage to throw an angry finger at Torny.

"Bliss buys you your life, all right?" Quik said. "She buys you nothing else. You try anything, I'll snap your neck or get the Najahn to do it for me."

Torny gulped, let that fear get nowhere near her eyes.

"YOu keep talking, Quik, if it makes you feel better. But how about we do it on their boat before they leave?"

The Najahn ship did seem like it was knotting up for the night. The crew that'd been loading some small crates looked to be gone, and evening lanterns had winked out around the ship's sides, getting it ready for a quiet evening.

"On that, at least, I can agree," Quik muttered, turning and leading them on.

"Real piece of work, your brother," Torny whispered to Bliss.

'He thinks we're his responsibility,' Bliss signed back, before remembering at Torny's confused look that the girl didn't know all the signs yet. A simpler message, then.

'He loves us.'

Torny, nodding in the twilight, seemed to understand that.

CHAPTER 32

ON THE WATER

How the people of Foti could stand to live in their towns with their squalor and smell mystified Quik. Smythe and Jarl's Tooth had, at the first, a certain wonder at the difference that'd compelled his fascination, but now the mist cleared. Everything on this industrial isle stank, its people walked with misery on their shoulders, and their desperate greed had stolen both Quik's purpose and his brother.

Now Bliss seemed taken with it too, collecting the bandit like some new accessory. Torny's cocky rebuttals and jabs wouldn't bother Quik so much—enough, anyway, that he nearly slipped on the water-splashed pier heading towards the Najahn ship—if the bandit didn't keep dashing looks at his sister like the two were best friends.

They should've left the bandit in the wastes, where Torny would've found the slow death she and all her kind deserved.

The Najahn, at least, ought to see things Quik's way. The Noctia forces rarely seemed tolerant of either banditry or foolishness, both areas Torny covered with aplomb. If they didn't run her off or throw her into the sea . . . well, Bliss would come around.

She had to.

Up close, the Najahn ship both paled against and exceeded the neighboring Foti galleon. Quik walked between them on a wide, long pier spaced here and there with leftover crates for the morning's work.

The Foti beast matched the isle in its sensibilities, blackened wood buttressed by metal rings, the vessel creaked in the soft surf as evening turned to night. No sails unfurled, great masts disappearing into the sky. Windows, dirty glass looked out Quik's way.

The Najahn sloop, by contrast, gave a svelte figure. Brighter, sun-bleached and almost gray in its wood, the craft kept its metal slimmer, its secrets hidden. Its own three masts were shorter, yet seemed decked out with more ropes, each catching Sichi's glow like a pink spiderweb in the sky. Secure lanterns flickered along the edges, rounded globes giving the boat a life the Foti ship couldn't match.

A life echoed by the Najahn ship's ramp, still down despite the hour. Near it, the voulge leaning against several crates and smoking some pipe, stood a guard. He eyed Quik long before the Vis man came near, had apparently sized Quik up and determined that, despite his muscles, the man posed little threat.

"Don't need any help," the Najahn said, loosing a mint-green puff into the air before he spoke. "Whatever you're looking for, it isn't here."

"Help is what I'm looking for," Quik said.

The Najahn crept his stare over Quik's shoulder. "Those two looking for help as well? A whole family?"

"It's not them that need it," Quik replied, drawing even with the guard. The man wore his Najahn leathers, a tunic and thick breeches beneath. A good plan with the night's chill descending, a feeling made more acute out here on the water. Quik's own rags let him know he'd be uncomfortable out here before long.

"You're expecting me to care?" The Najahn asked.

Quik nodded, "That's exactly what I expect."

The Najahn captain matched her guard in outfit, in skepticism, but at least the conversation happened aboard the ship, in the relatively warm confines of the captain's cabin. Quik told the story for the second time, the bandits, Wax, and the lava flow. When he finished, the Najahn captain looked at Torny.

The guard at the pier remained with them, no longer looking so lazy, his voulge at the ready. He stood back by the door, a position Quik noted would make any flight by Torny an impossible endeavor. Unless she planned to barrel past the captain and throw herself through a window to the sea.

A satisfying end that would be.

"You're one of them?" The Najahn captain asked. "These bandits?"

"Was," Torny said, no stress showing on her face, in her voice. "I'm making a career change."

The captain's return smile was all teeth. Bright ones too, something Quik wouldn't have noticed on Vis but stood out on this ash-blasted isle. In fact, the captain and her ship kept things clean all around. What Quik expected, and for once, he was gratified to see those expectations met.

"A wise decision," the captain said. "Thieves like you are heading for a swift end. The fiends'll take you, and if they don't, we will."

Torny snorted, drawing surprise from everyone save

Quik. Being dismissive to authority seemed to be the girl's default mode.

"The people I was with have been doing this for years," Torny answered. "Why would they stop now?"

The captain nodded, "Because the man who used to run this circuit's no longer here."

"What, you knocked him off?"

"Worse," the captain said. "He's been promoted. Sent back to Noctia almost a year ago now." She leaned forward, put her elbows on the sparse table before her, accompanied on its clean wood by navigation charts and things Quik couldn't read, didn't understand. "My names Pavarde, Captain Pavarde, and I've orders to put a stop to your nonsense."

Quik sat back in the chair, let a grin spread over his face. At last, a true victory. "Then you'll help us get our brother back?"

Pavarde snapped her eyes to Quik, "Don't call him that. He's not your brother now. He's the Renewal from Vis. That's what matters, and that's who I'm going to get. Tomorrow morning, we set sail south."

"And we're coming?" Quik asked, catching Bliss signing the same question his way.

"Of course," Pavarde replied. "Witnesses to tell the tale of how the Najahn keep its Renewals safe in the face of banditry are always welcome."

Pavarde stashed the trio with the cargo in the sloop's lower deck, a dire accommodation if the trip were to last longer than a day or two. Pavarde, though, claimed the sloop could travel fast, particularly with the winter winds. With that thought, Quik slept full and peacefully for the first time since leaving Smythe.

The journey south flew by, though Quik again found

Bliss spending too much time with Torny. Teaching the bandit her signs, while Torny replied with lessons on locks and picking them, on sleight of hand, on the sorts of things no Vis hunter would ever need to use. Yet, when Quik tried to remind Bliss of that fact, she shoo'ed him away.

Pavarde, thankfully, was happy to keep Quik by her side. The captain alternated questioning Quik about his isle, his experience, with stories about her own, and the Najahn.

The purple and gold couldn't be content any longer with the sidelines, with only their own interests, Pavarde explained. She'd been at the town as part of a patrol along the isle's western edge, looking for signs any fiends might be emerging, nesting.

"Nesting?" Quik asked.

"The worst," Pavarde replied. "On Kance and Tamas, already, we've found fiends trying to build homes for themselves. Attempting to reproduce. Not just wild destruction, as with the old ones."

The possibility some hostile creatures might try to make the isles their new territory explained the Najahn's growing reach, that and the isles themselves, who were proving more restless this time.

"Past Renewals, the Circle sends out the command and everyone plays nice with each other, recognizes the disaster for what it is," Pavarde said, stopping to spit over the sloop's side as it shot over waves, Foti's land always in sight to the east. The Wastes much more pleasant when Quik wasn't walking them. "Now they keep up their squabbles like they matter. Rana raids everyone, Kance's queens are locked in a power struggle trying to pull in Tamas and your eastern city."

"Mottilan."

"Sure. And Noctia, as ever, is filled with knives." Pavarde took a deep breath. Her purple and black uniform sucked in the sun, a noble icon. "Out here, at least, you can see the blade coming for your back."

"On Vis, these things don't happen."

Pavarde raised an eyebrow. "My naive friend, if you think they don't happen, then you aren't looking hard enough. It's in our nature, and if you want to climb to a better station, you'd better learn how to spot, and how to stab."

"Did you?"

Pavarde nodded. "The Najahn teach you well, and tie you enough to your fellow soldier to keep the truly bad to a minimum. The game, though, must be played." She laughed, shook her head. "But you don't have to worry about that. You'll walk your Guardian's path, and when your Renewal fails or succeeds, return to your isle, with its flowers and its hanoko, and forget all this."

The bandit camp emerged near the second day's end, cooking fish announcing its presence along with the squat structures up the beach. Pavarde called the crew, those not actively working the sails, to arms. She herself, clad now in gold, purple, and black mail, strode to the ship's bow. Behind her, another guard held Noctia's Crowned Circle flag high, letting anyone watching know what doom was coming for them.

Quik, Bliss, and Torny hung near the ship's center, both protected and, as Torny noted with her dry humor, kept encircled by other Najahn.

"What's our job again? To stay on the ship and do nothing?" Torny asked.

"What would you suggest?" Quik replied. "Or do you

want to run out there and join your friends as they get slaughtered?"

Torny shrugged, "The captain's all confident, sure, but to hear Sledge tell it, there's not a dozen out here but closer to fifty. More than there are pointy-headed Najahn on this boat."

"One Najahn's worth a dozen of yours."

Quik flinched as Bliss elbowed him. Torny, though, just laughed.

"Say what you want," Torny replied. "I'd just be ready to move."

Quik took a step away, put the camp in a good view as the sloop ran itself up on the soft sand. On either side, ramps slid down and Najahn stepped off the boat, armored, carrying voulges and chakram, ready to enforce the order that'd been so lacking on this cursed place. The sun bent low behind the shallow cliffs, painting them black save for the first on the beach, the shdows moving among them.

Shadows that would, no doubt, cease moving forever in a short time.

"Wax," Quik muttered, "I've come back for you."

CHAPTER 33

BRINGING HER BACK

The fallen fiend left more than its dusty bones and black cloak behind. The gray faces, six in all and with ever-so-slightly different versions of agonized howls stretching their lines, clattered to the rock floor. Trailing their sound came a discordant noise, one Svarde took a moment to parse as a dozen, a hundred conversations playing out at once.

Memories, leaking out and dissipating.

The Guardian held the whimpering man's head in his hands, already cooling, already so still. Svarde saw no wound, but the man's chest didn't rise and fall with any breath, nor did his lips move, his eyes open. At least, there in that moment, the fiend's final victim looked at peace.

"Kivi," Svarde said, setting the man's head down. "Go sniff around, make sure nothing else is hiding."

That there could be more monsters here, or even a second fiend, seemed the height of horror, but assuming otherwise would be worse still. Caution, guard, were necessary in the Dark Below.

"He's gone?" Rasslebeck asked, joining Svarde in looking at the whimpering man.

"Whatever's left of him, yes," Svarde answered. "He interrupted the fiend. Saved me."

"Found his courage at the end, then. No better time."

Svarde nodded, stood, slotted his axes back in their sheaths. Held the crossbow towards Maena as she emerged from her crumpled position. She stared at the weapon in Svarde's hand for longer than she should've, then grabbed it with a growl. Her hands worked fast, pulling and slotting another bolt in the thing, ratcheting back the string so it could fire in a split second.

"Ready," she announced.

"Then keep watch," Svarde replied. Behind him, Rasslebeck folded the whimpering man's arms. Burying the body wasn't an option in these stone caverns, yet another solution had itself ready.

The question was whether the whimpering man would be the only one left here.

"Pennifer, can you hear me?" Svarde asked. The woman had meandered to the room's far side. She ran her fingers along a quartz line, entranced by its smooth pink glow. "Do you have anything left in there?"

Pennifer did turn at his voice, but those eyes held no spark. She didn't speak, only watched Svarde for a muted moment before turning back to the quartz.

"Svarde," Rasslebeck called. "Come here, take a look at this."

Svarde put a hand on Pennifer's shoulder, squeezed. Hoped for, didn't receive a reaction. Two gone, then, and not much to show for it.

"Give me some good news," Svarde said, pacing back over to Rasslebeck.

"Don't know if it's good or bad, but it's news," Rasslebeck replied. At the whimpering man's feet, laid out along the fiend's bones, were those six gray faces. "Thought these were all the same ugly thing, now I'm starting to recognize a couple."

Rasslebeck wasn't hallucinating. What'd been smooth, if horrifying, while the fiend spun, now seemed to be growing personalities. Lines, bones, shapes. The mouths closed down as lips emerged along the gray tone, the cheeks rounded out. Foreheads flatted out from their rounded peaks.

"Only six?" Svarde asked, watching. "This thing only found six to kill?"

"You heard all that noise, right? Those words?"

"Most I didn't understand," Svarde said. "More than six voices, though."

"Best I can figure," Rasslebeck said, kneeling over the faces, "is it's like you and me having a meal. Take a punch to the gut after dinner and it's likely to come right back up. Wait a day before you take your licks, and you're fine."

"If you're right, then these are . . . us," Svarde said.

"Can't say I've spent a lot of time studying my own face, but that's my nose." Rasslebeck pointed at the fourth face. "Been broken enough times I'd recognize that ugly snout anywhere."

Five faces they recognized at the end, once the gray stopped moving. One for each of them, plus the whimpering man. Another, a mystery. A slim woman they'd not found, not heard. Rasslebeck set the whimpering man's mask on the body, while the other three held their own. Pennifer didn't seem to notice, didn't seem to care when Svarde offered her own face to her.

"What do we do with it?" Maena asked as the trio stood

in the quartz glow at the room's center. "I don't think I want to carry it all the way back up."

"What, no room in your heart for a little art?" Rasslebeck asked.

"That's not me," Maena said. "Or, it was. Not anymore."

Svarde held his own, frowned at its thin sculpt. Both his and Rasslebeck's were the least defined, features muddy, as if half-formed in the fiend's gray clay. Not a full meal, a design half-drawn. He turned the hard mask over in his hands, the back featureless and dark. Just like any real mask would be.

A scratch drew their attention back to Pennifer, whose feet had bumped her own mask. The dazed woman bent down, grasped the gray shape and held it up, looked at it with the same nothingness she'd had for everything.

"If she decides to keep it, Maena, you've got to," Rasslebeck said.

"I don't have to do any damn thing."

Svarde, though, kept his attention on their former friend. Pennifer turned the mask over in her hands, just as Svarde had done. She held it up before her face. A perfect match, the slim holes for eyes and mouth lining up with the blank visage behind it.

Pennifer pulled the mask closer, and the thing came alive. The stone seemed to shiver, sink into Pennifer's skin. The line between her grime-coated cheeks and the mask's stone fused, the two becoming one. She didn't scream, didn't cry even as Svarde started towards her.

Before he took two steps, the mask had vanished, sinking into and behind Pennifer's face. Leaving behind not the zombified ghoul, but a blinking, confused, and cursing Rana raider.

"Holy rivers," Rasslebeck breathed, putting his own

mask down and dashing towards Pennifer, wrapping her up in a hug. He spun the woman 'round, Pennifer trying to ask what'd happened. "You've missed one rotten tale, Pennifer, and it's one that'll be better in the telling than the feeling, you get me?"

Pennifer stepped back, separated herself from Rasslebeck, and looked around. Caught Svarde, Maena. Kivi, snorting the all clear, shuffled back into the room.

"Last thing I remember, some terrible wind went blowing through the cave we were walking," Pennifer said slow. "Now I'm here? You're all looking awful." She winced, glanced down at herself. "And why do my feet feel like they've been scraping nails?"

Rasslebeck grinned, "Because you decided to take a barefoot run through the tunnels, that's why."

The two broke off, Rasslebeck finding a spot to sit Pennifer down and tell the tale. As they did, Svarde turned to Maena, shrugged, and shoved his own ill-defined mask back into his face.

Like emerging from a dream, that's what it was. Pieces he'd been missing came back, his Foti childhood, years spent working the mines, the forges, hefting the axes. Svarde, thanks to the whimpering man, had kept his Guardian years, the decade lost on the Vis cliffside, and now parts he'd never realized were gone had come home.

"Your turn," Svarde said to Maena after taking a few deep breaths, stretching out his memory to see how far it could go, that all the good bits were there.

Maena, though, looked at the mask with narrowed eyes, a tight frown.

"That's not me," Maena said.

"'Course it's you. Who else would it be?"

Maena shook her head. Svarde noticed her hand trembled. The Rana captain raised the mask, higher than her own head.

"The person behind those eyes isn't who I am," Maena said. "If she comes back, then I'm not here."

Svarde loosened his fingers. Tried to catch Rasslebeck's eye, but the other two Rana were locked in conversation, starting to pull together their gear.

Kivi, though, found his look with her sapphires. Seemed to understand.

"Am I dead?" Maena continued, more to herself than Svarde. "If the other me comes back, was I ever alive?"

"You're the same damn person," Svarde said.

Maena flashed a glare at him. "You said I was different. And I know I'm not . . . myself. Her. Not her. I'm me. My own person."

"You have no past. You don't know anything about yourself, Maena. It's all there, in that mask. Put—"

"You could tell me," Maena replied, the anger fading into hope. "You could teach me who I was. It's a long walk back, right? By the end, I'll know what I need to know, I'll—"

"Can't tell you how you grew up, can't tell you your dreams, what's been burning in your heart all these years," Svarde said, moving a step closer. Maena still had that mask high. "This isn't the way, Maena."

"Easy for you to say, the man who lost nothing. Who didn't change." Maena's eyes flicked to the mask. "I want to live, Svarde. It's not your call whether I get to."

The Guardian whistled, low and smooth. Maena's face firmed up, she flung the mask down towards the rocky floor. Kivi, cutting behind the Rana captain, launched herself ahead, rolling in the air. The mask hit her claws, the ferrite's softest spot on her belly. Sparks shot up as the rock lizard's back ran across the stone, but the mask seemed safe.

Maena, not so.

Svarde closed while the Rana captain stared in shock at the ferrite's save. He wrapped Maena in a tight grip, clamping the Rana's two arms to her sides and lifting her off the rock. She tried kicking, but Svarde ignored the weak hits to his thighs, his knees. Slipping Maena into a tighter hug, Svarde moved a hand behind her head and pressed the Rana captain to the floor.

"Rasslebeck, Pennifer," Svarde shouted, and this time the two noticed. "Help, please."

"Help me," Maena tried as the other two drew near.

Pennifer made to do so, looking like she was about to kick Svarde in the face before Rasslebeck stopped her. The big Guardian pressed Maena into the rock, holding her there despite the captain's struggles. At Rasslebeck's ask, Svarde relayed what'd happened, over Maena's increasingly wild objections.

"You're killing me," Maena said as Rasslebeck went to retrieve the mask from Kivi's claws. "Murdering your friend."

"Bringing her back," Svarde countered.

At first, Maena's struggle with herself cut Svarde in a hard way. This new Maena wasn't the old, but she'd fought alongside them just the same, had helped face the fiend with nothing in her past, her future. That bravery deserved to be rewarded with something other than death, if that's what this was.

Now, though, Maena's protests, her pleas, shoved the sadness away. The real Maena, the one who'd sat with Svarde in the Rat's Fang and told him the goal lay down here, in the darkest deeps, wasn't scared like this, wouldn't have begged. If Svarde ever hoped to do what he'd sworn to Ami, he needed the old Maena back, the one willing to face whatever danger.

"Put the mask on," Svarde ordered when Rasselbeck returned. Maena tried to squirm away, one last burst stopped when Kivi settled her heavy body across Maena's legs. "Do it, Rasslebeck."

The Rana raider looked from Svarde to the captain, to Pennifer. When the last nodded at him, said she wanted her captain back, Rasslebeck found his spine.

"Sorry, boss," Rasslebeck said, kneeling beside Svarde. "If we're going down this road, we need you back."

Maena's final scream echoed long and far down the caves, into the tunnels, but through it all, Svarde kept his hold, kept his eyes locked on hers, and held to his hope.

CHAPTER 34
A SHORT CAREER

Wax began screaming when the water rose to his knees. Wordless cries, more spasms than real thought, pulled out by a body in crisis. Dark fell, a clouded night now hiding the stars, Sichi, leaving only the orange flickers up the beach and, of course, Sledge, returned now to her vigil.

A price, so Sledge said, to pay for those she lost along the way.

The bandit listened as Wax scraped his cords raw. The screams helped, each one stripping a second's pain. His feet had vanished into numbness, the line creeping higher with every wave. An incoming tide sure to kill him before long.

Quik, Bliss, weren't coming.

The two thoughts, that his certain death wasn't far and he wouldn't be saved by his Guardians, by his family, converged slowly, pushed back at first by the same will that'd helped Wax carry Pan down the Great Sana, that'd pushed him to distract the fiend and let Sawi escape.

The same will losing this struggle.

"Give it up, Wax," Sledge said between the mindless

shouts, and not for the first time. "No sense dying for nothing. And I could use some sleep. Your noise doesn't help."

The binds around his legs and wrists made the shivering rattle against the wood. Cold air primed Wax's skin for the water to follow, while thirst and hunger bit at his insides.

All told, Wax had been better.

All told, Wax didn't know why he was still there. Who was he proving anything to, now? Who cared what he did?

One of seven Renewals. Doubtless not the favorite to win it, to sit in Noctia's blasted isle and wait for a fiend to tear him apart. What a victory.

A wave crested higher than the ones before, lashed his back with icy spray. Another shout.

Honor for Kitaye? Who cared about honor. How many times did they celebrate the city's last Renewal? Wax couldn't even recall her name. Some weaver. That's what he was suffering for, here? A chance to be forgotten after it all?

"Say the word, Wax," Sledge called.

Say the word. That's all he'd have to do. Say that he gave up. Tell Pan, somehow, that he was sorry. That he wasn't strong enough.

Another wave. Wax convulsed, his head hitting the wood behind him. A fresh ache stealing some of the pain from his legs.

Unreasonable, wasn't it? The Najahn never told Wax this was what might happen. A fiend, maybe. An accident, possible. Torture? By the very people Wax was doing this all to save?

Say the word.

"I'm going in another minute," Sledge said. "You won't be alive when I come back."

Say the word.

. . .

HE WOKE WITH THE SUN. His back nestled into the sand, dry and warm. Someone had thrown a light blanket over him, but that wasn't what had Wax's attention. His hands, still bound, but now in a different way: to keep something clutched tight between them.

The whispers woke him, the familiar slips and sighs coming from the skar. Vis, welcoming Wax home.

"The man awakes," Sledge said, eating some stringy fish off the end of a knife. She sat on a driftwood log not a stride away. "Can you feel your feet, boy?"

Wax tried a wiggle, tried to flex his thighs. They twitched, they thawed, they wrestled back from the fathomless depths bodies go when surrounded by so much cold.

Sledge must've noticed the move beneath the blanket. She whistled.

"We were going to cut them off till Eggrad stopped us," Sledge said, digging the knife back into the crude earthenware bowl for another helping. "He wanted to prove to everyone that the skars are worth chasing."

Wax took Sledges words as an invitation, a chance to reconnect with his every toe, his every finger, his butt, his stomach, his heart. All were there, all responded to his search. A body that shouldn't have lived had endured, was thriving.

"How?"

"You feel it, don't you?" Sledge asked.

"It's like whispers. I can't understand them."

Sledge nodded, "Only felt it once myself. A Kance skar, the last time around. That one didn't work so well."

Wax turned in the sand, rubbing his shoulder into the

grit to get a better look at Sledge.

"What did you do with it?"

"The skar? Sold it like all the others." Sledge shook her head, chuckled in that hopeless way she had a tendency to do. "Not like we had a choice. Our buyers don't negotiate, and we don't get to say no."

"Who're they?"

"You'll meet them soon enough, if that sail is what I think."

Wax shifted, sat up. Saw, in the early light, a purple-black sail cutting across the horizon towards them. Behind Wax, the bandit camp sprang into a frenzied action, Eggrad's booming voice flying above it all demanding this and that.

"Early for a visit," Sledge said, setting the bowl down. "Must be desperate for more."

"How many do they take?"

Wax tucked away Sledge's comment about the skars speaking for later. A curiosity to follow-up on when he had more time. And, if he'd done what Wax suspected, he was about to be around Sledge for a very, very long time.

He'd escape back to Vis at some point, obviously, but when that would be, when Wax could attempt a solo crossing through the Wastes, back to Smythe, and afford passage home?

This Renewal would be done, and then some.

The Najahn sloop neared by the time Eggrad joined Sledge and Wax on the beach. Unlike the night before, Eggrad had on full Foti leathers, with two short swords on his waist. The sun-bleached helm pushed his bushy eyebrows down, covering his pupils in shadow, making it seem to Wax as if the bandit leader had no eyes at all, just fuzzy holes.

"Cut it loose," Eggrad said to Sledge. "He's well enough?"

"Seems to be." Sledge took the order, grabbed Wax's wrist and, with a single clean stroke, sent her mealtime knife slicing through the narrow strands holding Wax's wrists together.

Wax caught the skar in his freed hands, held it close and threw Eggrad a glare as the latter man held forth a hand.

"Reneging on your oath already, boy?" Eggrad asked, voice more curious than caustic. "Last night, you held out well, but you said the words. Going back on them now will give you the same fate, only faster, as I don't have time to listen to your pathetic screams."

"What if I throw it out there?" Wax said, getting to his feet, shifting the skar to his right hand.

"How will that spare your life?" Eggrad countered. "There's one move here, and that's putting the skar in my hand. You have one more breath before Sledge guts you so bad no skar will pull you back together."

A token display. That's all Wax had done, all he could muster. He'd have to live with that, as Sledge's cold stare showed no sympathy. She would do exactly as Eggrad asked.

So Wax did too, and the pair followed the bandit leader back into the camp. There he found the frenzy not all he expected: for every bandit embroiled in wrapping up spoils, arranging the stolen weapons, armor, and looted valuables, another made themselves ready for a fight. Some retreated behind the camp into the cliffs, crossbows and blowguns ready. More than one pregnant bandit among them.

"Just as deadly as you and I," Sledge said when she noticed Wax following the group, "but with more to lose from a dirty fight."

"I don't see any children?"

Sledge snorted, "They'll go to one of a dozen towns, each who'll pay for a body to raise, to work their mines, their forges. Everything's a trade here, Wax."

"The mothers let that happen?"

"Some go with their children, others don't." Sledge gave Wax a shove into Eggrad's tent. Stripped down, the dwelling seemed meager. "You and I get to wait here while Eggrad does the talking."

"Looks like you're expecting more than just a talk."

"Anyone trusting the Najahn to do just what they say is asking to get cheated."

When Wax pressed for more details, Sledge snapped at him to stay quiet. A soft rumble came up the beach as the sloop hit the shore, a rumble followed by surprised shouts, curses, and a sound Wax hadn't heard before: the clicks and clacks as crossbows let loose their quarrels.

Wax, sitting on combed sand, started up only for Sledge to push him back to the ground. Her right hand held Wax's own Foti blade once again, its brilliant blue contrasting the dusted beige around them.

"He gave you that back?" Wax whispered, sneaking the words over the growing shouts, calls, and now, a clash of metal on metal.

"A prize for getting your body back to ours," Sledge replied. "Apparently the Najahn aren't abiding by our usual deal."

"Killing you?"

A sharp scream cut above the battle. Sledge winced.

"I don't think they're playing." She glanced over Wax's shoulder, towards the tent's back. "Come on, let's go."

"Running?" Wax sat back. "Why should I? They'll just rescue me."

Sledge laughed, kept her eyes moving from Wax to the tent's front flap as the battle grew outside.

"They'll think you're a bandit, just like us," Sledge replied. "What's more likely, the Vis Renewal hiding in a bandit camp, or just another thief needing their head put on a pike?"

A persuasive argument, that.

Wax followed Sledge out the tent's back, Sledge using the Foti blade to cut a quick slit. Beyond, the beach met rocky cliffs, a venture Wax wasn't too keen to take with his bare feet, but Sledge offered no shoes and the battle said to wait was to die.

Outside the tent, Wax saw quarrels flying from holes in the cliffs to his left, black darts screaming towards the beach. Arrows flew back, lancing into the stone and bouncing off, blowing the soft rock into the air with every strike.

The camp itself blocked any view to the real fighting, no matter how many times Wax glanced back as Sledge led him further into the stone narrows.

"How far?" Wax asked as Sledge kept moving, the bandit ignoring options to travel left, reinforce her friends.

"Far enough," Sledge replied. "The Najahn won't waste the time to chase us all down. We'll be scattered, they'll get their damned prizes, and they'll be off."

"You don't think you'll win?"

Sledge stopped, the high gray stone around them muffling the battle's noise. Giving it a distance that allowed for full breaths, for a moment's thought.

"Eggred's spent years dealing with the Najahn," Sledge said. "He's soft. We're all soft now. If these Najahn press their attack, and it sure seems they mean to, we'll be carved up."

"But—"

Sledge whipped around, pointed a finger at Wax, at herself. "We're not fighters, you and me. Not like them. Thieves, adventurers, maybe. But the Najahn are warriors, armed and ready to do what their Circle commands. You fight them, you lose. It's why all the isles suffer their arrogance."

Before Wax could come up with a reply, Sledge had herself reversed again, putting more steps between them and the beach. Steps between herself and Wax.

Sledge might be right. The Najahn might mistake him for a bandit, but what Wax heard in Sledge's words was a life lived in fear, a promise that happiness, when found, would be fleeting. Not for him.

"Give me my sword," Wax said. Sledge stiffened, turned around and pointed Wax's own blue blade back at him. "You'll get away with your life. That's more than you deserve."

"Who are you to judge?" Sledge advanced, her pallor gray. Distant clashes, cries, curses bounced off the rock around them. "You're nothing but a boy. You don't know desperation."

"I know you're feeling it right now." Wax went right, side-stepping up the ridged stones, staying just beyond Sledge's reach. "The fighting's getting closer. They're looking for me, and they won't stop."

"They will if they find your body."

Sledge lunged, but Wax broke right. The Foti blade skipped off rock, scattering dust. Sledge cursed, followed Wax, saw he stood now between her and the trail away.

"I can dance for a long time," Wax said, refusing to let a smile come to his face. The blade. That's what he wanted. Sledge enraged might not give it to him. "You don't have these seconds. Give me the blade and you have a chance."

Sledge ran at him, a charge befitting a battle-cry, but she kept her mouth shut, teeth clenched. Wax feinted left before slipping his feet on the sandy ground and jumping back. Sledge swung, wild. The blade cut where Wax would've, should've been. Instead he remained, as ever, in Sledge's way. As she recovered, Wax scooped up sand, threw it in Sledge's face. The grains spattered her eyes, her mouth. She swore again, brushed away the dirt.

"I'll follow you, they'll follow me," Wax said, re-arming. "Maybe you'll get lucky, maybe you won't. But you don't have much time."

As if hearing Wax's threat, a sharp yelp came not far to their right. Someone's skewering scream. Sledge glanced that way. Fear had its grip now, a look Wax knew because it haunted so many of his own dreams: Pan, on the way down the Great Sana, the thorn in his side.

"I'm offering you a trade, and a good one," Wax continued, his voice level. "You told me to take Eggrad's offer, and that saved my life. Now I'm doing the same for you. Give me the blade and run."

Sledge eyed the Foti blade, waved it before her in a lazy slash. A heavy sigh. "That's all we get, don't we? One bad choice after the next." With a sudden snap, she whipped the Foti blade back behind her, towards the beach. "Take your sword, Wax. Damn you."

Wax didn't give Sledge a nod, didn't give her another word. He ran by her, keeping plenty wide, and he heard Sledge pick up her own pace. To the east, towards freedom, or what counted as such for her. As for Wax, the blue blade, the beach, and his brother and sister lay ahead.

His feet barely felt the hard rock as they ran.

CHAPTER 35
THE RISEN

On the road with Svarde and Catya, a common question after a few mugs of ale was whether they'd rather face one large fiend or several smaller ones. Svarde, of course, always bent his answer to the lone giant, wagering the one target made an easier hit with his axes.

Ami, for her part, wanted enemies she could cleave in a single swing. No worries about a counter, about the monster simply taking the sword and coming at her anyway.

Catya, as she always did, joked in the conversation's center, throwing weight one way or the other depending on who seemed to be winning the night's debate: what if the single fiend could fly, how about if the swarm split with every strike, multiplying into an infinite army?

Those conversations slashed by through Ami's mind as she watched the giant fiend, wrapped now in the canvas roof it'd destroyed, loop into a dive back towards them, its wings, legs, anger evident even as Sichi made the thing look more beautiful than it had any right to be.

Terrevin's voice cracked, whipping the Wards into faster action. Chakrams came off backs, found willing hands. The men and women around Ami bent, sent their arms with the flat discs back towards the earth, and as the fiend fell into range, Terrevin called out the throw.

Eight discs lanced into the air, not all at once but staggered in some invisible training so the pairs didn't strike one another but flew right at their target.

And hit.

The chakrams and their razor edges bit into the fiend, gnashing into its furred skin with splattering success, a raining ichor preceding the monster's wordless dive. Ami closed her eyes, took a single step towards Catya as the blood rain hit. She held Flamebreak over her head, its point straight up.

If the fiend was dumb enough to come down on her, its weight would likely mean Ami's death, but Flamebreak would ensure the fiend's own.

"Voulges up!" Terrevin shouted.

Curved spears rose as the fiend slammed home, an event Ami witnessed through half-closed eyes, a wiping left hand clearing the blood as she realized the fiend was not, in fact, going for a slamming kill.

Instead, the winged worm slammed into the lelune flowers behind Catya's throne, off the northern side. At impact, those chakrams that'd done such a nice opening assault flew off or shattered, their shards flying through the air in all directions.

"Down," Ami snapped to Catya, who'd tried to turn her head around her throne to see.

The Guardian, letting Flamebreak fall to the side, hugged Catya to her throne as rocks and charkam bits slammed against its back. Cries ran out as unlucky Wards had their armor battered, their vulnerabilities pierced.

"Charge!" Terrevin continued. "Wounded, retreat!"

To her left, Ami noticed the shieldwarden pushing another Ward up the path, the climb that'd take the Ward back to the tunnel, the guard station and Noctia proper. Reinforcements, or, more likely, witnesses to the dead left after the fight.

Six Wards remained up, Terrevin included, and they all brandished their voulges in a straight-on charge towards the fiend. The worm, for its part, struggled with its new home on the ground, writhing to rid itself of the last chakram bits. Any beauty the thing once held vanished now between lelune stems, dirt, and bleeding lines drawn by the attacks and the Aegis before them.

"What are you waiting for?" Catya asked as the Wards rushed by.

"Not waiting," Ami said, standing, holding Flamebreak again in her hands. "You're my objective. If the fiend gets by them, I have to protect you."

"You could save their lives."

In a melee like the one developing? Where the worm lashed its head and tail at the approaching Wards, driving some back, taking some light stabs in equal measure? The thrashing threw up more rocks too, a messy chaos.

"Selene's crew know what they're doing," Ami said, hoping that was indeed the case. "I'd get in the way."

The Wards did, at least, match up to Ami's words. Selene continued calling out orders, formations, strikes, and the Wards kept their composure, darting in when the worm's flailing rippled up the creature's long body to take deeper stabs, more devastating strikes. If one Ward fell, another pulled them back long enough to recover. The fiend's wings, too, seemed shredded from the fall. There would be no lifting off here.

A slow dance, this, but an inevitable one. Flamebreak wouldn't need—

"Ami," Catya said. "Look."

The Aegis had her eyes back towards the Wound. Ami followed the stare, saw a curious thing embedded into the rock just over the Wound's lip. A bronze color, a sick gold in Sichi's light, but solid and biting into the rock. Leading off its back was a golden chain, one falling over and into the Wound.

Taut.

Several injured Wards lay near the device, their attentions held on repairing gashes from the worm's initial strike. None had their eyes on the new hook. None, anyway, till a four-fingered hand swept up over the Wound's edge and planted itself on the earth. The hand mesmerized on sight, its fingers indistinct behind what seemed to be purple-blue flame, one that fluttered not the least in Noctia's cold early winter wind.

Indigo embers burst up at the hand's impact, sparks not falling to the ground and dying as they should, but instead drifting up into the air like a flower's seeds, winking out in a slow cadence.

Following the hand back up its arm, again a liquid-like purple-blue flame, sent Ami's stare to a shoulder, then down into the dark. At least, for one more quick moment.

A second hand rose, landing right of the first. Ami, already lifting Flamebreak, noted the hook's chain still pulled tight. A grip maintained, weight still held.

Another strange, new fiend.

It would die like all the others.

"Wards!" Ami warned, drawing the focus of the

wounded ones. Behind, the worm's fight continued, no notice taken of the new arrival. "To arms, or if you cannot wield them, leave."

As if in answer to her call, the fiend's head rose over the Wound. Like an obsidian arrow, the glittering silver-black triangle stuck out amid the purple-blue flame, all the more so because the fiend's own body appeared to be scorching its head again and again: orange lines followed where the fire burned, crossing the head before starting back again, splitting off at times to make random journeys.

All this was easy to notice as the fiend's head matched Ami's body for size. The first two hands still gripping the dirt, those not much larger than Ami's own, proved only a misleading introduction to the massive monster following. As the fiend's head came into full view, those first shoulders fell into a much larger spread, that of a giant thing, one triple or more Ami's own size.

One not worth giving a moment's advantage.

"Attack!" Ami cried, leveling Flamebreak at the creature.

Before, Ami would've noticed the skar's whispers, would've been curious as she readied the blade. Now, those slight sounds told a different story: Flamebreak was hungry, was delighted, wanted nothing more than what was about to happen.

And yet, Ami's charge faltered one step in.

Faltered, because the fiend spoke.

Those burning orange lines along its head coalesced, as if given sudden direction, into a single crackling oval, and from it, as the fiend continued to rise, emerged a rasping, seething speech.

The words, the cadence, resembled nothing Ami had

heard before. Nothing, save the same skar whispering in her head at that very second, calling for her to strike.

If Ami faltered, the Wards who'd regained their shaken feet, one with an arm hanging limp and the other two with bloody wounds to their stomachs and legs, did not. They staggered in at the giant, the first two thrusting their voulges at the arms and the last, coming from behind, launching his weapon at the fiend's head.

Najahn's finest weapons found their metal a poor match for their target. The curved points dove in, found the hands, glowed white and simply melted away, the dripping metal falling over the fiend's skin without a single twitch. The voulge soaring in at the head struck the monster's rocky skull, bounced off alit, and tumbled into the Wound's depths.

"Steady, Ami," Catya said behind her.

Right. Ami took a slow breath. Pushed aside the fiend's words as the three Wards backed off, their eyes casting about for more weapons. More useless attempts.

"What do you want?" Ami asked the fiend, a question she'd never uttered before in all her fights with the monstrous denizens of the Dark Below.

The fiend replied, its sizzle bright and snapping. Ami could make nothing of it. The skars, at least, seemed to give emotion with their whispering, an urging helping to guide her towards what the stones meant. The fiend held no such clues, though its continued rise suggested nothing good.

The gold chain went slack as a new hand appeared, this one doubled in size from the first. Heat radiated off the giant purple-blue limb, washing over Ami in a scalding wave. Flamebreak's skar leapt at it, pulling Ami forward of its own accord. The small stone called for the fiend's destruction, demanded it.

Time to give the Foti skar what it desired.

Ami leveled Flamebreak for a piercing stab right at the fiend's neck, a growing, glowing target as the monster continued its rise. As she made her first move, the golden hook drew back, its teeth peeling rock. It sank into the Wound, then rose again with the fiend's forth arm, its second giant hand holding the long chain's end, revealing the weapon to have not one but four great golden hooks. The fiend whipped the arm behind its head, drawing the hooks up into the open air.

Beautiful, in a way, soaring above the molten, burning thing. A race, under the glittering stars, to see who would die first.

Ami took another long stride, kicking off with her left into the final push. Her nose caught a whiff, her hair catching fire as the heat around her burned bright, sucked the air dry of anything else save blue-purple flame.

The skar guided her strike even as Ami's eyes found the falling hooks, each and all racing towards her, the fiend sending in what should be a devastating kill.

A flash. A voulge, flying perfect over Ami's right shoulder. The curved spear struck the snapping chain, the Najahn quality proving itself here even if it failed against the fire. The voulge dug deep into the large link, breaking its hold and sending the four hooks wide into a harmless crash far to Ami's right.

"You're clear!" Terrevin's shout snuck in between the skar's roar.

Flamebreak drove home, and Ami screamed as her skin tasted the fiend's fire. Above it all, filling her mind and running over her will, directing Ami to push ever forward, was the skar.

And Ami listened. For there was no other choice.

CHAPTER 36
THE RESCUE

The Lira had shown Bliss how to handle fiends, how to dash through the jungle unseen and unheard, how to master the night and conquer the day. Deshiva and the other hunters taught Bliss how to track, to live off the land, to fight with what she could find.

Neither showed her what it meant to go to war.

The Najahn streamed off the sloop, ready in their thin ranks to face the motley bandit resistance. Bliss, Quik, and Torny watched from the sloop, the Najahn leader bidding them stay while she cleaned up the rabble.

The bandits, for their part, came out expecting something different. Their leader—Bliss figured such because the man not only led the bandits, but carried a swagger with his steps—went down the sand with his arms out wide, no weapons drawn. Two bandits followed, each with ragged chests in their arms. Spoils, a bribe?

"She said things were changing," Quik added when the offering became obvious.

"Not so easy to bribe as the last," Torny said, her lower lip suffering a nervous bite.

'Worried?' Bliss signed to the bandit.

"This isn't looking good," Torny replied, then shrugged. "Good thing I've never met these people, or maybe I'd care more."

"Don't think she won't hold you responsible," Quik said. "Once Wax is back with us, you'll own up for your actions just like your friends."

Torny usually had a snappy comeback for Quik, but now she just kept silent, continuing chewing her lip.

Nervous, but then, Torny had every right to be. Gained a home only to watch it, now, be torn out away? Bliss wasn't sure how she'd react to that, only to know she wouldn't let it happen without a fight.

Which was, with Pavarde's whistle, what the beach turned into. The front Najahn ranks lowered their voulges and charged, not even bothering to play at negotiations. The back line slung chakram off their shoulders and threw the razor discs over their allies, the whistling circles cutting into the waiting bandits. Sand flew as boots dug in deep, and the first screams began.

Bliss winced, started to recoil only to feel Quik's hand on her back. Bliss looked at her brother, saw his face tight but his eyes stern, watching.

"This is important," Quik said as the conflict joined, quarrels like black hornets darting from the cliffs at the beach's back. "We brought the Najahn here. The least we can do is watch."

"Yeah, no thanks," Torny said, turning away. "Besides, I don't see your brother out there. Maybe he's already gone and all you're doing is getting people killed for nothing."

While Quik snarled off some dumb reply, Bliss tried to confirm Torny's assertion. The melee made it hard to tell, with bandits and Najahn mixing, voulges and swords flying, but she didn't recognize Wax among the fray. No blue Foti blade standing out above the rest.

"Think whatever you want," Torny said, heading towards the sloop's ramp. "I'm not waiting for a spear in my back or a noose around my neck."

Before Quik could do more than curse, Torny dropped over the sloop's side, splashing into the water and cutting along the beach towards the camp, away from the fighting.

'Good work,' Bliss signed to her brother.

"You're too friendly with her."

'She saved my life.' Bliss unslung her staff, watched Torny splash onto the sand, the thief almost glowing in the dawning sun. 'And she's right. Wax isn't out there.'

Bliss slipped from her brother's reach, heading towards the same boat side Torny had used. A glance down said the drop wasn't far.

"Where are you going?" Quik asked, moving to follow.

'After our brother.'

The water was damn cold, breath-stealing in its iciness, but the sand proved warmer, a gritty blanket coating Bliss as she ran after Torny. To her left, Pavarde's commands rose into the air, ordering the Najahn advance. A few quarrels still flew from the cliffs, but the bandits seemed to be scattering, running towards the slopes only to be cut down from behind by lancing spear or thrown chakram.

The Najahn, though, appeared in no particular hurry, tending to their wounded and making sure enemy casualties became corpses.

Torny, meanwhile, vanished among the tents.

Bliss picked up her pace, holding the staff in both hands and reminding her feet how to run light on the sand. They skipped across the top, leaving the barest print behind. On a full stomach, well-rested, Bliss found the run came easy, a rush following with it.

A hunt. For a friend, yes, and her brother, but a hunt.

The first tents were small, their dusted flaps blowing in a rising morning breeze. In them, Bliss saw skimpy bedrolls, satchels stuffed for a quick flight. Ones who'd gone to the beach, then, and who wouldn't be making it back.

Beyond them, Bliss found more leveled ground. Fire pits, racks for weapons and tools mostly barren. Breakfast's scent lingered on the air, dirty iron pans holding charred fish while earthen bowls owned leftover fruits from beachside trees and bushes, the few worthwhile plants on the isle that Bliss had seen.

"Sister!" came a voice unexpected and delighted.

Wax came around the largest tent at the camp's back, hands free and smile wide. Bliss matched it, the hunt's rush turning quick to victory's elation. Here he was, her Renewal, and looking healthy on top. No bad wounds, even freshly washed.

She didn't drop her staff to give Wax a tight hug, but he lifted Bliss up all the same, laughing, until another wounded one's scream cut through the air.

'We brought them,' Bliss signed as they both glanced through the camp towards the fighting. 'The Najahn came to rescue you.'

"I'll take it," Wax said, though the grimace said his feelings weren't guilt free. "That's your ship then?"

'It is.'

"Then let's go."

Bliss, though, didn't move after Wax, and her brother turned, the question obvious.

'I need to find someone,' Bliss said.

"Who?"

The answer to that question died with a sputtering, triumphant growl from Wax's far side. Bursting through a tent with his swords waving, blood streaming from several wounds, came the bandit leader. Dirt clung to his beard, his face, but the man's wild eyes rolled clear as they found Wax.

"My ticket out," the man said, frothy red spittle flecking as he spoke. "A Renewal for my life. A fair trade, wouldn't you say?"

Wax backed up a step, enough space for Bliss to round him, her staff at the ready. The bandit leader sighted her, stared for a lost moment, then clacked his short blades against one another.

"Thought you were Sledge for a moment, Lass, but I suppose Wax here's done away with her?" The bandit leader asked. "Come back to Eggrad for revenge?"

"I'm not—" Wax started as Eggrad lunged forward.

Bliss flicked her staff left, its end butting into Wax and knocking him further away. Eggrad looked to be heading straight at her brother, but after his first step, the bandit punched in his right foot and swerved hard towards Bliss, leading those twin blades in a low-high dance.

The Lira caught the high strike with her staff, retreating as she swung to dodge the low blow. A temporary save, as Eggrad pressed his attack, pushing the staff aside and leading again with his left blade for a gut-stabbing strike. One falling well short of home, thanks to a barreling, shouting form streaking in from the camp's seaward side.

Quik hit Eggrad from behind, throwing the bandit into the dirt. Quik fell after, catching himself with his hands and trying to stand, only for Eggrad, cursing his ill luck, to snap a kick into Quik's face. Bliss's brother toppled over into the dirt.

But taking one path left Eggrad open to others, namely a crack from Bliss's staff against the man's skull. The leather over his head blunted the blow, but the force jammed Eggrad's face into the dirt. Bliss slid her right foot back, sent the staff left for a sweeping strike that ought to end the whole thing.

The staff came in fast, but Eggrad stood up his right arm, planting the sword faster than any man should've after a head strike like Bliss had delivered. The blade served to block her staff's blow, shivering the wood even as Eggrad pulled himself back to his knees, his feet.

"Don't let him recover," Wax said, throwing an iron pan.

The missile swept in, smacked Eggard in the chest, causing a stumble. Bliss used it, jabbing the staff forward. Eggrad's left hand swept down, deflected the blow so it only struck his thigh, a hit still hard enough to bend, maybe break bone.

Eggard grimaced, spat out another fiery curse, but didn't fall.

What stamina the man had. Bliss pulled the staff back, readied her guard as Eggrad pushed forward again, only for the bandit leader to stop, pivot and stab.

Quik, coming again from behind, took the sudden strike in his chest, on the right side. In a flash, the sword went in, went out, and the Vis hunter dropped to the dirt. Wax called out his brother's name.

Bliss used the opening.

Going too low this time, with Eggrad's swords whirling back expecting a chest-level strike, Bliss hooked the bandit's ankles, upended him again into the sand. This time, Bliss slid her grip as the staff went up, reversing the swing and sending the metal end right into Eggrad's head.

The crack echoed loud, above the continuing fray to the north, and the bandit leader fell still.

"Quik!" Wax shouted again, sprinting past Bliss to his brother.

Bliss moved more slowly, kicking away both swords from Eggrad's hands before joining Wax at Quik's side.

The wound spread its sign into the sand, an oozing red delayed only by Quik's fingers. Wax already had his shirt torn, replacing Quik's hand as Bliss arrived with the wadded cloth. The cut, though, was deep, dangerous enough.

"Did the Najahn bring a healer, a doctor?" Wax asked as Bliss cast around for anything that might serve.

'I don't know,' Bliss signed. 'They didn't talk to us much.'

"Is it bad?" Quik asked, his voice already so weak, stretched. "It felt deep."

"I've seen worse," Wax snapped, then made another loud call for help, a call that would, Bliss figured, go unanswered as long as the Najahn had their own to deal with. "Bliss, we've gotta move him. Get him back to the boat."

'You take his shoulders, I'll take the feet.' Bliss stood while Wax scrambled near Quik's head. The staff went in its shoulder sling, and Bliss bent down, gripped her brother's ankles.

"Ready?" Wax asked, looking at her, then his expression changed, determination fading to horrified confusion.

Bliss whirled, dropping Quik's feet to the dirt. Eggrad rose up behind her, his swords gone but a hidden dagger in his right hand. He raisied the weapon, angled it in for a stab, and jerked. Once, twice, before collapsing to the ground.

Behind him, Eggrad's short sword in her hand, stood

Torny. Before Bliss could sign a thing, the thief tossed the blade aside and dove on Eggrad's body, tearing at the man's pockets, his ruined clothes.

"What're you doing?" Wax asked.

Torny glanced up, "Help me, if you want your brother to live."

There were times to question things, times to study the options and pick the best course, but there in that moment, Bliss used what she heard, what she felt, what she knew.

Torny hadn't abandoned them, hadn't abandoned her.

Together the two tore off Eggrad's armor, with Torny shouting a happy curse when she found what she'd been looking for, a familiar sapphire on a corroded chain.

"My skar," Wax said as Torny pulled the stone off of Eggrad.

At the move, as the skar lost its contact with the bandit leader, the man sighed, a withering exhale.

"No wonder he wouldn't stop," Wax said as Torny tossed the skar to him. "This thing, the Vis skar, it heals you."

"I know that, moron. Give it to your brother." Torny rolled her eyes, then went back to Eggrad's body, continuing to clear out pockets.

Wax pressed the skar to Quik's wound, while Bliss went to Torny, grabbed the thief's hands to get her attention.

"What?" Torny snapped. "This guy's the leader, which means he'll have any keys to the real valuables. I'm about to become a fugitive, so I'll—"

Bliss shook her head, 'You're going to stay. With us.'

Torny laughed. "Didn't you hear your brother? He's going to get me strung up at the first chance he gets."

Again, Bliss shook her head. 'I won't let him. Ever.'

Torny started up another quip, saw what Bliss poured into her face, her grip. Stopped, nodded slow.

"You promise?" Torny asked.

'On my life.'

"It's closing!" Wax shouted behind them. "The skar's working." Bliss turned round to see Wax slump into the sand, an exhausted smile on his face. "Bliss, I don't know how we're going to top this."

CHAPTER 37
THE GREAT FORGE

The bandits routed. The Najahn captain swept through the camp, taking anything of any value while Wax and the others, escorted back to the sloop, did little but rest, watch, and swap stories. The Najahn were thorough, burning any tents, materials they didn't take and leaving the camp a sundered ruin by the afternoon's end.

Among the taken treasure, presented by the captain to Wax from the spoils, were Quik's gauntlets. Wax's brother continued the recovery, though the skar didn't seem able to restore stamina so quickly: Quik slept the hours away, waking only to sip water and eat thin fish soup.

Torny, to Wax's eyes, seemed to take the dissolution of her recent tribe in stride. The bandit ate, drank, and joked with the Vis and any Najahn joining them, vanishing only towards the night's end to watch the camp remnants burn out on the sand.

"What changed?" Wax asked Bliss, the two of them on the sloop's deck, bulked out now in retrieved bandit clothes shielding them against the chill. The boat wouldn't sail till morning, a loose Najahn watch keeping eyes while most broke into looted ale and fruit wines for a raucous celebration.

'With her?' Bliss asked, and Wax nodded. 'She didn't try to kill me, and it was bleak out there. We helped each other.'

"And she stayed even after you found Quik?"

'Not that he helped, but Wax, I don't think she has anywhere to go.'

"You're angling towards something."

The little sister, Bliss had ever been a potent manipulator, able to squeeze her brothers into agreeing with just about anything, or playing them against each other till she had what she wanted. Wax already felt himself ready to agree, no matter what she said.

Bliss had come to his rescue, was the first one up the beach to find him. Wax more or less owed her whatever she wanted.

'She knows things we don't," Bliss started. 'About the world beyond Vis. We're lost, Wax. Admit it. Our first isle and we nearly starved, were nearly killed. There's six more, and Torny's savvy.'

"You want me to make her a Guardian?"

Now it was Bliss's turn to nod, the sincerity shining in the sloop's lamplight. Torny remained at the ship's bow, a shadow against Sichi's pink glow.

"Not all my choice, Bliss," Wax said. "But if she wants to come along, I won't say no. Though I don't think Quik will like it."

'We'll tell him Torny saved his life. That'll help.' Bliss grinned. 'And if it doesn't, too bad. You're the Renewal. It's your call.'

Wax's call or not, Quik kept up the grumbling, always

with Torny out of earshot, over the days that followed. The sloop took them up Foti's western coast, the Najahn captain promising an escort straight to the Great Forge. Not something always offered to Renewals, but given the stress, and the supplies the captain could donate to the Najahn garrison there, it seemed a harmless offer.

One Wax had no issue accepting.

They rode a ferrite wagon train across Foti's northern expanse, a mountainous but more verdant region than the Wastes below. Crops and livestock claimed grassy hillsides and leveled plains, with great gaping caves carved in here and there leading to mines.

The Great Forge itself didn't look much different than those ore factories at first glance, just a larger hole built into a silver-brown mountain sitting squat between other, higher peaks. At its base, a stone-and-stick Najahn camp parlayed its position with Foti enterprises, the latter bustling carts flush with raw ores inside the belching hot beast and springing them out with glittering spoils.

The entry, at least, gave some credit to the Great Forge's station, with Najahn and Foti banners snapping in the hot wind and carved statues lining the railed walkway down to the entrance. Torny, proving herself an adept tour guide, though she hadn't been to the Great Forge before, read off the names and deeds of every hammering man and woman they past by.

Most, it seemed, had earned their immortal honor by pioneering some new metal-working technique. Three, though, had necklaces added to their stoic gray statues: Foti's past Aegises, and farthest from the cave's mouth, their current one.

"Think she's still alive?" Wax asked as they passed by Catya's statue, a smooth figure showing the woman in a defiant pose, gripping the necklace with both hands as if to say any fiend would have to tear it from her grasp.

"If she wasn't, the road would be a lot more dangerous," Quik replied, taking a moment, with Bliss, to sign a Vis blessing at the statue. "The Circle made the call in time. We should finish well before she . . . falls."

"*If* they made it in time, you mean," Torny added. "Fassle's not infallible."

"The Circle's not just him," Quik countered as they continued past the statues, hugging the right side so carts could rumble past in either direction. Late morning proved a busy time for the Forge. "It's all the isles working together."

"It's Noctia doing whatever it wants."

"Good enough for me," Wax said, shutting down the argument. "I get some good food, some warm blankets, and a sweet trip all around the isles? I'll take it."

Torny looked like she was about to add on to that, but Bliss threw an elbow into her side and the bandit settled for an eye roll instead.

The Najahn guard waiting at the Forge's entry bade them to turn right, down the narrow bridge, rather than following the carts to the main smelting, hammering stations.

"What you're looking for is in the heart," the guard said, face and armor coated in black dust. "Don't stay down there long."

"Why's that?" Torny asked, to Quik's sigh. "We all going to catch on fire or something?"

The Najahn slipped the slightest smile, "The last thing I need today is to scrape your ashes into a bin."

'Well that's ominous,' Bliss signed.

"After what we've faced," Wax said, "it can't be any worse."

That statement found itself tested not long after, as the group, following the Najahn's guidance, found themselves walking along a narrow precipice overlooking a churning lava lake. In between the vast bubbles, pops, and hisses, far off hammering sounds rang throughout, a strange contrast between industry and natural fury.

Wax, when he wasn't wiping sweat from his eyes, followed Bliss along the ledge. They wore the lightest Foti canvas they could find, the shoes showing their worth as even a touch along the black rock walls proved able to burn the wayward palm or finger. The air shimmered, and every breath launched a battle to dodge a cough. They all resorted to Bliss's signs as a way to save breath, a move that, to Quik's smirking pleasure, cut Torny off from much of the conversation.

Not that they had much to talk about saving complaints about the heat and warnings of missteps and lava sparks. At least not till they reached the mentioned heart.

The Great Forge's center grew out from the narrow path into a wide square platform, one seemingly swept clean. Its broad base descended down into the lava lake, a crusted pillar glowing wherever the hot liquid splashed home. On its far side sat a stone growth, a bulbous thing larger than the wagon the group had rode here in and covered with glittering veins of gold, copper, silver, and more. Those veins ran down the shape and into the floor, spreading out all along the platform, intersecting here and there before ending at the group's feet.

"A puzzle," Torny announced, giving up on the signs.

Each vein had its own end, the tendril dropping into a shallow groove running across the platform's base. Those ends lay in cut out cubes, all floating in the simmering lava running through that groove. Standing up against the rock wall at their pathway's end were several forged poles, their purpose easy enough to guess.

"Push'em down," Wax suggested, hacked up some dust at the words.

Bliss didn't wait, grabbing the nearest pole—her staff would've worked, but like all their weapons and gear, it'd been left behind—and pushed down on the copper cube. It vanished beneath the lava, which began running up its bronzed line until it hit the vein's very first intersection, with the golden ore cutting it. There the lava sat, waiting as if unable to cross.

"Gold next, then," Quik said, grabbing a pole and pushing the vein down.

Again the lava ran down the gold vein, crossing the intersection with the copper before halting at . . . a second run in with the copper vein further along. Bliss's forced copper, meanwhile, didn't move any further.

"Now what?" Torny asked. "And please, if you know, be fast. It's damn hot in here."

That seemed to be the challenge. Solve the puzzle before the heat, the dust, the sheer intensity boiled you alive.

"To solve a puzzle," Wax said, "you've gotta know the rules. Bliss, pick it up. See if it resets."

Bliss lifted her pole off the copper cube, and the stone floated free from the lava in the groove. The lava that'd already traveled down the vein, though, sat still, glowing orange, hot, and waiting.

"Quik," Wax said, "now you."

The gold did much the same when Quik released it, save the lava dried out, cooling the gold vein black up until just past the intersection with the copper. Beyond it, between both copper touches, the gold remained covered by lava. Where it didn't, the gold turned black, coated now in fast-cooling lava rock.

And the copper used its free path, the lava left by Bliss's push streaking ahead to flow past the intersection with the gold till it was trapped by an encounter with the silver.

"Think we have our answer," Wax said, to the sweaty agreement of the others.

Knowing how the puzzle worked and solving it were two different things, but four melting minds worked better than Wax's alone, the group passing poles and ideas back and forth to get the lava along the veins, and the platform. When each reached the stone mound at the end, the lava wrapped its chosen vein. At the puzzle's finish, then, orange lines shone across the gray rock, before racing through some hidden hole inside. With a crackle and snap—Wax heard the sounds clear as he and the others made their way across the platform, stepping over the dried, but still hot, lava lines—the mound's center rose up. There, nestled beneath its stone cap, lay a glistening set of seven Foti skars.

Torny whistled as Wax reached the mound. Beneath the skars sat a small lava pool, one made by their puzzle-solving.

"Think I can touch it?" Wax asked the trio.

"Think if you don't, we're all going to fry," Torny replied.

"For once, I agree with the bandit," Quik added.

Just in case, Wax took his left hand and put it on the Vis skar, back again in its place on his neck. The skar's whispers grew, and the Forge's heat seemed less oppressive, his breath coming easier. A dangerous addiction, the skar could be.

But when Wax reached to grab his second, his fingers leading slow, he found the orange gem just as warm, and no warmer, than the Vis skar had been when he'd grabbed it atop the Great Sana not so long ago.

Wax pulled out the skar, turned and showed it to the group.

'Very impressive,' Bliss signed. 'Now can we get out of here?'

For once, nobody argued with that.

CHAPTER 38
SURFACE PRESSURE

The trudge back to the surface took longer than the way down. Tired feet, dwindling rations, and sheer emotional toll wore on Svarde and the others. Maena didn't snap back to her prior self quick, instead lingering in silence much of the way, at war within her own mind. Rasslebeck and Pennifer kept each other's council, while Kivi scouted ahead and kept them on the right path home.

All of which left Svarde to his own thoughts, and those bent towards the fiend and its stolen memories. The whimpering man and what they meant.

The Guardian had been to all seven isles, had heard their dialects, drank their ales, and experienced their cultures. None spoke the tongues he'd heard from the fiend, a chance Svarde might've tossed up to an ancient capture—who knew how long the fiend had survived in the depths—save for the whimpering man.

Without memory or much of a mind, the whimpering man didn't offer many clues, but in that absence he gave the most important one: the man's pallid appearance, slack skin, easy fit within the underground's tight tunnels and scant light suggested he hadn't been a rogue with enough luck to dive deep and get himself trapped.

That there were secrets in the Dark Below wasn't a surprise to anyone. That those secrets might include a people hiding beneath the surface?

A question for Noctia, perhaps. The Circle and the history books.

As for his quest to slay the fiend's heart, stop the spawning down in the deepest holes, Svarde felt his axes weighing on his back, the blisters on his feet, the dry scratch as his throat waited for water that wouldn't come.

The raid hadn't been enough. A small party wouldn't achieve what Svarde wanted. No, he'd need to convince the isles. Get, if not an army, than something closer to it. A steady supply chain, forays and forces willing to push deeper and claim the territory taken.

Not an expedition, then, but a war.

"Who'll you get to agree to it?" Maena said as they stomped through a damp cavern, ceilings and floors radiating Kivi's smoldering glow in an orange wash. "Rana, Kance, and Whent have standing armies, but they have them to fight each other, not to work together."

"Like every damn thing, Noctia will have to lead."

Maena laughed, a sharp cut, more bitter since before the fiend. "Now there's an impossibility. You said they wouldn't even help with this. Now you want to arrange something better?"

"I'll use the mask."

The gray plate sat in his satchel, carefully nestled between scrounged cloth scraps. Its features matched the whimpering man, and Svarde could only hope inside waited enough revelations to push Noctia to action.

"You don't even know if it'll work on someone else," Maena said, her voice dropping as she looked away. "And whomever you get to wear it will die if it does."

"Noctia has its prisoners. They'll give one up for this."

Maena winced. "Cold, even for you."

"The old you wouldn't have hesitated."

Maena sniffed. Fell into silence as they left the cavern, returned to the long single-file as the passage narrowed. Once more up and up and up, catching a breeze for a moment, a mysterious stench in another.

Had he become cold, unfeeling in his single-minded pursuit? Bitter, with Catya so far beyond any reach?

Didn't Svarde have that excuse? Didn't all who'd seen their once so promising dreams fade to shadows have a reason to damn their empathy?

Later, in what Rasslebeck declared would be their last break before the surface, the group gamely munching on dried mushrooms and mushy geahered moss, all of them lean, stomachs rumbling in a lurching backdrop, Maena told Svarde she'd go back.

"All the way down," Maena said, taking out her saber and polishing it, though fiends hadn't chased them on the return journey. "I feel I owe it to her."

"The other you?"

"She fought for me, even though she didn't know who I was, what would happen to her when I came back. I have to honor that."

"Even if I can't convince Noctia to give me a thousand Najahn soldiers?"

"Even if you can't convince them to give you breakfast."

Svarde chuckled, "I've had it. The better eggs are down at the water's edge. More grease, more flavor."

"Then what do we have to lose?"

The answer came at the exit, the first afternoon they'd seen in weeks making its gray-gold entrance at the cave's grand exit. The rock gave way to dirt, the air forfeited its damp ends, and for once Svarde took a whole breath without a cough, without wondering if some creature would dart from the darkness and snatch it from him.

Kivi, their fearless leader, stopped at the exit, the Ferrite's sapphire eyes turning back to Svarde with a warning snort.

"Guess we ought to be careful," Rasslebeck said, catching Kivi's meaning. "Going back to the surface means human problems."

"Nothing any Whent guard can do will measure up to the fiend," Pennifer countered. "I'd like to see them try to scare me now."

"Keep your arms sheathed nonetheless," Maena warned. "What a stupid thing it would be to come all this way only to take a bolt to the chest. We've not stolen a thing, hurt a soul on this isle."

Svarde wasn't sure he'd have the strength at this point to charge out, axes drawn, anyway. Lack of food, water, had his limbs trudging more from desperate habit than conscious choice. If the Whent wanted a fight, the least they could do would be to give him a few days rest, a proper meal or three first.

"Lead on, Kivi," Svarde said, but the ferrite stayed still, claws clamped to the cave's last end. "Fine, I'll go then."

Kivi's wisdom proved true: as Svarde walked onto the blustery land, the Whent outpost showed its newfound popularity. Whent archers, those rock-armored soldiers holding heavy crossbows, ringed the returners. Spacing them, bigger brutes with their Whent gauntlets and heavy shields, stood ready to advance.

At their center, stone armor painted over with an icy white coat, stood a Whent warlord, clad in thick, short furs and bearing the four-pointed beard demanded of every male Whent with any power.

Seeing Svarde, the man growled out a single word. The crossbows, already loaded, snapped to tight attention. That many bolts ought to have set off a panic in Svarde, but a dull numbness spread instead. A fatal acceptance.

"Lower your weapons," Svarde announced, keeping his hands well free of his own. "We're damn tired, hungry, and half-dead. We mean no harm to you and your people, and you can ask that town back a ways to prove my words."

Behind Svarde, the other three lurked at the cave's entrance for a long moment till retreat's obvious futility forced them forward. Kivi came up to Svarde's feet, plopped herself down alongside him, her tongue tasting the air and her eyes half-closed.

As tired as any of them, the ferrite, and as worthy of a rest.

"The town's already spoken of your bravery, and it's why you're not dead where you stand," said the Whent warlord, his brittle speech chomping through the words as if trying to attack every syllable. "They offer their thanks, and I'll repay it by not shooting you dead where you stand."

"I'll be sitting before long," Svarde replied. "Best not stake your triggers on a tired man's position."

The warlord hesitated, then laughed.

"You're not known for your humor, Guardian," the warlord said. "Found some down there, perhaps?"

"And much more besides."

"Then I'll be looking forward to hearing it from you," the Warlord flicked his two stubby arms forward, and those Whent geared for a melee approached the group. "It's a long way to the Pits. Time aplenty to fill your gut with food and my mind with tales. Then, of course, we'll see whether you can keep either of yours from being split."

"The Pits?" Pennifer asked as Maena cursed. "What're those?"

As Pennifer asked her question, Svarde found his hands moving towards his axes. A doomed effort, but then, waiting for the Pits would only be the same. Yet, looking into the nervous, determined faces of the approaching Whent guard, Svarde stayed his hand. Found his voice instead.

"The Pits are a chance," he said. "For you, and for the one who'll do whatever it takes to end your life."

The Whent Warlord, as his forces tore Svarde's weapons off his back, pulled the satchel away, didn't disagree.

CHAPTER 39
A NEW YOU

Ami saw herself when she woke, two copies, one reflected in each of Annalyse's wide lenses. The scientist leaned over Ami, her light breathing melding with crackling lantern flames as the only sounds in the quiet lab. Ami recognized the space immediately, a sort of home to her now in the weeks since she'd become Gladdring's experiment. Flush with anything Annalyse requested, the tower room defied familiarity, save for those lamps and Annalyse's goggles.

Cages lined the lab's walls, a circular ring leading to a broad slab in the center, one Ami figured she must be lying on, had been lying on, given by her stiff muscles. Her throat itched, her nose seemed crusted over. Ami tried to move her right wrist and found it strapped down.

"Awake?" Annalyse asked, blinking back at her. "Or is this another dream?"

"Dream?" Ami asked, a rasp.

"She lives!" Annalyse shouted, jumping back from the slab. "Here, let me get you some water. You'll need some."

Ami lay there—what else could she do—and explored

her own body while Annalyse scurried off. Her fingers, toes all seemed intact. While straps kept Ami from sitting up, she felt cloth along her body. Not the heavy armor she'd worn into combat.

The fiend. That blue flaming monster. Had it burned her armor away, metal forged in Foti's hottest furnaces?

Worse, the fiend hadn't just been a fiery beast. It'd used a tool, a weapon. Not something Ami had ever seen before. Claws, teeth, battering bones, fiends could have all those. Tools, real intelligence were left to the humans, the children of the seven gods.

If that was no longer true, then . . .

"Here, drink up," Annalyse said, tilting a cup towards Ami's mouth. After a too small sip Annalyse pulled it away. "Sorry, it's been a couple days. Don't want to overwhelm you. I've got the guards fetching some food."

"Several days? What—"

"She's safe, Ami. Don't worry. Noctia reinforced the Wards after the fight. Guess you provided them the evidence they needed." Annalyse gave Ami another sip, nodding as she did so. "That's always the issue with politicians, isn't it? Need to slap'em in the face sometimes to get them to notice."

As Ami embraced the water, she continued her mental tour of her body. She seemed to hear all right, to smell and taste. Her eyes saw much the way they had. And yet, things didn't seem right.

A tightness gripped her, and a feeling she wasn't alone. A feeling boosted by Annalyse's wandering eyes.

"Is it dead?"

"Is what dead?" Annalyse tilted her head, gears spinning. "Oh, you're still talking about the fight? The fiend? Terrevin said it fell back down into the Wound. Nobody knows, but it hasn't come back." Another water pour. "Good thing too. Not sure anyone could've done what you did."

Ami coughed, "I stabbed it with a sword."

"Not just any sword! You're too modest. And, speaking frankly, you could stand to be less so. You're representing us now, remember? The skars, Gladdring, our tower."

"What are you saying?"

"I'm saying your sword did the damage. Flamebreak, imbued with a Foti skar, felled the monster. That's the line we need to get behind."

Ami shuddered. Or tried. The straps kept the motion unsatisfying.

"I'm not playing politics."

"Look, I don't like it either, but it's the dance we need to keep playing with the toys." Annalyse bit her lip, her eyes flipping skyward for a moment before shrugging and bringing them back to Ami's own. "Besides, you don't have a choice now."

A latent fear spiked. Ami's heart sped up. The dry throat returned. She knew it, of course. The heat had been so intense, the burning everywhere.

"What happened to me, Annalyse?"

Pursing her lips into a sad, yet somehow still fascinated smile, Annalyse set the pitcher down and reached to Ami's face, her left cheek. The side that'd been closest to the fiend in the attack. Ami felt the pressure, but not the skin, the texture.

Instead, only cold came through.

"You should've died there," Annalyse said, her telltale curiosity leeching back. "Everyone said you lit up like a fresh candle. The fiend fell, and Flamebreak fell with it."

"My sword's gone?"

"Well, no. We know where it is. At the Wound's bottom."

"Annalyse."

"Right, anyway. You were lucky! Some Ward had come sprinting back, yelling about a bad fiend attack. Gladdring told me to grab our gear and come running."

Ami closed her eyes. Tried to remember. Lying there, on fire. Nothing came.

"Way too late, of course. Gladdring didn't get his show, but we found you and hey, he let me save your life."

Ami listened, growing more and more numb as Annalyse described popping a Vis skar from her own necklace, how she'd pressed it into Ami's hands and ordered her carried back to the tower. How the life-saving stone hadn't been enough.

"Minor wounds, it's a miracle. You're back and good to go in a few hours. More serious ones, it takes days, and even then there's some damage left the skars don't seem to touch." Annalyse frowned. "I don't know if that's the skar, though, or that we don't know how to use it."

"What did you do, Annalyse? Just tell me."

"You want to skip to the end?"

"Please."

Not the answer Annalyse wanted, but she sighed, scratched her nose, looked about as if hoping someone else would spring from the ether to deliver what Ami already decided was bad news.

"Every time I tried to take the skar away, you started dying," Annalyse said. "Something deep inside you must've been damaged. And your face . . . that side, anyway, it was all scarred over. So I came up with a solution."

"Untie me."

"Right, though I'd be careful. Don't know how the rest of you's doing, after all."

Annalyse undid the straps one by one, and after each, Ami tested her limbs again. Found them responsive, eager even to get going. It took a deep breath, another drink from Annalyse's pitcher, to bring Ami's healthy hands to her face.

The right side felt as it always had. A little dry, maybe, but skin. Warm. Healthy.

The left?

"It's the best Gladdring could find, and I crafted it personally," Annalyse said, though Ami noticed she'd put a meter between herself and the slab. "You won't notice it. Much." Annalyse tried a half-cocked smile. "And hey, no fiend's getting a claw through that."

Ami's hand went up, found Annalyse's work. Traced its contours around her left cheek, up to her ear and down nearly to Ami's chin, ending at the turn of her neck, the edge of her eye. Cold, smooth, hard.

"What is it?" Ami asked.

"The finest platinum in all the Seven Isles," a new voice boomed from above. Gladdring, followed by a food-bearing guard, made his way down the twisting stair into the lab. "It cost a fortune. I gave up more than one skar for your life."

Annalyse let Gladdring take her place, the scientist rushing over to a side table decked with notebooks, her charcoal pencil scratching away.

"Why?" Ami asked.

"You're too valuable to die," Gladdring replied. "And now, with that set in where everyone can see, you're my greatest asset."

Ami found the inset, there in her cheek. The skar's

warmth nestled into her. The whispers coming through, answering why she hadn't felt alone in her own mind. A different tune, than the Foti skar in Flamebreak, yet familiar anyway.

"You really know how to make someone feel good," Ami muttered, swinging her legs over the side.

"Good or bad, what matters is that you're alive." Gladdring turned 'round, grabbed the soup bowl from the guard and handed it over to her. "Drink up, Guardian. There's work that needs doing, and you've rested long enough."

Ami stared at the soup, her stomach ready to dig in. If she refused to eat, if she fought Gladdring's every effort, how long could Ami hold out?

Not long enough. The skar would keep her alive, if only barely. Gladdring would wait. And Catya, Catya still lived. Ami's oath stood.

The Guardian took the offered spoon, ran it through the thick broth, and lifted it to her lips. A sip and a swallow, a decision made.

"Tell me," Ami said, "what you need me to do."

CHAPTER 40
THE WIND QUEEN

Wax held up his hand on the dock, let the white snowflake land in his palm. A chill sting, as delightful as the crisp, clear air. Walk south but a few minutes and that same air would pick up Foti's industrial tinge, sulphur and heat. Leaving that behind was, in itself, a cause for celebration.

Leaving Foti with two skars and one extra Guardian, despite Quik's initial annoyance, was incredible.

"Sorry for what I said back there, Pan," Wax whispered, looking northward across the gray waves. Beyond that slate horizon, peppered with incoming and outgoing ships racing winter's arrival, lay Rana. "I'll try not to give up so easily this time."

His Guardians, his brother and sister had come through. Turning around, looking back down the dock, Wax saw Torny and Bliss about midway, the former helping Bliss play with a Foti spear-fisher. The device, a narrow tube with short-spear stuck inside, thin rope on its back end, could lance out and snipe anything foolish enough to be swimming around these waters. Far different from the poles and nets used back in Kitaye, and Wax found he didn't much care for the heavy metal resting in his hands, the clunky recoil after the trigger pull. Bliss, though, wore a wild grin as she aimed and sent the spear flying into the surf. Torny cackled.

Beyond them, at the dock's edge, Quik talked with Pavarde, the Najahn captain. The gilded commander had been Quik's companion of choice ever since leaving the bandit camp in ruins. From what his brother said, the two talked about Vis, about Noctia, about what it took to be a Najahn.

When Wax asked him why, Quik demurred, said only that there'd be Najahn everywhere they went. Might as well get to understand them better.

At least his brother's wound was healing up nicely. Every night, Wax handed over the Vis skar and Quik tucked it near the stab, holding it tight. He was almost back to running now, and everyone figured by the time they hit Rana's watery isle, they'd be ready to sprint right on to the next skar.

"Wax, watch out," Torny's voice snapped Wax home, saw him notice the slender ship carving fast near his dock.

Wax took a step back, then another and nearly fell off the pier's end as the vessel splashed in. The ship's sails, diamonds cut at too many angles, dwarfed the ship beneath, and they all spun in near-unison as the silver-blue hull slid into port. The ship's body came close, so close, to bumping the dock, but no touch sounded till the vessel reached a full stop. Even then, cushioning bags tossed over the sides buffered the contact.

A Kance ship, built to glide across the water's top, float from one wave's crest to the next. No straight lines, a light belly, designed to ferry quick rather than quantity. Even so, the north side of Foti would mean a far journey.

"Should be going to Noctia, not here," Torny muttered as she and Bliss came to stand by Wax, his sister coiling up the spear gun. "Unless there's something in Falska they really want." She threw a grimace back to the busy port city. "Can't imagine what that'd be."

'I can,' Bliss signed as the Kance vessel threw a step-stair over the side.

Far from a grim metal or wood piece, the step-stair caught the slight breeze and settled to the dock as if laid there by gentle hands. Yet once it touched, the thin pearl steps seemed as solid as stone.

"What? Ore?" Wax asked.

He needn't have questioned. The answer came a beat later, as a gilded soldier took the first step over the edge. Two thin rapiers clad the wirey man's waist, along with a willowy blue-and-white robe. He sighted the trio, judged them, and descended the stair without a word, ending with himself between the group and the Kance exit.

'Her,' Bliss said as the next one off made an appearance.

The woman bore her glittering regality with an icy discomfort, as if daring someone to call out her tight hands, her shifting eyes, and her bent knees. Quick steps were at odds with her obvious station.

As long as there'd been a Renewal, Kance had always sent one of its two Queens on the quest. Wax and the rest of Vis thought it a strange madness, but who cared what another isle did. Who cared, save this Kance Queen seemed to have speed on her side.

Amid her own robe, its collar decked in Kance sky diamonds, their sapphire speckled silver catching the gray morning and casting its light about, the Kance queen wore a Najahn necklace much like Wax's own. In it were two skars, the Kance diamond and Vis's emerald.

And here she was, docking a day or two away from the Great Forge.

"Looks like we'd better get a move on," Torny muttered.

Wax, though, met the queen's eyes as she descended the stair. She found his own necklace easy enough, and when she did, her look narrowed to one of pinched curiosity. Not hostility, not yet.

A competitor already beaten.

"Right," Wax said, his voice trailing off as the Kance queen, followed by a second guard, turned and strode down the dock. "Guess it's a real race now."

'Always has been,' Bliss replied. 'Now we just know what we're up against.'

"Want me to sabotage their ship?" Torny asked, a sly grin following the question.

"Think we've had enough violence for a fair bit, haven't we?" Quik announced, striding up to the group. "They're moving our boat down a pier to make room for this one. Guess she's a big deal." Quik took a closer look at the vessel, whistled. "Wax, think we're ready to ship out. Are you?"

"Wait to leave this blasted isle?" Wax laughed. "No thanks. Guardians, let's go find some rivers."

THIS CONCLUDES 'THE TRAIL OF FLAME' - read on for an excerpt from The Seven Isles Book Three - The Wrath of Rivers. For more adventures, visit us at www.blackkeybooks.com.

Thanks for reading!

An Excerpt from the Wrath of Rivers

THE SEVEN ISLES BOOK THREE

Maena, Rana captain, commander of her own ship and leader of sailors by the dozen, wiped her nose on the dirt-covered sleeve as the Whent wind whipped her dry, stringy hair into her face. The rest of her wasn't much better off, the weeks in the caves clinging to her as hard as the ropes binding her wrists, her ankles to metal loops on the rolling wagon.

She shared the rumbling trek across Whent's choppy tundra with the ones who'd followed her down into the cave, or at least the last few who'd remained till the end: Svarde, the hulking Foti Guardian and his loyal Ferrite sat in ponderous thought toward's the wagon's front. Near them, Rasslebeck and Pennifer, two Rana fighters who belonged slitting Whent throats instead of being held by the rockbiters, sat across from one another spitting old stories. Dire laughter seemed their default mode on this fourth day crossing Whent's massive isle.

Several nameless prisoners then filled the benches, ones Maena hadn't spoken to, would not, and they shared her lack of interest, spending their time instead picking at lice and lost in their own half-frozen minds.

At least they likely had only one.

Maena shifted her gaze right, out the wagon's scant back. The Whent prison train continued, another four wagons following them and five more in front, all heading towards that Whent dungeon known as the Pits.

Then again, Maena might not even know when she arrived, seeing as she spent so much time locked in a struggle with her own head.

The fiend in the Dark Below had shredded her memory, siphoned away Maena's past like she might eat a snack. What'd been left behind built, in the short time it existed, a version of her. One it fought to keep alive even when Svarde had smashed the old her, the original Maena back into being.

Why won't you die?

Because I barely had a chance to live.

The conversations pattered endless through the minutes, the hours, the days. Every thought Maena had would prompt an interjection from her other self, an opinion, a suggestion, a demand.

You'll never take me back.

It happened once. It can happen again. I'll wait.

Maena sniffed. Wiped her nose a second time. Blinked wind-bitten tears away. She wasn't a crier, but with her skin chapped, without guard from the cutting gales, the occasional snowy blusters, her body adopted other measures.

Can we live with each other?

Not with you at the till.

That was a laugh. A till. Maena had agreed with all the other sailors to give up that life with the expedition, an agreement that'd frayed soon after the dark grew too deep, the fiend cries too loud. She'd given up what she loved only to fail at what she wanted.

I didn't even have a chance at that.

Roars harkened their arrival before the wagon slowed, the echoes rising over the plains like a waterfall's wail. Soon enough the landscape followed suit, the wagon rolling through a palisade gate, one with the wood stakes pointing inward, the guards in watchtowers angling their eyes the wrong way.

Before the gate, tents sprouted across the landscape, their pitched sites offering fire pits and cheerful fur-clad Whents enjoying their days. Some raised flagons to toast the coming wagons.

On the gate's other side came what good trading could get you. Real buildings, stacked with Whent logs and buttressed by the rocky isle's stone. Smoke rose high from a hundred chimneys, but the air held none of Foti's mining stink. Maena saw shops, butchers, inns, and restaurants aplenty, all supported by roving livestock and hardy vegetable gardens, most now fallow harvests.

The wagons drew more cheers from passersby as they rolled along. Maena could only shiver in response, the glee in those stares a manic violence justifying all the Rana raids she'd pitted against the Whent barbarians. These people loved their bloodsport, so long as they could watch from their rocky mantels.

When the wagons came to a halt, their destination appeared less a prison cell than another rocky hole. Maena's stomach lurched at the downward sloping entry, the torches burning along its walls.

You can't be scared of that now, can you? I lived my whole life in one. Be brave, thief.

Thief? This is my life.

Think what you want.

"Pay attention," some Whent man shouted at her, untying her ropes from the loops and immediately stringing them through another, thinner chain. This one tied her ankles to the prisoner behind her, one in a loping line. "You'll follow me close, mind, or you'll get a beating. They won't hold off your turn either, so if you want a chance to get out of here, best keep your tongue shut and your eyes sharp."

Another man next to him, at the slopes mouth beneath that leering palisade, laughed. In one hand, he flipped a skinning knife.

"Barten," the man said, "You're giving them hope when there is none. Why do you torture them so?"

Barten rolled his eyes, a great thing given their size, nestled back in his wrinkled, bearded face. "Tross, they're more fun when they have something to lose." Barten stepped back off the wagon, tugged Maena upright. "There's a ferrite in this batch too. Damn Foti fire lizard won't leave its master."

"Can't we kill it?"

"Jochi says no, says it'll make the Foti a more interesting fighter."

Another tug and Maena took a step off the wagon. Farther than she thought, and her legs weren't quite awake yet. She fell forward, only for Barten to catch her with one hand, hoist her back upright.

Tross cursed, slotted his knife away, headed off towards the wagon train's front. Maena's eyes followed him as Barten pulled the others off the wagon.

"He's going to give your train master a talking to," Barten said, answering a question voiced by Rasslebeck.

"You're all looking less than ready. The Pits only wants healthy ones, and it's looking like we might have to spend a few days nursing you all back to contesting shape."

Contesting?

The Pits, so Maena knew, offered Whent prisoners, criminals, a chance at justice through prowess. Succeed at this or that contest and you'd get yourself let go. How possible that really was, Maena didn't know.

She'd never met anyone who'd escaped.

Then we could be the first.

Maena laughed, a hoarse rasp. There was an idea. In her condition, tired, half-frozen, and with voices talking in her head, Maena would be lucky to survive crossing blades with a baby.

Now, that's an exaggeration, no baby could lift a sword.

You don't talk like me, know that?

I am you, so that's an impossibility, Maena.

Barten pulled their prison train, once again fifth in line, down the hole and under the ground. At least, with all the torches, the chill disappeared. Stale air replaced it, but Maena would trade to feel her fingers and toes.

Barten lumped their wagon into a single cell, one with scattered, moldering straw slats. A hole in the corner served as the latrine.

"Meals will come as we see fit," Barten said. "Best you eat them when they arrive, as you'll need every bit to stay alive." He pulled the rope's end through a gap in the wood door, then tugged once, a single hard jerk. At the pull, all the knots around their wrists and ankles came undone, leaving a slithering rope Barten reeled in.

"Make any fuss, give us any grief, and you'll be dinner for something else," Barten continued, sweeping his scruff gaze among them all. "You're among the damned now, but not yet among the dead. How long that takes is up to you." A glimmer, a slight upturn among those scraggly curls. "Some lucky few might even make it out of here alive." That glint faded with a frown. "Not that I see any among you."

"Hold, Whent." The growl pulled Maena's attention to her left, to Svarde's figure, still hulking despite losing his armor, his axes. "Where's the ferrite?"

"The lizard's got the same chance as you," Barten replied. "If it earns its freedom, we'll send it back to your blasted isle."

With that, Barten twisted a key in the wood gate, locking them into the dirt and dust.

Seven people in a cell big enough for double that meant straw enough for everyone, though the latrine ruined what little comfort that provided. The first meal came quick enough, though, and Maena had to stare at it long to understand what she saw.

Better than what we ate down below, tell you that much.

Better than I've had at many inns.

Real meat. Cooked and tossed with potatoes. Carrots alongside. No ale, but a water barrel and earthen cups came with meal. One of the other prisoners started crying at the sight, shoveling the stuff into his mouth with his hands.

"Wash'em first," Svarde announced to the room, a little late for the one. "Go to Tamas and they'll tell you. The fastest way to die comes from disease in a place like this."

Another prisoner, a thin lady who bore a thrice-broken nose, laughed, "If you think disease is going to take you before a sword in here, or a beast's maw, then I envy your hope."

But she washed her hands, as did Maena and all the others. Even the first prisoner, once he'd finished stuffing his mouth, cleaned his grubby mitts.

So what are you going to do, thief? Sit here in silence?

After Svarde's warning, the group had settled into their places. Maena felt the Foti man's eyes cross to her from time to time, looks she ignored. He'd tried to rebuild their relationship on the walk out of the Dark Below, but Svarde had known the old Maena, the one still put together.

That one didn't exist any longer.

What, you have a better idea?

I didn't take charge in that cave, and I died for it. Don't kill me a second time.

Maena stiffened. Her second self had it right. The Pits could be a death sentence, but they could be something greater. If she could muster the energy to try.

Muster? If I'd known the real me was this pathetic, I'd have shot myself instead of that fiend.

Maena snorted a quiet laugh. Again, the second self had a point. How many raids had she led? How many swords had she crossed to earn the medals on her lost armor? This would only be one more challenge in a life filled with them.

Now, that's more like it. Show me who I really am.

Finishing her meal, Maena tossed the bowl against the gate and stood. The clatter drew attention to her, the prisoners watching as her torn, dirty, rag-clothed form found its spine.

"I don't know about any of you," Maena said, the rasp dying as she punched through her tired throat, "but I left a job unfinished back there, and I mean to see it through. That means fighting our way out of here, no matter what these Whent bastards throw at us. Who's with me?"

The prisoner cackled again, opened her mouth, then shut it as Svarde stood, the man glaring at her for a long moment before nodding at Maena.

"To the end, Rana. To the bitter, violent end."

"If I had a saber, you'd have it," Rasslebeck added, standing.

"My fists are yours, though they'd be better with a crossbow in'em." Pennifer stood too.

The other three prisoners eyed the quartet with confused wariness, but under Svarde's glare, they must have found a measure of confidence, because soon they too were on their feet.

Just in time for a bell's clarion ring to sound.

This concludes the excerpt from 'The Wrath of Rivers', The Seven Isles Book Three, available at your favorite retailer. For more adventures, visit us at www.blackkeybooks.com.

Thanks for reading!

Acknowledgments

There's this idea that writing is a solitary act, but that couldn't be further from the truth. Every writer depends on friends, family, and, yes, the readers to keep spinning their stories.

Specifically, I'd like to thank my wife, Nicole, who's endless love and encouragement make every day brighter. My brothers, Jonathan, Justin, and Matthew, and parents, Bob and Mary, who help keep a smile on my face.

And, of course, all of you readers that make this life possible.

Thank you.

About the Author

A.R. Knight writes sci-fi and fantasy in the frozen north of Wisconsin. With a pair of cats keeping him company, he enjoys delving into adventures that are as much about the villain as the hero.

After getting a degree in journalism and touring the country installing healthcare software, A.R. Knight thought it would be good to get back to what he loved. So now he's got a small office and early mornings to spin whatever tales come into his imagination.

When he's not writing, A.R. Knight tends to travel anywhere he can, whether that's islands off the coast of Ecuador, the rainforest, snowboarding in the Rocky Mountains, or sipping scotch in Edinburgh. That's the nice thing about the writing life, you can take it anywhere.

To contact or see what he's up to, visit www.blackkeybooks.com

arknight@blackkeybooks.com

For Kris

Copyright © 2023 by A.R. Knight
All rights reserved.
ISBN:
Ebook — 979-8-88858-016-5
Paperback — 979-8-88858-017-2
Large print — 979-8-88858-019-6
Hardcover — 979-8-88858-018-9

Published by Black Key Books

This book or any portion thereof may not be reproduced or used in any manner whatsoever without the express written permission of the publisher except for the use of brief quotations in a book review.

This is a work of fiction. Any similarity between the characters and situations within its pages and places or persons, living or dead, is unintentional and co-incidental.

www.blackkeybooks.com

www.ingramcontent.com/pod-product-compliance
Lightning Source LLC
Chambersburg PA
CBHW030741310726

48969CB00005B/1279